Take Her

Kinsley Kane

A Barbast Novel: Book One

Author Note

Take Her was previously self-published under the name Midnight Taylor in May of 2015. While that version will always hold a special place in my heart, after ten years of reflection, extensive rewrites, and an additional 56,000 or so words, this current version should be viewed and read as a completely different book. I hope you love it as much as I do.

While themes that make us uncomfortable are a great part of literature, they should never be at the cost of your mental health. I hope you enjoy these reads, but not all books are for all readers, please make your mental health a priority. Content warnings may be found on my site: authorkinsleykane.com

To those that find strength in themselves, even when it seems near impossible.

You're my hero.

To those that ever made me feel like I wasn't enough.

May the stars forgive you.

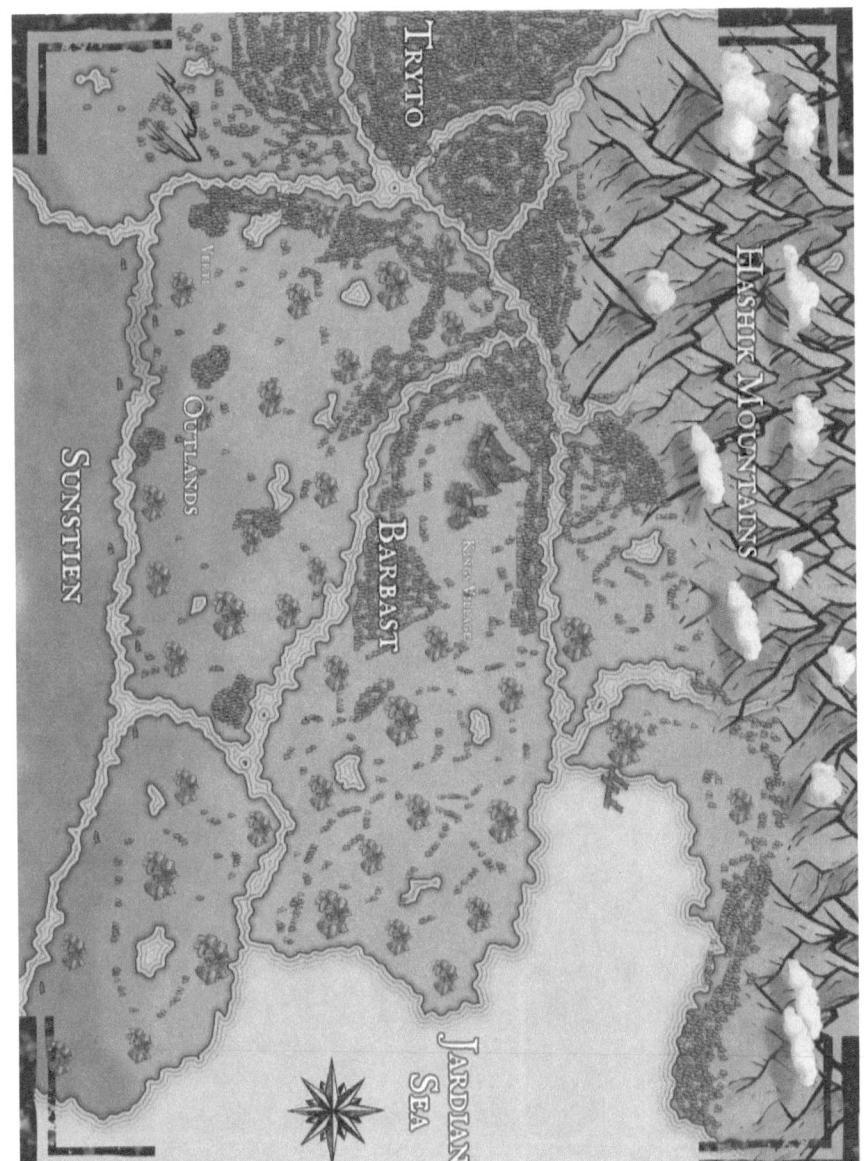

Take Her

Prologue

"Long ago, before borders scarred the land and fear drove kin apart, there was a time of harmony the world has nearly forgotten.

"The land was prosperous, lush, and impossibly alive. Inconceivably large trees soared; their magnificent branches caressed the skies. These pillars of life were proud, gentle, and strong, like trees are meant to be.

"Fields of wild grasses brimmed with vibrant flowers. Petals in so many colors it felt like a dream. People walked these fields to feel closer to the land, to breathe in the energy it offered. A simple stroll would lift spirits and lighten the soul.

"Soft breezes bowed the grass and whispered secrets to those who listened. They would tell you life's mysteries, revealing the beauty in the world and in each breath."

In hushed tones, the timeworn voice of the storyteller weaves her tale. The soft glow of moonlight casts the only light over her attentive audience. I used to believe in the whispered secrets. As a child, I'd hold my breath in the tall grass, listening for the wind to speak. Even now, part of me still wants to hear it.

She continues, "The people of the land regarded this beauty with respect and a fierce passion. They loved their land and tended to its needs. In return, it cared for and provided for them every day. Not only did they revere the land that gave them life, but they carried a passion for each other, too. There were no lines drawn in the sand, no harbored hate. They walked the land as equals and departed it the same.

The storyteller takes a staggered breath and even the breeze seems to pause, as if nature itself is listening in reverence.

"From the west came those cloaked in shadow and green, their skin marked by bark and sun. They carried the secrets of the soil. The knowledge of what grows in silence and what heals when all else fails. With quiet hands and knowing eyes, they tended the sick, eased suffering, and shared what they knew with any who came in need.

"From the south came those bronzed by sun and song, their footsteps steady on the soil. They knew how to speak to the land, how to coax abundance from it without taking too much. Give too little, and the land would grow wild and turn away. Take too much, and it would wither in silence. They welcomed all who wished to learn, teaching that the land was not a possession, but a giver of life to be honored.

"From the heart of the land came those shaped by stone and spark. Their hands knew the language of metal and gem, coaxing beauty and utility from the bones of the land. They crafted what others only dreamed of, tools, trinkets, wonders, and offered their inventions to guide, protect, and ease the burdens of the road.

"And from the north came those cloaked in snow and silence. They descended from their high white peaks, bringing with them the wisdom of the skies. Living so near to them, they had learned to speak to the stars. The sun was their brother, and the moon, their friend. They carried prophecies in their breath and saw truths written in light."

The storyteller's voice dips, brushing the edge of something I can't quite name. I shift, careful not to rustle the leaves behind me. I can't see the crowd, but I can feel the hush, like the story is casting a spell, even here, in the dark.

"The land thrived, as did the people who lived off her. Nomadic in nature, they wound their way across the lands and back again. They would come together as friends who simply had not met before. Circling a fire, they offered their companionship. At peace, with themselves and each other.

"Once a year, when the air turned cool and the moon graced the skies in her full form, they would gather. Under the moon's bright, smiling light, they would meet amidst fields of fading flowers and praise her, thanking her for her grace. They used this celebration to pass on stories, sing of their adventures, and rejoice in the life they had been blessed with." The quiet voice pauses, then continues with steel strengthening her words. Even now, I wish I could stop her, just once, before the story breaks.

"But greed took root at the center. The creators turned their gifts against the land and against the people. Knowledge, once shared freely, came at a price. They built themselves up, above others, above everything. No longer friends around the fire, they crowned themselves rulers. Women became prizes. People became property. And stone by stone, they raised walls to keep the rest of the world out."

"Ashamed of what their kin had become, the people of the north withdrew. They took their wisdom and vanished into the silence of the mountains, vowing never to return to a world divided by greed. The people of the west turned inward, vanishing into the shadows of their forests. There, the trees closed around them, hiding them from the animosity beyond.

"But the people of the south didn't just leave. No." The lone solemn beat of a drum is the only sound heard as the storyteller takes a breath, her attentive crowd waiting.

"They were outraged at the betrayal of everything that had been precious. They turned away from the rest of us. With such hatred scorching their hearts, their once prosperous land dried beneath their feet. Surrounded by only dust and red sand, hot as the malice they carried, they vowed those who had betrayed the old ways would never know peace.

"From a land that once glowed with harmony and serenity, people separated, lines were drawn, and knowledge... knowledge was lost." Deeply saddened by that truth, the storyteller repeats the last few words as barely a whisper.

It is a beautiful story, and she is confident in it. The words engraved on her heart, just as deep as any of the wrinkles on her skin. She has recited this story here at the Moon Festival for years in a tradition older than our country. At least, that's what the stories say.

The story might hold some truths, but no one believes it's real history. The Hashik mountains do lie along the northern border, but they're inhospitable, barren, wind-scoured, impossible to survive for long.

Barbast has two neighbors, not counting the sea.

The Tryto people live deep in their forests, rarely seen except when the peace treaty is renewed every few years. My only glimpse of them comes from a portrait in a history text. An image of a man painted in greens and browns, dressed in leaves and fur. Elders claim they can vanish among the trees in battle. As far as I know, there's never been any fights with them.

Pretty pieces of truth, sewn into a fable that could still land you on the wrong side of the monarchy and get you branded a traitor.

But the story lives on, told beside others tonight. The kind that dreams of a time with no ranks, no rulers. When anyone could learn a trade. When women had choices. When the unwanted weren't sold into slavery.

Such pretty tales.

I sigh. If only.

Of Verti's three festivals, only this one feels carved from quiet. The others are loud, merry, full of dancing and drink. But tonight is steeped in reverence. The only light comes from the full moon, casting silver shadows across the village. Wine and mooncakes pass freely from hand to hand, and thanks to Diamo sneaking some to our hiding spot, I've already had more than my share.

Silver and black streamers hang from every building, shimmering softly in the moonlight. Wind chimes dangle from each doorway, their gentle tinkling layered over the deep haunting rhythm of drums and the lone, sorrowful notes of a flute, threading through the night.

At the festival's center, the storytellers sit among plush cushions and swaying scarf-draped tents. Draped in dark robes, they look near ethereal with intricate silver markings adorning their bodies. They call them moon glyphs, said to be tied to the old stories. Most people say they're just decoration.

Both elders are relics of a dying art. No one trains to be a storyteller anymore. The tales they whisper are dangerous and forbidden. When these last voices fade, their whispered tales will disappear with them.

Around each tent, a knot of people gathers. Some standing, some curled into cushions, all leaning in like the wrong breath might make the story vanish. Tonight is the only night the people of Verti dare to set aside their loyalty to the crown. For a few quiet hours, they slip free of the weight of laws and pretend.

Diamo and I can't join them. Not yet. Unmated women aren't allowed, neither are children, or anyone the crown might call too fragile for dangerous stories. We're tucked behind a clump of trees just beyond the square, hidden from view.

The bark digs into my back as we sit in the hush of evening, sharing stolen wine and smuggled cakes. The sweetness lingers on my tongue, mingling with the night air. From our hiding place, the storyteller's voice reaches us, low and rich, heavy with memories long buried.

Diamo sits in the shadows beside me, moonlight threading through his dark curls. For a second, I catch the freckled bridge of his nose, the sharp angle of his cheekbone. He smells like woodsmoke and hay… heat, dirt, and something achingly familiar.

He's always looked more like a dream than a village boy. Tall, broad-shouldered, with a mouth that curves like it was made for secrets and smiling. But it's the eyes that undo me every time, deep amber in the dark, like honey warmed by flame.

He leans in close, breath warm against my ear. "I don't know why they bother keeping us away," he murmurs, voice thick with amusement. "We still hear the stories."

I smirk, taking another slow sip of wine. "Because if we're caught, they can pretend they had nothing to do with it when my father beats me." My voice is barely above a whisper, but he hears me.

He chuckles, low and quiet. "Ah, plausible deniability. Our favorite game."

The storyteller's voice rises slightly, pulling our attention back to her.

"Once, before the crown weighed heavy upon this land," she begins a new story, her words weaving a spell over the crowd, "the night belonged to the people." Her words slip through the square like smoke.

A hush falls over the crowd, the only sounds remaining are the distant echo of the flute and the rustling of leaves in the evening breeze. Even from our hidden perch, her words press against me, soft and sure and impossible to ignore. This is why the crown fears them, because stories have power.

Her voice blends with the rhythmic chime of wind bells and the steady pulse of distant drums, filling the air with a sense of something ancient, something lost. I close my eyes for a moment, letting it settle into my bones.

For tonight, at least, we can pretend too.

The storyteller's words settle over me like a ghost of something forgotten, something that should have been mine but never was. I take another sip of wine, letting it warm me from the inside, but it does little to chase away the wistfulness curling in my chest.

"They danced beneath the moon, unshackled by decree, unburdened by fear. They sang songs forbidden now, songs of old and forgotten freedoms."

I swallow hard. I can almost see them, spinning in the moonlight, laughter ringing without worry of who might be listening. No whispers of treason, no punishment for stepping out of line. Just freedom.

Diamo nudges my arm with his. "You've got that look again."

I turn to him, raising a brow. "What look?"

"The one that makes me think I'm going to have to talk you out of something foolish." He smirks, honey eyes glinting in the dim light.

I huff a quiet laugh. "Think we'll ever dance like that? Without worrying who's watching?"

"You know…" His grin grows. "We could go dance in the woods right now. No one would stop us."

"You'd like that, wouldn't you?" I shake my head, amused.

"Absolutely. You'd trip over your own feet, and I'd get to gloat about it for the rest of your life."

I shove him lightly, and he chuckles, but the humor fades quickly. My gaze drifts back toward the square, the shadows of people swaying in time with the music, lost in a world that isn't theirs to keep.

"Why can't it be like that?" I murmur, resting my head on his shoulder.

"The monarchy I suppose." He shrugs, too casual.

"Maybe they'd be liked if they actually tried to fix anything," I grumble.

Diamo laughs, clear and bright, a sharp crack in the hush. I flinch, glancing around. If someone hears us, I'll regret it later.

"You act like you're the only one who questions them, Narina. Not everyone has such a hard time following the rules," he lightly chastises.

"I just never bought into the illusion that they're perfect," I mutter. "It's not leading if no one gets a choice."

His shoulder shakes with silent laughter. He threads his fingers through my hair, pressing a gentle kiss to the top of my head. The familiar touch soothes some of my restlessness.

"Oh, Narina," he murmurs. "I can't decide if I should be grateful for your stubbornness or worried you'll get me executed for treason."

My stomach knots at the thought. Diamo has been my best friend since we were children, since he found me crying and spoke soft, soothing words. His affection and absurd antics are the only reasons this world hasn't broken me yet. The thought that I might cost him his life is unbearable.

He nudges my knee, pulling me from my thoughts. "Don't go brooding on me now."

"Why should I blindly follow a monarchy that doesn't even see me as a real person?" I ask, instead of dwelling.

"I never said you should, love." He tilts his head, staring up at the stars. "It's just not the world we live in."

"Maybe my father wouldn't hate me if it were a different world." The words slip out before I can stop them, the ache behind them heavier than I intended.

I asked for his permission to apprentice with the storytellers, but he dismissed the idea without a second thought. Blasphemous, he called it. In his eyes, they were nothing more than heretical spinsters who deserved to be whipped.

I would have accepted any apprenticeship he allowed but he claimed I lack the obedience for it. Worse, he said granting me a position would be an embarrassment, a disgrace to someone more deserving.

"Narina…" Diamo gingerly leans his head against mine. "My love, your father doesn't hate you. He just—doesn't understand you." His words are quiet against the night, consoling.

I pull away from his pity. "My father hates the fact that I'm not a son. I am nothing to him but a reminder that he will never have one."

Diamo doesn't argue. He knows the truth as well as I do. My parents tried for years to have another child, only to be told my mother was likely left barren from the fever she battled after my birth. I have been the living embodiment of his disappointment ever since.

"That," Diamo finally says, nudging me, "and you're the granddaughter of the craziest woman to ever live in Verti."

I let out a short laugh, but bitterness lingers. He stands, brushing dirt from his clothes.

"I'll get us more cake. Don't get lost in your own head while I'm gone."

I watch him disappear into the festival I'm not allowed to join. Not until I'm bound. But he's right. My father doesn't see me as the daughter he never wanted. He sees his mother when he looks at me, and he resents me for it.

Genevieve Brevou. Verti's favorite cautionary tale.

She was bound young. When her mate died, she didn't rebond like she was expected to. Instead, she vanished with my father for years, only to return without explanation. She lived alone in the house that technically belonged to her toddler son. Loud. Opinionated. Unconcerned with what anyone thought. She became the village's favorite scandal, a woman whispered about in hushed tones. When my father came of age, she left again, this time for good.

He spent his life trying to erase her shadow. Became a loyalist to the bone, a respected instructor of history and government, a pillar of the village. My mother says he isn't cruel because he hates me, but because he's afraid I'll end up like her.

In secret, I'm proud of the comparison.

She was strong. She spoke her mind. No one could tell her what to do.

I'm Narina Brevou, granddaughter of Verti's rebel, Genevieve Brevou.

I lean my head back against the tree and stare at the moon. Her silver light fills me with longing. Diamo is right. It's not the world we live in. That doesn't mean it's the world we have to accept.

I am Narina Brevou. I will not be broken.

The words are a silent promise to the Moon and her stars, something I tell myself when the world feels a little too heavy. An echo of ones I once saw scrawled in elegant script on the back of a portrait before it was burned.

Genevieve Brevou. She who was not broken.

I close my eyes, listening to the storyteller's willowy voice rise and fall in the distance, carrying me to another time.

Chapter One

Nearly Three Years Later

"It's such a waste." The whisper drifts through the curtain shielding me from the rest of the small space. "He's so handsome and kind. He could do much better than her."

I release a slow breath. Their topic of conversation is not unfamiliar to me, but a tickle of anger filters through me anyway. This is hardly the time *or* the place for such gossip.

"Oh, I *know*. I think everyone is still hoping he comes to his senses before the ceremony."

"I'd like to say he will, but he's been doting on that disappointment for years. I thought he pitied her. You know... just being kind. He's *such* a sweet boy."

"Yes, and then he announced their betrothal! I couldn't have been more shocked." The older woman's voice hushes slightly, but not quiet enough for the thick curtain to muffle. "The entire village was stunned.

Still is, I'm afraid. We were all hoping the extended betrothal meant he had reservations."

Rolling my eyes, I shift uncomfortably. Dress fittings are uncomfortable enough without being forced to endure their cruelty.

"And Master Blackwell was in earlier. Do you know what he told me?"

"Do tell, Meredith. Don't keep the goods to yourself!" the other woman urges, her voice tinged with excitement.

"He's chosen that boy for his new apprentice! Handsome *and* the village's new blacksmith! What a waste. She doesn't deserve him." I can clearly picture her curly grey hair bobbing as she shakes her head in disappointment. Despite their harsh words, a spike of excitement rushes through me: Diamo got the apprenticeship!

"How did such a respectable pairing like Keith and Pietra end up with a daughter like that anyway?"

"Lands only know, but here we are. Maybe it's in the blood. We all remember the disaster that was Genevieve. And me! I have the misfortune of being the one responsible for her dress! What an embarrassment."

The fabric bunches beneath my fingers as I clench my fists and bite back a retort. Meredith is the only seamstress in the village, and a friend of my mother's. Though I'm not sure you should consider someone who speaks like this about your daughter a friend.

My saving grace arrives when the bell on the door jingles.

"Ah, Pietra!" Meredith croons. "Rosanne and I were discussing your daughter's good fortune, her upcoming ceremony with the lovely *Diamo*." She practically purrs his name like he's her favorite dessert. "She's just trying on her dress now."

I suppose it's not technically a lie. They *were* discussing my ceremony, of sorts. Still, the insincerity of her comment turns my stomach. I smooth my hands over the fabric of the dress, taking the brief moment of respite to examine my reflection.

It's a simple gown, as expected in Verti. No one here has wealth to waste on extravagance. White cotton hugs my torso before flaring gently at my hips, falling to my ankles. My mother insisted on a touch of embroidery, so a delicate band of flowers encircles my waist. Tiny pink and blue petals with green leaves add a soft elegance I hadn't anticipated.

"Let's see you, girl!" Meredith calls.

Inhaling a steadying breath, I push the curtain aside and step out for inspection.

"There you are. You've been in there for ages." The greying woman huffs, hands poised on her hips.

"I wouldn't dream of interrupting your conversation." I shoot her a sour stare. "It seemed quite riveting."

She tuts, pursing her lips. "Eavesdropping is not an attractive trait, dear. It's quite rude."

"How do you feel about gossiping and disparaging paying customers?" I counter. "I can't imagine either being very polite or flattering, Meredith."

Rosanne gasps, reeling as if I had just spat at the seamstress. I roll my eyes and turn to my mother with a silent plea.

"Narina, dear," she sighs, her tone edged with warning. Her reputation and, by extension, my father's, is what matters, not defending her ill-tempered, outcast daughter. But her eyes are soft, a quiet reassurance beneath her rebuke.

"Meredith has done a beautiful job on your dress. Just look at you!" She turns me gently toward the adjacent mirror.

I do as she says, but the reflection is one I have seen countless times. Dark eyes, unruly brown hair woven into a thick braid, and a body filling out with soft curves.

At our first fitting, Meredith had subtly suggested I lose weight to better please my mate for our binding. I had firmly shut her down. When I told Diamo, he just scoffed and muttered that the old bat should mind her business. Then, scandalously close, he had whispered in my ear that he was looking forward to exploring my curves and if I did anything to change them before he could, he'd have harsh words for us both.

The memory warms me, a soft flush prickling beneath my skin. I shake it off with a small breath.

The mirror echoes their words, insisting I'll never be good enough for him. But this time, as I gaze into the reflective surface, I try to see what my mother sees. I ignore the whispers of the insulting biddies behind me and try to see what Diamo will see the day of our ceremony. The way he'll look at me, knowing that I'm his. Forever. I imagine the quiet words he'll whisper, the devotion in his eyes.

I study the white dress, flattering yet modest, with its belt of blooms. I see it all.

And I smile.

I am enough.

For *him*, I am enough.

I am Narina Brevou. And I am enough.

It's been three years since our betrothal. Three long, aching years of waiting.

At first, my mother insisted I was too young. Seventeen, she said, was far too soon, even though she'd been bound at that very age herself. Surprisingly, my father deferred to her, though perhaps he simply didn't want the argument.

Then Diamo's father fell ill, and he wanted to wait until the worst had passed.

And now, the blacksmith apprenticeship. He's spent the past year working from dawn to dusk, pouring every ounce of himself into earning that title.

We've waited. Patiently. Carefully. Always respectful of timing, of family, of every complication thrown our way.

But soon... so soon. I'll finally be his. Fully. Freely. Forever.

And no one, not even my father, will be able to take that from me.

I meet my mother's gaze in the mirror and find something rare.

Pride.

"You're beautiful, my daughter," she whispers. "And before you know it, you'll be bound." She smiles softly. "I hope you find infinite happiness with him."

13

I return her smile, just about to speak, when a derisive snort from behind us shatters the moment. I look skyward and bite my tongue, near to drawing blood, to keep myself from snapping and ruining my mother's friendship completely.

"I believe it fits fine, Mother. Let's not waste any more of Meredith's time." I hope my expression says what I can't, that I'm desperate to leave. She nods, and I quickly retreat behind the curtain.

A few blessedly short minutes later, I'm carrying the dress box with my mother strolling beside me. We walk in a comfortable silence toward Father's house. Soon, it won't be mine at all, once I am bound to Diamo, I will be his. No longer my father's property.

When Diamo and I are bound, he'll become the heir to both our families: his father's farm, my father's house. Tradition says the household passes to the new and stronger heirs, but most don't follow it to the letter. Sons take the title in name only, easing into the role as their fathers grow old. Few are cruel enough to cast their parents out.

Diamo has no desire to claim the farm before he's ready, and his parents will stay as long as they wish. If he earns the blacksmith apprenticeship, the farm won't matter. Diamo will have his own trade, his own path. The land can wait until it must pass.

And because my father has no son, that house will fall to Diamo too, in time.

I'm lost in thought until my mother's touch stops me mid-step as we turn the corner and see the gathered crowd. A hush blankets them, thick and stifling.

At the center of the square, a woman kneels. Her wrists are bound, her grey hair falling in wild strands around her face. Her eyes are proud. Her mouth, set in a stubborn line, even as a patrol guard shouts her crimes.

"Spreading false tales about the history of the monarchy," the soldier sneers. "Implying the crown's decrees are an egregious abuse toward its people."

My chest tightens. I recognize her now… the storyteller.

I remember her from the festivals. She wove legends from air and light, her voice strong even when it trembled. She spoke of courage and freedom, and I had wanted to be just like her.

And now she's being branded as a heretic? The crown's decrees *are* abuse, but they're just stories whispered underneath the moon.

The crowd seems to swell around me, bodies shifting too close. The air turns thin, my heartbeat loud in my ears.

A second guard approaches, a thick wooden rod in hand. My stomach turns.

"Mother—"

"Don't speak," my mother whispers, her grip tightening on my arm.

The rod is raised. I flinch, a cry caught in my throat. The crowd presses closer, and for a breathless second, it feels like there's no way out.

This is wrong. Why is no one standing up against this? Why is no one standing up for her? I open my mouth to argue, to defend her, to do anything but watch as the rod comes down on a woman I idolize.

"Enough!"

The voice cuts through the quiet square. A man steps forward, tall and broad, confident without a trace of arrogance. I exhale in relief.

Elias.

Diamo's father.

His hair is streaked with silver at the temples, his skin weathered from years working beneath the hot sun, but he holds himself with a quiet strength that reminds me so much of his son.

"Narina." The quiet whisper in my ear makes me jump, before the soothing hand catches my arm. Diamo's warm voice slides over me as he moves in front of me, partially blocking my view. His touch steadies me against the rising tide of dread.

"He will handle it," he reassures me quietly, already knowing the turmoil that twists inside of me. I nod absently, without looking at him, trying to look through the tight spaces in the crowd to the woman on the ground.

"This woman is no threat to the crown," Elias says, voice calm but firm. "She's a storyteller, not a soldier."

The guard holding the rod snarls, "Her words question the crown's authority."

"Is the crown truly so afraid of words now?"

Another man steps forward, an elder my father hosts at the house sometimes. He's respected as the village magistrate on the rare occasion when one is needed.

"She should be taken in for questioning," the magistrate says. The crowd begins to shift and murmur.

Diamo places a quick kiss against my temple. "Stay with your mother, love," he says before he slips into the crowd, heading for his father. He knows how badly I want to be the one defending her. It would be a bad idea though, for me, for him, for her, for my parents. It would just make everything worse to have a woman, one already seen as too rebellious, to speak up.

Elias steps back, arms folding across his chest. "What are you going to question? The stories you listen to as you fill your belly with wine?"

"The same tales half the village gather to hear every year?" Diamo's voice rings out as he steps from the crowd, placing himself between the guard and the woman.

"She is the one spewing treasonous lies." My breath stutters. Father steps forward. I hadn't even seen him in the crowd. My mother takes a step back, pulling me with her. Diamo's eyes flick to me. I see the war in him, speak or stay silent. If he defies my father, we could lose everything. But he holds his ground.

"They're just *stories*, Keith," Master Blackwell says, stepping forward. "No one believes they're true."

"She should be whipped for heresy," one of the guards snaps.

"For entertaining the village?" Elias approaches, laying a hand on my father's shoulder. "Come now, friend," he coaxes. "This old woman's stories won't start a rebellion."

"That is not the crown's view," the other guard voices.

"She shouldn't be beaten in the street like an animal," the blacksmith says flatly. The crowd murmurs in agreement.

"Then let her answer to the crown directly." Father turns toward the guards, expectantly.

"Agreed," the magistrate says.

"This is upsetting the women," a man mutters, pulling his mate closer as he steps forward.

"Be done with this ridiculous display," Elias demands the patrol guards.

"Take her in for questioning," the magistrate counters.

My lungs forget how to work. Justice teeters on a knife's edge, and all I can do is watch. The guards survey the crowd growing more restless by the minute before looking at each other.

"She'll be remanded to the castle. The crown will decide her fate." The guard still holding the rod grabs the woman's arm, wrenching her up out of the dirt. Diamo refuses to move out of the other's way, forcing the guard to move around him to join his comrade. Elias follows, still arguing for the woman even as the guards drag her away. Father halts the magistrate, drawing him into conversation.

The crowd starts to unravel, villagers peeling away in small groups. Mother tugs me from the square and onto the road home. I hadn't realized how tight my chest had grown until the crowd thins and I gulp down a full breath, my lungs stretching painfully against the space they'd been denied. But the relief is hollow, my thoughts still tangled with the storyteller, heavy with worry and restless with guilt.

Until I look up and can't stop the smile tugging at my lips.

It's him.

Diamo.

He stands at the end of the road, spotting me a second later. His pace quickens. He offers a nod of greeting to both my mother and me before his warm, timbered voice reaches us.

"May I escort you?" His smile is easy, deepening the dimple in his cheek. The same one I've known since I was six. The one that always makes everything feel a little lighter. He offers his arm, but there's a shadow behind his smile. Not fear exactly, but something quieter. The kind of look people wear when they're trying to make peace with something they know they can't fix.

"No, I'm afraid I have to hurry home." Mother takes the dress box from my hands with a practiced grace. "But I think Narina could use a distraction after her appointment and… everything else. You have my permission to escort her on a walk before returning her home."

She hadn't been in a hurry until now. While my mother may wish I was more obedient, as society expects, she loves me. She saw how the interaction at the seamstress unsettled me, how I mourned the storyteller. She also knows that Diamo and I crave time together in equal measure. She leans in, whispering a firm *"Behave"* in my ear before walking past him with a parting nod.

Diamo's hazel eyes hold mine for a long moment before he extends his hand. "Shall we?"

I don't hesitate. His fingers are warm as he tucks my hand into his elbow. Gravel crunches softly beneath our feet as we begin to walk. The image of the storyteller's bound wrists clings to me, even as Diamo's steadiness draws me gently back into the now. I let him lead. I don't care where we go. I trust him implicitly.

Instead, I watch him. The way the low light traces his profile, casting soft shadows beneath the sharp lines of his cheekbones. Freckles dust his sun-darkened skin, familiar as breath. His lashes flick low as he blinks, thick and long, like the kind that belongs to someone too soft for a world this cruel.

He looks calm, but I've seen the way he shoulders everything, quietly holding more than his share.

I've studied his face a hundred times before, but now, after what we witnessed, I want to memorize it all over again. Not just because I love him. Because I need to remember what *safe* looks like.

"What was your appointment?" he asks after a beat, his voice velvety and low. We won't speak of the storyteller. We don't have to. We both already know where we stand.

"A dress fitting," I reply shortly, wrinkling my nose.

"Did it not go well?"

I chuckle softly. What a complicated question. "The dress is beautiful and fits nicely." He doesn't need to know anything else. He knows the whispers that follow me, just as I know he's heard them all and never once let them change how he looks at me.

"I'm sure you look stunning in it, my love." My heart trips at the endearment. "And I hope no one told you otherwise."

Point proven. He knows this village. He knows how they view me. And he never lets it dim how he sees me.

"I can't wait for you to see for yourself." And I mean it. Because when he looks at me, I don't feel like an outcast. I feel like someone who belongs.

We round a bend, and the stables come into view.

My mother's voice echoes in my mind. Calm, sensible, and heavy with warning: *Behave.*

I should. After what I saw in the square, after the storyteller's wrists were bound and her voice punished, I know better. I know how this kingdom handles women who refuse to shrink themselves.

But what my mother didn't see was how that woman still held her head high, even with dirt on her knees, or how the crowd *almost* turned. How one voice almost shifted the tide.

I just want to breathe. To *exist* for one moment without being told who I'm allowed to be.

The horses are just ahead… freedom only a few steps away.

I glance up at Diamo. He's never tried to dim me. Never asked me to bite my tongue or be smaller. He gives me the kind of peace that makes you forget someone else is holding the leash. And right now, being near him feels like a promise. One I'm afraid I won't be able to keep.

If I stay this close, I might just kiss him. Or cry.

I pull my hand from his arm, lift my skirt, and spring forward.

Chapter Two

"Narina!" His deep voice calls after me. "Where are you going?"

I glance back, grinning at the raised brow he shoots me. Instead of answering, I quicken my pace, just fast enough to keep a few steps ahead of him. The familiar scent of hay and dirt grounds me, pulling me toward the fence line like a tether to something real. Diamo reaches me in moments, his arm wrapping around me, warm and steady.

He sighs, already knowing. "No, love. We can't take your father's horses without permission. He still has time to deny us."

I hesitate, but only for a breath. I should care. I *do* care. That woman in the square, kneeling in the dirt with her wrists bound and her stories silenced... she did nothing more than speak. And still, they tried to break her.

That could've been me. But I can't live small just to stay safe.

I look up at Diamo. Meeting his hazel eyes does very little to calm my pounding heart. They're like golden-honey, full of sweet promises. He's never asked me to be anything but myself. Never told me to shrink.

Right now, standing this close to him, I remember all the times we talked about leaving this place. It had always been a dream, half fantasy, half desperate wish. Not realistic. But still ours.

A breath of freedom. That's all I want.

His voice is low, his touch light, and for a second, I almost lean in. My fingers tighten around his sleeve. I want to stay here, to press pause and fall into the comfort of him. But this isn't the moment for softness. Not when everything inside me is already splintering.

I slip out of his grasp, grab the hem of my skirt, and vault the fence.

"Narina!" Diamo hisses.

I coo to Inez, my favorite mare, stroking her neck as she nuzzles against me. Then I swing onto her back, bare-legged and breathless. Inez senses my need, my urgency. Her hooves stamp against the dirt, ready. I close my eyes for a beat, savoring the anticipation.

I nudge her forward.

Diamo's boots hit the ground hard after scaling the fence, just as Inez leaps over it, clearing the wooden rail with graceful power. My breath catches, then releases into a whoop of joy as my stomach flips.

Freedom always tastes like this.

Diamo soon joins me in a gallop, matching my pace, and when I push Inez into a run, the race begins. The wind presses against us, cooling the midday heat. The wind, the speed, the open space... there's nothing like it. No rules. No eyes watching to see if I step out of line. Just Diamo and I, outrunning everything we can't control.

But the world has its own way of reminding us we're not free.

Verti is in the Outlands, along the southern border of Barbast. The fields we're riding through are as far south as anyone dares to go. Few know much about the people of the south. They only leave their deserts to demolish entire villages along the border. In their wake, they leave nothing but a burnt skeleton of what was.

It's said their skin is brown and taut, like leather, and they mark their bodies to terrify their victims. Stories swirl about raiders, deserters, and lawless warriors. Venture too close to Sunstien and survival is uncertain.

We don't speak as we ride. We don't need to.

Once the village is behind us, we veer east. Diamo gestures toward a wooded patch, and I nod, easing Inez into a slower pace. The wind fades, replaced by the soft rhythm of hooves and birdsong.

The grove is familiar. Not dense, but old, thick-trunked trees with sprawling limbs that have seen everything and still reach out. As we pass beneath their shade, I finally pull Inez to a stop and slide from her back, my feet landing softly in the moss. Diamo dismounts beside me, but his gaze lingers on me for a moment longer than necessary.

Warmth spreads through me, unrelated to the heat of the day, as his palm finds a familiar place against mine, our fingers entwining. Still recovering from the ride, we bask in the quiet moment. Then Diamo tugs me forward, guiding us through the shifting shadows, deeper into the trees. Leaves crackle beneath our feet.

"This is reckless, Narina." His voice is low, tense, as he tugs me along behind him.

"I know." I watch him carefully, gauging his reaction. Reckless, yes, but not out of character for either of us.

"Your father will find out. Too many people saw." His pace quickens with his words.

"I know." I keep my tone even. My father's anger is a familiar storm. Predictable. I stopped fearing it long ago.

"We're not bound yet. I can't legally protect you from him." His jaw flexes. "And after today?" There it is, not just frustration, but worry. For me.

I release a breath. "I know."

"Then why?" he asks quietly.

"She was just telling stories," I say, just as quiet.

He stops so abruptly I nearly collide with him. Whirling around, he grips my arms, eyes flashing.

"And that's all it took to put her in chains." His voice rises, desperation leaking into the words. "When I saw her today, bound in the dirt for speaking, for existing... all I could think was..." His eyes flicker between mine, searching. "All I could think was, what if it were you?" The last is just a breath of a whisper.

The world tilts for a second. His fear is real. Raw. And it's for me.

"You can't protect me from everything," I say gently.

"No," he agrees. "But I can try."

"I know." And I do. I know this man would protect me from the King himself if it came to it. I'd never push it that far. I'd never put him at risk for the sake of my freedom.

"Then why?" he repeats. "Why risk his ire, Narina? His belt? What if he revokes his permission?"

"The same reason we've been taking risks for years, Diamo." Because I can't suffocate in the life that's expected of me. Because sometimes I just need space to breathe. Because we're two people who would keep riding until we reached the horizon if we thought we'd get away with it.

"But we're so close, love." His expression tightens. "He could change his mind at the last moment. You know he could. He's asked me enough times if I'm sure you're the one I want." The words sting, even though I know he doesn't mean them to.

I reach up, smoothing the crease between his brows. "He won't revoke his permission. No one else would have me and he knows it. He's counting down the days until I'm no longer his burden. If he truly wanted to stop us, he would have long ago."

Diamo doesn't return my smirk. "That might be true," he says, "But it's still a risk. And I don't know what I'd do if he told me I couldn't have you." His fingers tighten on my arms. "You can't forget he has another option. He could sell you to the slavers."

"He wouldn't. They don't come through often enough."

Diamo's expression darkens. "That's not a comfort, Narina."

I pause, letting the silence stretch between us, before finally saying, "I'm sorry."

His eyes lift to mine. Surprised. Maybe even a little softened.

"Not for doing it," I add. "But for causing you worry."

He's not angry, just concerned. I can live with that. I'd never want to truly upset him. Tease him? Certainly. Push the limits? Always. But hurt him? Never.

He looks at me for a long moment, then finally lets out a breath, his tension easing.

"You have every right to want freedom. But it won't always come without a price." He rests his forehead against mine and whispers, "I don't know what I'd become if the cost was you."

"I couldn't help her, Diamo. I couldn't stop them. All I could do was stand there and hope someone else would. I know this was risky, but it was all I could do to feel like I still belonged to myself." There's a long pause before he speaks again, but I see the understanding flicker behind his eyes.

"If there's a way to keep you free and breathing, I promise I'll find it."

I smile then, small and a little sad. Because we both know that's a promise even he might not be able to keep.

But still, he'll try. He *tries*. He was one of the few who did today.

"You stood up for her," I say. "When no one else would."

His gaze falters. "She deserved better."

"You were better."

He blinks, like he doesn't quite believe me, but doesn't argue. He lets out a breath, half sigh, half dismissal.

"One day, someone will make you pay for being free. And I'll be standing there, helpless again. Just like today."

The words hang between us. I don't rush to fill the silence. Instead, I lean into him, pressing my forehead to his chest. His arms curl around me. He holds me for a long moment, his heartbeat strong beneath my cheek. Eventually, he lets go.

Spinning on my heel, I twirl, letting my skirt billow out before settling back around my legs. I glance back over my shoulder, a grin tugging at my lips.

"Would you like to know who the blacksmith chose?"

Diamo goes still. His brows lift, suspicious. "Is this a distraction?"

24

"Maybe," I say brightly. "Or maybe I overheard something at my appointment and just thought you deserved a little joy today."

He narrows his eyes. "Your teasing is unkind, love. You know how long I've waited to hear."

"Only because you insisted on pretending it didn't matter," I tease. "But every unplaced man in the village has been circling that forge like dogs around a butcher's scraps."

Diamo huffs a laugh and shakes his head.

It's rare for an apprenticeship to go to someone outside the family. Normally, the trade would pass from father to son. But the blacksmith's only son was lost to sickness last winter, and with no heir, the forge was left open for the first time in generations. Everyone wants it, but only one man can earn it.

I let the pause stretch a second longer, watching him squirm just enough to be satisfying.

Then I step back into his space, tiptoeing just enough to murmur, "Congratulations, apprentice."

Diamo inhales sharply, eyes widening.

I bounce on my toes, grinning as he stares at me, stunned. He sweeps me off my feet, spinning me in a blur of sunlight and green. The trees whirl past, laughter spilling from my lips.

"Narina, are you serious?" he whispers, the words barely breathed, like he's afraid to believe them.

"I promise. That's what I heard."

He sets me down, but his hands stay at my waist, steady and sure. His gaze roams over my face like he's trying to memorize every piece of it. Then, slowly, a radiant smile spreads across his lips, brighter than the sun breaking through after a storm.

"Do you know what this means? For us?" His voice is breathless with wonder. "Narina…" His hands slide up to cradle my face, his eyes shining. "We could have a good life."

I cup his face in return, forcing him to truly see me.

"I've never cared about that," I whisper, my thumbs brushing along his cheekbones. "It doesn't matter if I'm bound to a farmer or a blacksmith. If it's you, it's perfect."

And I mean it. With everything in me, I mean it. I am so proud of him. He's worked tirelessly for this, pushing himself past exhaustion, past doubt, past every obstacle thrown his way. This achievement is his and I'll celebrate it with him. But wealth, comfort, a life of ease? I don't need any of that. I just need him.

"Still," I add, smirking, "a few pretty things wouldn't hurt."

Diamo lets out a sharp laugh, his eyes darkening with emotion as he takes me in. The way he looks at me makes my stomach flutter, like I'm the only thing in the world that matters.

"Lands divine, woman," he murmurs with a slow shake of his head. "I don't think I can love you more."

Then his lips find mine, swift and warm, stealing my breath. The kiss is brief, chaste, almost reverent, but I feel the intensity behind it. The joy. The relief. The promise. When he pulls back, he's still grinning, his happiness radiating from him.

For a heartbeat, everything is perfect.

Then a shadow drifts across his face. Not fear, not sadness, just the weight of reality creeping back in.

"Are you alright?" I ask, unwilling to let the moment fray.

He exhales slowly, rubbing a hand over the back of his neck. "If I really get the apprenticeship..."

"When," I say without hesitation, squeezing his hand in mine.

His gaze holds mine, something unspoken moving behind his golden-honey eyes.

"It's not the work I'm worried about," he says. "It's the time. I'll be in the forge every day. Sunrise to dark. And once training starts, there won't be long before... before we're bound."

He doesn't sound regretful. Just quietly trying to hold onto all of it at once.

26

I squeeze his hand tighter. "We'll be bound in a little over a fortnight. A few weeks apart is nothing. Compared to forever?" I shake my head. "It's nothing at all."

I try to pour everything into the words: my certainty, my love, the future I see so clearly when I look at him. This man is everything. He needs to feel it in the press of my palm, in the way I say his name, in the way I choose him, always.

His shoulders loosen. His smile returns, softer now, a little wonder lingering behind it.

"I just don't want to miss a second with you," he whispers, lifting my hand to his lips. His kiss is gentle, almost sacred. "Forever still doesn't feel like enough."

I melt into him, breathing him in. Hay, smoke, and something that has always meant home. His arms gather me in without hesitation. The world falls away. For a little while, there's only the steady thrum of his heart against mine and the way he holds me like he never plans to let go.

"Shall we take a walk?" he asks, like he already knows I'll say yes.

I nod, but stay pressed against him for a moment more. He chuckles low under his breath, pressing a kiss to the top of my head before stepping away. But he laces our fingers together, keeping me close.

I groan softly at the loss of contact, lips pursed in playful protest.

"Always the gentleman," I mutter.

Diamo just laughs, a warm quiet sound that melts into the trees around us. "Come on, love. We'll have to head back soon."

He turns, already tugging me deeper into the woods, then glances over his shoulder with a teasing smile. "Let's take a walk."

Always the voice of reason.

Always mine.

Chapter Three

We meander through the ancient trees, their towering forms a sharp contrast to the dry, barren land that stretches beyond the grove. Here, the air is cooler, thick with the scent of damp earth and moss. The canopy overhead filters the sunlight into shifting patterns, dappling the forest floor in gold and green. It's quiet, eerily so. Only the rustling leaves and the soft stirrings of unseen creatures disturb the stillness.

Many in the village fear this place. You can feel the centuries it's lived, as though the trees themselves remember every whisper, every footstep that has ever passed through. This is one of my favorite places to visit with Diamo, though we keep our visits limited after...

I stop short, my lungs seizing mid-step.

The tree we've been avoiding for years looms before us, twisted and monstrous. The air sharpens around me, colder, heavier. My heart knows before my mind catches up. I hadn't realized how deep we'd wandered. A chill settles over me, curling around me like a vice.

Diamo's fingers tighten around mine.

"Narina." His voice is full of regret. "I'm so sorry. I didn't realize..."

I shake my head, swallowing hard. "Neither did I."

But it's too late now. The onslaught of guilt and grief surges up, clawing at the edges of carefully built walls. The air grows thick, suffocating, as I stare at the grotesque thing before us.

The first of many lurking in this grove.

The Blackbriar.

These invasive nightmares have plagued the Outlands for decades, choking the life from and replacing our towering oaks. Their bark is a deep, unnatural brown, so dark it looks black in the shadows, as if born from some hate-filled abyss. Their limbs, mostly barren, somehow thrive despite the lack of leaves. No one knows how. No one knows why.

This monster of a tree is easy to identify, its surface covered in vicious, dagger-like thorns, clustered together in jagged clumps. Some barely the length of a finger, others stretching nearly half the length of my forearm. They jut out like the spines of a beast lying in wait, their deep purple hue a cruel contrast to the sweet scent in the air.

Everything about the Blackbriar is death.

Its leaves secrete an oil that blisters skin, leaving behind angry, festering boils. The bark carries the same toxin, and when burned or crushed into a powder, it releases a smoke that kills. The worst of it all is the thorns. They hold a poison so potent, even the Sunstienians, with all their cruelty, seem merciful in comparison.

Warm arms wrap around me from behind, drawing me against a steady chest.

Diamo.

He's trying to anchor me, to pull me from the storm raging in my head, but comfort means little in the face of something like this.

Not when I'm staring at the very thing that took a life because of me.

Ky was one of Diamo's closest friends, practically a brother in everything but blood. Though he was a couple years older, they bonded easily, and because Diamo had taken to me, Ky became a friend to me as well. His sister, Lily, was just a year younger than I was, full of mischief and rebellion. We became fast friends, and together, the four of us were inseparable.

We spent our days chasing the thrill of adventure, skipping class to disappear into the grove, where we climbed trees for hours. We'd leap from branch to branch, racing through the canopy like we belonged to the sky. The boys were stronger and faster, always a few leaps ahead, but not on this day.

Lily and I were winning.

She had been complaining that she never won our races, so I let her take the lead, hanging back just enough to let her claim her victory. The harvest season was nearing its end, and leaves, brittle with age, had begun to fall in golden flurries around us. Maybe that's why she didn't see it.

I wasn't close enough to warn her.

Her scream tore through the trees, a sound so raw and piercing it turned my blood to ice.

Fear drove me forward, the crack of splintering bark sharp in my ears and my limbs burning as I closed the distance, barely catching myself before making the same jump. Bark scraped my palms as I teetered on the edge of the branch, heart hammering, breath frozen in my chest.

Lily lay sprawled on the ground below, her body curled in on itself.

At least six sickly purple thorns jutted from her skin.

"Lily! Lily, where are you?!" Ky's panicked voice shattered the air.

Before I could think, he was already flying through the treetops, too fast, not looking.

He was going to jump.

I lunged, catching his arm just as he leapt. His momentum wrenched me forward, and for a terrifying moment, we were weightless. The world blurred into a rush of color before we crashed to the ground, landing hard in a tangled heap.

Pain flared through my limbs, but there was no time to think about it. Diamo landed gracefully beside us, already pulling me to my feet. My body protested, but I barely noticed.

Lily.

Ky was at her side, his hands hovering helplessly over her trembling form. I scrambled to her, dropping to my knees beside them. My hands shook as I reached for her, clumsy and frantic, useless. She whimpered, eyes clenched shut, knees pulled to her chest.

Ky reached for a thorn.

"Don't," I said sharply, catching his wrist. His wide, frantic eyes met mine and I shook my head.

I tore a strip from my dress, wrapping it around my hand before reaching for the first thorn. The second I pulled it free, Lily cried out, shattering me.

"I'm sorry. I'm so sorry," I whispered, my hands shaking as I moved to the next. Ky held her hands, whispering to her, trying to soothe her.

The wounds were already swelling. Dark purple bloomed from the punctures, spreading like ink under her skin, turning an angry red at the edges. Heat radiated from the wounds.

Once I removed the last thorn, Ky pulled her into his lap, cradling her gently.

"It burns," she whimpered.

Ky shut his eyes tightly, his jaw clenched as if he could hold back the grief threatening to break him. When he opened them again, he gave her the softest smile.

"I know, Lil," he said, his voice threatening to fray. "It'll stop soon. I promise." His voice cracked. I grabbed her hand, willing the tears not to fall.

We knew.

We knew the truth and it was crushing.

Blackbriar is a poison no one escapes from. There was an antidote, but it wasn't shelf-stable. It only lasted a week before it broke down, and it wasn't needed often enough to justify the cost of keeping it in supply. No one had any. It could be made, but it took three days. The poison killed in one.

Even if we got her back to Verti, there was no saving her. Why put her through the agony of the journey?

"Ky," Lily sobbed. "My body burns."

Ky held her tighter, his face a mask of grief. "I know, Lil. It'll stop soon. Just hold onto me."

I squeezed her hand. Her skin seared beneath my touch, already damp with fever-sweat, her body trembling.

I hoped he was right. I hoped it was quick. Was that wrong? To hope for death? To hope she didn't suffer long?

Diamo slid an arm around my shoulders, drawing me close. His warmth didn't reach the cold settling in my bones.

"Tell her a story," he whispered. I turned to him confused. "It'll calm her. Give her something else to think about."

Ky met my gaze and gave me a quick nod.

So I did.

I forced my voice steady, even as my chest ached, and let the words spill from me. A tale of long ago. A place far from here.

When I finished one, I started another.

Diamo held me close. Ky rocked his sister in his arms.

And with stories drifting through the air…we watched Lily die.

"Narina."

Diamo gives me another squeeze, grounding me, pulling me back from the memory he was likely lost in too. His breath is warm against my skin as he nuzzles into the crook of my neck. But even his presence can't loosen the guilt lodged deep in my chest.

I will always blame myself for Lily's death.

Ky and his family left for King's Village not long after the incident, unable to live with the memories that haunted Verti. I can't blame them.

"It's a terrible way to die," I whisper into the stillness between us and the trees. The words linger in the air, heavy with grief, as if the forest itself remembers.

"There was nothing we could do. We were just kids," Diamo finally says, his voice quiet, unsure if he's speaking to me, himself, or Lily's memory.

I say nothing. My guilt is so palpable, that monstrous tree probably feeds off it. I know there was nothing we could do to save her after she fell, but if I had been—

"There was nothing you could have done."

His voice cuts through my thoughts as he guides me to face him. Strong hands frame my face, his calloused palms warm against my skin, forcing me to meet his honey-colored gaze.

"There was nothing you could have done," he repeats, more insistent this time.

I close my eyes, unable to agree with him.

Soft lips just barely graze across mine. Desperation coils in my chest, raw and aching. I need to feel something... else.

Clutching the front of his shirt like a lifeline in the dark, I pull him closer. He yields without hesitation, stepping into me as his lips find mine again, stronger this time, surer. His heat wraps around me, chasing the shadows away.

But, as always, the kiss doesn't last nearly as long as I want it to.

Diamo has never put my chastity at risk. That is a rule we both respect, a line we have never come close to crossing. Even now, with my face still cradled in his hands, he rests his forehead against mine, steadying himself.

"Narina," he breathes, his voice rough with restraint. His way of telling me this is all he can offer.

"I know," I whisper back. He's given me what I needed, a connection. I can wait for the rest.

"I love you," he whispers, pressing a kiss to my forehead, a fragile offering that can't erase the ache, but steadies me all the same.

"Endlessly."

I mean it with every piece of me. I will love this man until my last breath and beyond even that.

He straightens, his hands sliding down to linger at my waist, then squeezes lightly before stepping back. "Let's find the horses."

I nod and we turn our backs on the lethal tree, but its shadow clings to me with every step.

Chapter Four

The ride back to the village is unhurried, the silence between us comfortable. Each of us lost in thought, though our hands find each other as we ride side by side.

After stabling the horses, Diamo tucks my hand into the crook of his elbow, steady and sure as ever.

"I'll need to find Master Blackwell and confirm what you overheard," he says, the teasing lilt in his voice lightening the air.

I smile, glancing down at the hard-packed dirt of the road. "I'm proud of how hard you've been working for this, Diamo."

He tucks me a little closer to him. "I've been thinking."

He guides us around a wagon of grain heading the opposite direction, the wheels clattering over the uneven surface. Evening has settled over Verti. A few scattered torches gutter outside the tavern, and the low murmur of villagers heading home carries on the cooling breeze. The sharp scent of smoke and damp earth clings to the fading light.

Beside me, Diamo shifts his hold, his voice lighter now.

"The Moon Festival is just a few weeks after our ceremony." I look up at him, waiting for him to continue. "I was thinking we could go together. As a mated couple. No more hiding behind trees."

I stop mid-step, turning to him. "Do you mean it?"

His answering grin is soft but certain. "I know how much you love it. And how much you hate not being able to participate fully. I'd be honored to have you at my side." A small squeal of happiness escapes me. Diamo laughs, tugging me back into a walk. "I'm assuming that's a yes?"

"Yes! Yes, of course!"

To actually attend the festival would be the greatest gift. I might strain under the expectations laid on me, but with Diamo beside me, it's a life I could never resent. My steps feel lighter than they have in a long while. In just a few weeks, we'll be bound. He has the apprenticeship he's dreamed of. We'll attend the Moon Festival together. And I will finally... finally... be free of my father's hold.

But not soon enough.

My steps falter as we near my father's house. He's already waiting.

Leaning against the doorway, arms crossed, his sharp eyes track our approach. The longer I take to reach him, the harder his expression becomes.

"Come on, love," Diamo gently coaxes as he tugs me toward the wooden steps.

We ascend together, stopping just in front of the severe man. He straightens, pushing off the doorway. He's not much taller than Diamo and certainly not as strong, but the way he holds himself is enough to make my stomach twist.

"You can leave now, Diamo," he says, his voice like a blade against stone. His arms fall to his sides. That's when I see it. The strap. Cold dread floods my veins. Taking the horses had been a mistake. I swallow hard, fingers unconsciously tightening around Diamo's elbow.

A deep breath later, I make myself loosen my grip. This was my decision. Diamo had tried to warn me off. I won't let him feel guilty for leaving me here to my fate. But, as I release him, he catches my hand, stepping subtly between me and my father. He must have seen the leather, too.

"I must apologize before I go, sir." Diamo's confident words cut through the thick tension in the air. "I borrowed a couple of your horses to take Narina for a ride after we left Pietra earlier."

I hold my breath, watching my father over Diamo's shoulder. My Diamo, standing between me and the storm, taking the blame while subtly reminding him that we had my mother's permission to be together.

My father doesn't react, his weathered face unreadable, but I know him too well. The way his dark eyes slide to mine tells me everything—he's not convinced.

"I should have asked your permission," Diamo continues smoothly, "but I thought a celebratory ride would be the perfect way to tell Narina the news of my new blacksmith apprenticeship."

There it is. The key that might shift my father's anger, Diamo's rise in status, his growing importance in the community. For the first time, my father's gaze moves from me to Diamo, surprise flickering through his expression.

"That is quite an achievement." The words are begrudging, laced with lingering anger but underscored by an unmistakable thread of pride. I let out a quiet breath. If there's one thing that my father respects, it's position and standing. He cuts a look at me, then shifts his gaze back to Diamo. I see the question on his face. *Are you sure she's the one you want?*

"Thank you, sir." Diamo steps back, creating distance between us. "It is getting late. I'll take my leave." He takes my hand, lifting it to his lips and brushing a soft kiss across the back of it. A silent, yet undeniable answer to my father's unspoken question, I am *his* to claim.

"I do apologize if I caused you any inconvenience," Diamo adds. My father gives a stiff nod before turning on his heel and disappearing into the house.

I mouth *thank you* to Diamo. He winks, flashing me that quick, mischievous grin before hopping off the porch and making his way home. I watch him go, feeling a wave of gratitude. He's saved my hide more times than I care to admit.

Taking a steadying breath, I step inside. The door slams shut behind me.

I flinch at the sharp sound, my pulse kicking up. Father stands just inside the doorway, the worn leather strap clutched in his hand, his posture rigid with barely-contained fury.

"I'm no fool," he spits, the words cutting through the air. "And if you cared for him at all, you'd let him mate with someone who deserves him. Someone who doesn't make him debase himself."

"Diamo does what he wants." The words slip out before I can stop them. Quiet, but defiant. A mistake.

The strap slices through the air with a sharp snap. I barely get my arm up in time to deflect the blow. Pain flares across my forearm, the sting seeping deep into the skin.

"Do not talk back to me," he warns, his voice a low growl. The strap cracks again, harder this time. Again, I take it on my arm, biting back a gasp. Clenching my jaw, I resist the urge to take a step away from him. I learned that lesson long ago.

His anger trembles through his clenched hands, his breath ragged with restraint. But his arm doesn't raise again.

"Go to your room." He grinds the words through his teeth, stepping aside to let me pass. I keep my head down, my steps quick and careful, but he catches my arm as I move by. His fingers dig into bruising flesh.

"Take my horses again," he growls, his hot breath brushing against my ear, "and I will beat you black and blue. Mate or no." I nod, not trusting myself to speak. He releases me with a sharp shove and I don't waste a moment before hurrying to my room.

The door shuts behind me, a heavy barrier between him and me. I drag in a slow breath, relief flooding through me. Diamo's intervention, however subtle, had spared me much worse. If I'd known what kind of mood my father was in today, I never would have even considered taking the horses. Diamo's quick thinking saved me a beating, but I know I won't be welcome at the dinner table tonight.

I glance at my forearm, grimacing as the bruises begin to bloom beneath the skin. The marks are already deepening, and I can feel the dull ache settling in.

After dark has fully descended, the narrow door to my room creaks open slowly. A wave of exhaustion settles over me as I wonder if it's my father, come back to finish what he started. I glance up from the book I'd been reading, my heart tightening in my chest. But when I meet her gaze, a breath of relief escapes me. It's my mother. She closes the door softly behind her.

"I'm not sure how you thought stealing your father's horses would end well. I suppose my reminder to behave was too subtle," she says, tilting her head at me with an expression that's part amusement, part concern.

"It was impulsive," I admit.

"Indeed." She steps closer, holding out her hand and in the center of it rests a perfectly ripe, red apple. "I managed to calm him down a bit, but for the next few days, I'd recommend staying out of his way." I nod, accepting the apple from her. Staying out of my father's reach is always a good strategy. After all, the less we interact, the fewer bruises I'll wear.

"Which means," she continues, her gaze drifting to the book still nestled in my lap, "I wouldn't let him catch you with that." Her brow quirks up, her voice warning.

Reading. Another one of those things that's discouraged for women. We're allowed a few years of schooling, just enough to keep us from being completely ignorant, but anything beyond that is deemed wasteful, or worse, dangerous. Father had allowed me to read his texts after I left school, but it had been years since he'd mentioned it. And since I hadn't dared to bring it up again, it was safe to assume that it would now be a point of contention.

"I'll hide it and return it to his shelves when I can," I promise.

She glances around my small room as if taking it in for the first time, before returning her gaze to me. "Not long now," she says quietly, her voice soft with something like sorrow. "How are you feeling? Anxious?"

"Not in the slightest." Taking a glance around like she had, I grin. I love my mother, but this place has never felt like home to me. It's suffocating and I'd leave it without a second thought. "I'm ready. So ready."

She nods slowly, a wistful smile touching her lips as she sinks down onto the cot beside me.

"You're lucky," she says after a while, "to have found love so young."

I turn to her, surprised. "You were bound at my age." I remind her, but her gaze is fixed on the window, distant.

"My binding was arranged," she replies, her tone flat. "Your father cares for me, and I for him, but I would not call ours a love story." A soft huff of amusement escapes her lips as she seems to remember something. She glances back at me, her eyes softening. "Do you have any questions? About... anything?"

There's not much to question. We'd be bound and I'd be his. It's simple. Inevitable. "I don't believe so."

She watches me for a moment, her expression searching, before she asks gently, "The Claiming?" *Oh.* I feel the heat rise in my cheeks, flooding my face with a flush that's impossible to hide even in the dim light of the room.

"Diamo is a good man," she continues, voice steady as she rests a warm hand over mine. "He will take care of you I'm sure. But if you have questions... I am your mother. I'm here for you."

Her touch lingers, a silent offer of comfort and I squeeze her hand, grateful for the kindness she still gives, even as I feel like I'm slipping further away from her world.

We sit together in companionable silence for a while, the evening settling between us. Then, with a soft sigh, my mother gently rubs her thumb across the bruises blossoming on my arm. Her touch is tender; her eyes filled with quiet concern.

"He is a good man," she murmurs, her voice soft but steady. "He will take care of you." She places a fleeting kiss on my temple, her affection a balm. With a final glance, she stands and turns toward the door. "Good night, my daughter."

"Good night, mother," I reply, my voice a whisper in the stillness of the room.

As the door closes behind her, her words seem to echo in the air. *He is a good man.* Diamo is a good man. I finger the bruises on my arm, where her thumb had just been. I'm certain father has never left bruises on her. He has no reason to. Mother is the perfect, obedient mate. Submissive.

Almost.

I pick up the apple she'd smuggled me and take a bite, the sweet juice a treat to my dry mouth. He'd never strike her, but he has no such reservations with his child.

Snapping my book shut, I shove it under the thin mattress, the coarse linen scraping my fingers. The trouble it would cause wasn't worth it. I'll return it the next time my father leaves the house.

Diamo *is* a good man. Not just a good citizen. Not just a good friend. Not just a good example to the community. No, Diamo is truly good. I knew it from the first time I met him.

I crouched behind the old grain shed, small enough to fit between the crates and the wall if I tucked my knees in tight. My dress was smeared with dirt, and my breath kept catching in my chest. I didn't want to cry anymore. I didn't want to cry at all.

Father said I was disrespectful. That I didn't know how to hold my tongue. So, he'd made sure I remembered.

Take Her

The red sting across my legs still throbbed, but that wasn't what made my throat ache. It was the thought that maybe I did deserve it, because no one had stopped him.

I didn't hear the boy coming until he was already there. He cleared his throat, not loud, just enough to say I see you. I shrank back farther into the shadows.

"I won't tell anyone," he said.

I didn't answer. Didn't even move. If I didn't move, maybe he'd go away. He didn't. He sat cross-legged in the grass a few feet away. Not too close. Not far.

"I just didn't want you to be alone," he added after a moment. "I'm Diamo."

I kept my eyes on the ground, blinking hard.

He was quiet for a while. Then, softly, "You're Narina Brevou, right?"

I finally looked up, eyes puffy and rimmed red. He was a little older, with messy dark hair and a dust-smudged face.

"I heard your name before. You're the rebel's granddaughter."

I scowled.

His eyes didn't flinch. "That's kind of amazing."

I blinked. No one had ever said it like that.

He offered a crooked smile and picked up a pebble, rolling it between his fingers. "My pa says that makes you dangerous. But he also says dangerous people are the ones who change things."

I didn't know what to say to that.

"You look like someone who might be dangerous. Like someone who doesn't break easy," he added, soft now. "But it's okay if today's not one of those days."

My throat tightened and he fell quiet then. He didn't ask me what had happened. He didn't tell me to stop crying. He just sat there, humming something under his breath, picking at the grass. Not leaving.

And for the first time that day, I didn't feel so alone.

Chapter Five

The inked words on the page feel like my salvation, a lifeline in a sea of tension and dread. My father has not left the house in days. It's getting harder to avoid him, and the oppressive silence of my room is starting to drive me mad. Earlier, I sent a note to Diamo at the forge, asking if we could spend some time together after his shift. His reply came swiftly, and now, my mother is helping me pack a picnic basket.

Just as we finish, the sound of my name echoes through the house, sharp and demanding. The call is unmistakably my father's, filled with barely contained fury. My mother freezes, her lips pressing together into a thin line. She nods subtly toward the doorway, signaling for me not to keep him waiting. I sigh, brushing the crumbs from my fingers as I move toward the study.

The short hallway feels endless, each step growing heavier with dread. I try to figure out what I've done to provoke him, but my mind comes up empty. There's nothing I can pinpoint.

I knock tentatively on the half-open study door and wait for him to acknowledge me. Once a bedroom meant for an heir, the room had long since been claimed by my father, now filled with books and teaching papers. He sits on the opposite side of his desk and turns his cold eyes toward me.

"Get in here," he growls.

I step inside, keeping my distance, but it's not enough. He stomps around the desk, the heavy sound of his boots making my skin prickle. I flinch when he grabs my arm, the bruises from the other night flaring under his grip. He yanks me toward him, his voice low and seething.

"Can't help yourself, can you? Stealing from me, like a common thief?" His words are low, rhetorical snarls.

"I don't know—" My words falter, but I never get the chance to finish. His hand shoves mine down onto the desk, and I barely register the book before it crashes down on my fingers with a sickening thud. A sharp sting bursts through my hand, numbing my fingers almost instantly.

"Thief," he spits, driving the book down again. I bite back the cry that tries to tear free. I yank at my arm, but his grip only tightens, digging into the bruises already blooming beneath my skin.

"Why is *my* book under your bed?" he hisses.

"You—you told me I could read your books," I stammer, cursing myself for not returning it sooner. The words feel weak the moment they leave my mouth.

His face darkens. "*One* book. A long time ago." His voice drips with venom. "If you thought it was permitted, you wouldn't have hidden it."

He slams the book down again, harder. Agony flares up my arm, white-hot and blinding, forcing a whimper from my throat.

"A thief and a liar," he sneers. "You're a disgrace. I'd be wise to sell you to the slavers, let them break you."

Another blow lands, sharper than the last, sending a searing jolt up to my elbow and igniting a spark of fire that makes me gasp.

"Perhaps you should lose a hand like a common criminal." His eyes gleam and for a moment, I fear he will actually carry out the threat. A soft knock on the door freezes him in place, book mid-swing.

"Karth, dearest." My mother's quiet words fill the room. "Diamo is at the door for Narina."

I hold my breath. My father grunts in displeasure, his fury palpable. Without a word, he pulls me toward him, his grip unforgiving, and slams the book onto the empty desk. The sound of it reverberates in the still air and I flinch, a cold shiver running down my spine.

"The slavers are said to be in the Outlands this month," he growls. "If they arrive before you are bound, I will save that boy the trouble and sell you myself." My breath stutters. "I swear it. You *will* be broken."

I swallow hard, fighting the knot in my throat. He's threatened selling me before, but this is different. Hatred burns in his dark eyes, and I know without a doubt that it would give him a twisted satisfaction to hand me over to the slavers. To him, I am nothing but a wild animal to be caged.

He won't break off the betrothal. Not yet. The slavers might not even come to Verti, and my father can't risk being left with me. But if they do… I shudder at the thought. My fate is sealed.

"It would be wise of you not to give me further reason to tie you to a horse and seek them out." His breath is hot against my cheek as he hisses the words. His grip on my arm tightens for a moment before he shoves me away. I stumble, barely catching myself on the desk.

He stalks out of the room, brushing past my mother with a sharp tug on her hand, dragging her behind him as he leaves.

Once I'm alone, I suck in a shaky breath, forcing the air deep into my chest. My fingers throb with each pulse of my heart, stiff and tender, but not broken. I flex them carefully, pain flaring with the movement, then wipe the wetness from my eyes.

I smooth the front of my dress with trembling hands, willing them to still. Straightening my spine, I drag in another breath, heavier this time, and lift my chin.

I am Narina Brevou. I will not be broken.

The sound of the front door creaking open echoes down the hall. I linger a moment longer, the sharp sting of my father's words clinging to me. But I won't stay in the dark he left behind. I gather myself and step into the hall, drawn toward the one person who can still pull me back into the light.

Diamo stands just beyond the doorway, a little disheveled from the forge, streaked with soot and sunlight all at once. He looks like hope incarnate: a living, breathing promise that my life won't always look like this.

"Sir," he greets my father with a smile, though the black smudges on his face betray the hard work of his day.

"Diamo," my father returns tersely, barely acknowledging him. He gives a curt nod to my betrothed before moving past us and back into the house. His eyes narrow as he passes me, the warning clear. I bite my lip, struggling to keep my face neutral.

"I'm here for our day that you've arranged," Diamo whispers, a wink flashing in his eyes. He's supposed to arrange these meetings, but he always humors me when I ask.

I hold up a finger, signaling for him to wait just a moment. Stepping into the kitchen, I retrieve the picnic basket. I bid my mother a quiet good day. She smooths the front of her apron absently, offering me a small smile that doesn't quite reach her tired eyes. Her voice is barely more than a whisper. "Enjoy yourself." We don't need to say more. What's happened, has happened.

"Where are we off to, my love?" Diamo asks, as I join him on the porch. His grin is wide and warm as he looks down at me. I shift the basket in my hands, the easy rhythm of his steps beside mine, the familiar path we've walked so many times, soothing bruises both seen and unseen.

"I was thinking the river," I reply, my voice a little lighter than before. "I don't know about you, but I could definitely use some time away from this place." I skip down the steps, waiting for him to join me at the bottom.

"Narina, have you gotten yourself into trouble with your father again?" he asks, concern clouding his expression. For a moment, I want to fall into his arms and weep. To tell him everything. But no. I won't burden him with this. Not now. Not when we've finally carved out a moment for ourselves.

"No," I lie softly, forcing a smile to my lips. A prick of guilt tugs at my chest. I hate lying to him. But I hate the thought of worrying him even more. "All is well. Let's go." I stretch my sore fingers, the movement is a small but necessary distraction. It's not hard to smile at him, he's the sun that follows the storm. Diamo gives me a look that says he doesn't quite believe me, but, to my relief, he doesn't press the issue. With a smile of his own, he joins me, and together we head toward the river at a leisurely pace.

"Diamo, you're a mess." I laugh as I take in the black marks smeared across his face. As I look closer, I realize it's not just his face, his arms and clothes are streaked with the same soot.

"Your note said to come after my shift at the blacksmith," he says with a shrug, a sheepish grin on his lips. "I didn't want to keep you waiting."

"I suppose I should thank you for that." I smile at him, genuinely this time. "I hate waiting." Little does he know how much more I'm thankful for. Always my hero, even when he doesn't realize it.

"I should hope so," he hums, his voice light and easy as we walk side by side.

After a few minutes, I fall a step behind and let myself enjoy the way he moves among the villagers. He asks after their lives, exchanges smiles, and weaves himself into the heart of the village with an ease I've always admired.

Diamo has such a gift for connecting with people. It reminds me, in the quietest way, how incredibly lucky I am that we'll soon be bound together.

He turns back to me, his grin warm, and gestures for me to join him. "Narina, you remember Thomas and Ariel?"

I smile politely at the couple; they return the gesture. There's no pressure to speak, and I'm grateful for it.

In Verti, women are meant to be seen, not heard. Soft smiles, lowered eyes, voices no louder than a breath. I know how to play the part. But wearing the mask has never come easy. I've never quite grasped how to disappear quietly enough. I don't fit the mold they carve for their daughters. Normally, I'd make an effort for Diamo's sake. Say something polite. Pretend at grace I don't really possess.

But today?

Today, even pretending feels like tempting fate...

Diamo keeps the exchange brief, his hand slipping back into mine as we continue down the path. I shift the basket awkwardly, the strain biting into my sore fingers. Diamo reaches over and gently lifts it from my grasp, lightening my burden without a word.

"You didn't say hello?" he remarks, his brow raised in playful curiosity.

I kick a small stone in the path and it skitters away, kicking up a small puff of dust. I scuff my shoe against the ground, avoiding his gaze.

"Women are to be seen, not heard. They are not to speak unless spoken to." I numbly recite the words my father and others have drilled into me, the bitterness of them lingering in my throat.

"I invited you into the conversation, Narina," Diamo responds, his concern evident. "That's never stopped you before. Why now?"

The question hangs in the air. I can't answer him with the truth. *Because my father wants to sell me.* Actually *sell me.* The thought has my blood running cold.

"I just don't want to risk any more trouble," I offer, hoping he'll accept my excuse, though the words feel hollow. Diamo knows my father isn't the most forgiving man, but he doesn't know everything. I've kept the worst of it from him, not wanting to burden him with the truth, and to spare myself from his pity.

"That's not like you, love."

He pulls me closer to him and I sink into his warmth. The metallic tang of smoke clings to him, sinking into the folds of his clothes. Even though it's only been a few days since I last felt this comfort, I have missed it dearly.

Diamo guides us off the worn path, his arm casually draped around my waist. We pass through some light underbrush, Diamo parting the bushes gently for me. A few brambles tug at my skirts, whispering against the fabric as we slip through the undergrowth.

"We're here," Diamo announces, his voice warm with familiarity. The low rush of the river hums in the distance, and the scent of fresh water and sun-warmed grass wraps around us. I look around fondly at our spot. We've been coming here since we were young. It's secluded, tucked off the path and hidden behind a line of brush, with just a handful of trees standing guard to keep the village's disapproving eyes at bay.

Diamo places the basket gently on the soft grass. Before I can blink, he turns to me, his arms enveloping me in a sudden embrace. He leans in close, his breath teasing my ear, sending a wave of shivers down my spine. "Come take a swim with me."

Chapter Six

He releases me abruptly, his eyes sparkling with mischief, and races toward the water's edge. I laugh, calling out to him about the unfairness of his head start. Mimicking him, I kick off my shoes as I sprint after him, my feet light and quick. When he reaches the bank, he leaps into the river, sending up a bright, wide splash. I stop at the edge, waiting for him to resurface.

He pops up moments later, gasping for air, his chestnut hair dripping wet. My breath catches. The water clings to his shirt, outlining the strong muscles earned from years of working the field and the forge. His broad shoulders, strong arms… Land's divine, I could stare at him all day.

Laughing, he wades toward me, ripples trailing behind him. When he offers his hand, I take it without thinking… only to lose my footing as he tugs me off balance. An amused shriek escapes me as I tumble into the river beside him. The cool water swirls around me, and I flail for a moment, searching for footing on the slick stones.

A second later, strong hands under my arms lift me up. I sputter, spitting out river water, and Diamo bursts into laughter, his voice deep and bright against the sky.

"You alright there, my love?" His eyes twinkle.

I glare at him playfully through wet lashes and slap the water, sending a splash into his face. He roars with laughter, pulling me further into the river, where it's deep enough to swim. He stays close, never drifting far. I can swim, but dresses have tangled before, dragging me down. Today, I'd chosen one that floats light and easily around me.

The river is cool and refreshing, a soothing contrast to the heat of the sunny day. A perfect day for a swim. I lean back, arms wide, letting the gentle current rock me as I float. The sun kisses my face; the water hums around me. Diamo dives under and surfaces nearby, splashing playful droplets toward me.

For the first time in what feels like forever, the weight eases from my chest. Soon, I won't have to endure my father. Soon, this... this peace, this light... will be my life.

"Diamo." I call out when he surfaces from another dive, his hair slicked back, water streaming down his face.

"Yes, my love?" His voice is soft with affection as he swims closer.

"Thank you for today." A soft smile tugs at my lips. "This is exactly what I needed." I close my eyes again, content, letting the moment stretch on. This is exactly the escape I had been hoping for.

"Of course." He cradles me in his arms, his touch easy and familiar. "I needed it too. I definitely needed a break from the workshop." I relax into his hold, my hands finding their way around his neck. He swims us slowly toward the bank.

As he carries me, I run my fingers gently along his neck, rubbing at a lone streak of soot the river missed.

"Is it not what you imagined?" I ask.

"It is exactly as I imagined." His voice is content. "I enjoy the work, but it's constant." He reaches the muddy slope and sets me down carefully. "Let's see what you packed."

We climb out of the river, wringing out our dripping clothes. I wrestle with my soaked dress, wishing for trousers, though I can imagine the scandal that would cause. Diamo finds a shady spot under a tree, already digging through the picnic basket.

"They're at the bottom." I tell him as I settle beside him. He flashes me a wide grin before resuming his search. Triumphantly, he pulls out the bowl of berries, looking utterly delighted.

"I've been dreaming about these berries all week," he mumbles around a mouthful, juice dripping down his chin. I roll my eyes fondly and lean back in the grass, sunlight dancing through the swaying branches overhead. I can't wait until every day of my life has this goofy man in it.

"Only fifteen more days," he says, echoing my thoughts. Just fifteen days until our ceremony. I prop myself up on an elbow, watching him devour the berries, already moving on to the cheese.

"I know. It feels like the days are dragging," I admit. The last few weeks seem to stretch on endlessly, each day slower than the one before, like time itself is reluctant to move forward.

"I—What is that?" He cuts himself off, dropping the piece of cheese, frowning.

"What?" I ask, confused.

"*That.*"

He leans forward, gently taking my hand. When I flinch, his touch softens even more. His fingers trace over the yellow bruises fading on my skin, and the fresh angry marks pressed over them.

"Narina," he breathes. "What did he do?"

Tears sting my eyes.

What did *he* do. Not, what did *you* do.

My Diamo.

"It doesn't matter."

"It does matter! Look at you!" His voice sharpens, but his touch remains tender. "What happened?"

"I was thoughtless," I admit, though the words don't feel enough. A stern, doubtful look is all he gives me in return.

"I doubt it deserved this." He lifts my hand, turning it slightly before caressing it with aching gentleness. "Why didn't you say?"

"Say what? I did something stupid again, and I was punished… again. He's been more on edge lately, but it's nothing new and there's nothing to be done about it." I shrug and pull my hand from his, suddenly uncomfortable. I hate that he knows.

Diamo is quiet for a moment. I can feel the heat of his gaze, even as I look away.

"It still shouldn't happen," he says softly. "Even if there's nothing to be done."

I flinch. "You think I don't know that?"

"I think you know it too well," he replies, voice low but steady. "I just hate when you talk like it's what you deserve."

Something in my chest folds inward, the words settling sharp and raw.

"Narina," he whispers, and this time when he says my name, it's not just pity, it's ache. Ache for me, for the bruises he can't stop, for the fight I'm trying so hard to keep small.

"Fifteen more days." I look at the trees, speaking to him and myself both.

"Yes," he sighs, understanding my desire to change the subject. "How is planning going?"

"It's done. The dress was the last thing to be arranged."

He leans closer. "You would look beautiful in anything, my love." His hazel eyes lock onto mine with such intensity it sends butterflies fluttering in my stomach. It still amazes me how easily I can see every emotion in them. I push him away slightly when my heart threatens to race ahead of me.

"I have to at least try to look like I'm worthy of the great Diamo Reddrit." I joke, hoping to ease some of the tension between us, but he just continues to gaze at me, unwavering.

Jumping up, I beckon him back to the river, needing to shake off the weight pressing against my ribs. He rises slowly, catches my wrist, and pulls me to him instead. His arms wrap around me, holding me close. My heart pounds wildly. His gaze locks mine in place.

"You are worthy. You are everything. You are *my* everything." He leans in closer. Shivers run down my spine as his lips graze my ear when he whispers, "You are *mine.*"

Before I can even begin to think of a reply, his lips find mine.

This kiss isn't soft or tentative. It's heat and wanting and too many words unsaid. My hands fist in his shirt as time seems to slow down. The world narrows to the feel of him, the taste of river water and sun-warmed skin. His arms tighten around me, grounding and dizzying all at once. The kiss deepens, restrained, but trembling on the edge of something bigger.

We both know we can't cross that line.

But part of me aches not to care.

He pulls back first, smirking against my skin like he knows exactly what I'm thinking.

Laughing breathlessly, I shove at his chest and take off running.

"Oy! Headstarts aren't fair, love!" he calls after me.

"You're one to talk!" I shout back, laughter bursting out of me as I dart across the field. Dust kicks up beneath my feet as I race in wide, looping circles. Diamo is faster, stronger. He could catch me easily if he wanted.

But he doesn't.

He lets me run.

Lets me feel free.

This.

This is my Diamo… laughing, loving, playful.

The boy who made me believe in freedom.

I want him to chase me forever.

Chapter Seven

I only stop laughing when Diamo's shouts of warning cut through the air.

But it's too late.

Dust erupts around me as hooves hammer the earth, too fast, too close.

I stumble, heart slamming against my ribs, struggling for balance, but the hem of my dress tangles around my legs. I hit the ground hard, pain ripping through my knees.

The horses skid to a stop just short of trampling me, hooves kicking up a blinding spray of dust and grit. I shove myself upright, coughing, blinking through the haze. My skirt is ruined. The damp fabric clinging, the dirt turning it heavy and dark with mud.

Frustration flares sharp as I lift my head, ready to lash out at whoever nearly trampled me. The words die on my tongue.

A man sits astride one of the horses, the reins loose in his gloved hands.

Take Her

He wears a deep red riding cap, dark hair spilling beneath it, but it's his eyes that stop me cold.

The bluest eyes I've ever seen, stark against his light skin.

Recognition jolts through me. I've seen those eyes before. Not in person, but in the portrait that hangs in the village hall.

Those eyes belong to the King.

Chapter Eight

Why is the King here? We're in the Outlands. He never comes this far from court. Yet, here he is. And I was nearly trampled by his horse.

He sits tall in the saddle, silent, staring.

I'm staring too.

Panic squeezes my chest. I know my place. I should lower my gaze, bow, do anything but stand here frozen beneath his piercing stare.

Too many moments too late, Diamo reaches me. He skids to a stop, he's breathless from the chase, his hands brushing my arms, checking me for injury. Once satisfied, his gaze lifts. The moment he recognizes the man before us, every muscle in his body locks into place. Whatever words he meant to say die in his throat. He bows deeply.

I should bow too. I *know* I should. But those eyes hold me captive.

The King regards me with a raised brow, his expression unreadable. Only when Diamo grips my hand and pulls me sharply down do I finally tear my gaze away. For the second time in minutes, my knees hit the ground.

"Milord," Diamo says, his voice steady but reverent. "It is an honor to be in your presence. I fiercely apologize for my mate's actions. She has forgotten herself."

I know better than to look up. I know. But something inside me fractures, refusing to obey. I lift my eyes.

The King is still watching me.

A flicker of amusement crosses his features, gone almost as soon as it appears. My stomach knots. The fleeting smile unsettles me more than any reprimand would.

Barely sparing Diamo a glance, he nudges his horse forward with a grunt, his escorts falling in line behind him.

Diamo exhales sharply the moment they're out of earshot. He bends to help me up but pulls me into a tight embrace. His arms lock around me, steadying my trembling hands. Over his shoulder, I watch the King ride away, swallowed by dust and distance.

"What were you thinking? Land's divine, Narina, what were you thinking?!" The words are a furious whisper against my ear. He pushes me out to arm's length, searching my face. Frustration, fear, and something rawer than either flash through his eyes.

I have no answers. I wish I did.

"I love your strength. Your stubbornness," he says, voice taut with urgency. "But you know better. Especially when it comes to men like him." He pulls me against him again, one hand cradling the back of my head.

"Especially the King," he whispers, more to himself than to me.

When he leans back, his hands still framing me, his gaze hardens. "You froze."

I flinch. "I didn't know what to do."

"You *always* know what to do." His voice isn't angry, but heartbroken. "You're brave. Fierce. I love that about you. But today…" He trails off.

I brace myself. "Today I was reckless."

He nods slowly. "And loud. And bold. And wild. And I love that too." He swallows, his jaw flexing. "But if the King had taken that as defiance... if he'd decided to make an example of you..."

He doesn't finish the sentence. He doesn't need to.

"I want a future with you," he says instead. "I want *forever*, Narina. And that means surviving the next fifteen days without giving *anyone* an excuse to take you away from me."

I nod, staring past him at the path where the King had disappeared.

"I wasn't thinking," I whisper.

"It's alright," he says softly. "You're alright." He says it like he's trying to convince us both. He tucks a damp curl behind my ear. "Let's go home."

We gather our shoes and the picnic basket from the riverside, the silence between us stretching on. Diamo walks beside me without speaking, his hand brushing mine now and then as if to remind himself I'm still here. I don't try to fill the space. I don't know how.

Shame gnaws at me, unrelenting. Not only did I put myself in danger, but I risked Diamo's safety too. The King could have punished us both with a word. I hate... *hate*... that I've disappointed him. He'd never say it outright, but it lingers in everything he doesn't say now.

My father is cruel in his own right, but the King... the King is something else. Renowned for his unbending will. His ruthless rule. His ability to make people disappear with a nod. I know my place. I should have lowered my gaze, bowed, done anything but stare.

But I hadn't.

And it wasn't just fear that had rooted me to the spot.

It was something far more dangerous.

Curiosity.

The thought twists in my gut. I try to shove it away, but it lingers, sharper than the sting of scraped knees or the ache in my bruised fingers.

The walk home drags on, stretching unbearably long. When we finally reach my father's doorstep, I hesitate, staring at the scuff marks on my shoes. My heart aches with unsaid apologies. It's impossible to make up for earlier, but Diamo deserves one, no matter how inadequate it might be. I turn to him.

"Diamo, I—"

He lifts a hand, silencing me.

"Don't, Narina. Just… don't." His voice is quiet. Weary. "I had a wonderful day with you at the river. Thank you for the picnic."

Guilt squeezes tighter. He presses a chaste kiss to my cheek, so gentle it breaks something in me. He lingers a moment longer, then turns toward the steps.

I watch him go, aching to fix what I've broken.

He pauses on the second step, head tilting slightly though he doesn't look at me directly.

"I'll be busy at the workshop. I don't know when I'll see you next." Another pause. Then a sigh. "Stay safe, love."

Then he's gone, jogging down the lane toward home, taking my heart with him.

Sadness wells up, threatening to spill over, but I force back the tears. Crying won't change anything. Self-pity won't undo today. This is my fault. There's no one else to blame. Diamo deserves better. I know that. He always has. But he wants me. And stars help me, I want him, too.

I slip inside the house, moving quietly. I don't dare face my parents. Not tonight.

Too tired to care, I let the mud-streaked dress fall to the floor, tug on my nightdress, and crawl into bed. Maybe tomorrow the world will feel less… broken.

I fiddle with the thin silver band around my finger, Diamo's promise, and notice my finger is starting to swell. Grimacing, I twist and pull the ring over the purple knot of my knuckle, heart sinking as it slips into my palm. I can't help but feel the sting of irony as I stare at the ring in my hand. Maybe it's the world's cruel way of telling me I don't deserve the promise it represents.

I can almost hear Diamo now, if I said that aloud. It's always the same with him anytime I doubt our betrothal. *My promise is eternal.*

Still, I set the ring carefully on the table beside my cot, next to the knotted pendant I slip from my neck. An ache tightens in my chest. His promise may be eternal, but tonight, I feel unworthy of it. Tomorrow, I tell myself, I'll do better. I'll be better. For him.

I am Narina Brevou. I will not...

The thought crumbles. Not tonight. Defeated, I lie back on my cot, and sleep soon pulls me under.

The sun hung low in the sky, casting a golden glow through the window. My father's voice cracked through the stillness.

"Narina, are you paying attention?"

I blinked, trying to focus. Diamo was outside the window, laughing with one of the village boys. I couldn't help but glance out at him. My father's voice pulled me back to the lesson, and the books spread across the table.

"Yes, Father." I answered quickly, dragging my attention back to the open books before me.

"Then what did I just say?" My father's tone hardened and I froze. Of course I didn't know.

"Something about taxes?" I offered weakly.

He slammed his palm on the desk, the sound making me jump. "You're not listening."

"I'm sorry," I said quickly, "I was just... thinking."

"You're wasting my time, Narina." His voice rose with each word. "You think you need to learn all this government nonsense? Ask your mother to teach you proper things." He stood, gathering the books roughly into his arms.

I was lucky that he'd agreed to teach me at all. I suppose the educator in him couldn't resist. Or maybe he'd hoped to shape my mind into something obedient. Or maybe, just maybe, he had agreed because I was his daughter, and I had asked.

"I want to learn," I insisted, reaching to stop him.

He scoffed, his voice dripping with disbelief. "You skip school more than you attend." A huge exaggeration, but one I knew he believed. He'd never understand that I hadn't skipped because I didn't value it. I skipped because I knew they'd take it from me when I turned thirteen. Skipping with Diamo was my way of controlling that loss.

I wanted to know how things worked in the world built to exclude me. Knowledge was a weapon that I wasn't allowed to wield, and that made me crave it even more.

"Cooking. Cleaning. Managing a household. Those are the lessons you need to learn. That's your place." He folded his arms and glared at me, as if that were the final word. "I will not waste my time on this further."

I bit my cheek, pushing back the urge to argue. Starting a fight with him wouldn't help. Anything beyond domesticity was a waste in his opinion.

"Will you leave the books?" I asked. "I can read them on my own."

He looked down at the pile of books, his brow furrowing as he considered. For a moment, I saw something flicker there, hesitation maybe. Or memory. I was still just a child to him. I bit my lip as the silence stretched.

"You may choose one," he finally said, begrudgingly. "More than that is unnecessary."

"Thank you," I muttered, my fingers already reaching for one at random. I slipped it under my arm, relief flooding me. I'd finish it quickly and swap it out for something else when he wasn't looking.

He waved me off with a grunt. "Get out of here. Don't waste my time any more than you already have.

Chapter Nine

"Narina. Narina, wake up, my dear." My mother's urgent voice cuts through the dark. Light floods the room, and I squint against it, still blinking through the fog of sleep.

"Narina, come quickly." My father stands in the doorway, a lit lantern in hand.

I sit up slowly, trying to piece together what's happening. Their faces are drawn, not panicked, but something close.

"What's going on?" I croak. My voice is rough, my throat dry. It's the middle of the night. Why are they awake?

"Do as you're told. Get up," my father snaps, already turning away.

My mother helps me to my feet and leads me out of the room. I'm still shaking the fog from my head when a loud pounding echoes from the front door. Father glances back at each of us just before he pulls it open.

"Everyone in your household is to report to the square immediately," a guard commands, low and clipped. I open my mouth to ask why, but my mother's firm grip on my hand tightens. I bite my tongue and follow.

We step out into the night. The cool air prickles my skin. I shiver in my short nightdress, wishing I'd thought to grab shoes, a shawl, or anything at all to cover myself. The dirt beneath my bare feet is sharp and biting. The path is already crowded. Torches flicker between bobbing lanterns, lighting faces pinched with confusion and fear. Babies cry. Children cling to their parents. Guards shout orders, moving door to door, herding us toward the square.

I scan the crowd as we move, searching for a familiar face. My heart beats faster as my eyes dart over the sea of people. I almost crash into my father when he stops. A thick-set guard stands ahead at the junction to the square, blocking the path as he directs people.

Father steps forward, leading us into the growing line. I continue to scan the faces around us, searching. As we reach the front, the guard glances over us but lingers too long on me.

"Is she bound?" he asks.

"Not yet," my father says flatly.

The guard flags another nearby. "This one's not bound." I don't catch the order he gives, but the second guard approaches me without hesitation. Unease prickles beneath my skin as he advances.

"She's to report to the front," the first guard says. "Take your mate and proceed."

Father doesn't hesitate as he tugs Mother away. She squeezes my hand once before letting go, her face soft with concern.

A sharp spike of panic stabs my chest, as the second guard grabs my arm. His pace is fast, his hold tighter than necessary. I stumble trying to keep up as I'm half-dragged across the square. My eyes dart through the crowd, near desperate. And then I see him.

Diamo, standing with his family. His eyes find mine at the same moment. He starts to smile, until he sees the guard's hand on me. The smile dies. He says something to his father, then starts forward, but stops when his father places a hand on his arm. I take a steadying breath.

The guard deposits me at the front of the square, alongside a line of other girls. I watch as the rest of the girls are gathered into the same area, the youngest barely fifteen. The crowd in front of us grows. Torn between nervousness and a deep, gnawing sense of dread, my stomach churns.

The crowd gradually quiets. I glance up and immediately wish I hadn't. They part like water, bowing as they clear a path for him.

The King.

He strides toward us like he owns the world. His shoulders are set, his posture unshakable. I'd thought, hoped, he was just passing through earlier. But this?

I quickly glance around, hoping for an opportunity to slip away unnoticed. The square is surrounded by guards, royal guards, not just the usual local patrols. Realization settles in. There's no way to escape.

Slowly, agonizingly slow, the King makes his way to the front of the crowd, to us. When he finally reaches our line, he pauses, turning to face the people. He raises his hands, and the deep, resonant voice that follows easily carries across the square.

"Good people of Verti. Thank you for your hospitality. It is late. I know you work hard during the day. I will not keep you long." He turns back to us with no further explanation.

With a nod, two of his guards fall into step behind him. The King moves slowly down the line, his eyes glancing over each girl. In turn, each girl offers a curtsy. Some trembling. Some practiced. All silent. All know their place. A blush heats my cheeks as I think of how I had behaved earlier. I wonder if Diamo is thinking the same.

The King pauses briefly in front of a couple of girls but moves on after only a few seconds. When he reaches me, I manage a weak curtsy and, thankfully, remember to keep my gaze firmly down. I fixate on his boots as they stop in front of me. They gleam without a trace of dust. How? It's such a mundane thought, but one that keeps my mind occupied. But it's not enough.

"Look at me," he commands. Reluctantly, I obey. I'm once again caught in the icy blue of those eyes. Cold. Certain. Remembering. Of course he does. There's no way he can't. I take a deep breath. It doesn't steady me.

"You're the girl from the field. The one who interfered with my horse." I bite my tongue to keep from pointing out that it was he who nearly ran me down. Instead, I give a small nod. "Your age?"

"Nineteen," I say, trying to sound confident, though I'm not sure I succeed. His eyes hold me in place, cold and calculating. He strokes his full, grey-speckled beard, once, thoughtfully. His expression doesn't change, but the air feels like it's thickening between us. What is he thinking? Surely, he can't take the foolish actions of a girl from the fields seriously.

Finally, he releases me from his gaze, turning toward the crowd.

"To whom does this girl belong?" His voice booms across the square, demanding attention. I feel every eye in the village on me, the weight of their stares pressing down. I glance at Diamo and silently plead with him, though I know he can't do anything without endangering himself. Still, he meets my gaze, worry tainting the sweet honey.

"I am her father, milord," my father calls out. "This is the man she will be bound to." The crowd shifts, creating space around him as he motions toward Diamo.

"When are you to be bound, boy?" The ground slips from beneath me as Diamo tears his gaze from mine to the King.

"A matter of days, milord," Diamo responds, his voice still as steady and confident as it was earlier in the field. The King narrows his eyes, scrutinizing Diamo.

"How long have you been promised?"

"Two years, milord."

"A long time to wait to claim her." The King raises an eyebrow, his words probing.

"The time wasn't right, milord," Diamo says, his voice faltering slightly. My heart skips a beat.

"How unfortunate," the King murmurs.

I didn't realize how fast I was breathing until now. The dizziness begins to set in as those blue eyes lock onto mine once again. He watches me in silence. His lips curl into a slow smirk.

And I know.

He raises a hand, his voice calm.

"Take her."

Chapter Ten

Time collapses, stretching and vanishing all at once.

The guards seize me before I remember how to breathe. One takes each arm as the ground falls away beneath me. The King still wears that blasted smirk plastered to his face as he watches.

My mother wails. I snap my head toward her. She's crumpled in my father's arms. He never even glances my way.

Diamo does. He's pushing through the crowd, ducking under arms and around guards. His expression is a storm of rage and fear.

"Narina!" His shout pierces something in me. "Narina!"

I breathe.

I dig my heels into the dirt, resisting with everything I have. I don't know where they're taking me, but I won't go quietly. Whatever I did, it can't warrant this. I twist against their grip. Two more guards rush in.

"No, no! Let go! You can't do this! Let go of me!" I kick, thrash, scream. They hold on tighter as they drag me through the street.

"Narina! Narina!" Through the shifting bodies, I catch another glimpse of Diamo, just before he's seized. Blood streaks the side of his face. He's still fighting. Of course he is.

I scream until my throat burns raw, kicking at the guards. They dodge easily and barely flinch, only tightening their grip. I twist harder. Fight harder. But it's like trying to move stone.

Diamo vanishes from view. I can still hear him shouting, but it's fading. He's no longer in the square. The King's men drag me toward a carriage, half-carrying me now. I lash out again, blindly, desperately. One of them swears.

The door of the carriage flies open. I'm shoved inside, into the hands of more guards. One of them curses as I twist free for half a second before another pins me back down. It's too fast. Too inevitable.

The carriage jolts into motion, and my struggle turns clumsy and chaotic with the sway of the road. I fight until my muscles give out, my breath breaking in shuddering gasps. My arms hang useless. My legs refuse to move.

They don't release me right away. Just sitting, gripping my arms like they expect me to strike again. Eventually, they loosen their hold and lean back, watching me like I'm a wild animal.

I don't blame them. One has a red line carved down his cheek. I don't remember drawing blood, but I remember the curse and the threat on my life. The other clutches his shin. I almost feel proud. But my own arms throb. Bruises are already blooming under my skin. And the pride withers into something hollow.

I curl up in the seat opposite them. It's ridiculous how lavish this prison is. Red velvet cushions beneath me, gold trim gleaming at the edges of the curtains and walls, tassels swinging with every bump in the road. Even the windows are glass. Actual glass. I've never seen that before. All the carriages that come and go from Verti are simple, practical things.

I hug my knees to my chest, pressing my cheek against the sharp bones. The air inside is warmer than outside, but I still shiver. My skin crawls from cold and leftover adrenaline. My heart refuses to settle, pounding like it still thinks there's time to run.

I shut my eyes. Not to sleep; there's no way I could sleep. Just to escape. To block out the image of my mother fainting, imagining her disappointment. To shut out the thoughts of what came of Diamo after fighting for me. To drown the quiet, creeping dread of what they'll do to me.

All of it. I just want to go back. To the river where we laughed. To my room, to my mother's arms. I want to go back to Verti, where I belong. To Diamo.

To the life that just got ripped out from under me.

Fifteen.

The age when a young lady was first allowed to walk the village without a family member. So long as she had an escort. It was my fifteenth birthday, and there had never been any question who mine would be.

As expected, Diamo stood on our doorstep that morning. We'd been out alone before, of course, plenty of times. Just never with permission. But today he was here to ask properly, to take me to Merchant's Valley.

While my father spoke with him, my mother braided my hair in my room. When Father returned and gave his approval, excitement fluttered in my chest. I couldn't sit still. My fidgeting tugged a few strands loose from my mother's careful hands, and she clicked her tongue at me before gently guiding them back into place. Her hum was soft, steady. I forced myself to sit still, barely containing my impatience. The moment she finished, I leaped to my feet and hurried down the hall, stopping just short of Diamo, who was already smiling.

Taking his offered arm, we started toward the door.

"Narina."

My mother's quiet voice floated after me. A reminder. A warning.

I turned. She stood beside my father, the perfect vision of a proper woman. Hair twisted into a tight bun. Eyes downcast. Hands folded neatly in front of her.

Always a step behind. A knowing look and a small smile graced her face, as they always did. I studied her, trying to etch the image into my mind. Then, with a nod, I acknowledged the chastisement. Straightening, I attempted to emulate her demure demeanor and simple grace as I left with Diamo.

Merchant's Valley sat just beyond the village square, a stretch of road lined with wooden stalls and canvas awnings. The scent of fresh bread and smoked meat mingled with warm smithy smoke. A hammer rang in the distance. Somewhere, someone played a flute. The melody threaded through the morning air, weaving between the voices of merchants and hagglers.

I darted from stall to stall, wide-eyed and full of questions. Anyone else would've found me exhausting. My father certainly had. The one time he brought me here, he left so annoyed he never took me again.

But Diamo just laughed. He knew the vendors by name but let me set the pace, trailing behind with amused patience and only stepping in when I floundered.

We stopped at a jeweler's booth, where Diamo introduced me to his friend Bailef, the merchant's apprentice. As they fell into conversation, I wandered, drawn to the glittering trinkets. Near the back, I spotted a pendant. It hung from a simple black cord, half-hidden in shadow. Copper loops twisted around each other in a web of knots, the metal darkened with age. It looked ancient, otherworldly.

I reached for it, and was startled when Diamo appeared beside me. I pulled my hand back, embarrassed. He said nothing, just unhooked the cord and slipped it over my head. The pendant landed against my collarbone like it had always belonged there.

I stared up at him, silent.

"To commemorate today," he said softly, smiling.

Lands, the butterflies that smile sets loose.

"Thank you," I whispered. "It's beautiful."

We walked on, the valley alive around us, our arms occasionally brushing. Here, amidst the hum of voices and the scent of spices on the breeze, he whispered his thoughts of the future.

Low and soft in my ear, he told me he liked me just as I was. He didn't want me to change, didn't want me to become what society expected. He thought I was strong, brave ... different. His words made me blush, made my heart race.

Take Her

Diamo was my beloved friend. Today, he was my escort. And almost always, an escort became a mate.

Chapter Eleven

Numb. Completely numb.

I don't feel the cold air against my skin. I don't feel the sway of the carriage beneath me. I don't feel the soft cushion I've been sitting on for hours. I don't feel the soreness in my body from newly acquired bruises. I don't feel the gripping pain in my heart at the thought of Diamo. I don't feel the tear in my stomach when I think of my family.

I don't feel anything.

I'm just numb.

The carriage bumps along, steady as ever. I suppose it's time to face the world again. After all, I *should* feel something. Anyone would, especially after losing everything. I draw a breath and gather what little strength I have to open my eyes. The guards are still in their places, both asleep now. A sign of how long we've been traveling, or maybe just proof that it was the dead of night when this journey began.

Reaching for the familiar warmth of my copper pendant, my fingers close around nothing. The unwelcome realization that I left it on my table hits. The chill seeps in then, and I let it. The bitterness of it dulls the pain that's spreading across my chest. If only it were an injury, something that could be treated and wrapped. But this pain goes deeper. It cuts and throbs until I feel like I'm going to choke on it.

I won't cry though. Not now. Not here.

I'm Narina Brevou. I will not be...

I am Narina Brevou. I...

I am...

The carriage dips hard and jerks to a violent stop. My stomach drops. With a startled squeal, I throw out my arms as I'm flung sideways. I slam into the corner, hitting the wall hard enough to send pain lancing through my arm. One of the guards hits the floor; the other barely catches himself before landing on top of me. Considering they were asleep seconds ago, I suppose I'm lucky he has fast reflexes.

Groaning, I clutch my shoulder and try to right myself. It's a feat as the carriage is now sharply tilted toward the back corner. Lands divine.

The guards recover faster than I do. One moves to stand near me while the other edges toward the door and peeks outside. His expression when he looks back is grim.

"It's the wheel," he mutters. He jerks his chin toward me. "Stay with the girl." Then he disappears into the night.

I straighten myself the best I can, but the slant of the carriage makes it impossible. Giving up, I lean my head back against the plush wall. I thought this night couldn't get any worse, but here we are. We're stuck on a road, who knows where, with a wheel that is either stuck or broken. I close my eyes against the pounding in my skull. When I hear the door pop open again, I don't bother looking.

"It's broken. No signs of tampering, just bad luck. Guy says he can't fix it in the dark. We're here until morning." It's the guard. His voice is easy to recognize, higher pitched, with a distinct inflection. "It's only a couple of hours until dawn. Better bring the girl out and get her settled."

No, just leave me here. But they don't hear my thoughts.

A hand grabs my arm and hauls me upright. I finally open my eyes, just enough to find my footing. The guard near me braces himself and helps me fight gravity, guiding me to the door. The man waiting offers his hand. Accepting the fact that I'll probably fall on my face if I don't, I take it and let him pull me safely to the ground.

The night is moonlit but dim. A sliver of silver casts just enough light to see the remnants of the broken wheel on the ground just a few steps away. The cracked and broken wood looks eerily haunted in the shadows.

I shiver in the open air. My thin nightdress offers little protection against the creeping chill. If I'd known I was going on a midnight journey, I might've dressed more sensibly. I wrap my arms tightly around myself as the guard leads me to a fallen tree in a patch of grass.

"Sit here." I do. I'm too tired to argue. He watches me shivering and hesitates. "We'll get a fire started soon. Try not to freeze to death until then. His Majesty would have my head." I can't tell if he's joking. I'm not sure I care. He walks off toward the carriage driver.

I squint into the dark. I have no idea where we are, but we're definitely not in the Outlands anymore. The land is too green, too alive. Lush grass replaces red dirt. Trees line the horizon behind me. On the other side of the road, an open pasture stretches out, the tall grasses bowing in the breeze.

I shiver again. This is ridiculous. If I sit here much longer, I might just end up freezing to death or at the very least catch a cold.

Standing, I carefully make my way through the grass. It's wet and icy against my bare feet. I gather sticks as I go, arms slowly filling. When I have enough, I return to the fallen tree and kneel a few feet in front of it.

Diamo and I have been out late on cold nights more times than I can count. He spent one entire evening teaching me how to build and start a fire. I never thought I'd need to with him around, but I asked and he taught me, patient as ever. *Diamo.* My heart tugs at the memory as I take my time stacking the sticks the way he showed me.

A boy, a page maybe by the look of his uniform, comes and stands near me. He's tall but his face and build mark him at maybe thirteen or fourteen years. He doesn't say anything, and I'm in no mood to engage, so I continue my task in silence. As I finish stacking the wood, he kneels beside me.

"I can finish it, Miss." I move aside. I don't have anything to light it with anyway.

He works quickly, pulling out a bundle of dried cotton. He strikes his flint until a spark catches. Nursing the tiny flame, he sets it at the base of the stack I'd made. I watch the boy feed it slowly, coaxing it to grow.

He reminds me of Diamo; the surety of his movements, the way he hunches his shoulders. A shiver shakes me from getting lost in those memories again. I retreat back to the fallen tree and sit, leaning against it as I watch the fire slowly grow.

Gradually, it builds and gives off enough warmth to take the chill from the air. The boy settles on the other side, curling into the grass.

We were lying in the sparse grass just beyond the fence line, the last stretch of Verti before the fields and desert took over. The stars were clear out there, so many, you couldn't count them if you tried. Diamo lay beside me, hands behind his head, his elbow brushing mine whenever we shifted.

"It's still out there," he said softly. "That dream. You and me, heading east, slipping past the border patrols, getting to the sea and just... sailing."

I smiled at the memory. It was our oldest dream, half rebellion, half escape plan.

"Past the charts," I said, echoing our old rhythm. "Until we find something they haven't named yet."

He chuckled. "A place where no one tells us who to be. No patrols. No punishments. No one watching to see if you speak too loudly or take up too much space."

For a long moment, I let myself picture it again, the boat, the open water, the quiet life built from nothing but freedom and salt wind. But the longer I stared at the stars, the more fragile the vision became.

"What if it's just more of the same?" I said finally. "New names, new laws, new rulers."

Diamo didn't answer.

I shifted onto my side, the dry grass crackling beneath me. "At least here," I whispered, "I know where the lines are. I know when to duck, when to be quiet. Verti's far enough from the capital that the crown only looks this way when it wants something. The patrols are predictable. The people talk too much, but they're not cruel."

His gaze found mine in the dark, steady and unreadable.

"I have some freedom here," I went on. "In the stories whispered. In the space between punishments. In you. Maybe that's all we're meant to have. Maybe we should just… be glad for what we've carved out."

Diamo sat up, brushing dirt from his palms. "No."

The word cut through the stillness like flint striking steel.

"You used to say we were meant for more," he said, not unkindly. "Not just scraps of silence. More. A world where you didn't have to calculate your every breath."

"I still want that," I said. "But maybe we can't have it."

"Not unless we make it," he replied. "Not unless someone starts. They just don't know how."

He looked out toward the empty road, the faint silhouette of the village behind us. "I've been talking to my father. Quietly. He wants things to change too. Master Blackwell has mentioned it, as well." He turned back to me, his voice low. "What if we know how?"

I blinked at him. "You're planning a rebellion with a hammer and forge?"

A grin tugged at the corner of his mouth. "Change doesn't always come with fire, Narina. Sometimes it comes with work and patience and people willing to speak just a little louder each year."

I studied him in the dark. Strong, quiet, steady. The kind of man who could break a system without shouting.

"I still think about the sea," I whispered.

"I know."

We sat in silence for a while, the kind you can only share with someone who knows all the pieces of you and still stays close.

I let my fingers find his, and we lay in the quiet. Two people dreaming the same dream, not realizing it was already slipping out of reach.

Chapter Twelve

The sun is just starting to peek over the horizon when I wake. *Dawn.* I hadn't even realized I was drifting off.

If I'd known what was coming, I would've kissed him, said his name like a prayer, promised I'd meet him at the sea, even if I had to burn the world to get there.

But I didn't know.

And I didn't kiss him.

I sit up gingerly. Everything aches, probably made worse by sleeping against a tree. Stretching my stiff back, I take in my surroundings. The fire has burned down to embers. The boy is curled on the ground, still asleep. The guards are near the carriage, voices raised as they gesture wildly at a man kneeling beside the broken wheel. One throws up his hands and spins away. He catches sight of me and stomps over. It's the one who sat me here last night.

"Looks like we're here for a while." He tosses a bag. It lands beside me with a soft thump. "There's some food in there. Share with the boy."

He moves to leave, but then pauses, turning back. "Do *not* wander off. This isn't an area for a young woman to get lost in. It won't end well."

I nod mutely. I have no idea where we are, but I'm aware that there are areas of Barbast crawling with unrest and crime.

Hungry, I open the bag and investigate the contents. *Ugh.* Pulling out a folded piece of cloth, I am both grateful and irritated. This would've been appreciated ages ago. Still, I wrap the wool blanket around my shoulders before I continue searching the pack. There's salted meat, fruit leather, and tough bread. Splitting off a little of each, I pull the blanket tighter and settle back against the tree.

Mouth watering from the salty meat, I watch the three men trying to force the broken wheel into cooperation. They're not having any luck piecing the shards of wood back together. The rest of the guards are a few feet away, tending to the horses and rummaging through their own packs.

With everyone distracted it really would be the perfect time to escape back to Verti. I'm caught between the sweet lure of freedom and the sour taste of becoming the victim of something much worse than a trip to the capital—when the rattle of wheels bumping down the road draws my attention.

My bite of jerky catches in my throat at the sight. A wagon approaches, drawn by three horses and topped with a metal cage. Four gruff men walk alongside it, with one more in the driver's seat. Tanned from long travels through southern Barbast, the scars on their arms are pale and jagged. One man has a matching scar slashed across his cheek. Swords hang at their hips. Their clothes are worn, but not ragged.

It isn't the sight of the men that makes my stomach twist. It's the people behind the bars.

Ten, maybe more, men and women hunched in the too-short cage. There isn't enough room for all of them to sit at once. Bile rises when I spot a child no older than seven peeking out from behind a woman's skirt. I want to look away but their faces hold me.

Despair.

Desperation.

Fear.

Defeat.

It stains every expression.

"Slavers." The boy's voice, soft beside me, startles me from my stare. I glance at him briefly before returning my gaze to the wagon.

"Don't you pity the beasts?" he whispers, as if afraid they'll hear him.

Pity? No. This doesn't fill me with pity. It fills me with horror. Horror. Rage. Disgust. Those are the emotions filling me right now. How could anyone look at this and think it was acceptable? Pity isn't appropriate here. Pity has no place in this moment. Outrage. Revulsion. Grief.

"No," I whisper back. "I grieve for them." I push to my feet, needing the distance. "And they're not beasts. They're people, no different than you or me." I walk away from the page boy before I say something more dangerous.

How could the monarchy deem this travesty anything but abhorrent and appalling? The rolling dungeon had been a threat my father threw at me many times in an attempt to make me obedient, but it had never been a fate that came to fruition. Unless, that is the same fate my own carriage is delivering me to. It may not be made of bars, but the ending could be the same. A fresh emotion washes over me… sharp, cold, and impossible to ignore. Fear.

The slavers' cage stops beside our wagon. The driver speaks to the guards near the wheel. I pull the blanket tighter as they exchange words. I've only seen a slaver's cage in Verti once before, but I know their routine. They sweep through the Outlands buying and selling "unwanteds." Then they make their way to the capital where they sell their remaining "cargo." The words disgust me. "Cargo." "Unwanteds."

If the slaves make it to the capital, most end up in the King's castle, or in service to his nobles.

After a few minutes, one of the slavers claps a guard on the shoulder and heads for the back of the cage. He hauls down a spare wheel and pushes it toward the group. I don't see what the guard gives him in return, but I release a breath of relief that it wasn't me.

One wheel lighter, likely a few gold richer, the slavers snap their reins and urge their own horses forward. I watch them go, unable to tear my eyes from the people inside. They grasp the bars for balance as they're hauled toward a fate no one deserves.

The guard who seems to be in charge, Harrow, if I overheard right, turns to where I'd been sitting. A small kernel of satisfaction tickles me as a flicker of panic crosses his face when he doesn't see me. It fades quickly when he spots me nearby. He stomps over, irritation radiating off him.

"I told you to not wander."

I look around, genuinely confused. "I'd hardly call walking a few steps wandering," I say dryly.

"We're leaving as soon as the new wheel's on. We're already behind schedule," he snipes, clearly on edge.

"Don't rush on my account." I flash a too-sweet smile. I'm in no hurry to reach whatever misery awaits me. He grunts. Of course the brute can't just *ask* me to move. Instead, he grabs my arm and steers me back to where the page waits by the fire.

"Watch her," he growls to the boy, who looks thoroughly frightened to even be addressed by the large man. He nods shakily. Harrow releases me and marches back to the others.

I study the boy. He must be from a decent family to have landed a page's apprenticeship. Pages aren't common in the Outlands, but in the capital, nearly every wealthy lord and ranking officer has one. In return, they get education, lodging, and a path toward becoming royal guards, knights, generals, and the like.

"What's your name?" I ask.

He hesitates, eyes flickering to mine. He must decide that I can't hurt anything because he quietly voices his answer.

"Peter."

"Who are you page to, Peter?"

"Why do you want to know?" he snaps, straightening.

I shrug. I don't actually care, but a little conversation might make the wait pass quicker. When he doesn't answer, I sidestep around him and return to my spot by the tree. He follows close behind, quiet as a puppy waiting for praise.

Leaning back, I nod toward the smoldering embers.

"Think you can resurrect it? Harrow might pop a vein if I *wander* off for more wood."

"Captain," he mumbles.

"Pardon?"

"It's Captain Harrow." His voice is small but he is sure in his defense of the man's title. "We probably shouldn't," he gestures to the fire. "He'll be in a hurry to leave once the wheel is fixed."

"He's the one you serve, then?" I tilt my head. He looks surprised by the guess, mouth opening and closing like a startled fish before replying.

"It's not official until the King approves it at the castle. No one is sure if he'll accept an Outlander in his court."

"Seems like he's collecting us," I mutter. "Though, I'm sure your fate is more promising than my own." I glance at him. "Do you happen to know what my fate entails?" Sitting beside me, he shakes his head, his floppy golden curls bouncing.

"I'm not even sure the King knows," he admits.

"What?"

He shrugs and stares out across the field.

"It didn't make any sense. He didn't want to stop at any villages. He was actually avoiding them. We were just passing by your village on the way to the castle. We were well past it and about ready to make camp for the night when he suddenly called for us all to turn around and return to Verti. I didn't hear anyone say why... or why he took you."

I wave away the apology in his eyes. I know why. The King is vain and I disrespected him.

"Why was he in the Outlands if he didn't want to stop anywhere?" Another shrug then leans back on his hands.

"They stopped in my village to collect me, but the King didn't make an appearance. I heard he stopped in a couple villages, sat on a dais, watched for a day, then moved on."

"Peter!" Harrow's voice is loud and harsh. "Put out those embers! We're moving." Peter jolts upright and shouts back his acknowledgement.

"Let's go, girl," he barks. I assume the second part is for me. I pull the blanket tighter and rise.

The carriage has been righted, the new wheel in place. Harrow stares down at me, finger pointed like I'm a mutt in need of taming.

"We've got a long haul ahead. You act up, and my men won't hesitate to tie you down. Understand?"

I'm not sure whether to feel flattered that he thinks I'm that much trouble or insulted that he's speaking to me like an unruly hog. I remember why I'm here and I can't afford for Harrow to report anything worse. Mute obedience is probably the wiser choice. He squints at me, then shoves me into the carriage where two guards wait.

Chapter Thirteen

With occasional stops to rest the horses, rotate the guards, and tend to other needs, the rest of the day passes without incident before they finally make camp. I'm left to sleep in the carriage with a guard at the door after being told the area isn't safe enough for me to be outside.

The next day passes in a similar fashion. Midmorning, Peter is allowed to join me and the guards in the carriage. His youth and inexperience make the long ride hard on him. His head lolls as he sleeps away the day in the corner of the lush carriage, and I envy his ability to relax. The closer we get to King's Village, the tighter my chest becomes. I'm drawn back into the aching void that's taken up residence in me.

The carriage pulls into a turn and the jostling abruptly stops, replaced by a smooth ride. The shift is so sudden I sit up straighter, instantly alert. Odds are we're now on the King's Path, the one and only road that leads directly to the castle and the village before it. Of course it's well-maintained. The road to the throne gets special attention.

Take Her

Curiosity gets the better of me the longer I think about our destination and what awaits me. Pulling back the short curtain that hangs across the door, I peer outside. It's dusk.

Guards are posted intermittently along the path, likely to deter any would-be thieves. Robbing a royal carriage is foolish, but not impossible. Beyond the path, thick woods stretch in every direction, the trees packed tightly with undergrowth twisting madly at their base.

Then I see it, and freeze. The wooden houses and thatched roofs packed tightly together being cast into darkness by the stretching shadows from the setting sun and the massive castle looming behind them. The castle rises in stark silhouette, its turrets and towers climbing toward the sky, nestled in front of the mountains like a beast in wait.

Even in the Outlands, stories of the castle are everywhere. Endless, twisting corridors that swallow intruders. Secret tunnels that have saved monarchs... and doomed them. Glorious stories of festivals and celebrations in the square. Dances and parties in the ballroom. Tales filled with color... and others drowned in darkness.

Control. Torture. Death.

Like they did with her.

The thought stabs through me: the storyteller. They dragged her off too. For imagined disobedience. For defiance. And now they're doing the same to me. I'm being pulled down the same road. Straight to the crown. Straight to punishment.

As we draw nearer, details sharpen. Villagers make their way home beneath lanterns and torches flickering to life. Candlelight glows in the castle's many windows, making them look like a haunted garden suspended in stone.

Suddenly I have no more desire to see it and the horrors it holds than to sit in this carriage for another second. I'd rather face the dark woods.

I am Narina Brevou. I will not be broken.

Without another thought, I fling open the door and jump out. My feet stumble on the landing, but I manage to stay upright. I don't look back. I run, straight into the trees, ignoring the shouting guards behind me.

I run blindly with no idea where I'm going and even less sense of which way is home. I hear them. Heavy footsteps crashing through the brush, crushing leaves and limbs beneath their boots.

Branches claw at my arms and brambles snag my nightdress. Stones and roots bite into my bare feet. But I don't stop. If they want me, they'll have to catch me.

My breath comes in shallow gasps, my lungs screaming for more than I can give. Under the thick canopy, the woods are darker than the road had been, the last rays of sunlight swallowed by leaves.

I can hear them struggling too, tripping on the same limbs and brush that slow me down. But they're getting closer.

I force myself to keep going, to ignore the pain in my soles, the tearing in my side, the fire in my legs. Slowing down isn't an option. Getting caught means never seeing home again. Never seeing Diamo again.

My foot snags on a root and I trip over a stone. Shouts echo around me, closer now. Panic sweeps over me, either I am slowing down or they're catching up. In the dimness, I spot a fallen tree. I lunge for it, but I don't clear it. I fall, crashing awkwardly on my arm. My wrist twists beneath me and a bolt of pain shoots up my arm. I grit my teeth to keep from crying out.

The fall is my undoing as the guards catch me easily, surrounding me. One guard reaches for me and I kick out at him. My heel connects with his nose and he reels back, cursing through blood.

I am Narina Brevou.

They will not take me without a fight.

Two more approach me, slower, warier this time. Their hands outstretched. I lash out at them in any way I can when they get close. I dig my hands into the leaves and debris around me, searching for anything I can use to defend myself. I hurl a stone at one of them. It narrowly misses, and he curses. I grab another.

Take Her

A crack echoes off the trees. Pain explodes at the back of my head. My vision blurs. Dizziness overtakes me. And then—darkness.

I was curled up behind Father's house, arms wrapped tight around my knees, face buried so no one would see. My back still stung where the switch had landed. This time, I'd spoken out of turn.

I'd tried to hold it together afterward. Had walked away with my head high, the way I'd promised myself I always would. But as soon as I was out of sight, I broke.

I didn't hear Diamo coming. I never did when I needed him most.

He crouched beside me, the dirt shifting under his boots as he nudged my shoulder.

"Narina." His voice was soft, coaxing. I ignored him.

Instead of leaving, he rocked back on his heels. "You know, I've seen you take worse than this and still spit fire." I didn't respond. My throat full of heat and shame.

He sighed, dramatic and theatrical, bumping against my shoulder again. "Come on… rebels' granddaughter. Who. Are. You?"

I peeked out from under my arm to glare at him. He was grinning like an idiot.

"I'm not playing this game right now," I muttered.

"It's not a game," he said brightly. "It's a sacred ritual. I ask. You answer. Balance is restored to the world."

I sniffled and wiped my nose on my sleeve.

Diamo grinned, bouncing where he crouched, gaze light and playful. "I know you know," he pressed. "So say it."

I drew in a shaky breath. "Narina Brevou."

"Good." He nodded, pleased. "Who are you?"

I blinked at him, then straightened my trembling shoulders. "I am Narina Brevou."

"And…?" He was insistent, unwavering.

I swallowed hard, my jaw tightening. Then, with a deep breath, I lifted my chin, my voice steady this time. "And I will not be broken."

Diamo grinned wider, satisfaction glinting in his eyes. "There she is."

Chapter Fourteen

Surrounded by darkness, I'm not even sure my eyes are open until I spot a sliver of light beneath the door across from me. I groan as my shoulder protests against the cold, unforgiving stone I'm lying on, and a burning tingle tortures my fingers. Rolling to my back, I shiver and silently curse the fallen tree that landed me here.

Eventually, I convince my aching muscles to support me enough to sit up, though the headache that blooms immediately makes me wish I had stayed sprawled across the stone. Pressing the heel of my palm to the throbbing between my eyes, I try to shake the tingling from my hand before taking stock of the rest of me.

My run through the woods left its mark—scraped legs, sore arms likely bruised, aching soles of my feet, and the worst of it, a throbbing wrist that flares with every movement. I blow out a breath and mutter under it. Could this impossible situation get any worse?

A thought I should have kept silent. Fueled by the foul stench of this dungeon and the sheer terror of my situation, my imagination has no trouble conjuring worse. Punishments. Interrogations. Rotting down here alone. I shiver at the possibilities and almost find myself hoping they forget about me entirely.

No such luck.

The door creaks and groans open. I squint against the sudden brightness as I sit up straighter, shielding my eyes. Once the spots fade, I make out a woman standing in the doorway, flanked by four guards holding torches.

She wears a modest long-sleeved black dress that frames her collarbone and hits just above her ankles, the only adornment is a black fabric belt at the waist. The guards wear the typical black uniform with the royal symbol on the left arm, but these four also bear a deep red band around their right biceps.

"I'm Mistress Myra," the woman says. Her voice is high and clipped, as severe as the bun that pins her hair in place. "His Majesty has summoned you. We must not keep him waiting." She inclines her head toward the hallway.

I eye the guards on either side of me, weighing the odds of refusing to move. Mistress Myra huffs and purses her lips.

"They will drag you if necessary." She waves a hand toward the corridor. "We must not keep His Majesty waiting."

I take a breath, remind myself that the stronger I appear, the harder I'll be to break. *I am Narina Brevou. I will not be broken.*

Not relishing the idea of adding fresh bruises to the collection, I push to my feet, wincing as dizziness swirls and fire burns the soles of my feet. I steady myself with my arms until the world stops spinning, then hobble to Myra's side. The guards follow close behind.

The halls are empty as we walk, a small mercy considering my state. Myra's pace is unrelenting, and I quickly learn the rumors about the castle's layout are true. It feels endless, with twisting passages that loop back on themselves. I've already lost my sense of direction, and I swear this is the fourth time I've seen that statue of a nearly naked man holding a bow.

"The castle was designed to confuse intruders. So don't go wandering," Myra says, as if reading my thoughts. "You'll get lost and we're too busy preparing to come looking for you."

If only that were true. I could vanish in this place and be forgotten.

"Preparing for what?" I ask, doing a half skip to keep up. Each step on bare stone sends a flare through my feet.

"I was told your... education was lacking." Her sigh is heavy with practiced tolerance. "So, to avoid us both getting in trouble I'll help you." She takes a sharp left and continues, "When you are in the presence of His Majesty you will keep your head down, eyes averted, and remain silent. Obedience is not optional. Disobedience will be punished. We hold higher expectations for our women here than *those people* in the Outlands." She spits the words *those people* like they taste foul. Insulted, I glance at her, but her eyes remain fixed on the corridor ahead.

"What are you preparing for?" I try again.

"When we reach the throne room, you will continue to the center and kneel, head down, and wait for His Majesty's instructions." She doesn't miss a step.

"Do you know why he's summoned me?" I press, heart thudding. She doesn't answer. Apparently done with her speech, the only sounds left are the heavy thud of guard boots and the slap of my bare feet.

Before I can ask again, we stop at a pair of wooden doors. They're nearly twice as tall as I am and intricate carvings cover their entirety. The guards swing them open and to my surprise, Myra drops to her knees by the door, head bowed, hands folded neatly in her lap.

Obedience is not optional.

The two guards behind me guide me forward into the vast room. The same cold stone continues from the hallway, but my gaze is drawn past it to the expansive windows on the opposite wall. Peaked stone arches reach the ceiling, framing a clear view of the fields beyond the castle wall. Heavy gold drapes hang down to the floor between the windows. A small platform sits before them, topped by a single red velvet throne. We stop just short of the royal crest etched into the stone floor, a sword piercing a twisted crown of vines and jewels.

"Kneel." The command slices through my awe. I turn, disoriented.

"Wha—" A swift backhand sends me tumbling to the ground. Pain explodes across my cheek and through my wrist. Gasping, I cradle the injured arm and look up, just in time to catch a boot to the ribs. Air leaves my lungs in a sharp wheeze. On my knees, I lean forward, press my forehead to the cool floor, blink away tears, and fight the urge to cry out. I hold my breath.

After several heartbeats, a door to the left opens and boots echo across the chamber. Too sore to lift my head, I stay perfectly still. Another set of boots follows. Then more. They stop in front of me.

This is it. They've brought me here to face my fate.

"Ah, my son. Welcome." The familiar deep timbre of the King reverberates through the room. I must be hallucinating. *Son?*

"You summoned me, Your Majesty." The unfamiliar voice is low and smooth, laced with either boredom or irritation.

"I did. I have news." Footsteps pace in front of me. "It is your twenty-fifth year and subsequently the year of your binding." He continues moving. "Traditionally, the girl is chosen for traits that will strengthen the royal line. Now, we choose one from the wealthiest noble families."

"Yes. Your Majesty has chosen Coraline."

"I've decided to return to an older tradition. One where the girl is taken from an outlying village." I try to follow what he's saying, to understand, but it's difficult to focus around the sharp stab in my ribs.

The other voice sounds skeptical. "That tradition involved kidnapping a village head's daughter to force their submission, Your Majesty."

"Exactly." The King's tone sharpens. "A show of power. A reminder that *all* belong to the crown. On my recent travels, I found the perfect girl. Unexpectedly, in fact." He chuckles. "Stand, girl."

For a second, I don't move. I don't dare. I whisper Myra's warnings to myself and keep my head down. This is just a terrible dream and I'll wake up in the dungeon any moment. But a hand seizes my arm and yanks me to my feet. The pain steals my breath again.

"This is the girl you kidnapped from the Outlands." The Prince confirms. I risk a glance. A look of surprise and skepticism matches his distasteful tone. I'm suddenly all too aware of how I must look. My nightdress, covered with mud and torn beyond repair. The rest of me, just as dirty, scraped and bruised. All culprits of the disastrous last three days of my life and no doubt the reason for the Prince's look before schooling his face into blank neutrality.

"Yes. She is your mate. Or will be in a few days."

The word echoes through me, sending a shock down to my core. *Mate.* I can't be the Prince's mate. I already have a betrothed. This has to be a mistake.

"Coraline is—"

"Coraline is ill and too weak to contribute any sort of strength to the line. This girl has every quality that is desirable in an heir." His voice grows sharp. "Which is after all, the entire purpose of a mating." My mind reels as I fight the nausea curling in my stomach.

"I do not see any valuable qualities here, Your Majesty," the Prince says, gesturing to me.

I try to hide my frown. So we're just skipping over the whole kidnapping bit?

"My horse nearly trampled her and she didn't flinch as she stared me down. I do believe she would have lectured me had her betrothed not put her in line." Surprise flickers briefly across the Prince's face. "My guards did not intimidate her in the least when we were at her village. Just last night, it took no less than six of my personal guards to track her and restrain her after an escape attempt." I listen to him explain and a tickle of self-hatred starts to nag at me. I *am* here because I acted foolishly. "She is obviously in need of training. Something you are more than capable of handling."

94

The Prince looks at me fully now, scanning me from head to toe and back again. His unreadable face makes my skin crawl. I bite my lower lip to keep myself from speaking. The taste of dirt fills my mouth. *Perfect.*

"Lord Tro—"

"Lord Trovy," the King interrupts, "will fall in line. *As. Will. You.*" The monarch leaves no room for argument as he starts to make his way toward the door. "This is your betrothed. See that the preparations stay on track."

"Yes, Your Majesty." The Prince bows low. The King turns and leaves, most of his guards following.

Four guards remain, two by me, two lingering behind the Prince.

Chapter Fifteen

Once the King leaves, the Prince sighs, his shoulders drooping slightly. He rubs a hand down his face before turning back to me. The radiating pain makes it easy to stay still under his scrutiny. My body starts to sag with exhaustion and I'm tempted to give in to it. Longest few days of my life and now I'm supposed to bind myself to this man? The Prince?

"Your name." Not a question.

I have to clear my throat before I'm able to respond without sounding like a strangled goat.

"Narina." I manage, barely a rasp.

"Untrained indeed."

He scans me again, and this time I do fidget, the raw soles of my feet shifting on the stone. He lets out a halfhearted chuckle and runs his fingers through his dark brown hair. The ends brush along his ears when it falls back.

"The King kidnapped you and now you are mine."

Not yours.

Out of habit, I push the stray hairs from my braid out of my face, freezing when a flash of anger cuts across the Prince's features. Perfect. I've broken some kind of rule. I force myself to stay put when he takes two quick steps forward and grips my chin. His hold is firm but not painful. He tilts my head to the side, his thumb skating across my cheek.

"Many bruises cover your body, Narina, but this one is fresh." His tone sharpens. "Tell me who struck you." I blink, too stunned to do anything but stutter. Without letting go, he turns a harsh glare on the King's guards. "Who." His voice is ice.

The culprit takes a single step forward. Steel-grey eyes meet my own before the Prince finally releases me. I cradle my ribs, trying to steady my breath.

"Mistress Myra," he calls, already striding toward the guards.

She hurries over, offering a curtsy. "Your Grace."

"Tell me what happened."

"We retrieved the girl from the cell and brought her here as instructed," she says, her voice far smaller than it had been when bossing me around. "When we entered the throne room, she was told to kneel. She didn't, so the guard struck her..." She hesitates but continues when the Prince raises a brow at her. "And then he kicked her, Your Grace."

Quick as lightning, he strikes, backhanding the guard. The man shows no reaction except for stumbling back a step. The Prince follows.

"No one knew who she was," the Prince says coldly. "You are spared this time. Touch her again, and you will lose a hand—if not your life." A shiver runs down my spine at the way he never once broke that emotionless mask.

"Yes, Your Grace," the guard replies, bowing his head.

"Dismissed."

The Prince returns to my side as if the incident never happened and tilts my chin again to inspect my cheek.

"You are quite battered, darling," he mutters, catching my gaze. He holds me for a moment before dropping his hand and looking away.

"Mistress," he calls, turning to leave, "take my betrothed to her quarters and have her washed up. I will have Moots visit her there."

Myra no longer seems concerned with my pace. She leads me through the corridors in silence, and though I have a thousand questions, I stay quiet for several minutes. Eventually, I muster the energy to ask the one at the forefront of my frenzied thoughts.

"Does the Prince strike people often?"

If I'm to be bound to him, I need to know. Myra stops and turns to face me. For a moment, I think she might answer. She shakes her head slightly.

"Not anymore," she whispers, then continues walking.

"What does that mean?"

I wait, but she's back to being silent without any indication of saying more. Giving up, I don't ask anything else. It's too difficult to try to walk and talk when every breath stabs.

The King should have chosen anyone but me. I'm a far cry from the perfect mate and he knows it. He said I have "qualities desired in an heir." I agree with the Prince, what possible qualities could those be? Every scenario he listed was me being impertinent, defiant, and disobedient. Aren't those the exact things they *don't* want at court?

Heir. Qualities to pass to an *heir.* I can't...

"We're here."

Myra's words pull me back to the present instead of falling down that particular spiral of panic. We're standing in front of a large wooden door and thankfully it's not the one that leads to the dungeon.

"These will be your quarters until the ceremony," she says, pushing it open.

"Then what?"

She rolls her eyes and herds me into the room. Right. Then I belong to *him.*

"I will go fetch servants to bathe you and see if Moots is on his way."

Before I can ask who Moots is, she has closed the door, leaving me alone.

Finding a mirror on the opposite wall, I move to it, bracing myself. I look just as terrible as I imagined. My dress hangs in shredded pieces, barely decent. My hair's half out of its braid, sticking out at odd angles. Scratches crisscross my skin, and my cheek has swollen into a blotchy red mess. No wonder the Prince looked at me like that. I would've too.

After failing to convince the servants I can wash myself, I sit silently as they clean and tend to me with warm water and cloths. They say nothing. Once I'm dressed in a plain cotton shift, they vanish. Perched on the edge of the solitary bed, I try to keep my mind from spiraling as I wait for whoever Moots is.

A quick knock precedes the door opening. Myra enters, followed by a large man. He pauses to speak with her, towering over her. He rests a massive hand briefly on her shoulder, which she steps away from with a polite bow of her head. She gestures toward me, drawing his gaze. His eyes widen. He crosses the room in a few long strides.

"Oh, my dear child." A surprisingly gentle hand touches my cheek. "What's happened to you?"

I don't answer, positive that it's a rhetorical question.

"I'm Moots, the Prince's personal physician. I work for, and am paid solely by, His Grace." He smiles. "Let us see what we can do to fix you up, shall we?"

Definitely rhetorical.

He pulls bottles and bandages from a bag I hadn't noticed. Murmuring to himself, he cleans and wraps the deeper wounds. I study the darker tone of his skin. The villagers back home are tanned from the sun, darker than most in King's Village—but I've never seen skin like his. It looks stained by ink. Fascinating.

Realizing I'm staring, I look away and focus on his movements instead.

He dabs salve on my bruises, poking gently. He pays special attention to the older ones on my arms and fingers, then the new one on my cheek. When he reaches my wrist, he clicks his tongue and bows closer, testing movement carefully.

Finally, he wraps it tightly. It already feels better.

"Not broken," he says quietly, before moving on to my feet. He coats them in salve and bandages them, creating makeshift socks.

"Have you any more injuries?" he asks, straightening. I'm about to answer no, then remember.

"My ribs. On this side."

He adjusts his position on the bed and carefully prods along my side, murmuring to himself again.

"Not broken, just badly bruised," he confirms. "Mistress Myra will wrap it for you. I will return in the morning to check your progress. Eat and rest. Most of your injuries should heal by then." With an impossibly large smile and his bag in hand, he leaves me here in Myra's questionable care. Myra watches him go, then crosses her arms and looks me over, scowling.

Chapter Sixteen

"Children! Come back here! Both of you!"

We raced away from the schoolhouse, hands entwined, laughing at the large man trying to chase us down.

"You just wait until your parents hear of this! You just wait!"

Diamo and I didn't stop running until we'd rounded a corner and lost him. We made it to our secret spot by the river, breathless.

"That was hilarious!" Diamo laughed, resting his hands on his knees.

"Did you see how red his face got?" I fell backward onto the grass, still laughing.

"I thought he was going to explode!" Diamo dropped beside me, grinning.

"What a perfect idea." I turned my face toward him, the grass tickling my cheek. His smile reached his eyes, crinkling the corners.

"I was bored. I'm a farmer's son. I learn everything I need out in the field. I'm surprised you agreed."

"You are?" I wrinkled my nose at him. It was my last year I'd be allowed to attend school. He shouldn't have been surprised.

"No. Not a bit. I saw you falling asleep in your chair. Your father's going to be cross, though."

"My father is always cross." I folded my arms behind my head and watched the clouds drift above us.

"Maybe because you hardly listen." He leaned over me, blocking my view. "I'd feel bad if you got punished for this."

"It's boring being a girl. You wouldn't listen either." I shoved him away, and he toppled back laughing before springing to his feet.

"Are you sure you're a girl? You don't act like one."

I stuck my tongue out.

"Narina Brevou, that is not very lady-like."

I jumped up and gave him an exaggerated curtsy.

"My lord, Diamo. I apologize for my indiscretion."

Puffing out his chest, he stepped toward me.

"My lady Narina," he said dramatically, pushing my shoulders. I dropped back to the grass with a squeak. "There are not enough apologies in the world to cover your indiscretions."

Mouth gaping, I stared at him as he smirked down at me.

"Then perhaps I should just add to the list and knock you in the river!"

I leapt to my feet and gave chase. He easily outran me, but the game kept us busy for the rest of the afternoon.

I wake from a restless sleep, staring at the stone ceiling above.

My father punished me for that afternoon… and many more after.

I'm sorry, I say silently to the memory.

There *aren't* enough apologies in the world to cover my indiscretions.

And now they've landed me here. Away from Diamo. Away from everything we were supposed to have.

There are no windows, but it must still be the middle of the night. I don't hear anything beyond the faint echo of boots pacing outside my door. A single patrolling guard, by the sound of it. I wonder idly how long it takes to learn this place. Is there a trick? Or do you just memorize the maze?

Slowly, I swing my feet off the bed and rise, mindful of my wrist and ribs. The chill of the floor seeps through the bandages on my feet, but it's oddly soothing. I shrug into the robe I was given and pad to the door. I don't know what I'm doing. I don't even know what I'd say if I'm caught. Still, I ease the door open and peek out.

The hallway is dim, with only the occasional sconce casting light. No sign of the guard. I step out and quietly tiptoe to the left.

Sticking to the shadows, I hug the walls and move forward. While I don't know where I'm going, I'm sure that I'm probably not supposed to be out of my room. When the familiar echo of boots sounds again, I freeze and listen. Behind me. I pick up my pace, just enough to stay ahead of the patrol. Eventually, the steps fade in the opposite direction.

There are several doors that line the hallway. I pause to listen at a few but hear nothing. All the handles I try are locked. With no side corridors branching off, my only choice is forward. I could turn back. But I'm not ready to return to that silent room and wait out the night. Pulling the robe closer around me, I shiver. Nights are still mild in Verti. Here, the cold creeps in fast.

Realizing I must be getting closer to open air, I quicken my pace.

"Narina."

I jump and nearly stumble at the sound of my name. I spin around, pulling the robe tight like armor. The Prince steps from the shadows.

"I hope you are not lost." He's dressed in loose black pants, his nightshirt unbuttoned just enough to reveal the top of his chest. His hands are tucked into his pockets, his tone casual.

"Ah... no." I scramble for words. "I'm not lost."

"Running again, then."

His expression doesn't change, giving away nothing. He almost looks aloof. *Almost.* I remember his quick mood shifts from earlier and tread carefully.

"No. I'm not running," I say truthfully. The thought had crossed my mind, but it wasn't the reason I'd left.

"Then tell me what you are doing roaming the hallways, Narina." The flicker of torchlight reflects in his steely eyes. I search for an acceptable excuse.

"I couldn't sleep." It's all I've got, and true enough. He tilts his head slightly, watching me. I shift under his gaze, suddenly remembering I never bowed or used a title. His eyes follow the movement down to my bandaged feet before returning to my own.

"Moots tells me you have sustained some significant injuries." He leans casually against the wall, arms crossed.

"Yes, but they're already much better. Thank you. Moots was very helpful."

"Indeed. He can be. I will tell him to make you a sleeping draft."

"Oh…" I hesitate, panic swelling.

How do I tell a Prince *no*? I haven't taken any drafts, drugs, potions, medicines, or unreliable drinks since the solid month my father drugged me in an attempt to *tame me*. It's a different sort of vulnerability when you feel like a stranger to yourself. When your mind is slow and doesn't feel like your own… it's not an experience I ever want to repeat.

"That's really not necessary. Thank y—"

My knees buckle as I take a step past him. I start to fall, but he catches me under the arms before I hit the ground. I press my palm to my forehead, dizzy and rattled.

"You have clearly been through quite an ordeal," he says. "You need rest. Moots will prepare a draft."

"Please. . I really don't think—" I nearly take us both down when I try to pull away but my legs fail me again and he catches me a second time.

"That's enough." He cuts off my protest. "Sleep is important, Narina. You need to be well rested for upcoming events. It will also prevent any more hallway wandering." He smirks. "We would not want you getting lost."

Bending down, he scoops my knees out from under me, cradling me in his arms. "I will return you safely to your room where you will stay for the remainder of the evening." His firm tone makes it clear he will not take any more arguments from me.

I nod, unwilling to push him when I can't even stand properly. He shifts his grip when I wince, careful around my ribs.

During the journey back to my room, my muscles grow heavy. I struggle to keep my eyes open. Somehow, he knows which door is mine. He pushes it open with his foot and carries me inside. He sets me gently on the bed, laying me on top of the furs. Leaning down, he brackets me with his arms, meeting my eyes.

"No more wandering, Narina. Not tonight. Not ever."

Too tired to protest, I simply sink into the warmth beneath me. As sleep pulls at me, I catch a glimpse of him looking back before shutting the door.

I want to be angry that he just confined me to my room, but my eyes are too heavy to think about it for long.

Chapter Seventeen

Last night feels like a lucid dream as I swing my legs off the bed. In fact, all of yesterday feels like some horrible nightmare. I don't even remember my actual dreams. With my eyes still closed, part of me pretends that it *was* all a dream, but one look around the room shatters that hope.

This space is easily twice the size of my bedroom at home. A fireplace fills one corner, the bed another, with a wooden chest at its foot. The mirror sits in the last. That's it, simple furnishings, and I'm grateful for that. I make my way over to the mirror.

It takes a moment to reconcile the reflection. Moots has far exceeded any expectations I might've had. I hadn't taken him seriously when he said most of my injuries would heal overnight, but somehow, his medicines accomplished just that. The bruise on my cheek has faded to a pale purple, barely distinguishable from a shadow. Thin pink lines are all that's left of my bramble scratches. The rest of my bruises are nearly gone. My feet still ache, but the swelling has gone down. The only thing that still throbs is my wrist.

There's a quick knock on the door before it creaks open. I catch sight of Myra entering in the mirror's reflection and roll my eyes. Of course she doesn't wait for a reply. Why even knock?

"It's time to dress." Myra ushers in two other women.

"I can dress myself, Myra." I huff.

She gives me a pointed stare. "These events are too important to leave to you." She waves the women forward, dismissing me entirely.

"What are you talking about?"

"Come, come! We're on a schedule ladies!" Myra claps, ignoring my question.

Not long after, I'm dressed in another simple white gown. A heart-shaped neckline sweeps up to fluttering sleeves, and the fitted bodice flows into a skirt that brushes the floor. It's modest but elegant. It's nicer than anything I ever dreamed of owning in Verti. A pair of surprisingly comfortable white slippers and a braid crowning my head complete the look.

Myra has been circling and inspecting me for the last two minutes. I resist the urge to make a rude comment, but eventually hold out my arms in annoyance.

"Well, I think that's as good as it's going to get today," she says finally.

"Don't feel the need to flatter me, Myra."

"Mistress. *Mistress* Myra," she corrects crisply, then turns to the door. "Come along. I expect it's about time for your entrance."

I start to follow her but stop short.

"What entrance?" Tired of her not answering any of my questions, I cross my arms and wait. She just raises an eyebrow at me, perfectly composed.

"His Majesty and His Grace will be very cross if you're late," she states simply.

I bite the inside of my cheek, this woman is *really* starting to grate on my nerves. Still, curiosity and the desire to avoid more bruises, push me forward.

We walk in silence through the winding halls. I'm still tired from last night and don't have the energy to ask more questions I know she won't answer. Eventually, we reach the engraved wooden doors from last night, the throne room. Two guards stand at attention, ready to open them.

"This is as far as I go," Myra says, pausing. I glance at her, remembering the last time she led me here.

"Rules I should know?"

She tries to hide a smirk. "Stay silent. Do as you're told. His Grace should be on the other side."

With a slight bow of her head, she retreats down the hall.

Of course.

Stay silent. Do as you're told.

Simple enough.

I hope.

The guards pull the doors open. Two more stand on the other side, beyond them is the large room… full of people. I freeze. Shock and anxiety take hold as heads begin to turn my way.

Great. *I'm* the entrance.

Scanning the crowd, I spot the Prince walking my direction. I never thought I'd be relieved to see him.

Stay silent. Do as you're told.

"Narina." The Prince greets me as he nears. I nod at him, unable to speak. My focus is fixed on the sheer number of people and how many are still turning to stare. Somewhere in the room, a voice announces the King's approach. The murmuring crowd begins to find their places.

"A curtsy is appropriate when you greet your royals, darling," he whispers close. The tingle of his breath against my ear jolts me from my daze.

"Sorry," I mumble, still eyeing the crowd wearily. He steps in front of me, blocking my view with his broad shoulders.

"Give me your hands."

I lift them automatically but snatch them back when he produces a rope.

"The King has kidnapped my intended mate and is fond of theatrics," he explains quickly. "It will come off right after...unless you forget to bow." A crooked smirk plays across his mouth.

Still, I hesitate.

"Hands, Narina."

I glare, but I remember Myra's words. Reluctantly, I offer them again. He binds them with care, being especially gentle with my injured wrist. Once he's finished, he lifts my chin, and our eyes meet. They're a dark blue today, matching the color of his uniform blazer. He looks... anxious?

"You do not have to do anything," he murmurs quietly. "Just walk with me. And bow." He moves to stand at my side. The room hushes as the King enters and crosses the dais to stand in front of the throne.

"Thank you to everyone who has attended this session of court," he says, his voice echoing. "I acknowledge the special circumstances were announced last minute."

I wonder if his voice *naturally* carries like that, or if it's something trained for the throne.

"It is my heir's twenty-fifth year and the year of his mating. The old traditions of selecting women with desirable traits to strengthen the royal line have long been ignored. But I have revived that tradition of might and of power."

He pauses.

"I trekked to the edge of Sunstien and brought back a suitable mate for my only heir. A good hunt demands worthy prey that puts up a fight, and she didn't disappoint, showing strength, intelligence, and perseverance." He chuckles. A few others do too.

He called me prey.

"All desirable attributes. And she now belongs to us. Today marks the beginning of formal preparations leading up to their ceremony. May I present to the court, my heir and his captured future mate."

Every eye turns toward us. The Prince's bow beside me prompts a curtsy of my own. It's unsteady and far from graceful, but I manage it despite my bound hands. Straightening, the Prince takes my elbow and leads me through the murmuring crowd.

I fight the nausea rising in my throat.

So many eyes.

Tied up.

Paraded like prey.

So many people.

When we reach the royal symbol etched into the floor, the Prince stops.

"Your Majesty," he says, bowing low. I follow with another curtsy, his hand helping me stay balanced. "I am grateful for the capture and gift of my betrothed."

He rises, pulling me up with him. I fix my gaze on the shaft of light illuminating the tip of the sword at my feet and my mouth firmly shut. Despite the evidence of the last few days, I'm not foolish enough to tempt fate now.

"You will be bound in eleven days."

The floor tilts under me. The Prince tightens his grip to steady me.

"Thank you, Your Majesty," he says smoothly. "With your permission, she will attend court with me this morning."

The King must have agreed because the Prince bows once more. Then he steers me to the side of the dais and into a small antechamber.

Chapter Eighteen

"That *bastard!*"

The words rip out of me as soon as the door shuts behind us.

"He knows. He *knows* what that day is."

I whirl on the Prince. He raises his eyebrows, with a thoroughly bemused smirk playing across his face. I seethe.

"It's not enough that he had to rip me away from everything, *everything*... but to make our ceremony on the same day that I was supposed to..." My voice shakes. "That *BASTARD.*"

I know I'm not making any sense to him. I don't care. I don't owe him anything.

Wincing, I try to yank my hands free of the rope binding them and start pacing the small room. There's not much here, just four paces wide, no furniture, and a single narrow window.

The Prince reaches out, and I sidestep him, his smirk only fueling my anger. I keep tugging at the rope despite how much it hurts, letting out a frustrated yell when it refuses to give.

"You are going to hurt yourself," he says gently, like someone coaxing a spooked horse. He reaches again, and again I avoid him.

He raises a brow. "You will not be able to do it yourself, darling."

The door to the throne room swings open. The Prince lunges, grabs my bound hands, and pulls me sharply to him... just as the bastard himself walks in.

The door closes behind him. The King turns, his gaze sweeping over us.

Between the King, the Prince, me, and my rage, the antechamber is crowded. The Prince sketches a half bow before the King turns to me. Unflinchingly, I meet his cold blue stare. The pleasure I find there stirs the hot anger in my chest. After a handful of heartbeats, he smiles. It's not a pleasurable thing, but wicked and cruel. Triumphant. I'm *done* being silent.

"You ba—"

My step toward the King is cut short as the Prince yanks me back and shoves me behind him. I'm not sure whether I trip over my feet or the dress, but my shoulder slams into the wall, tearing the fabric.

"Well, Your Majesty, you certainly did choose a wild one." The Prince chuckles, his body a solid wall between me and the man now glaring at my audacity. His icy gaze slides to the Prince before he exits through the opposite door.

Without releasing me, the Prince turns, no longer amused. No one speaks as we watch each other, my breathing still rapid with fury. Finally, he looks down and starts working on loosening the ropes that tightened in my struggle.

"You have now been presented to the court," he says flatly. Begrudgingly, I don't fight him.

"Is that supposed to mean something to me?"

"I am not surprised it does not." A slight smile tugs at his mouth. I nearly slap him. Thankfully, my hands are still bound.

"No one tells me anything."

"It is not your place to know anything."

I bite my cheek to stop myself from saying the first thing that comes to mind and manage to grind out something slightly more civil.

"So, you're telling me it's not my place to know about things that *drastically* affect my life?"

"No," he says simply. "Not unless you are told it is."

"My life's been turned upside down and I'm not even given the *courtesy* of knowing what's going on." My words break at the end despite my effort to stay calm.

"You are becoming my mate."

I release a hollow breath. Of course. His fingers pause on the knot.

"Tell me why you do not want that."

"Do you care?" The question slips out before I can stop it.

Does he? Does he care that he has a mate who doesn't want him? He tilts his head and resumes working the rope loose.

"Tell me anyway."

"I don't love you." I'm not sure he hears the barely whispered words until he nods.

"But you love someone." He looks up expectantly, and I give the smallest nod.

"And in eleven days you were supposed to be bound to this lover of yours."

The rope falls away. He straightens and gently circles my wrists with his hands. The rage has ebbed into pain. Or maybe that's what it always was.

He runs his thumbs across the red marks where the rope chafed. For a moment, I think he's going to call me battered again, but he doesn't.

"The King does nothing without purpose." He pulls me close until our chests brush, and I'm forced to meet his eyes. "The more you push him, the more he will punish you... until he demands that you are broken." He leans closer, his voice low. "Breaking you will fall to me."

I can barely breathe.

He steps back, releasing me, and air returns to the room. With a brief motion for me to stay where I am, he disappears through the same door the King used. Collapsing against the wall, I rub my wrists, taking the reprieve to collect myself. They burn—raw and red. Fitting, perhaps; they're a match for the raw knot in my chest.

I am Narina Brevou. I will not be broken.

He returns a moment later, carrying a finely made cloak. Draping it over my shoulders to hide the torn dress, he slowly fastens each of the three buttons.

"It is borrowed," he says. "From a noble."

He adjusts the fabric until the rip is completely concealed.

"Being presented to the court is a formality," he explains. "First is the taking, the King sets out in search of a woman to be the heir's mate. Then, you are presented to the court for the King's formal approval and your introduction to the nobility. There is a celebratory banquet that will follow the court proceedings, but not everyone will choose to stay, the proceedings are rather dull. Tomorrow is a feast in our honor. There are more events throughout the week, but you are not required to attend."

He steps back with a sigh, watching me. His tone is unusually open, and it catches me off guard. I don't know what to say.

Satisfied that I'm covered, he meets my eyes again.

"Narina, this is not some grand sweeping romance—"

"Oh, *trust* me. I have no grand illusions of romance with you." I have to stifle the urge to slap my hand over my mouth for cutting him off and letting the words leap out.

I wince, giving him an apologetic look, hoping it will soften the blow. The blow doesn't come. He only gives me a cutting look.

"But you are mine now." The words are ice. "It would be wise to let the lingering thoughts of your lover go." He extends a hand toward me. "They will only cause you trouble here."

Never.

I hate him.

I will never be his.

I hate him.

But I accept his hand anyway.

Chapter Nineteen

Even with the fineness of the borrowed cloak, I feel overwhelmingly underdressed compared to the rest of the noblewomen throughout the room. With my hand tucked into his elbow, the Prince silently guides me through the crowd and around the long wooden table at the room's center.

Despite the elegance of the attendees, the room is simple and clearly designed for function. The table has seats for eight—the King, the Prince, and the six advisors. Beyond that is terraced seating for those attending the proceedings. A few nobles are already seated, but most are still entering or exchanging pleasantries. Some appear to be saying their goodbyes.

We pause when an older man in dress uniform approaches and bows.

"Advisor Kensington." The Prince nods. Straightening, the man glances at me, barely polite, then leans toward the Prince.

"May I have a private word, sir?"

"After I show my betrothed to her seat, Advisor."

"It cannot wait, Your Grace."

With a barely veiled scowl, the Prince pats my hand and steps away, turning to the man expectantly.

I'm still watching their exchange when a quiet voice whispers too close behind me.

"You don't belong here."

I turn to face the young woman, taking a step back to recreate space between us. She's tall and lanky, her custom-tailored blue gown clinging to her narrow frame, blonde curls piled high on her head.

"I agree," I say with a shrug. I have no idea who she is or why she's so upset by my existence. She folds her arms, clearly annoyed.

"Outlander scum should stay in the Outlands." I smirk at her obvious attempt to rile me. She apparently didn't understand the kidnapped portion of this arrangement.

"If you could tell the King that, I'd be grateful."

"I'll make sure you regret—"

"Careful, Mariselle," comes the Prince's voice, smooth as velvet. A hand rests warmly on my back. "That nearly sounded like a threat to my betrothed."

Panic flashes in her eyes as she stumbles back, nearly tripping over her own feet as she curtsies. "Your Grace, I—"

He takes a step, closing the distance between them. A small part of me feels for her as she lowers her gaze to his boots, frozen.

"Remember your place, Miss Kensington."

She says nothing, only dipping lower into the curtsy. He stares down at her a moment longer, then turns back to me and guides me toward the waiting seats, leaving her bowed in rigid submission behind us.

The exchange draws a few glances from nearby nobles, but they quickly return to their own conversations, no one's eager to attract a royal's attention. I don't blame them. The Prince's entire demeanor has shifted, his expression sharp, his presence bristling. He cuts across the room with me in tow, every step radiating controlled intensity. The contrast between his velvet voice and the razor edge beneath it unsettles me, even more than the confrontation itself. How many versions of this man are there?

We reach an empty chair set apart from the rest. He gestures to it, his hand dropping away as I lower myself into the seat. I glance around. Several nobles are still watching us, far less subtle than they seem to think. My skin prickles under their attention, but I force my spine straight. Wordlessly, the Prince returns to the long table and takes his seat. A moment later, the King calls court to order, prompting the remaining nobles to scramble for seats or quietly file out of the room.

The Prince hadn't exaggerated, court proceedings are mind-numbingly dull. The advisors debate military placement, village conditions, crop yields, and the war with Sunstien. The only burst of excitement comes when the Treasury Advisor gets so worked up he knocks over his chair yelling at the Commodities Advisor. The table shakes when the King slams a hand on the wooden surface. With one icy glare, both men fall silent and reclaim their seats.

Thanks to my father's books, I understand most of what they're discussing, but it doesn't make it any more interesting. After a while, I stop trying to follow and let my attention drift. By the third topic change, most of the attendees have finally lost interest in staring at me. With no one left to glare back at, my gaze slides to the man at the end of the table.

He's leaned back in his chair, relaxed but with impeccable posture. His eyes follow the conversation, and occasionally he nods. Sometimes, he looks as bored as I feel. He rarely speaks. As heir, I expected more involvement.

His gaze flicks up, catching me staring.

I look away quickly, warmth flooding my cheeks. When I dare another glance, his steel-blue eyes catch mine—and hold them. His face remains unreadable, as always, but his stare is unwavering. The knot that's been sitting in my chest since I arrived pulls tighter. Is he really as unaffected by all this as he seems? I stay locked in his gaze until an advisor addresses him, and the tension between us snaps as his focus shifts.

That impossible man is now my betrothed.

You are mine now.

A twisted echo of words that had sounded like sweet honey dripping from Diamo's lips and a cold dagger from the Prince's.

He wanted me to forget Diamo.

Impossible.

Diamo is my everything. He's always been my rock, my support, my strength… I don't know who I am without him. To forget Diamo, I would have to forget who I am. To not love Diamo would be akin to not having a heart. Not loving Diamo just might break me.

You are mine now.

Never.

A small group of nobles rises from their seats and begins quietly making their way toward the exit. I can't blame them. It feels like a lifetime has passed since the proceedings began. It's a wonder more haven't left already.

My spine straightens as I realize they'll pass right by me on their way out.

A voice from last night drifts back to me: *Running again, then.*

Yes.

I won't stay and let them take Diamo from me.

I am Narina Brevou. I will not be broken.

I pull the borrowed cloak tighter and lift the hood over my head. Two of the women already wear theirs, so mine won't stand out. My heart hammers in my chest as I glance toward the Prince. He's still focused on the debate, his posture relaxed, his attention elsewhere. Good.

The group passes.

I stand and slide into their midst like I belong.

Each footstep feels louder than it should. I keep my head down, shoulders hunched, the cloak brushing lightly against my skin with every step. I wait for someone to notice the extra presence among them; to whisper, to point, or to call out.

No one does.

No one notices as we pass through the open door into the hallway.

No one says a word as we wind through the twisting corridors.

No one stops us as we exit into the daylight beyond the castle walls.

At the outer gate, the nobles begin to break apart. Some drift toward carriages, others toward horses. Only a few continue down the path toward King's Village. I ease back just enough to avoid their notice, keeping close enough so the guards on the wall don't give me a second glance. Just another noble, not a stolen girl from the Outlands.

Shouts begin behind us, quiet at first, then steadily growing louder from within the castle. The nobles ahead of me slow, glancing over their shoulders in curiosity. I don't. Skirt brushing my ankles, hood low, I slip past them, heart racing. Every step puts more distance between me and the stone walls behind me.

Please, please, please… I beg no one.

The heart of the village has to be dense enough to disappear into. I just have to reach it. The smooth cobblestone gives way to packed dirt, and each hurried step kicks up small bursts of dust around my feet.

The guards' voices spill out into the open air. They're outside now. I glance back. Dozens of them spread across the path, the walls, the gaps in between. None close, yet, but fear still clamps down hard. My heart pounds louder than the footfalls beneath me.

Run. Run. Run.

Escape. Escape. Escape.

Home. Home. Home.

Diamo.

Small buildings begin to dot the landscape on either side of the path: new, uneven, the village's edge. They grow closer, tighter, forming narrow lanes and crooked shadows. I don't stop.

Every step is a fight against panic. Each breath comes sharper, harder.

Take Her

If I can reach the crowd, I'll disappear. No one will find me. Not him. Not them.

No more ropes. No more orders. No more staring eyes.

I clutch the cloak tighter, jaw set.

Nearly there.

Chapter Twenty

The air is knocked from me when something collides into me from the side. I'm shoved off the path and behind one of the larger buildings. Hot fire sears through my sprained wrist, shooting up to my shoulder and stabbing through my bruised ribs as I land in the hard dirt on my hands and knees.

How did the guards sneak up on me so quickly?

Groaning, I push off the ground and wrestle myself free of the cloak tangled around my legs.

"Give me everything," a hoarse voice demands.

I freeze. Not a guard.

"I don't have anything."

I turn slowly, hands lifted to show they're empty. A scruffy man with hollow cheeks and sunken eyes stares me down, disappointment flickering across his drawn face when he realizes I'm not adorned in court jewels. Still, he holds a dull, rusted knife steady in my direction.

"You have something. Give it."

Swallowing hard, I inch a step backward. He mirrors me, closing the gap again, forcing me to stop. I lift my palms higher in a wordless plea. I can't believe I escaped one trap only to land in another. His eyes rake over me in quick, greedy sweeps.

"The cloak," he says, jerking his head toward it.

I nod and carefully unclasp it, tossing it to the dirt in front of him. When he bends to snatch it up, I take another step back. He's quick and matches the movement again, raising the knife higher. His lips peel back in a sneer, exposing cracked teeth.

"I have nothing else," I say, my voice trembling on the edge of a plea. I can't die here. And I can't scream for help, not without the guards finding me and dragging me back to that gilded cage.

"The shoes," he says.

I hesitate. Getting home barefoot would be near impossible.

"Give me the shoes!" he shouts, waving the blade.

My hands rise again, fingers trembling as my breath shortens into sharp, panicked bursts. I'm not trained to disarm a man, but I can try not to die.

"Alright, alright... here."

I kick one shoe off to his left. He doesn't move. The sun glints off the knife as he lifts it again. I kick the second shoe harder, sending it behind and to the right. He squints at me, annoyed. I hold still, barely breathing, and wait for him to decide if I'm worth the trouble.

At last, he turns to gather the shoes. I bolt.

Holding the hem of my torn and dirty dress in one hand, I put as much distance between me and the thief as I can. The cuts on my feet sting as they split open with every step. I still run, pushing them to carry me until the din of noise from the village's center reaches my ears.

With shaking hands, I brace myself against the nearest house, dragging air into my burning lungs. The rough timber under my palms grounds me while I try to breathe past the lingering panic.

How in the stars am I going to make it home?

How am I going to make it home *alive*?

Tears prick the corners of my eyes as self-pity, panic, and pain twist themselves around like vines trying to choke me. Going back isn't an option. I can't go back to that. I won't.

I squeeze my eyes shut, holding the tears back.

I am Narina Brevou. I will not be broken.

I will not be broken.

But my lungs refuse to cooperate. I can only manage shallow gasps. And in the darkness behind my eyes, all I see is a shaky, rusted knife and a rope pulled too tight around my wrists. A rope that'll likely be around my neck if they catch me.

If something worse doesn't find me first.

I wrap my arms around my middle in a feeble attempt to hold myself together. The knot in my chest just gets tighter and tighter, squeezing from the inside, suffocating me. My lungs are cracked and refuse to hold air, the broken pieces stabbing me with every attempt. My thoughts spiral in impossible circles, refusing to listen to reason, refusing to cooperate enough to breathe.

Breathe. Breathe. Breathe.

My love.

Diamo's cool, crisp voice cuts through the twisting thoughts.

I sink to my knees and put every ounce of energy I have into focusing on that sweet voice in my head. Leaning my head against the weathered boards of the house, I struggle against the torrent of panic.

My love.

Air fills my lungs as I force breath into them, clinging to the lifeline that's always been Diamo.

You are my everything.

Tender words spoken in private. Words from a man who cherishes me just as much as I adore him. Will he be waiting for me? Yes. I know that answer with every fiber of my being. There's nothing we wouldn't do for each other.

You are mine.

Not a claim of ownership. A vow of love. From the man who lends me his strength and reminds me of my own. Fighting the tightness in my chest, I try to find that strength now.

I am not helpless. I am not powerless. I am not feeble.

Who are you?

The memory of his voice rings clear and playful. He's beside me again, crouched in the dirt, daring me to rise.

I am Narina Brevou.

I drag in a deeper breath. The knot loosens.

Who. Are. You.

I am Narina Brevou.

I can picture him nodding, encouraging me, those honey eyes waiting, filled with pride.

I am Narina Brevou. I will not be broken.

Trembling, I pull myself out of the dirt and lean against the house. Counting to five, I pull in a ragged breath with each number, the air moving easier each time. Finally, I'm able to open my eyes to the pinking sky and blow out a heavy breath, sending the wave of anxiety with it.

I shake my head and smile. Of course Diamo is still saving me, even when he's not here. I don't know what I'd do without him. I don't know *who* I'd be without him. And I never want to find out. It's time to get home to him.

Chapter
Twenty-One

The village center is easy enough to find, the constant din of noise like a beacon calling me. Winding my way through the dirt streets until they turn to cobble, the noise of voices and market sounds steadily gets louder as I get closer. None of it prepares me for what waits around the last corner.

I stop short, caught off guard by the sheer number of people weaving their way around one another and the rows of vendor stalls. I knew King's Village was the capital of Barbast, a bustling center of trade and life, but this far exceeds anything I imagined. The incredible crowd reminds me strangely of a colony of ants. Too many to count, each with their own purpose, their own agenda, and yet they move seamlessly around each other—a smooth, functional colony. I stand frozen in disbelief, until someone bumps into me hard from behind, jarring me into the chaotic current of movement and vendors shouting for attention.

"Fresh bread!"

"Two coppers! Only two coppers!"

"Best silk in Barbast! Shipped from the East!"

"Tryto cures! Don't forget your Tryto cures!"

The press of people around me keeps me moving through the maze of stalls, the foreign scents and cacophony of noise quickly overwhelming me.

"Move, rat."

I turn toward the gnarled voice that just bumped into me. A middle aged man sneers down his long nose before moving off into the crowd. I wince as someone else steps on my bare toes.

"Beggar trash," a woman scoffs as she shoves past me.

The realization that my plan to disappear into the crowd isn't much of a plan at all hits me with a sudden certainty. I stand out in this bustling colony and they know it. Silent eyes scan and decidedly judge my torn dress covered in dirt, the unraveling hair that had once been pinned into a noble updo, and the bare, bandaged feet that scream I don't belong here.

I won't be disappearing here, if anything, it'll be easy for someone to point me out to the first guard who comes asking.

As much as I'd love to stay and wander through the maze of vendors, despite the crowd, I have to get away from the stares, the shoves, and the sharp judgments. Even if I did blend in, what would I do when the sun goes down and the market closes? I can already feel the cool air of evening seeping in.

Stars above, what had I been thinking walking into a crowd this size?

I push the creeping panic away and resolve to focus on one problem at a time. A major one in the form of a black jacket with the royal seal on his left arm not ten paces in front of me scanning the crowd. He doesn't seem to have any urgency to him, word from the castle must not have reached him yet, but it's only a matter of time.

I push through the mass of people, mumbling an apology to a woman with an armful of purchases as I slip past her and duck behind the next stall into a quieter side street. I pause just long enough to catch my breath and force back the remnants of that tight, constricting feeling left by the crowd.

Focus.

Move.

Unsteady and lost, I put one foot in front of the other across the cool cobblestone, distancing myself from the chaos of the market. I have no idea where I'm going, what I'm doing, or even what I *should* be doing. I feel like I'm six years old again and lost without someone to tell me what to do. Drifting through the unfamiliar wood and stone streets, balancing on the edge of panic, despair, and self pity.

A shiver travels down my spine, warning of the cold night ahead. Maybe returning to the castle and pleading for mercy is my best option. I'd never see Diamo again. Perhaps that would be better for him, a life without trouble.

No. I have no doubt he longs for me just as I ache for him. There might only be a sliver of hope out here, but it's more than I'd ever have trapped in that stone prison with the Prince. I don't even know which direction the castle is anymore, the buildings are too tall to see over.

I slow as I turn a corner and spot a small yard. Not unusual, but this one has a clothesline. A line full of garments that haven't yet been brought in for the night. And at the end of it, a shawl. A very warm-looking shawl.

Stealing is wrong. I answer the thought that flared the moment I saw it. But my feet ignore it, stepping toward the short fence before I can convince myself to stop.

It's right there, the answer to a couple current problems of mine— warmth, protection, concealment. Right there. Just hanging a few feet away. My stomach twists with the decision. It's wrong, but what's the alternative?

I carefully step up onto an empty fruit box and ease over the small fence. Landing softly, I scan the yard and the windows for movement.

The last thing I need is to get arrested as a thief. Then, I'll be locked in the castle *and* missing a hand. When nothing stirs, I tiptoe through the dry grass to the shawl and run my fingers over the fabric. Wool. Thick and soft. I lift it from the line and press it to my nose.

"Vivi?"

I spin toward the quiet questioning voice, caught between terror and shame. Holding the shawl to my chest like a shield, I watch the woman carefully. She stands on the steps of the house, silver hair swept back, a small hunch to her stance. I could just drop the shawl and run. I could outrun her and her shouts. But I don't move. My muscles lock.

She studies me from wild hair to bare feet. Then her eyes dart around the small yard before she beckons me toward her.

"Well, get in here before someone sees you," she hisses.

Chapter
Twenty-Two

I don't move, frozen with the fear of what if. What if she knows they're looking for me and it's a trap?

"Quickly, girl!" Then her face softens a fraction. "You are welcome here."

Something in the words thaws my frozen joints. I move across the short distance. She holds the door open and slips in behind me, closing it quietly.

I stop just inside what looks like a kitchen. She circles around to face me, eyes scanning me again, brow creasing.

"Slave?" she muses curiously.

This was a mistake. I should have never come in here. I glance around the kitchen, suddenly sure I've walked straight into danger.

"You're safe here," she whispers. She looks at me then, as if she's realized something. I take half a step back, afraid of what that might be. "You weren't sent here," she says slowly, more to herself than to me.

I frown, she's expecting someone? I shake my head. She studies me for a moment longer, something unreadable in her expression.

"Vivi always said the stars bring the lost ones home. I used to think she was full of nonsense. Now I'm not so sure. You weren't told that this is a safe house, were you?"

I don't answer, not sure what she's saying.

"I am Andreya," she says gently. "And my home is a safe house. A place for runaways to stay a night or two before moving on. You look like you could use some help. You are safe here." She pauses, tilting her head. "Your secrets are safe with me."

She nods once, as if sealing a pact.

"Are you a slave?"

I shake my head, reeling from her words. A safe house. I didn't even know such things existed. What are the odds I stumbled into one meant to help escaped slaves?

Her face hardens just slightly.

"A criminal?"

Another shake of my head.

No. I'm a runaway soon-to-be princess. It sounds ridiculous even in my mind. But I'm not interested in the crown. Let them find someone else.

She looks at my dress and bare feet again, and her face softens with her voice.

"Bad mating?"

I nod, that's about as close to the truth I'm willing to get with a stranger.

Offering a small smile, she nods back. "Can I have your name?" she asks, reaching out for the shawl I'm still clutching. I hesitate, then hand it over, feeling sheepish. She seems kind. She's opened her home. The least I can do is give her my name.

"Narina," I say, my voice cracking. "And I'm sorry for taking your clothing."

With a wide smile she wraps the cloth around my shoulders and steers me to the small wooden table at the center of the room.

"Nonsense. That's exactly what they're there for. I switch them out a few times a week so it doesn't look suspicious having the same clothes always hanging out." Shrugging at her own thoughts, she sits me down in a chair. "It's a pleasure to meet you, Narina. Welcome to my home. Let's get you something warm to eat."

She bustles about the small room, setting a kettle on the iron stove and rummaging through cabinets with surprising agility for her age.

"We'll get you fed, a warm bath, and clean clothes. I'll show you where you'll be hiding, and tomorrow, after a decent night of sleep, we can talk about your plans and get you to the next safe house." She never stops moving as she prattles off the list.

Next safe house. Plans.

I don't really have a plan.

Get home to Verti. To Diamo.

But then what?

My last attempt at a plan had failed miserably. We wouldn't be able to stay. They will undoubtedly look for me there. Though I could foolishly hope they'd decide I'm not worth the trouble and find someone else for the Prince to mate. Someone more suitable. Someone who wants to be Princess.

I'm pulled from the panicked thoughts when a steaming bowl of stew is placed on the table in front of me.

"My dear. Take a breath. You look like a panicked rabbit caught in a snare. You're safe here," she croons. "Focus on filling your belly and getting warm. We'll worry about the rest tomorrow." Aged fingers with knuckles starting to twist pat my own before she returns to the now steaming kettle.

Worry about the rest tomorrow... I suddenly realize I haven't even had a moment to think about today or yesterday. I've been so focused on surviving now - tomorrow isn't even in my peripheral. With another look around the warm kitchen, I pull the shawl tight, settle back into the chair, and breathe.

Andreya hums as she moves, filling two mugs with steaming water. The tune is almost familiar but I can't place it. Music isn't common in Verti. Lullabies, ceremonies, and festivals are about the only things involving song. For a place so far from court, they're rather strict on some things.

She places the steaming mug in front of me and sits in the opposite chair.

"Eat," she urges, before blowing across the top of her mug before sipping with her eyes closed. A strange feeling flits across my chest. I feel… comfortable in her presence, relaxed almost.

"Thank you," I murmur, spooning stew into my mouth. I hope she knows all that thank you encompasses, because it is for much more than a bowl of stew and mug of tea. I think she does, because she simply nods, eyes still closed as she cradles her own tea.

The broth is hot, but it warms me as it fills my belly. Andreya sits with me as I eat, but doesn't prod or push. She just hums and sips her tea, letting me process in silence. When I return the spoon to the bowl for the last time, she places her mug on the table and folds her hands.

"I know you've been through a lot, but if you're going to stay here I need to ask a couple of questions, so I know best how to keep us both safe."

I nod immediately. She obviously knows what she's doing and I'm just grateful to be out of the cold and away from guards who'd drag me back without a second thought.

"Are you being looked for?"

I nod again.

"Family? Guards?"

Another nod. My eyes drop to the table. This is foolish. I shouldn't be putting this poor woman in danger.

"Palace guards?"

"I'm sorry." The words rush out. "I shouldn't be here. I don't want to put you in danger."

"Nonsense. This is what I do. You're not going anywhere, especially if it's the castle that's after you."

She glances at my wrists and the raw skin circling them.

"Were you assaulted?"

"No." The answer comes out firm.

She meets my eyes, not quite convinced.

I shake my head again, trying to reassure her.

"Beaten?"

I look down and fidget with the speckled brown stitches of the wool draped over me.

"I don't..." I falter.

I don't know how to answer that. I was struck, yes, by my father, by the guard... by life. I feel beaten. Beaten down to the point that I don't even know the words to describe what I've been through. Beaten to the point of surrendering my fate to an old woman with kind eyes and a warm shawl.

"I understand," she whispers reassuringly. "Let's get you a bath, and some salve for those bruises."

The bath is nothing special, but it's enough to ease the ache in my muscles and warm the chill that's settled in my bones. Andreya gives me a simple cotton nightdress and insists I keep the shawl.

Now we sit again at the table, a tin of salve and a roll of bandages between us.

She gently dabs the salve onto the remaining wounds and bruises on my hands before moving on to the rope burns on my wrists.

How does it feel like it's been ages since I stood in that antechamber, raging at the Prince, when the bright red speckled flesh from the rope burns says otherwise. I watch mutely as she works, once again humming. She asks no questions. Something I am infinitely grateful for. I don't think I have the strength to answer.

After insisting I can bandage my own feet, she allows it but watches closely. Andreya motions for me to move before dragging the table off to the side. I watch as she stoops and lifts a door in the floor I hadn't seen. Wooden panels lift in one smooth motion, revealing a small hollow just big enough for a grown man.

"It's not much, but it's comfortable enough and safe," she says. "You'll be hidden for the night."

I shove the panic that tries to rise, right back down into the box it belongs in. I won't be ungrateful and I don't have any other options. She must see something in my face.

"I promise it's safe. And I promise you'll be out first thing in the morning."

I nod and offer a small smile. "Thank you," I say earnestly. "For taking the risk."

"You are quite welcome." She gestures to the opening. "It's only a couple feet down."

I lower myself in. My feet meet a soft mattress layered with blankets and furs. When I sit, the door can close easily above me. I try not to let that thought go too far.

"Good night, dear. Try to rest. I'll see you in the morning."

"Good night," I whisper as the trapdoor closes. I watch candlelight spill through the slats as she moves the table back. Then, one by one, they go out until the last of the light trails out of the room, following her retreating footsteps.

Darkness.

Trapped.

I'm in a hole beneath a stranger's floor.

I try to stay calm by reassuring myself that Andreya is a kind woman and this is a safe house. Of course 'runaways' have to be hidden. It's for her protection as much as it is for mine. If she were to be caught with a runaway slave, she'd be in just as much trouble as they were. If she were to be caught hiding me... I don't know what they'd do to her. This is best.

I repeat it as I curl into the blankets, but I know sleep won't come easily. Not as the dark presses in closer. Not as the King's voice echoes from the corners. Not as the Prince whispers in my ear.

Chapter Twenty-Three

Morning is slow to come, but it arrives with the scrape of wood on wood before the small door above me opens.

"Good morning!" Andreya's full face beams down at me. She reaches for my hand and helps me climb from the hiding space. "How was your night?" she asks, closing the door after me. I move to help her return the table to its original spot.

"It was quite comfortable. Thank you." A truth.

"You look like you didn't sleep a wink," she says, eyeing me through her lashes.

"Just everything catching up with me, I suppose." Another truth. She's been so kind. I'm grateful and it was the whirlwind of recent days that kept me awake most of the night.

"Understandable. Let's get some food in you, then we'll talk plans. I don't like to discuss such serious things before I've seen the sun."

A glance toward the window confirms it's just before dawn, a sliver pink-tinged sky peeks between the lace curtains.

"May I help you? I'm not much of a cook despite my mother's best efforts, but I can get the kettle started, or anything else you'd like me to do." I turn from the growing light to find her already bustling around the stove.

"Oh, that's not necessary. You just have a seat and relax," she says, waving a hand over her shoulder without looking back. "Change your bandages if you must do something."

I don't know why I'm surprised when I take the bandages off my wrists and find nothing but faint lines on the skin that was chafed and tender just hours ago. I shouldn't be surprised, after what Moots did for my other injuries.

"I've never seen anything work like this salve," I muse aloud, wondering if it's just available here, in the richer part of the territory. Nothing like this reached us in the Outlands.

"Mmm, I get it from the nicest man. He's a physician from Tryto, and I swear he knows secrets no one else does."

I chuckle. "His name wouldn't be Moots, would it?"

She spins around, spoon in hand. "Oh! You know him?"

"I've met him. He was very kind."

"So kind. He's usually up at the castle, but comes down to the village now and then. I hear he's training an apprentice. Not something he's ever done before. Such a nice man. And aren't his eyes just beautiful?" She turns back to the stove, prattling on.

I listen quietly as I apply a light layer of salve to the remaining marks on my skin. There's something comforting about her easy chatter. She just rambles on like I'm an old friend, not some runaway stranger. It's difficult not to wish that we *were* friends. To wish that I weren't a fugitive in hiding, but someone this compassionate woman would know and welcome into her home for a casual chat over a cup of tea. To wish for a different life. To wish that I didn't have an entire castle hunting for me. It's hard to not wish that I were still the girl in an Outland village, mildly disliked, betrothed, and *unknown*. I'd happily go back to that reality and be grateful for my luck.

Swallowing thickly, I don't realize I've been staring at a knot in the tabletop until Andreya places a bowl of oats and fruit over it. She gives me a few rules that include staying away from windows and not opening the door, then leaves for the market.

Left alone with breakfast and a storm of thoughts, I eat, clean up, and dress. I pace the house anxiously, counting every creak of wood, until finally, the door opens again. Andreya returns. Relief sweeps through me when I see she's alone. I'd been half expecting her to return with guards, but the look on her face quickly unsettles me again.

"Did something happen?" I nearly whisper, afraid of the answer. I wring my hands as she sets her bags down and meets my eyes.

"You… are a very wanted woman." She exhales slowly. "All is well. No one knows you're here. But… there are guards crawling the entire village looking for you. Someone wants you back very badly."

Her thin eyebrows raise but I stay quiet. She might change her mind if she knew it was the King himself. She gestures for me to follow her into the sitting room.

I'd wandered into it earlier but didn't linger. It felt personal. Paintings of various sizes and subjects litter every surface in the room. The supplies used to create them equally spread about. Scattered in between are plants in every type of vessel imaginable. Pots, vases, pans, teacups, bowls - all filled with greenery from full climbing vines to tiny cuttings just starting. Walking in here feels a bit like walking into the midst of someone's mind.

We sit in two matching armchairs with soft green cushions and a low wooden table between us. She leans back, hands folded across her stomach.

"Normally, I suggest laying low for a day or two. Wait out the search for a bit." She jumps right into her thoughts, leaving me to catch up. "But getting you out of the village is going to be difficult and as…

desired as you seem to be, I think the sooner we move you, the better. Tomorrow I think." She nods, agreeing with her own thoughts.

Tomorrow. It feels too soon, and not soon enough. It means I get farther from the castle quicker. It means I get to see Diamo earlier. But tomorrow feels too quick, rushed almost. It doesn't take much to realize why.

It feels safe here. *I* feel safe here.

I've only ever felt safe looking up at the stars. Racing horses. Swimming rivers. I felt safe with Diamo. I'll feel safe again after I leave.

"So, do you know which direction you'd like to head? There are safe houses all over, but I'd rather not send you the wrong way." She pulls a piece of paper on the table closer and digs through the clutter, searching for something.

"Verti. I need to go to Verti first." The answer comes without hesitation. I *need* to get to Diamo. After that, we'll figure things out. Maybe we'll make our fantasy of sailing east a reality.

"Verti, huh?"

"It's in the Outlands, near Sunstien."

"Oh… I know it. Little village with too much attitude in recent years." Her tone is amused, but she narrows her eyes. "You said first. You're not planning to stay?"

She triumphantly pulls out a charcoal pencil from under a pile of paintbrushes. Shaking my head I drop my gaze.

"They know I'm from there. It's the first place they'll look."

"Is that wise? From what I know of Verti, they're more in line with the crown than most of the Outlands. Not exactly welcoming for anyone trying to live outside the lines."

She's right. They won't hesitate to hand me back to the monarchy. It's a risk I have to take. I can't run and not at least try to return to Diamo. My heart won't allow it. The thought of never seeing him again squeezes my chest painfully.

"I have to," I say quietly.

"Alright, then. Verti it is." Her weathered hands are steady as she sketches a map. She marks key locations and lines the margins with directions and signs to look for. Listening closely, I admire the artistry of how beautifully her script flows across the page. Something about the way the letters curl stirs something familiar.

"Memorize it carefully. We'll burn it in a few minutes. Can't have this information just lying around but we don't want you getting lost either. I'll fetch us some tea." I nod and whisper a thank you as she rises.

Studying the map closely, I repeat the landmarks over and over in my head, committing them to memory. They are my key to freedom. To Diamo. Closing my eyes, I attempt to recite them without the assistance of the paper and I miss at least one. Sighing, I look around the room to clear my head.

I'm on my feet and moving before I fully register why, the paper slipping from my fingers to the floor. My mind refuses to accept what my eyes are seeing. Slowly, I reach out and lift the painting, fingers brushing over the textured canvas. I follow the strokes of dark hair with trembling hands, then trace the dark eyes that mirror my own.

"She who was not broken," I whisper. It's been so long, but there is no mistaking it.

"Genevieve Brevou."

I jump at Andreya's quiet voice behind me, nearly dropping the frame. She sets two mugs on the table but doesn't come closer.

My grandmother's portrait is in this house.

"You knew her?" My voice is barely more than a breath. As if speaking too loudly would chase off the truth of it.

Andreya laughs softly, "I knew Vivi better than anyone." She watches me clutch the painting. "I wondered, when I saw you. Then you mentioned Verti, and I knew. I was just trying to decide whether it was something you'd want to know. You're the spitting image of her, you know."

She pats the seat beside her. I hesitate, then sit, still holding the painting like a lifeline.

"How did you know her?" I'm still whispering, unwilling to break the fragile hope that had blossomed in my chest.

Genevieve Brevou. The woman whose image and words had kept me going through every dark moment in my life. A woman my parents and village refused to talk about. The reason my father hated me.

"Genevieve was..." she looks past me and smiles, "the love of my life."

The words settle softly, but I know how sharp they could be in the wrong hands. It wasn't safe to say such things aloud. Not then. Definitely not now. A truth like that could earn her a whipping. Worse, if someone cruel enough were listening.

But she trusts me.

And she loved her anyway.

She continues on reverently.

"Her mate, John, was a mean bastard. He had too heavy a hand and never a kind word. There was no grief there when he died, but Vivi was distraught, lost without him controlling her. She came here to King's Village hoping to escape the oppression of Verti and the watchful eyes of everyone who knew her as a child. But I'm afraid she found that life was no kinder in King's Village. I took her and her son in when I found them on the street shivering and starving. They weren't running from anyone, just down on their luck." Andreya gives me a half smile as she lives through the memory.

"She was beautiful. And kind. But oh she was as smart as a whip and didn't hesitate to give anyone a piece of her mind, which landed her in trouble more often than not." She chuckles, eyes misty. "She was... a light."

"Vivi and I became friends quickly and I made my home hers. She and her baby boy filled this house with joy and an irresistible love. She became my whole world. And then she left."

Leaning forward, she takes a mug in hand and blows across the top, scattering the steam.

"I lost a lot of years with Genevieve when she returned to Verti with Keith. She promised she'd come back, but that's a long time to hold onto a promise. That's a long time to wait for the person who stole your heart to return."

"Why did she go back to Verti if she was happy here?"

She takes a long sip before answering. "She let her mouth run away from her and ran into some trouble with the market guards. We're in the heart of the capital, there's no more dangerous place for a woman without a mate. Even though Verti is tight knit and difficult to endure, it's better than being on the doorstep of the man who rules it all. They beat her, and threatened to take Keith. She left that very night. Took Keith back to Verti to raise him in peace. Well, in as much peace as you can as a widowed, unmated mother."

"But she came back," I say, half asking.

"Yes. She came back to me." Another smile wrinkles her cheeks. "She returned as soon as Keith reached the age to run his own house. She fulfilled her duty to her son, and then came here to live for herself. We had a beautiful life." She takes another sip of tea.

I let her words settle. My heart aches with everything I didn't know.

"I saw a painting once, inscribed with 'She who was not broken.'"

Andreya's curly hair bounces as she nods. "I painted that for her, after she'd been here a while. I was still learning and she was stunning. The perfect subject—my favorite subject. I added the words to the back and gave it to her when she left... to remind her."

"Remind her of what?"

"That she was a survivor. She didn't let John break her. She didn't let his loss break her. She didn't let raising a son on her own break her. She didn't let King's Village break her. I needed her to remember that Verti couldn't break her either, nothing could, and nothing did." She leans forward and catches me in a stare.

"Genevieve Brevou was a force all her own, and if I were to guess... you are too. You won't let anything break you."

I shake my head as tears well without warning. She pats my hand, and with a single blink, they slip free, trailing down my cheeks.

"I try," I mumble, the emotion thick in my throat. "I only saw the words once, but I recite them every time I need to remember who I am." The realization hits hard that the woman saving me now has been saving me my whole life, and the tears come faster.

"You're Keith's daughter?"

I can only nod.

"I'm honored I was able to help you, even in some small way."

But I can't let her keep helping, not without knowing the truth. Genevieve, my grandmother, loved this woman. Andreya saved her. Just like she's saving me now. I can't put her in more danger than I already have.

"I have to tell you something." My voice cracks as I swipe at the tears on my cheeks. She watches me, waiting. "I... I'm not just wanted by anyone."

One of her eyebrows lifts in quiet curiosity as she leans back.

I blow out a breath and steel myself. She deserves the truth, deserves to know exactly what kind of trouble I've dragged to her door.

"I'm wanted by the King. And the Prince. They're the ones searching for me." The words spill out in a rush, but saying them feels like exhaling a burden I didn't realize I was carrying. "I'm running from the crown. That's why there are so many guards."

I fidget with the edge of the frame still resting in my lap while she simply watches me, her face unreadable.

"I'm sorry," I add quickly, when she stays silent. "I shouldn't be here. It's too dangerous. I couldn't live with myself if something happened to you because of me. I'll leave."

I set the painting gently on the table and start to rise.

"Sit." Her voice snaps, firmer than I've ever heard it. I freeze. "Vivi's granddaughter is in need. I won't let you walk out into a village full of guards hunting you down. Not happening."

She shakes her head and points to the chair I just stood from.

"Sit. I've been doing this a long time, girl. I know the risks. They're mine to take, not yours to carry. No one makes my choices but me. Guilt doesn't live in this house."

Stunned, I blink at the sudden fire in her tone and sit.

"Good," she says with a short nod. "You said it was a bad mating. So why are the royals so invested?"

"They want me bound to the Prince."

Her eyebrows nearly leap into her hairline, her mouth forming a perfect O.

It's my turn for storytelling, and I tell her everything that's transpired to get me from Verti to here. Every sordid detail and event that's been the nightmare of my life the last few days spills from my lips like water breaching a dam.

Chapter
Twenty-Four

I spent the rest of the day with Andreya in the sitting room, cocooned in warmth and quiet. The afternoon sunlight filtered in through lace curtains, casting soft patterns across the floor. Dust motes drifted lazily through the golden air, and for a few fleeting hours, it felt like the world had stopped chasing me. We sat together in mismatched armchairs, a pot of tea between us, speaking in low voices and long pauses. I couldn't remember the last time I'd been able to sit still like this, without fear driving every breath.

I recited the directions to the next safe house over and over until she was satisfied I knew them well enough to survive. Then we burned the paper together in the fireplace, watching the edges curl to black, as if sealing a promise between us.

After that, she told me dozens of stories. About Genevieve. About the village. About ridiculous things that made her laugh so hard she cried. Her voice took on a softness when she spoke of my grandmother, equal parts reverent and raw. She didn't gloss over the hardships but always returned to her strength.

The more I listened, the more I felt the shape of Genevieve forming in my mind, not as a legend or whispered warning, but as a woman. A fierce, brilliant, imperfect woman who had made people love her despite the risks. Despite the loss. Andreya's voice filled the space with color, and it painted my grandmother back to life in bold, defiant strokes. I asked questions I didn't even know I had. She answered each one. I committed every story to memory like I was starving for them.

As the day faded and shadows deepened across the walls, the soft rhythm of life in Andreya's home settled around me like a blanket. She made supper while humming under her breath, something wistful I didn't recognize but wanted to. I helped where I could, grateful just to be useful. We washed the dishes slowly, speaking less now, letting the silence say what words couldn't. When the time came, I didn't want to leave her side. I didn't want to vanish beneath the floorboards again. But I did. She kissed the top of my head like I was her own, handed me a folded quilt and a candle stub, and reminded me that morning would come.

I curled beneath the house, and listened to the soft creak of Andreya's rocking chair. That sound, more than anything, told me I was safe. It was the sound of a home. Of someone waiting. Of stillness. I held on to it until sleep found me.

Now, it's morning.

And I'm leaving today.

The room is quiet, still blanketed in the grey hush before sunrise. A kettle simmers softly on the stove, and the smell of dried herbs lingers faintly in the air. Andreya moves through the space with the ease of someone who has already lived a full day before most have opened their eyes. She hasn't said much, neither have I, but something unspoken hums between us. A sense of ending.

I don't want to go.

Part of me aches to stay, to pretend that yesterday wasn't a pause in the chaos but the beginning of something real. I want more time in this quiet house with the woman who welcomed me like I was hers. More hours of stories and warmth and stillness.

But the illusion of safety doesn't hold against the truth. King's Village is crawling with guards, and every one of them would drag me back to the Prince if they found me. I can't let that happen. Diamo is waiting. I don't know what the future holds, or even what direction we'll run, but I know I have to find him. The rest, we'll face together.

"Here you go, dear," Andreya says, handing me a folded bundle of clothes. "These were Vivi's. I know she wouldn't mind you having them for your journey."

I take them in both hands, holding them longer than I should. The fabric is soft, worn in the way only well-loved things are. It feels sacred somehow to be trusted with something that belonged to a grandmother I never met, but feel tethered to all the same.

"You don't want too much to carry, but you'll need a couple changes in case something gets wet or torn. Don't want you catching cold," she adds, already moving about the kitchen, slipping fruit and dried meat into a cloth bag.

"Go change. I'll finish packing this."

When I emerge from the bathing room dressed in a long-sleeved blue cotton gown with a floral-stitched corset over the top, her hands go still. She just stares.

"Oh, goodness," she whispers. "It's like taking a step back in time. Vivi would be so proud of you."

I smile faintly and finish tying a ribbon at the end of the braid I've managed to tame my hair into.

"Thank you. That means more than you know."

She nods once, and though she blinks quickly, her eyes are shining. Then she tucks a tin of salve into the bag and reaches for something else, the small portrait of Genevieve.

"For you," she says, offering it with both hands. "You won't let them break you. I know it in my bones."

My throat tightens as I take it from her. I don't have words. What do you say to someone who saved you with more than a hiding place? Who handed you back pieces of yourself you didn't know were missing?

"Andreya—"

Three sharp knocks land on the door.

The sound freezes everything. My voice. My breath. The fragile calm that held the morning together.

Andreya presses a finger to her lips. I nod without speaking, heart hammering. I jam the portrait into my pocket, and we move, sliding the table aside carefully. I lower myself into the hiding space, pull the hatch shut above me, and curl inward.

Three more knocks, louder and sharper now.

"I'm coming! Give an old woman a minute!" she calls. Her tone is strong. Annoyed, even. But I can hear the tight edge under it now. She's stalling.

The table scrapes slightly as she slides it back into place. I wince, pressing my body into the corner, trying to make myself smaller. Her footsteps move toward the door, slow but steady. The door creaks open. A low voice responds, definitely a man's. I strain to make out the words, but everything is muffled. Then the door shuts again. Her steps return, and I finally let myself breathe.

"They're looking for you door to door now," she says, just barely loud enough for me to hear. "We'll get you out today. Just give him a minute to move on and I'll shift the table. There's a cart—"

The next knock isn't a knock at all. It's a bang. A fist. Full force.

Her footsteps stop. My breath catches again.

Then the door explodes open, crashing against the wall. Heavy boots trample in, three, maybe four sets. The sound alone makes my stomach lurch.

"King's Guard. Your home is subject to a search for a fugitive of the crown. Tell us where she is," a gravel-edged voice barks.

Recognition slams into me. *Captain Harrow.*

"I just told you—there is no one here, sir," Andreya snaps. "This is ridiculous. You're going to give an old woman a heart attack barging in like that."

"Do not interfere," the man growls. "If you're aiding her, your punishment will be severe. Take her outside."

There's a shuffle, a gasp, and the sound of dragging footsteps. I cover my mouth with both hands and fight the sudden rise of nausea. This is wrong. I want to scream. I want to do something.

But if they find me now, we'll both be lost.

I close my eyes. Breathe. Count.

One. Two. Three.

This is spiraling out of control so fast I can't think, can't move, can't do anything but listen as the search begins.

Furniture is overturned. Cabinets wrenched open. I flinch at the sound of something heavy crashing against the floor, wood, maybe a chair. Then the brittle sound of pottery shattering. Something glass. A picture frame? I imagine the little green teacups on her shelf. The paintings stacked in the corner. I imagine them breaking, scattered across the floor, trampled under boots, treated like trash, as if none of it ever mattered.

They're destroying her home. Her treasures. Her life. Because of me.

Please let them leave. Please let her be okay. Please, just let this end.

The boots stop. The shadows go still.

Then Harrow's voice again, crueler this time, calm in the worst kind of way.

"Come out, girl! We know you're here."

Statues have more life to them than I do at this moment. I don't breathe. I don't even blink. If I'm still enough, silent enough, maybe they'll give up. Maybe they'll leave.

"Do you care for the woman at all?"

I close my eyes.

"She'll have five lashes for every minute you waste my time here! I have no more patience for you."

My heart sinks.

No. No, surely not.

He doesn't mean it. He's bluffing. He has to be bluffing.

He wouldn't. Not without proof.

Not without—

But this is Barbast.

This is King's Village.

And he is a servant of the King.

There's silence. Then he starts counting.

"Five. Four. Three. Two. One. One minute wasted." A pause. "Five lashes for the woman!" He shouts the last through the door.

Crack.

A scream.

Andreya's scream.

It rips through me.

I dig my nails into my skin, clench my jaw until it aches, anything to stop myself from moving. If I come out now, what good will it do? They'll hurt her more. They'll take me.

Crack. Another scream. Shorter. Sharper.

Please stop. Please stop. Please.

I tell myself not to move. I tell myself she would understand. That if I stay hidden, I'll survive and she won't suffer for nothing. But each cry punches through that logic like it's made of paper.

Then silence. A long, excruciating breath of it. Then...

"Five. Four. Three. Two. One. Two minutes wasted. Five more!"

Another crack.

I try to cover my ears, but it's like the sound is inside me. Tearing something loose.

Another.

My breath hitches. My body starts to tremble.

And with the third blow, something inside me shatters.

"Stop!" I scream. "Stop, please! I'm here!" My voice cracks on the words. "I'm here!"

The table crashes aside. The hatch is yanked open.

Captain Harrow's shadowed face appears. His eyes flick over me like I'm just another chore.

Another cry from outside, higher this time, nearly broken.

I shoot to my feet. "Stop them! I'm right here!"

He shrugs like it doesn't matter. "You earned her five. She gets five."

Then he grabs my arm and hauls me up like I weigh nothing.

The room is in ruin. Paintings torn. Chairs splintered. Dishes ground into shards. Every beautiful thing she ever loved, reduced to trash on the floor.

They drag me through it like I belong with the wreckage.

Outside, the crowd has gathered along the low fence. Curious, watching. Faces half-lit in morning light, half-shadowed by cruelty or boredom. I don't know which is worse.

Andreya is on her knees in the dirt. One guard on either arm. Another stands behind her, whip raised. It falls. She jerks forward with a ragged cry.

"Andreya!" I scream, lungs burning. "I'm so sorry!"

Tears pour down my face. I can't stop them. I don't try.

Captain Harrow binds my wrists, rough and fast, then drags me toward the gate.

She lifts her head, her eyes meeting mine, and smiles.

"I regret nothing."

"She will when she gets back to the castle," the gruff guard mutters in my ear as he pulls me away.

His voice is flat, almost bored, and the cruelty of it turns my stomach. Equal parts fear and fury flood through me. I dig in my heels, trying to plant myself in the dirt. I won't let him drag me away from her like this. I won't.

But he yanks me forward, chest to chest, and lowers his voice to a growl. "If I get punished for your bruises, she'll suffer twice. Move."

I look back. Andreya is still pinned to the ground. The back of her dress is torn open, the green fabric soaked dark.

My feet move.

Not because I want to. Because I don't know what else to do. I don't know how to fight this.

Satisfied, the guard leads me through the gate and over to a waiting horse. He passes me off to another man and climbs into the saddle. Then he reaches down, expecting me to come.

I hesitate, heart thudding.

I don't want to ride with him. I don't want to be anywhere near him.

"Ride the horse or be dragged behind it," he says. "Makes no difference to me, girl."

Heat prickles across my skin. Slowly, I raise my bound hands. Another guard lifts me from behind, and they shove me up into the saddle. Harrow settles behind me, boxing me in with his arms as he takes the reins.

"Burn it," he calls out.

I twist, heart seizing.

"No—"

Two guards approach the house. They toss flaming torches through the window and door.

Andreya's scream cuts through everything. She collapses forward in the dirt, not from pain, but from the kind of devastation that can't be measured. She sobs, helpless, as the flames catch the curtains and smoke pours out into the sky. She watches her home, her memories, her history, her peace, go up in flames.

I can't look away.

The house crackles louder as the fire climbs higher, hungrily devouring everything she loved. Everything she gave me. Everything she risked to keep me safe.

There is no undoing this.

It's gone.

I watch.

Take Her

Helpless.
Powerless.
What have I done?

Chapter Twenty-Five

The ride back to the castle is silent. The Captain and I don't speak as his horse carries us at a steady trot, the rhythmic strike of hooves on stone the only sound. Not a single word is exchanged as we pass the castle walls, and even when he pulls me from the horse outside the castle entrance, the silence stretches on.

The numbness from the night I was taken has found me again— a familiar, hollow feeling I welcome all too easily. It's easier to bear than the guilt and shock that threatens to drown me. I let the emptiness settle in, until I feel detached from my emotions. It's as if my body is no longer mine. It's an unfeeling stranger walking past the giant engraved doors. It's an apathetic girl that stands next to the captain in the center of the throne room.

I don't have to ask what we're waiting for. I already know. The numbness whispers that I don't care. I deserve whatever punishment comes. The destruction my choices have caused is proof enough.

The King enters the room with swift, heavy steps, his anger palpable with every click of his boots against the stone. The Captain bows low behind me as the King stops before us. I meet his frostbitten glare without flinching, refusing to give him the satisfaction of seeing me cower.

In a flash, his hand shoots out, seizing my face with a brutal force, squeezing my cheeks between his thick fingers.

"You wretched brat," he growls, his grip digging into my flesh. "Do you have any idea what you've done?"

"Your Majesty," the Prince's voice echoes through the almost empty room, smooth and controlled.

The King sneers, his expression darkening as his son steps forward, giving a short bow when he reaches my side.

"You should thank him," the King spits. "If he weren't so insistent on not having a bruised bride, I'd have you beaten within an inch of your life." He shoves my face away, making me stumble back a step.

The Prince places a steadying hand on my arm, the warmth of his touch too stark against the cold threading through me. Copper fills my mouth as I bite my cheek hard, refusing to let any words escape.

Taking a step back, the King demands a report from Captain Harrow. The man eagerly obliges.

"We've suspected the woman of smuggling slaves for some time. We held off on arresting her, hoping a slave would lead us to the rest of the chain. When the girl disappeared, we watched all of the suspected homes. She was seen purchasing supplies outside her normal routine."

"And you found her there," the King cuts in, impatient.

"Yes, Your Majesty. We gave the woman a chance to hand her over. When she didn't, we forced entry. The girl was hiding under the floorboards."

"She's been dealt with?"

"The woman received ten lashes at the scene. The home was burned. I brought the girl straight here."

Revulsion rises in me at how casually they recount the ruin of a woman's life. I waver on my feet. The Prince's hand on my arm tightens slightly.

"Bring her," the King orders.

"Your Majesty." The Captain bows low and swiftly exits. We wait in silence for the sound of his boots to fade down the hall. The King spins a large onyx ring around his middle finger.

"Tell us where the next safe house is," he says, breaking the quiet.

I let out a quiet, half-formed scoff, more breath than sound. They're delusional if they think I'd help them hunt down more people who risk everything to free others. I promised Andreya I'd never give up the locations. I've already let her down, I won't do it again. I watch the revolution of the dark gem around the monarch's finger, detached.

The Prince draws me closer, until my back is flush with his chest. His breath stirs my hair as he leans in. "Tell him what he wants to know and we will be done here."

I don't acknowledge his ignorance. We can stay here all day.

But his arms wind around me, his fingers tugging gently at the binding on my wrists. My lungs stutter, his nearness unsettling. Diamo's the only man whose arms have ever enveloped me, and with him, it felt like shelter. This feels like a cage. A stifling cage I failed to escape.

"Come on, darling," the Prince coaxes softly, throwing the rope behind us. "His Majesty is waiting."

My eyes snap up to the King's.

"He will die waiting."

Satisfaction flickers through my chest as the King's face distorts with rage. He moves quickly, but the Prince is faster, pulling me impossibly closer and turning to the side.

The King stops a hair's breadth from the Prince's shoulder, breath puffing and face red.

"With respect," the Prince says, his voice low but firm, "I will remind Your Majesty that you chose her for her resilience."

The air thickens with tension. My pulse thrums as I watch them, locked in a silent battle of wills. Neither of them flinches away. I hold my breath, the Prince's grip on my arms is painfully tight, but I don't dare move, don't dare break the stillness.

"The insolent bitch will find her place, or I will show it to her," the King snarls, his voice soaked in venom.

The sound of the throne room doors opening captures everyone's attention, cutting off any reply the Prince had. My stomach plummets, and a fissure of pain cracks through the numb shell I've built around myself.

Chapter Twenty-Six

Two King's guards step into the room, the older woman draped between them, a stark contrast to their imposing figures. Her silver hair, once glossy and full, now falls in tangled waves around her weathered face. Her dress, torn and stained, clings to her small frame. The men's expressions remain impassive as they drop her limp form near us. Her breath comes in ragged gasps as she struggles to hold herself up. Angry, raw whip marks cross her back where the fabric has split.

My heart stutters at her broken body, and the Prince's grip loosens as I slump against him, my knees weakening.

I did this.

"Perfect," the King says, stepping toward her. He doesn't look at her with pity. He doesn't see her as a person. To him, she's an object, a pawn. Just another subject to either be ruled, or crushed.

His voice breaks the room's heavy silence, drawing Andreya's attention. Her head snaps up. Her eyes find mine. And I realize, her body may be broken but her spirit isn't. Her sharp gaze pierces through me, undefeated.

"Tell me where the next safe house is." The King turns to me, but I don't tear my eyes from the woman on the ground.

"I can get it from her," he continues, his oily voice sliding down my spine, "but haven't you put her through enough?"

"I don't know where the next safe house is." The words leave me flat and devoid of emotion, yet I'm surprised by the steadiness in my voice. It should have cracked or trembled, but I managed to sound convincing, certain.

Andreya's eyes soften with the smallest hint of a smile. She gives a subtle nod and I know I've made the right choice in my lie. I promised her. Swore to her, on everything that matters, that I would protect those safe places with my silence. I feel a strange sense of relief, knowing that despite all the pain I've caused her, I can keep this vow. I can do this for her, for all the runaways that follow.

"Where is the next safe house?!" His shout lashes through the air, jarring me upright.

"Narina," the Prince whispers behind me, barely audible. But my resolve doesn't waver.

"I don't know," I repeat.

"Pity," the King says, his voice turning quiet again, lethal.

"And you?" he asks, turning to the battered woman.

"I will not break." Her voice is steady, her gaze locked with mine. There is no hesitation, no flicker of doubt. She's not just speaking the words, she's carving them into the space between us, and in that moment, I know with an undeniable certainty, she isn't speaking to the King.

"We shall see."

The King flicks a hand in silent command. The guard behind her obeys without hesitation, raising a long leather whip and bringing it down in a vicious arc. The crack of it connecting with her already broken skin echoes through the cold, empty chamber, reverberating off the walls.

She flinches, a brief, involuntary action, but she does not cry out. The sight knocks the breath from my lungs, but I do not look away. I will not look away. She will not endure this moment alone.

Another flick of his wrist. Another lash.

The leather slices through the air before it lands against her back with another sickening crack. This time, her body jerks forward, her breath shuddering out of her in a ragged gasp. I clench my fists, nails biting into my palms. But I do not look away. I hold her gaze, pouring every ounce of strength into the space between us.

Again.

The whip whistles before it lands. She bites down on her lip, and her arms tremble as she fights to stay upright.

Again.

Red blooms against the torn fabric of her dress, dark and wet, trailing down in thin rivulets that vanish into the floor's cracks. Sweat beads along her temple, her breaths coming faster now. Still, she doesn't make a sound.

Again.

A choked breath slips past her lips as her body recoils against the pain. My gut twists when her head drops, breaking our connection.

The King sighs, slow and exaggerated, as if this is some minor inconvenience. He watches her with something bordering amusement, then leans forward.

"Where are the safe houses?" His voice is smooth, almost bored.

I hold my breath.

She does not answer.

The silence stretches between them. A single drop of blood slips from the curve of her shoulder, falling soundlessly to the stone floor.

He sighs again before looking over his shoulder at me.

"Narina?" My name is a dagger on his tongue, sharp with false patience.

I do not answer. I'm not sure I have the strength to lie again. Not after the consequences she has borne for my faults. His lips press together, the briefest flicker of irritation crossing his face before he gives the order.

"Continue," he says flatly.

The whip cuts through the air and lands with a brutal snap. Her body stiffens, and she whimpers.

Again.

Her fingers clench against the stone as the force of the blow drives her forward. She barely catches herself. My chest constricts. The King watches, his head tilting as if evaluating an injured animal before him.

Silence hangs in the air, heavy with her labored breaths. She is shaking, barely able to hold herself upright.

"You are quite stubborn," he muses. "But everyone breaks eventually." His gaze slides back to me. "Everyone."

A chill crawls down my spine. He's seen how I look at her, how I refuse to look away even when every lash feels like a blade to my own ribs. He's not breaking *her*. The King smiles, slow and satisfied, like a predator watching its prey finally understand the inevitable.

He gestures lazily toward the guard holding the whip. Something snaps inside me. An explosion against the shell that had been holding me together.

"NO!"

The word tears out of me as adrenaline floods my veins. Before anyone can react, I twist hard, throwing my weight sideways. My shoulder slams into the Prince's chest and he stumbles, his grip slipping just enough.

I break free.

My feet barely touch the ground as I spring forward. The guard raises his arm, preparing to strike, but I throw myself between them before the blow can land.

Pain explodes across my back, fire lashing through my nerves. The impact knocks me forward, but I'm already pressing myself against her, shielding her with my own body, my arms wrapping around her trembling frame.

A sharp gasp rips from her lips as I press against her, my body shaking from the force of the blow. Her blood seeps into my dress, hot and thick. I tighten my hold on her, refusing to move, refusing to let them touch her again.

"I'm sorry," I whisper into her ear, too quiet for anyone else to hear. I will not let her continue to suffer for me.

The room is deathly silent.

Then... footsteps. Steady. Measured.

A hand clamps down on my arm, firm and unyielding.

"Narina." The Prince's voice is low, almost quiet, but there's an edge to it. A warning.

I shake my head, clutching her tighter, anchoring myself to her. She was my refuge when I needed one, I will be her shield now.

"Let her go," he says. "This will not help her."

I don't. I can't.

His grip tightens, and then, with a sharp tug, I'm yanked backward.

"No!"

I struggle, twisting in his grasp, but he's stronger. My feet skid against the stone as he drags me away from her.

Andreya makes a broken sound, something between a gasp and a whimper, as I'm torn away from her. My fingers claw at empty air.

"*Please.*"

The word slips out before I can stop it, raw and shaking. The Prince's hold on me falters for the briefest second, something unreadable flickering across his features.

Then the King hums, amused. "My, my. Quite the little martyr, aren't you? Just tell me what I want to know, and this will all be over." His voice drips with the promise of further suffering.

"Stars damn you," Andreya curses, her voice ragged, barely a whisper, yet it cuts through the air like a blade.

The King merely raises a brow, unbothered by her words. She lifts her chin slightly, a silent defiance, an echo of strength. Her gaze heavy with pain and unspoken resolve meets mine.

"I regret nothing. Remember the strength you come from."

Her words hit like a blow to the chest.

I twist again, desperate to return to her, to tell her what she means to me. To make sure she knows I am here with her, for her.

But the Prince tightens his grip, locking my arms against my sides.

"Enough," he murmurs, tension lacing his voice.

"Do not let them break you," Andreya whispers, her words a prayer to the stars themselves. She nods once, the slight movement barely perceptible. It's enough. For a moment, time stands still. Her strength wraps around me.

The King watches us with something dangerously close to satisfaction.

"Take her to her room," the Prince says, his voice cold. The command is final.

The guards move swiftly, grabbing my arms with brutal efficiency. They drag me toward the door, my heart hammering painfully in my chest. Every step pulls me further from her. The Prince follows closely.

I glance back one last time at Andreya. She's watching me, her expression pained, except for... a smile.

It's a small thing. But it's enough. It's not a smile of defeat; it's a smile of strength, of knowing that no matter what, we will not break.

Then the Prince steps into my line of sight. The guards pause. Silence presses down on us, broken only by the sound of my breath.

"You'll regret this," I say suddenly, my voice low but fierce.

I don't know where the words come from. I don't know if I'm speaking to him, myself, or the stars themselves, but the words come anyway. Born of fury. Of grief. Of helplessness dressed up as defiance. And I don't take them back.

He doesn't flinch. Doesn't yell. Doesn't threaten. He just stands there, still as stone, his steel gaze locked on mine. His indifference settles over me, cold, unmoving, and unfeeling. Exactly what I expect of him.

"I doubt that," he murmurs at last. Then he turns and closes the door between us.

The latch clicks too loudly.

The guards push me forward. I don't fight them.

The hallway feels narrower than before. Their hands tighter. The air harder to breathe.

The hollow finality of the Prince's words settles deep in my bones.

Chapter
Twenty-Seven

I will not be broken.

I curl into a ball on the pile of furs atop the wooden bed in the room I'd hoped never to see again. Failure presses down on me, squeezing the breath from my lungs. The air feels thick and heavy. I can still hear the echoes of leather meeting flesh. The scene replays in my mind, her body broken and bleeding.

I will not be broken.

I press my face into the fur, willing the images to go away. I should have fought harder. Should have found a way to save her. I want to move. To scream. To throw myself to the ground and cry. But my body feels like stone, frozen by guilt and the crushing knowledge that this is all my fault. I failed her, and now I'm stuck in this cold, empty room while she suffers. I want to rage against the walls, but all I can do is lie here, swallowed by helplessness.

I will not be broken.

My grandmother's greatest love. Someone who took a chance on me. Someone who opened her home. Who protected me. She's suffering *because* of me. If I hadn't shown up, she might've had years of a happy life, creating beautiful art and helping those who need it most. I ruined that.

These thoughts and images have been plaguing me all night. Swirling in and out of my mind, a relentless storm I can't escape. Every time I close my eyes, I see her tremble with pain. And then, the crack of the whip again. It's a sound that echoes in my bones, as if it will never stop, never fade.

She didn't deserve this.

I failed her.

And now I have to live with that.

I will not be broken.

A sharp knock sounds on the door. I don't move. Whoever it is, I have no interest in entertaining them. But of course, Mistress Myra isn't one to be ignored. She bustles in without hesitation, a white gown draped over her arm like a banner of my defeat.

"Up you get," she trills, far too bright. "Time to change."

"No," I say simply. I'd rather rot in these bloodied clothes than wrap myself in another white dress. I know what the color symbolizes. White—pure, untouched, innocent. A lamb dressed for slaughter. A sacrifice to the crown. A bride for the heir.

Myra sighs, clicking her tongue. "You're an absolute mess, and His Grace is on his way."

"Get out." My voice is flat. Unforgiving.

She falters, hand hovering over the pristine dress. But her hesitation is brief. She recovers quickly, straightening with a huff before laying the gown across the chest at the foot of the bed.

"You're covered in blood," she tsks, planting her hands on her hips. "You can't receive him like this."

"Get. Out." I repeat, sharper now.

"These clothes will have to be burned. They're simply awful," she mutters.

"Get! OUT!" I snap.

Her high-pitched voice grates against my frayed nerves, but it's the casual dismissal of my bloodstained dress, the last connection I have to Genevieve and Andreya… intolerable.

"I will fetch the guards if I must!" she threatens, raising her voice to match mine.

"Enough." The deep measured command cuts through the room.

I close my eyes in frustration even before I hear the steady approach of boots against stone. He couldn't just leave me alone.

"Mistress, you are shouting," the Prince says coolly.

With a sharp exhale and rustle of fabric, Myra's skirts whisper against the floor as she dips into a quick curtsy.

"Your Grace," she murmurs, her tone smoothing into practiced deference. "She refuses to dress."

I don't look up. I don't move.

I just breathe, bracing for whatever comes next.

I don't need to look to know he's watching me. I can feel the weight of his gaze pressing against my skin, assessing. I keep my eyes shut, willing him to disappear, willing all of them to leave me in peace. If you can call the press of guilt, rage, and helplessness, peace.

He says nothing for a moment, and then, "Wait in the hall with Moots."

Myra hesitates but knows better than to argue. She gathers her skirts and slips out. The door clicks shut behind her, sealing me in with him.

I do not move.

I do not speak.

For a long while, the only sound is the faint crackling of the fire in the hearth. Then his boots move, slow and deliberate, until he stops beside the bed.

"I would have let you rest," he says, voice unreadable. "But we must speak before I leave the castle."

I let my silence stretch.

"It is unusual for a Mistress to lose her composure," he muses. "I may need to have a word with her."

"What do you want?" I mutter.

He ignores the tone. "First, tell me what happened between you and the Mistress."

I open my eyes and meet his storm-grey gaze. "She's pushy."

A smirk pulls at his lips. "There has to be more."

Rolling my eyes, I give in. He won't leave until he gets what he wants.

"She wants to burn my dress."

His gaze flicks over the ruined fabric. "Well, it is in a sad state."

I burrow deeper into the furs, hoping he'll take the hint and leave. But instead he crouches beside me, lowering to my level.

"Tell me," he demands quietly.

"It's mine," I whisper. The knot in my throat tightens.

He nods, eyes scanning me before his fingers brush the lone tear down the back of the dress. I shiver at the contact.

"Very well," he says. "But you will clean up so Moots can have a proper look at you."

I nod. If it means I can keep this last scrap of her, I'll do anything.

He watches, like he expects resistance. The room is too quiet, pressing in. Still, I manage to ask what's been clawing at me all night, afraid of the answer.

"Andreya?"

He exhales through his nose and rises. I sit up, stiff and aching.

"She's in the dungeons."

I curl my fingers into the furs, bracing myself. "And?"

His jaw tightens. "The King will have her moved to the stocks by morning."

A sharp breath hitches in my throat.

"She will remain there until she gives him what he wants." His voice is steady, impassive. As if she wasn't sentenced to humiliation and suffering under the eyes of the entire court.

"She'll never give him anything," I say, my voice tight with conviction and fear.

"Then he will break her," he replies.

Something inside me cracks, a fracture spreading through the numbness I've been clinging to.

I shake my head. "You can't let him do this. You have to see that this is wrong."

"It is not my decision."

"But you're the Prince. You have influence. You stopped him from having me beaten. You could—"

"Enough, Narina," he interrupts. "This is treason, not a bride with a sharp tongue."

I clench my fists, nails digging into my palms. The helplessness returns, coiling tighter, suffocating. I can still see her blood. Still hear her voice telling me I won't break.

"She won't break," I force steel into the words.

The Prince studies me for a long moment, then moves toward the door.

"I have business outside the castle today," he says. "You will remain here until I return."

I blink. "Excuse me?"

"You are not to leave this room."

The words settle like iron bars slamming shut.

"So I'm to be caged like some disobedient pet?"

His jaw ticks. "It is for your own good."

"My own good?" I push off the bed, the exhaustion momentarily forgotten in the face of my growing fury. "Why not the dungeons then, if you don't want to deal with the hassle of me running off again?"

In two strides, he's in front of me, towering. His eyes are hard steel. The heir to the throne, shaped by power and untouched by mercy, here to keep me in line.

"Running again is not something I would advise, darling." His voice is low and deliberate. "You will stay in this room. I do not want to return to another mess."

I take a step forward, refusing to let him intimidate me. "You can't just leave me to—"

"I do not have time to fight," he says, cutting me off. His voice is impassive once again. "You will stay. Or next time, I will lock you in the dungeons you seem to crave."

He exhales sharply, adjusting the cuffs of his jacket. He steps back and gestures to the discarded white dress.

"Myra will clean you up. Moots will examine you. Then rest. I will return before the feast this evening."

I blink. "What feast?"

"I told you. The court will hold a feast in our honor."

My stomach clenches. I stiffen. "That was supposed to be days ago."

"The King did not want the embarrassment of his captured prize missing. It was postponed."

A cold laugh bubbles up before I can stop it. "How fortunate for him that I've returned."

He doesn't respond, but his gaze sharpens.

Fury sits tight in my chest, burning through the last remnants of exhaustion.

"So that's it?" I ask. "I'm expected to put on a dress and smile for the court like all is well? Like I haven't lost everything? Like Andreya isn't suffering because of me?"

My voice cracks, but I push through. "Don't make me do this."

His expression darkens. "You have left me no choice."

A bitter laugh scratches at my throat, but I swallow it down. He turns toward the door, opening it with controlled ease.

"Behave, Narina."

He says it so simply, as if it's that easy. As if I haven't been stripped of every choice that ever mattered.

Then he steps into the hall, addressing Myra waiting outside. "Send the clothes to Thalia for repair."

I refuse to look at him. But I feel his gaze linger, before he turns to the man at Myra's side.

"Moots."

The large man gives a short nod. The Prince says nothing more as he walks away.

And just like that, he's gone. Leaving me alone in this cage of a room with the two people assigned to mold me into a presentable captive.

Left him no choice?

As if I ever had any.

Chapter
Twenty-Eight

I reluctantly allow Myra to clean the blood from my skin and dress me in the insufferable white gown, a constant reminder of my place in their world, of what I am to them. Moots' gentle hands tend to the old wounds and the new one streaking down my back. His coaxing voice and soft touch are too kind for my mood, nearly pushing me to tears.

When they finish, I ignore the food they left and lie down, trying to rest for the events later. Despite the exhaustion weighing down every part of me, sleep refuses to come. My mind churns. Hours blur. I lose track of time.

Then a sudden flurry of movement outside the door snaps me to attention. Shouts ripple through the hallway. Whistles pierce the air. Boots pound against stone in every direction. I sit up, heart racing, straining to make sense of it, but the chaos only escalates.

Curiosity claws at me, pulling me out of bed. I approach the door and pause, listening. I reach for the handle, expecting resistance. A lock. A guard. Some reminder of control.

It turns easily.

A nervous flutter settles in my chest. I crack the door open, expecting a guard to slam it shut at any second, but the hall is empty. Just a few soldiers rush past in the distance, their whistles shrill as they vanish around a corner.

I pause, frowning. Of course he didn't lock it. He expects me to follow his order simply because he gave it. I'm supposed to listen. Obey. Sit pretty in my white dress and wait for the next command.

My gaze lingers on the hall beyond. I'm not planning to run. I'm not looking for an escape route. I just need… air. A moment to breathe. To think without the walls pressing in.

The room behind me feels smaller with every passing hour. The bed like a trap. The dress on my skin like a collar. The silence is loud with things I can't bear to face.

He warned me what would happen if I disobeyed.

But I also remember the way the Prince looked at me. The control in his voice. The way he made the decision for me.

I stare at the open door, breath shallow.

I don't owe him my obedience.

I'll just see what the noise is. Just for a minute. Just long enough to feel human again. Then I'll come back. Slip back into the room before anyone notices.

I slide on the matching white shoes left at the foot of the bed, their soft fabric useless for anything but quiet compliance, and step into the corridor.

My pulse quickens with every step. I already know part of the long hallway to the left, but most of the noise is coming from the opposite direction, so I follow it. Not to run. Not really. But because the stillness behind me is worse.

The hall narrows and branches into a dozen unfamiliar directions. I try to commit something to memory, maybe a turn or a landmark I could retrace, but the castle lives up to its reputation. It's maze-like, cold, and deliberately hard to navigate.

My slippers make no sound as I walk, but the air buzzes with footsteps and shouts in the distance. No one pays me any attention, but that does nothing to ease the tension in my spine. Every heartbeat reminds me I'm defying orders. I wonder if he's back in the castle yet. I wonder if he'll come looking.

The longer I walk, the more lost I feel. Stone corridors twist and repeat, tapestries drape heavy against dark walls, doors loom with no markings to guide me. I don't belong here. Not just in the castle, but in this life they've forced me into. Every step reminds me I'm playing a role I didn't choose, dressed like someone I'm not, in a place that was never meant for me.

I slow, debating whether I should turn back. Return to the room, to the silence, to the waiting. But turning around feels like surrender.

So I keep going.

A sudden rush of footsteps echoes ahead. A squad of guards rounds the corner, moving fast.

Panic rises. I freeze, breath caught in my throat. Before they can spot me, I dart sideways and slip behind a tall tapestry hanging against the stone wall. My fingers clutch the fabric as I press myself into the shadows, heart pounding.

The sound of boots grows louder. Closer.

I try to make myself smaller, barely daring to breathe. Their voices are low, clipped with urgency, but they don't stop. One by one, they pass. Relief washes over me. Just for a moment before I stumble backward—into nothing. My heart lurches as I fall, landing hard. Pain ricochets up my spine as I hit the ground with a muted thud.

I sit up slowly, brushing grit from my palms. It takes a moment for my eyes to adjust. A sliver of sunlight filters through a small window high on one wall. Dust drifts in the beam, turning slowly in the quiet air. The walls are bare. The sconces unlit.

For one brief, impossible second, I wonder if I've found something I wasn't meant to. An escape route, maybe. A forgotten passage. Some way out.

But there's nothing here. No door. No tunnel. No stairs. Just stone, silence, and the sound of my own breathing.

No one followed me.

No one saw.

I rise, slowly, back aching from the fall. The hush settles over me, muffling the faint echoes of commotion from the corridor outside. I cross the room and lean back against the far wall, the chill of the stone steadying me. I need to think. To breathe. To feel something besides this gnawing pressure in my chest.

No one knows I'm here.

The idea tempts me more than I want to admit. I could disappear down another hallway, deeper into the castle. Slip out before anyone realizes. The Prince isn't here to stop me, and for once, no guard at my back.

As soon as that thought forms, another follows, sharper and more biting.

If I run now, who will pay the cost?

My hands curl against my sides. I see Andreya, knees in the dirt, her dress torn open, her blood soaking into the stone. Her screams echo louder here than they did then. She paid the price for my last attempt to flee. And she never once hesitated.

Diamo wouldn't either. If I showed up at his door, he'd take me in without question. He'd fight for me. Protect me. Even if it cost him everything. But the thought of that… the idea of him suffering like Andreya did… It twists something deep and sick inside me.

I want to run. Stars, I want it more than anything.

I *can't* be the reason that happens again. I won't survive it.

But don't we deserve to be happy?

Is it selfish to still want that?

Is it selfish to still want *him*?

Is it wrong to want more than this cage?

To not want to be bound to a man I hate?

I squeeze my eyes shut and press the heel of my hand to them, trying to push the thoughts away, but they won't go. They just keep spinning... guilt, longing, fear, defiance. All tangled together until I don't know what's right anymore. I don't know what choice leads to freedom, and what choice leads to more ruin.

I sink down, pulling my knees to my chest. The stone seeps cold through the thin fabric of my gown. My thoughts churn until they blur at the edges. Somewhere, hope still stirs. It's a dangerous thing, and I hate that I don't know what to do with it.

The sounds outside begin to fade. Fewer voices now. The sharp whistles and shouted commands give way to the low hum of order being restored. Whatever pulled the guards away is settling down.

Time is slipping.

I tilt my head back against the wall and let my eyes close, just for a moment. I tell myself I'll figure it out later. The right choice. The right moment. Right now, I don't have either.

And I'm tired.

I should go back before someone notices. Before I make things worse. I'm not ready to decide anything, and this isn't the place I want to be caught. I'll return to my room. Pretend nothing happened.

I draw in a long, quiet breath and uncurl myself.

A soft rustling at the entrance makes me freeze. Then the quiet, steady sound of footsteps. I hold my breath, trying to make myself as small as possible, hoping whoever it is will pass by.

But the steps don't fade. Steadily, they come closer, slow and deliberate.

I look up just as a figure steps through the dark entryway. He stops short, hand going to the hilt of his sword as I scramble to my feet. He's younger than most I've seen, maybe the Prince's age. A blue band circles his sleeve, marking him as one of the Prince's personal guards. His sharp gaze sweeps over the empty room before settling on me, and I know the stark white dress gives me away instantly.

"Are you injured?" His voice is quiet, but not exactly gentle.

175

"No." I shake my head, fidgeting with my hands. "I just got overwhelmed by all the commotion and…ended up in here."

He studies me for a moment before releasing his grip on his weapon. "The King is looking for you."

I wince. That can't be good. "I was just about to find my way back to my room."

"He wants you in the throne room." There's something almost reluctant in the way he says it, and a chill runs down my spine.

A tense silence stretches between us as his words settle in. The King wants me in the throne room. I force a swallow past the lump in my throat and straighten my shoulders.

"Now?"

The guard nods once. "Now."

Chapter
Twenty-Nine

"Has the Prince returned?" I ask.

A slow shake of his head gives me the answer and with it, dread.

I glance toward the tapestry-covered entrance, weighing my options. I could refuse. Try to run again... but to what end? I'd only make things worse. With a resigned breath, I step forward. The guard watches me carefully, his posture rigid but not aggressive. He doesn't reach for me, doesn't force me forward. He just waits.

"Shall we?"

As I brush past him into the dim hallway, my pulse quickens. The castle is quieter now. The frantic shouts and running footsteps have faded, replaced by hushed murmurs and distant voices. Whatever chaos unfolded earlier has been contained, and now, the attention has shifted—back to me.

The guard falls into step beside me, his boots echoing against the stone floors. The corridor feels too still, thick with the weight of unspoken words. The silence stretches until it presses against my skin. I can't stand it. I can't take the sound of our footsteps, the thrum of my heart growing louder with every step.

"What was all the commotion about earlier?" I ask, my voice softer than I intended. I half expect him to ignore me like the others. But he glances at me from the corner of his eye, considering. Deciding.

Finally, he answers. "There was an assassin in the castle."

I falter mid-step. *An assassin?* I stare at him, searching for more in the rigid line of his jaw.

"No need to worry," he adds as if that's possible. "They were caught quickly."

"That's a relief, I suppose." But my skin still prickles with unease. "Were they after the King?"

"No."

"Then… who?"

"You."

His answer lands like a hammer blow. I stumble. His hand is there, strong and steady, gripping my elbow to keep me upright. His touch is fleeting, gone the moment I find my balance, but his words hang in the air, impossible to ignore.

Me.

I stare ahead, but my focus is shattered. My mind won't settle, too full of questions and dread. Someone came to kill me. Not the King. Not the Prince. Me.

Why?

I replay the moments of the past few days, searching for some clue, some name, some misstep. Is this punishment? Retribution? A warning? The corridors blur as the echo of the word rattles in my mind.

Assassin.

He'd said they were caught quickly, but how close did they get? How far would they have gone if they hadn't been caught? What if I'd still been in my room?

The silence between us grows heavy again. I don't know what to ask next. My mind is too busy spinning, unraveling with disbelief and denial.

The throne room doors loom before us, tall and final. The guard says nothing, just waits while I gather myself. I inhale slowly. My skin still crawls, my thoughts still spin. But I lift my chin.

I am Narina Brevou. I will not be broken.

He pushes the door open, and I step into the foreboding chamber.

Sunlight pours through the towering windows, stretching long shadows across the polished stone. At the far end of the room, the King lounges atop his throne, half-draped in shadow.

A spike of unwelcome fear lances through me, but I push it down. I force one foot in front of the other until I reach the curve of the crown etched into the floor. I lower into a small curtsey. I have no desire to invite any further punishment.

"Where is the woman?" The King's cruel baritone carries easily across the room.

Confused, I risk a glance up. He's traded his uniform jacket for a thick, dark robe, the fabric rich and heavy. The gold crown on top of his dark hair gleams in the sunlight—an exact replica of the one I stand on.

"Where is the woman?" he demands again, his voice void of patience.

"I don't—who?" The words catch on my tongue, uncertain.

His movements are swift. Controlled rage radiates from him as he rises to his feet.

"Your *friend* from yesterday," he says, taking a step toward the edge of the dais. "Somehow vanished between the dungeons and the stocks. *Where. Is. She.*"

I stare, slack-jawed. She's gone. She escaped. Shock and relief collide and tangle into disbelief. I scan the stones in front of me for any evidence of the suffering that she endured here yesterday. Not one spot stains them.

"I—I don't know." I manage, my voice uneven.

Take Her

The King watches me for a long, unnerving moment, his icy gaze cutting through the space between us. Then, with a slow exhale, he dismisses me with a flick of his fingers, as if I'm not worth the effort.

"Where did you find her?" he asks, shifting his focus to the guard at my side.

The man straightens. "Not far from her room. In an old safe room, Your Majesty."

His voice is steady, but I swear I catch the slightest tension in the way he holds himself.

The King hums and settles back into the throne. Drumming his ringed fingers against the gilded arm, he turns his attention back to me.

"You were told to stay in your room."

My stomach knots. "I—"

"By the Prince himself," he continues, eyes narrowed. "And yet, they find you *elsewhere*. Ignoring a direct order."

"I was only—"

"Defying a command," he interrupts smoothly, though his tone is anything but calm. There's a sharpness in his gaze, an unspoken threat beneath his words.

"If I may, Your Majesty," the guard interjects.

I blink in surprise.

"I don't believe she was—"

"You may not." The King silences him with a wave of his hand. "Leave us."

The guard's jaw tenses. He bows low, then turns and strides from the room. A King's guard steps closer, filling the void.

The King leans forward now, studying me as if I'm something small and breakable... something he *wants* to break.

"Tell me, girl," he murmurs, his voice thick with condescension. "Do you *relish* disobeying your betters?"

I meet his gaze. The familiar flutter of fury that's never far when I'm near him stirs. There is nothing that makes him or the Prince *better* than me except their pompous titles. I bite my tongue to keep from saying so.

He studies me for a long moment, the corner of his mouth twitching in something close to amusement. As if he knows what I want to say.

"You have nothing to say for yourself?" he goads, tilting his head. "Perhaps you need a reminder of what happens to those who fail to follow orders in *my* court."

The scrape of wood against stone makes me flinch.

A chair is placed in front of me. It's a sturdy, high-backed thing that I hadn't even noticed in the room before. The King's guard steps away, his expression impassive, but his hands are tense at his sides.

He knew this was coming.

They *all* did.

My stomach drops, I know what this is.

I've been here before—the chair, the sneer, the breath before the blow.

Different room. Different man. Different chair. Same control. Same cruelty.

"Brace yourself," the King commands, his voice emotionless.

My pulse roars in my ears as I step forward. Ignoring the tremble in my hands, I grip the back of the chair. The wood is cool beneath my fingertips, grounding me in the moment, even as dread pools in my gut.

The room is too quiet.

Then—*crack*.

A gasp rips from my throat as the first blow lands across my back. The sting blooms instantly beneath my dress. But it's not a whip.

A strap.

I bite down on my lower lip, a breath of relief slipping free. I know this pain. I know how to bear it. It burns, but it could be worse. I've seen worse. Endured worse.

Looking up, I meet the King's gaze, and let him see nothing but defiance.

Another strike.

Another.

And another.

I squeeze the back of the chair, knuckles white. The pain climbs, searing and raw. I don't know if there's a pattern to the blows. I just know that I refuse to crumble beneath them.

The King is watching. *Waiting.* He wants to see how far I'll bend before I break. I refuse to give him that satisfaction.

I am Narina Brevou. I will not be broken.

I keep my eyes on him, even as the fire in my back steals my breath. By the time his voice cuts through the haze of pain, I barely register it.

"Enough."

Chapter Thirty

The air in the throne room still crackles with tension. I don't move at first. My breath comes in slow, controlled pulls, my back throbbing beneath my dress. I steady myself, only straightening when I am sure I won't collapse.

The King regards me with an unreadable expression. Then, with a flick of his fingers, he dismisses me. A smug smirk tugs at my lips as the guards approach, ready to escort me out. And that's when I see the emotion flickering beneath all that cold indifference.

Hate.

I shrug off the guard's guiding touch, though the movement sends a sharp ripple of pain through my back. I grit my teeth against it, refusing to let it show.

We walk in silence. My steps are steady despite the lingering sting. The heavy aftermath of what just happened clings to me, but I push it aside. I didn't break and the King hated it. That alone is enough to keep my chin high as I approach my door. Until I spot her, at least.

Myra stands outside my room, arms crossed, her lips pressed into a thin line. The flickering torchlight casts shadows across her face, but there's no mistaking the look in her eyes, knowing and utterly disapproving. I release a heavy sigh as we reach her. She gives the guards a respectful nod.

"Must you always undo my hard work and make such a mess of yourself?" she huffs, sweeping into the room after me, her black skirt billowing.

I roll my eyes. Of course she's somehow made this about her.

"I need Moots," I say instead of the five far less polite things that come to mind.

"You *need* to clean up before the feast." Her voice grates like a whetstone across my patience.

"I need Moots *first*." I turn to her, arms crossed. She mirrors the stance, looking down her long nose at me with that ever-present air of disapproval.

"Now… please." I add, hoping to avoid any more arguments.

With an indignant sigh, she spins and exits. The door snaps shut behind her.

Exhaling, I lean against it for a moment, grateful for the brief solitude. I tentatively stretch, wincing as pain flares along my back. It's manageable. I've survived worse. *Stars know my father left me in this state more than once.* But with the feast looming, some of Moots' miracle salves wouldn't be remiss.

Gingerly, I loosen the ties on the dress, each movement slow and deliberate. With a quiet sigh, I let the fabric fall from my shoulders and puddles at my feet. The cool air brushes against my bare skin, but does little to ease the fire still burning beneath the surface.

Stepping free of the dress, I crawl onto the bed, seeking the comfort of its softness. I sit facing the door, pulling a couple of furs over myself, the weight offering some warmth against the dull ache spreading through me. My thoughts spin as I lean forward against my knees. The silence is only interrupted by the sound of my own breath, deep and steadying, as I wait for Moots.

184

A quick knock on the door cuts through the quiet.

"Come in," I call, pulling the furs up tighter.

Moots' familiar, comforting face peers around the edge of the door. A small sigh of relief escapes me.

"I heard you needed me," he says, voice smooth and soothing.

I nod. "If you're not too busy."

"I'm never too busy for you, child." He steps inside and closes the door behind him. "Though, I must admit, I'm seeing you for injuries with more frequency than I'd like." He chuckles. I offer a faint smile.

"Now, let's see what we can do to fix you up, shall we?" He moves toward me with ease. His presence is already easing the tension in my shoulders.

Relief is almost instant as Moots gently applies salve to my back. The cool ointment soothes my inflamed skin, and I slump a little as the sting begins to fade.

"Thank you," I murmur, blowing out a slow breath. "I could have managed, but—"

"That is unnecessary when I am here," he cuts in without pause.

A knock sounds on the door again. I ignore it, assuming Myra will either wait or barge in like usual. But my body stiffens in surprise, instead of Myra's dark eyes, it's ashen ones that meet my own.

"Your Grace," Moots says from behind me.

I don't speak, choosing to watch him instead. His eyes remain locked on mine as he crosses the room, until he's behind me. Uncomfortable with the idea of him seeing the evidence of my disobedience, I shift slightly, angling myself away. The bed shifts as Moots stands, vacating the space behind me.

"I am finished." Moots gives my shoulder a gentle pat, his touch warm. "You should feel much better now."

"Thank you," I whisper, barely audible. I can still feel the Prince's gaze even though he doesn't speak.

"No breaks in the skin," Moots says quietly. "And the whip mark from yesterday doesn't look like it's going to scar. Let me know if you need anything else, Your Grace." He bows.

Take Her

"Narina, child, I say this with love, but I hope we don't see each other for a while." With a large grin, he slips out the door, leaving me alone with the Prince.

I turn, fully blocking his view of my back, clutching the furs tightly around me. His gaze is cold and unyielding. I can almost feel the weight of his disapproval. Disappointment? It's unsaid, but heavy.

He looks at me like he expected something else. Something better. Maybe obedience. And I don't know if that makes me angry... or ashamed. I bite my lip, unsure if I should speak, or if silence is my ally right now.

Just then, Myra bustles back in, her arms full with yet another damn white gown. She halts mid-step, dropping into a hasty curtsy.

"Oh! Your Grace."

The Prince turns toward her, his expression shuttering further, as if she's just shattered something. Without a word, he brushes past her, his movements sharp, like he's leaving something unfinished. The door closes behind him with a quiet thud.

Myra lingers, glancing between me and the empty doorway. She purses her lips when she sees me sitting on the bed wrapped in nothing but furs.

"Let's get you dressed for the feast," she mutters, her usual perk dulled.

I don't respond, but I stand anyway.

Still unsure what just passed between us.

Chapter
Thirty-One

It doesn't take long for Myra and the two servants she brought to get me ready for the feast, as if the last hour never happened. Myra frets over the ointment still coating my back, worried it might ruin the dress, while the servants work efficiently, weaving my hair into an elegant updo.

Once they finish, I find myself standing in front of Myra once again, awaiting her critical inspection.

"Well, I suppose you'll have to do." Myra tilts her head with a sigh. I wonder if I'll ever hear a compliment from her. Or anything besides the same resigned acknowledgment.

I meet my own gaze in the mirror and pull my shoulders back, ignoring the pinch of the bodice. The dress is a more formal version of what I usually wear. Off-the-shoulder sleeves sweeping delicately along my arms, the soft white fabric of the full skirt brushing the ground with every step. It feels excessive, meant for someone else.

Myra leans forward, adjusting a fold of fabric with careful fingers. "Now, remember what I told you. Stay quiet. Do as you're told. Do not ruin this." She scans me a final time. "The guards will escort you."

With a dismissive wave, she motions for me to go. I open the door and step into the hallway, immediately freezing in my tracks.

Leaning casually against the wall with his arms crossed, the Prince watches me. His deep navy-blue uniform stands out against the pale stone, the intricate gold details catching the light. He doesn't look angry or even impatient, but there's a quiet intensity in his gaze that makes my skin prickle.

For a moment, I can't move. He stands there, silent, and yet the corridor feels smaller with him in it, like his presence alone commands attention. Then, with effortless grace, he pushes off the wall and straightens to his full height. Every movement is deliberate. Controlled. Impossible to read.

I blink, trying to gather myself, trying to remember how to breathe. I should speak, say something, anything, but my mind won't cooperate.

Before I can find my voice, he extends a hand.

He doesn't speak. Just waits.

After a beat, I place my hand in his, hesitating only slightly. He threads my arm through his. His grip is firm but not forceful. The fabric of his jacket is cool and structured beneath my fingers.

His pace is steady as we walk, the torchlight throwing soft gold across the stone walls, our footsteps the only sound in the hallway.

I steal a glance at him, searching his profile. The warm light catches the sharp angles of his face. Something about how calm he looks only twists the tension tighter in my chest.

I swallow, gathering my courage.

"Andreya is gone." It isn't a question.

I need to hear him say it.

"Yes."

His step doesn't falter.

The single word hits hard. He doesn't elaborate, doesn't offer an explanation. I can feel the conversation closing before it's even begun.

For a moment, relief flickers. If she's gone, maybe she's safe. Maybe they won't be able to hurt her again. But the comfort is selfishly short-lived. I am alone here, again. She was the first person to believe in me since Diamo. And now she's gone too.

I hesitate, then try again. "Do you know—"

"She disappeared without a trace. It is done." His voice is calm, final.

I press my lips together, frustration curling.

"Will he look for her?" I press.

"Of course." The words are clipped, leaving no room for doubt. No room for argument.

A quiet command to let it go. But the ache and worry linger anyway.

The Prince slows us to a stop as the hum of music and voices filters through the passageway. The air is tinged with the scent of roasted meats and spiced wine. He releases my arm and turns to face me.

"This feast is important to the King," he says, evenly.

"Stay silent. Do as I'm told?"

"And bow," he adds, the faintest trace of amusement in his voice.

I realize I failed to do so with him earlier. Schooling my features, I execute a sweeping curtsy, one my mother would be proud of. When I rise, his brow is lifted in mild surprise.

"A beautiful sight," he remarks, the corner of his mouth twitching.

I roll my eyes but take his offered arm once more. With that, he leads us forward through a grand archway, and the full splendor of the feast unfurls before me.

The room is vast, its soaring ceilings lined with carved beams, its walls adorned with banners bearing the royal crest and intricate tapestries. Candles flicker in massive iron chandeliers, casting a golden glow over the polished stone floors. Long tables stretch across the space, laden with silver platters piled high with roasted game, fresh fruits, and delicacies I can't name. Goblets gleam under the candlelight, filled to the brim with dark wine. Servants weave between guests, refilling plates and cups with practiced ease.

Toward the rear of the room, a lively group gathers on a dance floor, the swirling movement of their gowns and tunics blending in a mesmerizing display of color. Laughter and conversation rise and fall over the lilting melody played by a group of musicians tucked into the corner.

My gaze drifts to the raised dais on one side of the room, where the King sits in an ornate chair, his presence commanding even from a distance. He watches the feast before him, his expression bored. On the opposite side of the hall, a matching dais holds an empty table set for two.

I tighten my grip on the Prince's arm without thinking. The sheer grandeur of the room, the press of people, the inevitable weight of expectation… it's overwhelming.

He feels the shift in my posture and leans into me.

"Breathe," he murmurs, barely loud enough to hear.

I force myself to inhale deeply, straightening my shoulders as we step fully into the room. There's no turning back now. At least there's no rope around my wrists this time. The thought is meant to be comforting, but it does little to steady me as the room hushes. The musicians stop playing, their melody trailing into silence, and every eye turns toward us.

My throat tightens. The walls suddenly feel too close, the air too thick. I focus on keeping my steps even with the Prince's, not letting the rising panic show as he guides us forward.

We cross the room with slow, deliberate movements, the Prince's stride unwavering beside me. Heat crawls up my neck beneath the piercing stares of the gathered nobles, their whispered speculations just barely reaching my ears. I keep my gaze forward, forcing myself to breathe through the unease.

At last, we reach the King's dais. The Prince waits for me to sink into a low curtsy before bowing beside me. Silence stretches. I can feel the King's eyes on me, heavy and assessing, but he says nothing. A mere nod, dismissive yet absolute.

It's over in seconds, but it feels like an eternity.

The Prince straightens and mirrors his father's gesture. I rise, resisting the urge to flee as he leads me away, across the grand hall toward the second dais. My pulse pounds with every step. The elevated table looms ahead, set apart from the others, a clear display of status.

After we ascend the short steps, the Prince nods once, a signal. The moment he does, the room exhales. The music resumes as though it had never stopped. Conversations pick up, the tension dissipating in an instant.

But I can still hear my pulse pounding in my ears.

I glance around at the sea of unfamiliar faces, the laughter, the clinking goblets. It swirls together into an unrelenting blur of noise and movement. The Prince remains unaffected, his gaze sweeping the crowd with quiet authority. I, on the other hand, fight the instinct to shrink into the shadows as a line begins to form before us. Nobles, eager to greet their Prince.

He doesn't release me as he motions the first guest forward. A broad-shouldered noble, draped in fine silks steps up beside a woman adorned in colorful jewels that sparkle in the light. I suddenly feel very underdressed again. They bow low before us.

"Lord Mackey," the Prince acknowledges with a small nod.

"An honor, Your Grace," Lord Mackey replies smoothly before stepping aside, allowing the next guests to approach.

I stand stiffly at the Prince's side, uncertain what's expected of me. The nobles bow, exchange pleasantries, and move on. I don't know if I'm supposed to respond, to bow in return, or even acknowledge them at all. The Prince offers no cues, and I refuse to embarrass myself by guessing wrong. So, I do the only thing I can. I keep quiet, my hand clasped tightly around the Prince's arm, my expression carefully neutral. If anyone finds my lack of response strange, they don't show it.

One by one, the nobles cycle through, each bowing in respect, each addressed by name before retreating back to the festivities. Their greetings are all formal, practiced, and impersonal, though some cast curious glances my way.

At last, the line dwindles. The Prince guides me toward the table, where a servant boy dressed in a plain grey tunic pulls out my chair, before doing the same for the Prince. I lower myself into the plush seat, my back rigid, hands resting uneasily in my lap.

Moments later, the same boy reappears, carefully setting a silver tray before us. The sight is staggering. Seared meats glisten in thick sauces, ripened fruits gleaming in the candlelight, steaming vegetables are arranged in careful, deliberate excess.

The extravagance of it churns my stomach. In Verti, a meal was a necessity, simple and measured, never more than what was needed. Here, it's a display of decadent abundance.

"Take it slow," the Prince says, as if sensing my unease.

I glance at him, but he doesn't look at me. His focus remains on the food before him. There's no mockery in his tone, no condescension, just an awareness of the contrast between this feast and what I'm used to.

I reach for the smallest portion of roasted meat and take a cautious bite. The taste is startling. The rich, smoky flavor melts on my tongue, layered with spices I can't name. I blink, caught off guard by the explosion of warmth and depth, nothing like the bland, salted meats of home. I take another bite, slower this time, savoring it.

Though I feel him watching me from the corner of his eye, the Prince doesn't acknowledge my reaction. Instead, he lifts his own food in the same effortless way he does everything else.

The servant boy steps forward again, a polished silver pitcher in hand. He pours crimson wine into the Prince's goblet and then moves to do the same for me. I speak before he can pour.

"Could I have water instead?"

The boy freezes. His gaze flicks toward the Prince, waiting for approval.

I press my lips together, irritation flickering. It's a simple request, why does it require permission?

The Prince gives a small nod, barely a gesture at all, and the boy changes course. He returns quickly and pours clear water into my goblet before stepping away.

Even now, even in something as small as a drink, my choices are not entirely my own.

Chapter Thirty-Two

The King briefly interrupts the festivities to make a speech, one similar to the one he gave when he announced our betrothal to court. The Prince gently pulls me to my feet, guiding me to stand beside him as the King drones on.

Once again, all eyes are on us and I fight not to fidget under the attention. Their stares are expectant. Celebratory. As if this union were something joyful. At last, the King finishes, and we return to our seats, the revelry resuming around us.

But my unease transforms into something darker as I watch the celebration unfold. Boisterous laughter rings in the air, and my fingers tighten into the fabric of my skirt. Nobody seems to mind that the reason behind the celebration is kidnapping. Sudden, hot, boiling hate rises in me.

I hate these people.

I hate how they follow without question. I hate that they don't acknowledge the cost of this charade. I hate that they can be here having a joyous time, while I have to push back the pain of being ripped from my life. The pain that threatens to overwhelm me every second I'm here. I hate that they can't possibly know what it's like. I hate them for not caring.

The Prince, unconcerned by the fanfare and empty smiles, takes a sip of his wine, unbothered.

I don't belong here.

"I'd like to leave now." The words leave me suddenly.

The Prince stills, then deliberately sets his goblet down.

"That is rather rude, Narina. This feast is in your honor." His gaze shifts to me with a condescending glint.

"No," I counter, meeting his eyes with as much defiance as I can muster, "I'm positive it's in yours considering I'm not here of my own volition." I don't bother pretending otherwise.

He smirks, his lips twisting into a knowing expression. "Foul mood."

"What reason would I have to be in a foul mood?" I ask, the words dripping sarcasm as I hold his gaze.

"Perhaps you are regretting the consequences of your earlier disobedience." He leans back slightly, eyes glinting as he watches me. "I would be remiss if I saw it repeated."

His gaze flicks to the King across the room before returning to me, the unspoken threat clear.

"I am no stranger to the bite of leather." I reply steadily, refusing to back down.

The Prince's gaze narrows, but his attention is diverted as a guard at the corner of the dais gives a subtle signal. The guard's face is grim, his stance rigid. The Prince tilts his head, a slight shift in his posture.

Leaning close to me, he says, "If you are not here of your own volition, I suppose I should not let you leave of it either."

He gestures to the platter in front of me.

"Eat."

He doesn't wait for me to respond, already standing and moving toward the guard without another word.

I grip the table, my fingers pressing hard into the polished wood. His response was cold and dismissive, like I'm some puppet meant to obey without question. I glare at the Prince's retreating back, rage burning low in my stomach.

My gaze drops to the opulent display before me, to the food I never asked for. My stomach twists with hunger, but the sight of the lavish spread only fuels my contempt. It's an insult after his casual command. A reminder of his control. The longer I stare at it, the more it mocks me with every glint of silver and spice.

I force my gaze away, only to find two finely dressed women lingering much too close to the dais. Their brightly colored gowns shimmering in the light. One of them, a blonde with keen eyes and an all-too-familiar smirk, gives me a look that's far too appraising for my comfort.

Mariselle. My fists tighten. The way she looks over me now, like I'm a curiosity to be examined, tells me nothing has changed since our last encounter.

She turns slightly, whispering something to her companion, a strikingly elegant woman with dark hair and sharp features. The other woman watches me with stiff distaste, her expression bitter.

"How quaint," Mariselle muses, her voice carrying just enough to ensure I hear. "Look where the Outlander has found herself."

The sweetness in her tone drips with condescension, rubbing raw against my already fraying patience.

"How lovely to see someone from such a humble background at a feast like this." She sighs, feigning admiration. "I imagine it must be overwhelming, being so far from the *dirt* you're used to."

I clench my jaw. I will not give her the satisfaction of a reaction.

"Must be nice," she continues, her smile sharp, "but I wonder how long it'll take before your family forgets about you. After all, if you truly meant something to them, they would've fought harder to keep you." She tilts her head in mock concern. "Wouldn't they?"

The words cut deep and before I can think better of it, I'm on my feet. The chair scrapes against the stone floor as I lean over the table, my heart pounding.

Mariselle's smirk deepens.

"Mariselle."

The Prince's cool tone slides between us, and she stiffens instantly. He steps in front of me, his presence a barrier between us. Mariselle's smugness vanishes, and she quickly drops into a curtsy. Her companion follows suit, looking suddenly sheepish.

"I do not see your chaperone." His voice is measured, authoritative.

The Prince's gaze flicks to the dark-haired woman. "Coraline." It takes me a second to recognize the name, and then it clicks. She had been the one meant to stand here. She was supposed to be bound to the Prince before the King dragged me here. No wonder she looked ready to carve me from existence.

"Lord Trovy is by the King," the Prince continues, leaving no room for argument. "I suggest you return to him immediately." The slight woman barely manages another curtsy before practically fleeing.

The Prince turns his full attention back to Mariselle. "I believe I have already put you in your place when it comes to my betrothed." His voice is like ice. Mariselle's head lowers slightly, her earlier bravado wilting.

"I think I should have a word with Advisor Kensington," he adds, and she blanches.

To my surprise, the Prince steps beside me and nudges my chair forward, guiding me back into it. He leans down just enough for his next words to be meant for me alone.

"Eat." An unmistakable firm command.

I don't know if it was protection or possession. And I'm not sure which would be worse. Without another glance, he descends the steps, his hand closing around Mariselle's elbow, less than gently, as he leads her away.

I exhale a shaky breath as I watch their retreating forms, my skin still burning from the exchange. The anger inside me simmers dangerously, but I force myself to swallow it down.

Mariselle's words cling to me like a stain. *I wonder how long it will take for your family to forget about you.*

The thought pierces deeper than I care to admit. They did fight for me... didn't they? I know my mother wept. I know Diamo fought for me. And Andreya... Andreya gave more than I deserved.

And yet, I am here. Alone.

A soft clink startles me as a servant appears, to refill my goblet. I don't even look at the wine before I shake my head.

"Water, please."

The boy hesitates. His gaze flicks toward the direction the Prince disappeared, waiting for confirmation. The silent deference stokes my irritation further.

"I asked for water," I repeat, my voice tight. "He already gave permission." I huff, exasperated.

Still, he hesitates.

Of course. Even in his absence, something as simple as a drink is not my decision to make.

The servant finally looks relieved when the Prince's voice cuts through the air behind him. "Give her what she asks for."

I startle slightly. I hadn't even noticed him return. Mariselle is nowhere in sight.

"Do not make her ask again."

The servant boy nods quickly and scurries away to fetch the water.

The Prince settles into the seat beside me, reaching for his own goblet. He doesn't say anything, doesn't look at me, as if the entire ordeal had never happened. He drinks, calm, unruffled, while I sit here still seething.

"You should eat," he says finally. He shifts slightly in his seat. "Mariselle is hardly worth your energy."

I stare at him, at his effortless poise.

"She insulted me."

"She wanted you to react," he counters. "And you gave her exactly what she wanted."

I stiffen. The way he says it, like *I* was the fool in all of this, dents my pride.

"You didn't have to interfere."

His gaze darkens, "No one disrespects what is mine."

I bristle. "I'm not some doll you can dress up and parade around. I'm not a possession."

"You are mine."

The words are calm, matter-of-fact, as he leans back in his seat.

"Free will is still a thing." I snap.

"Not here."

My stomach betrays me with an audible rumble. The Prince's eyes flick to me, giving me a pointed look.

"Eat, Narina." He says firmly, before turning to address a noble couple that is approaching the dais.

I slump back in my chair and cross my arms, stubbornly ignoring him. And my traitorous stomach.

I can't stay here. Not like this. If I do, I'll disappear a little more each day, until I don't recognize myself at all.

Chapter
Thirty-Three

I winced as the old wood of the windowsill creaked beneath my weight. I had nearly made it inside when a lantern flared to life.

My father stood in the doorway, his face a thundercloud of barely contained rage. My mother was beside him, solemn and silent, her hands folded tightly in front of her.

"Where have you been?" My father's voice was low and deadly.

I swallowed, forcing myself to meet his gaze. "I—"

"Don't lie to me, girl!" he thundered, stepping forward. "Sneaking in through the window, creeping around like a common criminal? Did you think I wouldn't notice?"

"I wasn't—I just—"

"Have you been indecent?" His voice cut through my feeble protests. "Has that boy touched you?"

"Karth, she's too young to—" my mother tried to defend me, but he cut her off with a look.

My face flamed with fury. "Diamo respects me. He respects you and Mother too much to try anything!"

My father scoffed, his lip curling. "Respect," he sneered. "You think sneaking around like some shameless harlot is respect?"

Mother flinched at the word but said nothing.

"I've done nothing wrong," I insisted, my voice shaking. "We only talked—"

"Talked?" His laugh was cruel. "Is that what you call it? Slipping out in the night like some common wench? What will people say? Do you want to disgrace this family? To ruin yourself?"

"I haven't done anything to be ashamed of," I snapped, nails digging into my palms. Diamo and I spent many secret evenings together, and no one ever found out. Until now.

"You haven't?" He took a slow, deliberate step forward. "You are mine, *Narina. My daughter. My responsibility. You don't get to make decisions like this. You don't get to risk my name, my honor, because you want to play at foolish fantasies with some village boy you'll never deserve!"*

I clenched my jaw, burning with humiliation and fury.

"I won't be your possession," I whispered.

His hand twitched at his side, but he didn't raise it. Not yet.

My mother remained silent, her gaze lowered.

Father exhaled sharply through his nose, shaking his head in disgust. "You are a foolish girl," he muttered. "You think you have choices? That you can run around, doing as you please?"

I stayed rigid, refusing to look away, but the weight of his glare pressed down like an iron shackle.

He stepped closer, and for a breath, I thought he might strike me.

"You will not disgrace this family," he continued, his voice cooler now, more controlled. "I won't allow it."

"I think you have proved your point, Narina." The Prince's tight voice pulls me from my wandering thoughts.

The room has slowly emptied. First the King, then the nobles slowly trickling out one by one. The musicians stopped playing not too long ago, and now only a handful of servants remain, clearing away the remnants of the feast.

I don't move. I barely acknowledge him, instead peeking at him from the corner of my eye before returning my gaze to the goblet I've been staring at.

"You are acting childish." He tries again, irritation creeping into his voice.

I fill my lungs and let the air out in a long sigh.

"The feast is over," I say blandly. "May I go now?"

A startled squeak escapes me as he suddenly shoves my chair back, the scrape of wood against stone loud in the near-empty hall. He stands between the table and me, blocking my view of the goblet. Now, I'm staring at the last gold button on his jacket. He leans back, casually resting on the table's edge with infuriating ease.

"The feast is over when I say it is," he says smoothly, crossing his arms. "It is ours, after all."

"Yours." I correct him flatly.

His eyes flicker with something unreadable before he pushes off the table, leaning down, bracing his hands on the arms of my chair. Trapping me.

"You cannot behave like this here," he says, voice low and controlled.

I meet his gaze without flinching. "I was quiet. What more do you want from me?"

His jaw ticks. "Not everything has to be a fight, Narina."

"I don't belong here!" The words fly out and I don't regret them.

His lips press into a thin line. "And yet, here you are."

I give a humorless laugh. "Through no choice of my own."

His hands tighten on the chair, but his voice remains maddeningly composed. "I have given you more leniency than most, but you are testing my limits."

My eyes narrow. "Am I supposed to be grateful?"

His gaze hardens. "This," he gestures between us, "is unacceptable."

But acting like a pompous ass... well, now that is acceptable. I bite my tongue to keep the words in, my expression giving away nothing.

He exhales through his nose. "You are making this far more difficult than it needs to be."

"Good."

His mouth slants into something that isn't quite a smile. "I do not care how intimate you are with the feeling of a strap across your back, darling. But I assure you, you will not test that here."

A thinly veiled warning. One I don't care about.

I lean in, closing the little space remaining between us. "I don't owe you obedience." My voice drops, as I meet his steel gaze. "Or allegiance."

"No," he agrees, eye dark. "Not yet."

His words are meant to rattle me. They don't.

Because that day will never come.

And I will not be broken.

He stares at me for a long moment before straightening. Coming to some kind of decision, he signals to the ever-present guards. "Escort her to her room."

I hold my ground for a beat longer than necessary before finally rising. Two guards step forward, one leading the way, the other falling in step behind me. I expect him to turn away, to dismiss me as he always does, but as I take my first step past him, his voice halts me.

"Narina."

I glance back. His gaze rakes over me, his expression composed but something simmering just beneath the surface.

"Do not assume I will always be so patient," he says quietly.

I meet his gaze, unflinching. "I don't recall asking for your grace."

A flicker of something, annoyance, amusement, something sharper, passes over his face before he smooths it back into cold detachment.

"No," he muses, low and thoughtful. "I suppose you wouldn't."

His eyes drag over me once more before he steps back.

A dismissal.

I don't hesitate this time, turning on my heel and letting the guards usher me from the hall.

The air outside the grand room is cooler, the stone halls quieter now that the feast has ended. The lingering scent of candle smoke and spiced meats cling to the air as we walk. I say nothing, keeping my stride steady, my expression impassive.

The guards keep formation at first, one ahead, one behind, remaining stiff, disciplined, as expected. But as the steps between us stretch, as my silence lulls them into comfort, their posture shifts.

One rolls his shoulders, exhaling a breath like he's shaking off the long hours of the evening. The other rubs at his neck, muttering something to his companion. Slowly, the distance between them closes and they begin walking side by side, falling into easy conversation.

Their voices lower, but I catch fragments. Complaints about the length of the feast. A passing remark about the Prince's mood. They barely glance back at me, as if I am an afterthought now, harmless.

They've grown overconfident. Lazy, almost. They shouldn't drop their guard, not after the assassin. But I'm not a killer. Just a girl in silk and silence. They see no danger in me.

I'd watched where I could. How they moved, how often they looked back, which corridors they seemed to favor. I hadn't seen much, not really, but I'd paid attention. Enough to know which turns felt riskier than others. I didn't know exactly where I'd go. Only that I couldn't stay.

I wet my lips, adrenaline buzzing just beneath my skin. My heart kicks hard. What if they catch me? What if there are more assassins? They caught the last one, but who sent them? What if they're still watching?

I force a breath. Fear has kept me quiet long enough. I made my choice back in the hall.

I don't belong here.

Andreya is gone. There's no one left to be punished in my place. I won't lead innocents into danger. I thought for a moment about not going to Diamo. About running somewhere else. Anywhere else. But I couldn't follow through.

I know he'd stand by me without hesitation. He'd risk everything, with or without my permission. This is different. But I have to trust that we were never meant to survive this world apart. And maybe, just maybe, that love is still enough.

One of the guards glances back, his gaze briefly settling on me to ensure I'm still following. The second his head turns back, I feel the shift in the air. It's now or never, I won't get another chance.

I scan my surroundings quickly. There's a small hall to my right, shadowed and quiet. But the larger intersection we passed earlier feels like a better option. I make a split-second decision, veering back toward the intersection.

My slippers barely make a sound as I move. I pass a young servant girl carrying an empty tray. She startles at the sight of me and halts. I pause too, my breath catching.

"Please," I whisper. "Which way leads out?"

She doesn't speak. Her eyes dart to the left, then snap away. She moves on without a word.

But it's enough.

I veer left, my heart slamming against my ribs. The halls twist and turn, unfamiliar doors and paths blur together. I continue on, hoping I don't get lost in the maze.

"Thank fate," I whisper to myself, my breath quickening, when the hall miraculously opens up into an iron staircase. The moonlit sky and cool night air greet me. Hope blooms in my chest. I lift my skirt, my legs moving faster as I make my way down the staircase, each step feeling lighter than the last.

When my slippers finally touch the soft, damp grass below, my spirit soars. The breeze sweeps past me, a quiet whisper of freedom.

Chapter
Thirty-Four

I run.

Pushing forward and abandoning caution completely.

My feet slam into the ground. My skirts are bundled in one hand, the other pumping at my side. I move as fast as I can, determined to get as far away from this place as possible.

Shouts carry across the yard, sharp and frantic.

Glancing back, I see the two guards racing down the stairs and into the grass, their footsteps heavy. The panic in their movements drives me to push harder, my breath coming in ragged bursts. My heart pounds, the blood roaring in my ears.

I glance back again, and I spot him. The faint outline of the Prince stands at the top of the stairs, a silhouette against the moonlit sky. My chest tightens. I can't afford to stop now.

The burning in my legs becomes unbearable, my muscles screaming for relief, but I ignore it. I refuse to slow. I won't go back to that cage. I won't pretend to be something I'm not, and I won't let them make me into something else, something that bends... or breaks.

Luck continues to be on my side as I near the gate. The guards stationed there are distracted, moving up the path to see what the commotion at the castle is. This is my chance. With swift, silent steps, I come from the side, slipping by them with ease, heart hammering in my chest.

I pause for just a moment, debating. Should I make my way back to the village and the King's Path? The familiar route, but with the higher risk of people. Or should I follow the wall and go into the woods?

The decision comes quickly. The woods. It's easier to slip into the dark and I'd rather take my chances with the trees than people.

The moon is full tonight, casting a soft, pale glow that outlines the castle walls. I stay close to the rough stones, my breath shallow, hoping the sentries can't see me from their vantage points. The shadows are long and I press myself into them, trusting the darkness is enough to conceal the stark white of my dress.

I can still hear the shouts, but they're not close enough to trigger panic yet. Nervousness gnaws at my gut, but I don't let it overwhelm me. Finally, with a release of breath, I push through the tree line, the cool air of the woods welcoming me like an old friend.

I stop short, bracing my hands on my knees, dragging in fast, ragged breaths. I can't stop for long, but my still-healing injuries need a brief reprieve from the strain. The woods stretch ahead, dark and dense, the full moon casting long shadows between the trunks.

I straighten, my heart still pounding, and immediately realize a problem, my skirt. The long, flowing fabric will slow me down, snagging on branches, tangling around my legs. I can't afford that. Not now.

Frantically, I scan the ground and snatch up a jagged rock. The first stab into the fabric is the hardest, but once I have a small tear, I yank at it, ripping the skirt up to my knees. The sound is loud in the quiet of the forest, but there's no time for care. I gather the discarded fabric, shoving it beneath a thick bush to hide any trace of my passage.

The cold night air bites at my now-exposed legs, raising goosebumps on my skin. I ignore it. I have to move.

I dodge low-hanging branches and weave through the undergrowth, moving as quickly as I can. After a few minutes, I pivot, turning so that I'm running parallel with the tree line. If I follow this route, I'll skirt around King's Village, keeping myself hidden, and eventually find the King's Path. If I can reach it, I can find my way home.

Home.

A shout cracks through the night air like a whip.

They're too close.

They've split up. I count at least three different groups calling out commands, scattering through the woods. I don't look back. I can't lose focus. That's what happened last time. That's how they caught me before.

Losing focus means getting caught.

Getting caught means going back.

Going back means losing everything.

Home.

The word pulses through my mind like a drumbeat, keeping me moving. Faster. Stronger. My breathing turns ragged, my still-bruised ribs aching with every inhale. I press a hand against my side, trying to hold them together even as they threaten to break apart.

Hold it together. Hold it together.

My back screams with every stride, the soles of my feet burn, but none of it matters.

I have to get home. I have to get to him. It will all be okay then. We'll figure it out from there, together. Because Diamo *is* my home.

An unmistakable sound rings through the air.

My breath freezes in my throat, my heart seizing.

No.

I beg every star in the sky it isn't what I think it is.

I slow, straining to hear past the rustling brush, the distant shouts of the guards. Maybe I imagined it. Maybe it was the wind, or a fox, anything but—

There it is again.

No. No, no, no.

Dogs.

Their baying is faint, but unmistakable… and growing closer.

I beg my feet to move faster, pushing my battered body beyond its limits. But it's not fast enough. I *know* it's not fast enough.

I scan my surroundings frantically, searching for anything… anything that can save me. The trees blur, my vision narrowing as pain stabs through my ribs with every breath. The harder I push, the worse it gets. My focus wavers.

Another howl splits the night.

I *can't* outrun a dog.

I grit my teeth. I have to think.

Think.

My foot catches on a stone and I stumble, catching myself against the rough bark of a tree. My ribs scream in protest, my back searing.

The memory crashes into me like lightning.

Tree races.

I look up at the canopy above me. Diamo's laughter echoing through the woods, the way we used to launch ourselves through the branches. He always teased me that I was too slow when I lost.

Not this time.

I lurch forward, scanning for the right tree. I don't have time to be picky, I just need something tall, with enough branches to get me high enough. Dogs can't climb trees.

There.

A sturdy oak stands a few feet ahead, its limbs stretching toward the sky like open arms. I rush toward it, my legs heavy, each step like wading through deep water. Not fast enough. I don't stop.

Because if I stop, I lose.

And if I lose this time, I go back.

Chapter Thirty-Five

I stretch upward, fingers curling around the first sturdy handhold I can find. The rough bark digs into my skin as I pull myself up, biting back a whimper when pain lances through my ribs. Every breath is sharp and shallow.

Breathe, Narina. You have time.

I drag my feet up, my slippers struggling for purchase against the rough bark. I push myself higher. My skirts snag on a jagged bit of bark, but I yank them free, uncaring if the fabric tears. The baying grows louder, echoing through the trees.

Reach, pull. Reach, pull.

Each movement is slow, agonizing. My muscles scream. My fingers tremble against the strain. This used to be easy, racing Diamo up the trees, breathless laughter mixing with rustling leaves. But that was years ago, when I was lighter, when my body was unburdened by pain and exhaustion. Now, every movement is slow, unsteady.

Reach, pull. Reach, pull.

I gasp as a sharp crack splits the air as the branch I grab snaps off in my hand. My heart lurches when I drop, my injured wrist taking the brunt of my weight. Fire rips through my arm, white-hot and unforgiving, spots dance in my vision.

Don't fall. Don't fall.

Gritting my teeth, I make my other hand move, fingers scrambling against the bark. One breath. Then another. The pain threatens to drag me under, but I won't let it. With everything I have left, I swing up, grabbing another branch, locking my arm around it. My grip steadies. My heart pounds.

I'm shaking, breathless, but I'm still here.

Inching over to another branch, I ease myself onto it. I lean back against the trunk for support, giving my body a moment to catch up.

Just a minute. I just need a minute.

Deep breaths come in ragged pulls as I nurse my searing wrist and hold my throbbing ribs. I close my eyes briefly, trying to steady myself, when suddenly I hear the dogs again. They're closer now. Too close. I snap upright, my heart leaping into my throat. I have to move, now.

The dogs will lead the guards straight to this tree if I don't act fast. It's time to fly.

Cautiously, I pull myself upright, ignoring the sharp protest in my ribs. I extend my arms for balance and creep out further onto the narrow but sturdy branch. I can feel the bark pressing into my feet through the thin soles of my slippers. The night air seeps cold into my skin. I force my mind to calm and focus.

Sure, I'm out of practice, but falling isn't an option.

I inch closer to the edge, feeling the branch bend slightly under my weight. I bend my knees, my body swaying as I find my balance.

And then I leap.

For a heartbeat, I'm weightless, arms stretching toward the next branch, my chest tight with fear. Relief floods through me when my fingers close around a limb of the neighboring tree, and it holds. I breathe before hauling myself up.

Closing my eyes, I try to capture that feeling and confidence I had when younger. Back to the days when this was easy. When running and jumping through the treetops felt like flying.

I continue.

Faster now, I reach the next thick branch. The muscles in my legs scream at me, but I jump again.

I have to get as far as I can before they get close enough to hear me.

The pain intensifies with each jump. My limbs are on fire, my side aching with every stretch. My wrist feels like it's going to snap with every desperate reach. Without layers of fabric to protect my skin, the jagged bark tears open my knees, but I can't stop.

I push on.

I am Narina Brevou.

I am a fighter.

Home.

I need to get home.

My arms are shaking now. It's been a long few days and it's all catching up with me. I'm beginning to regret my earlier stubbornness. I should have eaten. After a full day without food, my body is starting to feel the effects. Weakness creeps in, making every movement more difficult.

I freeze mid-motion when I hear the first guard's voice. They've reached the base of the tree I climbed. My heart hammers in my chest. Moving quickly, and as silently as possible, I find a large heavy branch. Climbing onto it carefully, I settle into place. The bark is rough across my back as I brace myself against the trunk, forcing my breath to slow.

I hold perfectly still, listening.

"Where'd she go?" one of them grumbles.

"I dunno. Dogs stopped 'ere," another responds, his voice slightly muffled by the distance.

"Well, where'd she go?" The first guard demands again.

"Dogs think she stopped *'ere*." he repeats, annoyed.

"Damn dogs," the second voice mutters. "King will have our heads if we don't bring her back."

"What's so special about this one?" a third voice asks. He sounds young, nervous even.

"I dunno," the second one says.

"Damn dogs." The demanding one is clearly fed up.

"It ain't the dogs. She came 'ere."

"Maybe she's a ghost," the young guard offers, voice trembling.

"Or maybe she went up the tree, dimwit."

I don't like the conclusion he's come to.

"How she gunna git up there?" he scoffs.

"Climb."

"She's a girl." the young one says, as if he can't fathom the possibility.

"Look, a broken branch!"

Stars damn me.

They're getting much too close to the truth. The evidence I left behind doesn't help. The broken branch. My own doing. I press myself tighter into the tree, sure they're going to find me from the pounding of my heart alone. I can't afford another mistake.

I hold my breath, not daring to move despite every muscle in my body aching to flee. The guards' voices drift up to me, their frustration mounting.

"She's gotta be up there. Where else would she go?" The irritated guard growls.

"She ain't a bird."

"But your dogs stopped here." The young one reminds him tentatively.

"She coulda gone 'nywhere."

"Quit your yapping!" The other one snaps. "Help me search the damn tree."

I close my eyes, willing my mind to stay calm. Panic won't help anything. But I can't go back. I force in a quiet deep breath. My ribs scream in protest, but the pain grounds me.

I strain to listen, trying to pinpoint their location. Their boots crunch in the leaves, drifting through the trees. They seem to be moving in different directions now, searching frantically.

"I—I think I saw something up there." The young guard stutters from a little too close.

"Shut it boy," the irritated one cuts him off. "Just keep moving."

I need to move. But there's nowhere to go without being spotted.

Then I feel it. A skittering sensation along my arm. My skin crawls with dread as I look down. A large spider, its long legs and fat body an ugly black, crawls its way up my arm. A moment of panic has me quickly swatting the creature off, but the *thud* it makes as it hits the ground is louder than I ever expected.

"Did you hear that?" the young one whispers furiously, obviously nervous.

"Somethin's over there!"

Their feet crunch toward me. I hold the branch tighter, willing the tree to swallow me whole.

"There! There's something white in that tree!"

No, no, no...

I curse under my breath.

The pale gleam of my white dress shines through the leaves. I will never wear another white dress for as long as I live...

"Oy! Girl! Come down before you break your neck!" One of them shouts.

Like he really cares, I think bitterly.

I can't be caught here. I *won't* go back. Making a split-second decision, I stand quickly and jump, grabbing for the next branch. I hear a bowstring twang behind me and an arrow barely misses me, striking the trunk I just left.

"He wants her alive!" The irritated one growls.

"Alive, don't mean not hurt."

"Greg."

"*Relax…*"

Shock paralyzes me for a moment, they're *shooting* at me? Before I can think about it for too long, I jump again. But in the chaotic motion, my slipper catches a branch and I lose my footing entirely. My now bare foot misses its mark and I flail.

No… My eyes water as I cling to the branch by my fingertips.

The snap of the bowstring sounds again and the next arrow shoots through the air. I gasp when it strikes just inches from me.

Focus, I plead silently, but I can feel the weakness in my muscles.

In the next moment, my grip falters.

My sprained wrist burns with a sharp jolt and my strength gives out.

I lose my hold on the branch and drop, the ground rushing up to meet me.

Chapter Thirty-Six

A dull throbbing pulses through my skull, spreading down my spine in slow, aching waves. My body feels heavy, pinned to the cold ground beneath me. Distant voices filter through the fog in my mind, broken and scattered pieces of a conversation I can't quite grasp.

"… ain't gunna know if we 'ave a little fun first…" The words are slick, curling with amusement that makes my stomach turn.

"She'll tell," one says with a shake to his voice.

"'Er word 'gainst ours."

A pause. A shuffle of boots in the dirt.

"He'd listen to her," the irritated one snaps, his voice taking on a warning.

My stomach twists as I realize they're talking about me.

I fight to open my eyes, but even that feels like a battle. My lashes flutter, but the world above me is a blur of shifting shadows and fractured light. Faces swim in and out of focus. My head pounds, my ribs scream in protest with each shallow breath, and the whole world tilts at an unnatural angle.

"Nah…"

"… orders… find her and return her…"

The treetops above sway and blur together, the moon's bright beams filtering down through the near-bare branches, casting eerie patterns across the forest floor.

"… don't mean… a little fun…"

"… would find out…"

My ears ring, drowning out half their words, but I still hear enough.

Enough to know I have to move.

"He'll cut off your hands."

"… just an Outlander… fugitive…"

"I'd bet you… wages…"

I try to push up, but a wave of dizziness slams into me, forcing me back down. My fingers dig into the dirt, cold and trembling, as I fight to stay conscious.

"Hold 'er boy…"

"I'd rather live."

I try rolling over instead. If I can't run, I'll crawl. Anything to get away from here. But before I make it an inch, a rough hand clamps around my arm and yanks me back. I try to pull away, but my body won't obey. His breath is sour and too close. Every nerve in me screams *no*.

"Where you goin' beautiful?" The vile one sneers.

A whimper slips out, my weak attempt at swatting him away lands on nothing but air.

"We're taking her back. Now." The one with too much snap in his voice says.

"Not 'fore I have my fun."

My stomach lurches at the sound of his voice, bile rising in my throat. I can feel the dirt against my cheek, the sharp grit grinding into my skin. I want to scream, but my mouth won't open.

"You're risking your life." The young one stutters.

"She ain't gunna tell. 'Nd even is she did, he ain't gunna believe 'er."

His hand slips toward my waist. I try to twist away, but everything hurts. I can't breathe. I can't move.

"I assure you, he would."

A new voice cuts through the night, low and deadly, smooth as silk and sharp as steel.

The grip on my arm loosens instantly.

"Remove your hands. Immediately."

Never in my life did I think I would *relish* the sound of that voice.

There's a scuffle of hurried boots over leaves. Someone curses under their breath. The grip on my arm disappears entirely. I don't need to see to know they're putting distance between themselves and *him*.

The leaves crunch beneath steady, deliberate steps as he approaches. I try to lift my head, to find him through the haze clouding my vision, but another wave of dizziness keeps me pinned. My limbs refuse to cooperate. My breath comes in shallow gasps.

"Take him to the dungeons." The words are a command, absolute and final. I hear the guards mutter hurried affirmations before dragging their struggling companion away.

A shadow moves over me. Instinct flares to life and I flinch away.

"Easy." His voice is softer now, but no less firm. A light, gentle brush of fingers over my cheeks feels warm in contrast to the cold night air.

"Shh," he soothes. "You are safe now."

A tear slips down that same cheek, a silent betrayal of the tangled emotions inside me. Relief, because I've been saved. But also despair, because I know the truth. I am *not* safe. I am anything but safe. And in moments, I will be dragged back to that gilded cage, that suffocating castle that I fought so hard to try to escape. Safety isn't safety if it comes with shackles.

As if to confirm my worst fear, his voice murmurs above me, gentle but unyielding.

"Come on, darling. Back we go."

Before I can protest, his arms slip beneath me, lifting me effortlessly. I barely register the warmth of his body before the movement sends a fresh wave of vertigo crashing over me. A choked whimper escapes my lips as the world tilts violently.

I squeeze my eyes shut, desperate to block out the spinning, to anchor myself in the darkness behind my lids.

"Open them." His command is quiet.

Even now, when the world is spinning off-axis, he's in control.

I shake my head weakly.

"Narina." His voice is sharper this time. "You need to stay awake."

I let out a broken breath, knowing he's right, and hating it. Forcing my eyes open, I blink sluggishly up at the moonlight sky. The stars blur and swim together. Tears slip silently down my cheeks, but I don't fight him. I don't have the strength to.

I feel...*broken.*

The Prince strides forward, his steps smooth and sure despite carrying my weight. I can feel the shift of his muscles as he moves, his grip steady. The dizziness still has me in its grip, every motion sending another jolt of nausea twisting through my stomach.

"Tell me how you got past the gate." His voice carries that quiet authority it always does, demanding an answer.

I swallow thickly, trying to gather the strength to speak. I try to smother the tears, willing myself to pull it together. My voice is little more than a rasp when I finally manage to force the words out.

"They left it—for a moment. Went to see what was happening at the castle. I—" I pause, throat tightening. My body trembles, exhaustion bleeding into every limb. "I slipped through."

I shift slightly, just enough to shake my head, but regret it instantly. The motion sends my vision spinning and the Prince doubles before my eyes. My stomach roils violently and I let out a strangled breath.

His arms tighten around me.

"Don't move," his voice is soft, but no less commanding. "Just talk."

I nod weakly, just the barest of movement, and clutch at his shirt, my fingers twisting into the fabric, desperate to steady myself. The warmth of him seeps through the material, solid and real. I press my face into his shoulder, seeking some small reprieve from the overwhelming sickness and pain.

I don't even realize I've closed my eyes until his voice cuts sharply through the haze.

"Wake up."

My eyes flutter open, dazed and unfocused.

I breathe in slowly, trying to hold on. I have to stay awake.

"Tell me what happened next." His voice is insistent, pulling at the edges of my fading consciousness.

I try to grasp the words, pushing them past my lips. "Shadows... the wall..." The effort is immense, my throat raw, my body drained.

"Tell me how you lasted so long in the woods with the dogs."

I blink slowly, struggling to focus.

"Trees." The word is sluggish, drawn out. It's all I can manage.

I can feel it... the life slipping away from me, the energy leaking from my limbs, my head lolling slightly.

Am I dying?

"Look at me."

I hear him, but the command feels distant, as if spoken through water. I want to listen. I do. But I just... can't.

"Let me see those eyes."

What eyes? Whose voice is that?

It's familiar. Strong. Steady.

But it's getting further away.

Take Her

The world tilts and suddenly I feel weightless, like I'm floating. No pain, no exhaustion... just air beneath me.

Flying.

Home.

Chapter Thirty-Seven

The world tilts and spins every time I try to open my eyes. Voices swirl in and out, blending together, warping into something unrecognizable. Words twist, garbled and distant. Why won't they stop? Why won't everything just stop?

Shapes shift in the darkness, stretching, bending. Shadows reach for me, curling at the edges like they're laughing, like they know something I don't.

"Shh, Narina." A cool hand presses against my forehead. "Just relax."

The voice is soft, but it doesn't belong to the shadows. Or does it? I can't tell. I don't want to listen. There are places in my mind I can't bear to go, places clawing at me, trying to drag me under. They want me to remember. They want me to feel the depth of my failure, the hollow ache of everything I've lost.

"Just rest," the voice soothes.

I don't want to. But the shadows have already decided for me.

The hay beneath us rustled slightly as I settled deeper into Diamo's warmth. The crisp night air was cool against my face. I knew we shouldn't be out that late. If we were caught… but we never got caught. We'd done this so many times before, sneaking behind his house to lie beneath the endless sprawl of sky, wrapped in the kind of quiet that only existed in the dead of night.

Diamo shifted beside me, his arm tightening just slightly around my shoulders, pulling me closer. He's always warm, even when the night air carries a crisp bite. Above us, stars were scattered across the darkness, winking in and out, shifting ever so slightly as if whispering secrets to one another.

"There," he murmured, lifting his hand. I followed his fingertip as it traced the sky. "That one looks like a horse."

I squinted, tilting my head. "No, it doesn't."

He gasped dramatically. "Are you blind? Look at those strong legs, that proud head. It's magnificent."

I snorted. "That's three stars in a lopsided line."

"You're right. I see it now. It's a chicken. A very dignified chicken."

A laugh burst out of me. "You're ridiculous."

"Ridiculously talented at constellation spotting? Yes, I know." I could feel his silent chuckle next to me.

We lapsed back into silence, watching as the stars shimmered, reshaping themselves with the passing time. Diamo pointed out another, something about a hunter, and then another. His voice was slow, unhurried. We weren't in a rush. We never were. This moment could stretch forever. I wouldn't mind.

A gust of wind stirred the hay around us, and I burrowed deeper into him. He shifted again, the movement slight, but I felt the press of his chin at the top of my head, the steady rise and fall of his breathing. Safe. Warm. Home.

224

I sighed, closing my eyes for just a moment, letting myself sink into the kind of peace I only ever seemed to find in moments like this. Moments with him.

"Narina?" I know that voice. At least I think I do.

"How are we feeling, child?" Oh, I *definitely* know that voice. I reach for it, trying to make my body cooperate. I manage a sound, but it comes out as nothing more than mumbled mush.

"It's okay, my dear. Take your time."

A voice rises outside the door, muffled but unmistakable. "You will get her under control, or I will take other measures to ensure her obedience."

My stomach sinks. My will to wake up vanishes. Another voice responds, too quiet to make out.

"Yes, we'll just take our time, my dear," Moots says, his tone light but his eyes flickering toward the door. "We had quite a fall, so I'm told."

With effort, I pry my eyes open. Everything is fuzzy and distorted, but after several blinks, the world sharpens just enough. I was right. I *do* know that voice.

Moots' full, warm face hovers above me. "There we are."

His whole face smiles. His eyes crinkle at the corners, his eyebrows lift, even his ears twitch slightly. It's genuine and I like it.

Another rise in volume from the hall, "Train her, or I will have someone—" The voice is abruptly cut off again by the quieter one.

Moots' gaze darts to the door and back to me. I try to shift, but a sharp, pounding pain in my head stops me cold.

"Stay still," he insists. "I've got a draft here that will help the pain—"

"No." My voice is a croak, but the refusal is clear. "Just water, please."

He hesitates, clearly ready to argue, but I hold his gaze. After a moment, he relents, nodding. Moving off the bed, he approaches a nearby tray holding a teapot and a small, purple vial.

"At least have some tea," he offers, pouring a cup of the steaming liquid. "It's very relaxing."

He nods toward the vial. "And this is the sleeping draft the Prince requested for you a few days ago. It will help you rest."

"Moots!" His name is barked from the hallway.

His eyes meet mine once more before he sets the tray beside me.

"Try the tea. And the draft." Then, reluctantly, he steps away. The door shuts softly behind him.

I glare at the offending purple vial. How convenient it would be for them to drug me until the ceremony. My throat is unbearably dry, but the tea smells like a lovely floral blend, tempting me. With more effort than it should take, I lean over and lift the cup, taking a few small sips. The warmth soothes my raw throat and settles in my stomach, a small comfort in an otherwise unbearable situation.

Before Moots returns, I push myself up onto my elbows, my limbs trembling with the strain. Carefully, I unstop the vial and pour its contents into the teapot. I have no intention of drinking it, but if I don't at least pretend, it'll cause a fuss.

My hands shake as I try to set the empty vial back on the tray, but it slips from my fingers, hitting the floor, shattering. I let out a quiet huff and drop back against the pillows, exhausted from the simple act of deception.

The door creaks open, and Moots peeks his head inside.

"Are we all right?"

They must have heard the glass break. I give a weak nod and wave toward the mess on the floor. That's all the explanation I can muster.

Moots' sharp eyes flick to the tray. "So, we took the sleeping draft, then?"

I nod.

"And the tea?"

Another nod.

"Good. It soothes the body wonderfully."

I don't reply. Instead, I stare at the ceiling, my thoughts sluggish and muddled.

"Is it still evening?" My voice cracks, barely above a whisper.

Moots crouches, carefully gathering the broken glass.

"A few hours before dawn," he answers. "There are no events for you today, so you've been given permission to remain in your quarters to rest and recover."

"How thoughtful," I murmur, intending sarcasm but the words are barely audible.

My eyelids grow heavier. Memories resurface, unbidden and unwelcome. The endless stretch of woods. The sharp snap of the bowstring. The moment I lost my grip.

I rub my thumb over the empty place where my silver band used to be. I close my eyes against the unshed tears starting to burn them.

I *failed*.

I failed to get home. I failed Diamo.

And now, I may never see him again.

Sleep, or perhaps unconsciousness, greedily pulls at me. I don't resist. I'm not ready to face it. I let the blackness pull me under.

The river murmured beside us, its gentle currents swirling around smooth stones, filling the silence between us. The sun was warm against my skin, seeping into my bones, relaxing. I lay on my stomach, my head resting on my folded arms, while Diamo stretched out beside me, one arm slung lazily over his eyes. His other hand traced slow, absentminded patterns against my back, nonsense shapes that made my skin tingle.

I should've let myself enjoy it, let the quiet settle over us like a blanket, but the thought had been gnawing at me too long.

"Are you sure it's me?" My voice barely carried over the rustling leaves. "That I'm the one you want?"

Diamo didn't move at first, just exhaled a slow breath, his fingers pausing before resuming their path. Then he turned his head toward me, eyes still half-lidded with sleep, but sharp.

"Love," he murmured, as if the very question was absurd. He shifted onto his side, his fingers slipping up to the nape of my neck, tangling gently in my hair. "You know the answer."

I swallowed, pressing my cheek into my arm. "Do I?"

He huffed a quiet laugh, then before I could stop him, he plucked the leather cord from his own wrist, the one he always wore, darkened and frayed, and looped it around mine instead.

"You're part of me. You always have been," he said, tying it with ease.

I stared at it, at the familiar knot, my throat tightening.

"Now you won't forget." His voice was soft, teasing, but his grip lingered, grounding me.

The river kept moving, the world kept turning, but for that moment, I let myself believe him.

Chapter Thirty - Eight

The ceiling is stone, just like the rest of this place. I don't know why I had expected it to be different. It's not. It's the same unassuming, dull, grey stone.

My limbs feel heavy, weighed down by something unseen. My thoughts drag like they're wading through thick mud. I squeeze my eyes shut, then open them again, trying to shake the sluggishness clinging to me. I know this feeling... groggy, unnatural. Like waking up from a deep, forced sleep.

But I didn't take the draft. I know I didn't.

My gaze shifts to the empty tea cup on the tray beside me. The only thing I had was... the tea.

A bitter taste curls in my mouth, though the tea itself had been sweet.

Take Her

My stomach clenches as I realize the truth. I may have outwitted them with the vial, but they had outwitted me with the tea.

I won't drink it again.

I press the back of my hand to my forehead, trying to will the fog away. Everything feels slow, dull. But that doesn't stop the thoughts pressing in, circling.

I've counted the bricks twice. There are sixty-seven.

When I woke up this morning, Moots told me that my head injury looked worse than it really was. I might experience some dizziness and nausea, but with rest I should be just fine for the ceremony in a few days.

Perfect.

One, two, three...

A plate of fruit and cheese was delivered to me earlier, with the relayed instructions to eat slowly. Accompanying it was a red vial filled with something for the pain. I was free to take it if I felt like it.

I ignored both.

Seven, eight, nine...

I've replayed the events of last night over and over, trying to figure out where I went wrong. What could I have done differently? If I had just moved faster. If I could have just held on a little longer.

Thirteen, fourteen, fifteen...

I blame the white dress. I blame the spider. I blame the dogs.

Twenty-one, twenty-two, twenty-three...

I blame the trees. I blame the guards. I blame the slippers.

Twenty-six, twenty-seven, twenty-eight...

I blame myself.

A quick knock on the door interrupts my spiral of self-recrimination, followed by the sound of it opening. The Prince enters, impeccable as always, his presence filling the room. The door clicks shut behind him, trapping me with him. He stands there for a long moment, just watching me.

I glance at him briefly before returning my gaze to the ceiling, uninterested, too busy wallowing in the guilt and heaviness of failure.

Finally, his voice breaks the silence, harsh and demanding. "I told you, you cannot behave like this here."

I don't respond, still counting the bricks in the ceiling...

Forty-three, forty-four, forty-five...

Lost in my own world, my thoughts too tangled to care about his words.

"You do not know how hard I had to fight the King to keep you from punishment for your reckless actions," he adds, frustration seeping through his voice.

Some small, awful part of me knows I should be grateful for that. I'm not.

"I'm not interested in making life easier for you," I mutter, my voice still hoarse. I don't look at him, don't care enough to give him my attention.

The Prince's voice hardens, growing angrier. "He wanted to have you trained and broken." The disgust is clear in his tone.

I don't react. The numbness wraps around me like a blanket.

"He chose me for my strength and resilience, if I recall." My reply is flat, tired.

"You and I both know that was not the reason," he replies. The harshness has been replaced with something colder.

That comment shouldn't sting, but it does. Because he is right. It's because of my stubbornness, my refusal to bend, that led me here. If I had only played along. If I had only been what was expected of me...

No.

I clench my jaw, forcing the thought away.

I am Narina Brevou. Diamo loves me.

I will not be broken. I will not lose myself.

I exhale slowly. "Why are you here?"

He's silent for a moment, like he wants to continue the previous line of conversation but then says, "To tell you that you are free to walk the castle."

That gets my attention. I turn my head towards him, brow furrowing. He says it like it's a gift. Like I should be grateful for the privilege of pacing my own cage. I'm not.

"With a leash, I assume?"

I thought the inside of this room would be my only view until the moment of our ceremony.

"With a guard," he corrects. "At all times."

I scoff quietly, "Of course."

He does not react. "I will be in meetings all day. If you need something, tell your guard."

"And if I need nothing?" I challenge.

"You will keep your head down and stay out of trouble," he says. "I may not be inclined to risk treason and fight for you next time."

He does not wait for a reply. He simply turns and walks out, leaving me alone once again.

Slowly, painfully, I rise. The ache in my body is overwhelming, but it's not the physical pain that makes me falter. It's the sudden realization that I've been cleaned up. Redressed. My injuries rewrapped. A deep sense of violation washes over me. I wish the Prince were still here so I could demand who did this. Logic tells me it was probably Myra and Moots, but after last night, the idea of being touched without knowing makes my skin crawl.

I shake the lingering unease and force myself toward the door. My steps are slow, unsteady from the lingering effects of the tea, but I push through it. I look around for new shoes and find none. They probably think it'll deter me from escaping, but I won't let that stop me.

My fingers tighten around the handle and for a moment, I hesitate. The Prince said I could walk the castle, but that doesn't mean his guards will be so accommodating. And I doubt the King would approve.

Still, I refuse to stay locked in this cage.

I pull the door open.

The guard outside does not stop me. He does not speak. He merely falls into step behind me, his presence noticeable but unobtrusive. A silent shadow.

I don't know where I'm going, only that I can't go back. So I walk. Slowly at first, and then with more purpose, my bare feet silent against the cold, stone floors. And then, they weren't. With a couple turns, I find myself in a completely different part of the castle.

The halls are grand, impossibly tall, lined with towering windows and gilded sconces that cast a soft, flickering light. Everything here is cold beauty, perfect and unyielding. The paintings along the walls depict monarchs and battle scenes, stories of victories won, legacies secured. The ceiling above me is adorned with intricate carvings, the king of craftsmanship that must have taken decades to complete.

It is beautiful. It is suffocating.

I let my gaze trace the curves of marble columns. I marvel at the way light filters through stained glass, casting fractured colors onto the stone. Anything to keep my mind from circling back to the night before. Anything to ignore the ache of what I've lost.

I turn another corner, admiring a particularly long mural, when the soft murmur of voices reaches me. Turning my head, I immediately regret my decision to wander.

Mariselle.

And Coraline.

And a few other noble girls, draped in silk and jewels, their laughter delicate and practiced.

They see me before I can slip away. Mariselle's lips curve into a slow, knowing smile. Coraline's eyes narrow just slightly. The others fall silent, watching, waiting.

Like wolves scenting blood on the wind.

"Hello, there." Her venomous voice slides down the hall. "Daisy, Arabelle, this is…" she tilts her head considering me. "The Outlander, that stole the Prince from Coraline."

"Mariselle," I say, flatly. "Coraline." I shift my gaze to the slight woman whose place I took.

And hate her for being weak enough to need a replacement.

Mariselle's smile widens, sharp as a blade. "Oh, how rude of me. You must still be exhausted after your little… adventure last night." Her gaze sweeps over me, taking in the bare feet, the simple gown, the bruises I can't quite hide. "Tell me, are all Outlanders this uncivilized, or is it just you?"

I don't rise to the bait. Not yet. Instead, I let my gaze drift lazily over her, then to Coraline, who stands just behind her, lips pressed into a thin line.

"Is that why you always seem so interested in me?" I ask, voice smooth despite the exhaustion. "Curiosity? Jealousy?"

I let my eyes flick over Coraline again. "Or insecurity?"

Coraline's mouth twitches, but she doesn't speak. Mariselle, however, laughs, delighted.

"Oh, she has claws after all," she purrs. "How charming."

She steps closer, her perfume sickly sweet. "And yet, here you are. No crown, no silks, no shoes. Just a pretty little prisoner in a borrowed dress."

I tilt my head, meeting her gaze without hesitation.

"And yet, here you are," I echo. "A pretty little viper with too much time on her hands."

The girls behind her stifle giggles, but Mariselle doesn't falter. If anything her amusement grows.

"Oh, it is a shame, really."

Something in her tone shifts, just enough to make my stomach twist. I don't let it show.

Mariselle sighs, feigning disappointment.

"It seems your family will forget you sooner rather than later." She brushes an invisible speck of dust from her sleeve.

Cold dread slams through me, cutting through the false sweetness of their laughter.

Mariselle tilts her head. "Oh? Have you not heard?"

She leans in, lowering her voice as if she's sharing a secret just between us.

"Verti is burning."

She draws out each word, savoring the effect.

"Or it will be soon when the Sunstienians are done with it."

The hallway tilts. My breath locks in my throat.

She's lying. She has to be.

But she looks too pleased, too entertained by my reaction.

I take a step closer, my heart pounding. "The King—"

"The King?" Mariselle smiles, "Oh, do keep up. The King does not tolerate defiance. And your dear little home..." She sighs, mockingly wistful. "Will be the price of yours. He has no intention of intervening."

A roaring fills my ears. I'm moving before I can think, but the guard's hand clamps onto my arm, halting me before I can reach her.

Mariselle's smile turns wicked.

"Oh, look at you. So full of fight. It is almost sad."

She leans in just enough to whisper.

"Tell me, do you think they will cry for you while they burn?"

I don't realize I'm shaking until my nails bite into my palms.

I can't breathe.

Mariselle's laughter is still hanging in the air when my hand moves. A sharp crack sounds through the hall as my palm meets her cheek, snapping her head to the side. The sound is almost as satisfying as the stunned silence that follows.

Chapter Thirty-Nine

Mariselle jerks back, eyes wide with shock, hand flying to her face

"You *hit* me."

"Yes," I say, deadly calm. "I will do it again if you keep speaking."

Gasps ripple through the gathered noble girls, scandalized and delighted all at once. Coraline's lips part as if she wants to intervene, but Mariselle regains herself first. Her expression twists, half fury, half disbelief.

"You *barbaric* little—"

I turn away from her before she can finish, my body vibrating with rage. I fix my gaze on the guard still gripping my arm.

"Take me to the Prince."

His grip doesn't loosen, but he shakes his head. "That is not—"

"The Prince said," I interrupt, my voice steel, "that if I needed anything, I should tell the guard." I lift my chin. "I need the Prince. Now."

He hesitates. I can see the war behind his eyes, duty clashing with whatever orders he has been given. But I don't back down.

My entire world has just shifted, the ground cracking beneath my feet, and I *will not* be left standing here helpless while my home... my family... *Diamo*...

"Now," I repeat, my voice trembling, but not with fear. With fury. With panic. With something deep and dark clawing at my insides.

For a long moment, I think he'll refuse and I'll have to go searching on my own.

Then, with a sharp nod, he releases my arm and turns on his heel. "Follow me."

I do. I don't look back at Mariselle, at Coraline, at the smug little nobles who think this is just another entertaining afternoon.

I walk, because if I stop, I'll shatter.

The guard leads me through the halls, but he is not moving *fast enough.*

Every step feels like it's dragging through sand, like time itself is conspiring against me. My mind is a storm, panic tightening around my ribs. My mother. My father. *Diamo.* They're going to die.

They are going to die.

My feet ache to run, but the guard keeps a steady, deliberate pace, as if he can't hear the blood pounding in my ears, the breath tearing in and out of my lungs.

We turn a corner, and he finally slows, pointing to a heavy door at the end of the hall.

"His Grace is in there, but he's in a meeting. You should wait—"

I don't hear the rest. I can't.

My feet move before my mind can catch up. I *run*, ignoring the guard's startled shout behind me. The door is right there. I throw my weight into it, the heavy wood swinging open with a force that makes it crash against the wall.

A dozen men turn toward me, their expressions shifting from shock to disapproval in the span of a heartbeat.

The room is cavernous, a long table stretching down its center.

Nobles.

They're all nobles, dressed in fine silks, their sharp gazes cutting into me like knives. Guards line the walls, hands drifting toward their weapons at the intrusion.

The guard behind me stumbles to a halt, stiffening before quickly bowing.

I should feel the terror then, the regret of what I've just done. I've broken every rule, every unspoken law of this place.

But my eyes find sharp grey ones at the head of the table, and whatever rationality I had left vanishes.

I take a step forward, my chest heaving, my heart ready to crack in two.

"You have to help them." My voice echoes in the shocked silence. "*Please*, you have to save them."

The Prince doesn't move at first. He just *stares*. Horrified. Then the horror melts into shock, and finally, his jaw tightens and his face heats with anger.

I don't care.

"Please," I beg, stumbling forward. "They'll all die. You have to help them."

A few of the nobles laugh, low and amused, as if I'm nothing more than an entertaining spectacle. I ignore them. My feet carry me forward, desperate, unthinking. A guard steps in my path, moving to stop me, but the Prince lifts a hand. The guard hesitates, then silently retreats to his post.

I barely have time to register his movement.

The Prince is on me so fast I can't react. His hand clamps around my throat and before I can suck in a breath, I'm shoved backward. The edge of the table digs into my spine as he leans over me, his grip like iron.

"I do not take orders from you," he grinds out.

His hold tightens. I gasp, my fingers flying to his wrist, struggling for air.

"Out," he commands.

For a second, I think he is talking to me. Then there is a grumble of voices, the screech of chairs sliding against the floor. I can hear the nobles rising from their seats, the shuffle of movement as they begin their exit.

"Everyone," the Prince snaps. "Out."

The guards hesitate. Then, one by one, they fall into line, filing silently from the room. I can't move. His stare pins me as much as his grip does, the table biting into my lower back.

I stare into his eyes, wide and terrified.

The doors shut with a heavy finality and I am alone with him.

"I do not take orders from you," he repeats low, lethal. "Do you know how easy it would be to break you?" He leans in, the heat of his breath brushing my skin. "I can do anything I like with you at this moment and not a soul would care."

His grip tightens just enough to make my pulse hammer against his fingers.

"You. Are. Mine." His breathing is heavy. "Understand that, Narina. You. Are. Mine."

I stare up at him, my breaths coming in quick, shallow gasps. His eyes burn into mine, hard and angry.

"Do not ever come in here, demanding anything from me." The words strike sharply. "*Nothing.*"

He looks away, taking a deep breath, as if trying to reign himself in. When he looks back at me, his grip relaxes, though his fingers still rest against my throat.

"It would be easy. So easy," he whispers, almost to himself.

Then, just like that, he releases me, straightens, and smooths his jacket.

He moves to the nearest chair and drops into it, lounging back, throwing one leg over the arm as though utterly unbothered. His sudden ease is somehow more unsettling than his fury.

I force myself to stand upright, resisting the instinct to rub my throat. My legs are unsteady as I lower myself onto the edge of the seat, wary, waiting.

"Narina," he sighs, "I do not *want* to hurt you."

He folds his hands in his lap, inspecting them casually.

"No one ever interrupts a meeting of the state. Certainly not by *barging in* and making demands of their royal." His gaze flicks up, trapping me in its cold grasp. "And yet, I do not even want to train you."

I'm held captive by his stare, confused by his words. I'm too wary to ask what he means, but he continues before I can make sense of them.

"Tell me what it is you want, darling." His voice is quieter now, but no less sharp. "You may *ask* me now."

Surprised, I clear my throat. I don't trust my voice, don't trust my instincts around him, but I have to try. *Diamo.* I have to chance it. I have to save him.

"My village. I heard my village is in the path of the Sunstienians."

He doesn't react at first. Just watches me. Calculating.

"Is it true?" I press.

He tilts his head. "I would be interested to know where you heard this."

"Does it matter?" My heart pounds. "*Is it true?*"

"Answer for an answer, darling." The corner of his mouth picks up in a smirk.

Of course this is when he decides to toy with me. Even with blood on the line, he wants to turn it into a power play. I should refuse. But I can't afford to.

"Mariselle."

"It is true," he says with casual finality.

The air in my lungs vanishes. "And the King doesn't intend to save them?"

He studies me for a moment before answering, "Correct."

"He *can't* do that!" The words burst from me.

"Of course he can." The Prince lifts a shoulder slightly, all effortless indifference. "He is the King."

"Why would he let his people die?" I demand, my voice shaking.

His gaze sharpens, locking onto mine. "For the same reason you are here."

"I don't understand." I shake my head.

"I thought we agreed earlier on why you are here," he says, as if it's the simplest thing ever. He rises, pacing behind his chair.

Still tense, I push to my feet, refusing to let him loom over me.

"It doesn't matter why I'm here, Verti—"

"It *matters*." He turns, his stare like steel. "You are here at *his* will."

"Then tell me! Tell me why the King chose *me*!" I yell, my voice cracking. I know I shouldn't be shouting at him, but frustration and fear are unraveling inside me. I'm barely keeping myself together.

The Prince doesn't flinch.

"You defied him."

"And?"

He steps closer, slow and deliberate. "There are grumbles in the Outlands that our might does not outweigh Sunstien's. Whispers of seceding from Barbast. Your defiance confirms that for him." His voice drops. "He will not let it stand. He will break you to show them he is in control."

"I will *not* be broken," I say firmly, my voice steady despite everything.

The room seems to go still. The air between us shifts, the tension tightening. I don't care to explain myself further. I said what I said.

Without warning, his fingers are around my throat again. But this time, he doesn't squeeze. His grip is firm, controlling, but not cruel. His thumb rests against the hollow of my throat, feeling the frantic pulse there.

I can feel him staring at me, but I don't meet his eyes. Partly out of defiance, partly out of fear. The Prince watches me for a long beat before speaking again, this time with a quieter, more dangerous edge to his voice.

"Tell me what you think that means here."

I finally look at him. His demand is too loaded for me to answer in my state and I know he wouldn't be satisfied with whatever response I did have. I remain silent. His eyes search mine. Whatever he finds there makes his expression darken.

"You do not know what it means to be broken in this castle."

He looks at me, like he's deciding something, and then with a finality that makes my heart drop, he speaks again.

"Come."

I blink at him, confused. "What?"

"If you are so determined to test the limits of what he will do to you, you should at least see what you are risking."

I hesitate, but he doesn't relent, his eyes narrowing, daring me to defy him.

"Come," he says again, leaving no space for refusal as he releases me and heads for the door.

Chapter Forty

The twisting hallways seem endless as the Prince leads me through them. I struggle to keep up with his quick pace. My bare feet ache against the cold stone as my ribs throb and my head pounds.

I stop to brace myself against the wall, struggling to catch my breath and clear the wave of dizziness that had set in. The Prince notices me lagging immediately. Without a word, he drops back to my side and grips my elbow, pulling me forward. His silence, his indifference, feels like a punishment in itself.

"How... far... is it?" I gasp between ragged breaths.

He ignores my question, his pace not slowing. At this point, he's practically dragging me alongside him, deeper into the castle, into the lower levels. A deep unease takes root as the air grows colder.

The few guards and courtiers we pass bow to the Prince but make no move to approach him, offering only the briefest glances at the girl he's all but hauling through the corridors. I realize it is not my presence that keeps them at bay, but the energy radiating off *him*.

Finally, he stops in front of an unassuming door. The only thing distinguishing it from the rest of the doors is the royal crest carved into the wood.

I seize the reprieve, sagging against the wall, cradling my ribs and fighting for steady breaths.

The Prince turns to face me, arms crossing over his chest. His fingers tap idly against his sleeve. But something about the way he's hesitating makes me pause.

When his gaze meets mine, I see something I never expected to find.

Not concern. He doesn't concern himself with people like me.

But a flicker of something. Like he's second-guessing the choice to show me what's beyond that door.

The thought is so out of character, so absurd, it unsettles me more than if he'd dragged me through without a word.

"I do not *want* to take you in there, Narina."

The words are calm, almost too even. But the fact that he says them at all… it throws me. He doesn't want to take me in. Does that mean he *cares* what I see? Or does he simply know what it will do to me and doesn't want the mess?

I don't know. I don't think I want to.

Whatever it is, it passes quickly. He takes a sharp breath and I know… he's already made up his mind.

He moves closer. Too close. I press back against the wall, but there's nowhere to go. He bends down until our gazes are level, his face just inches from mine.

"I will make this very clear for you." His voice is controlled, betraying none of the doubt he had a moment ago.

"You will stay by my side. You will stay silent. Do not look anyone in the eyes. Do not react to anything you see or hear. Do *not* incite the trainers." His fingers lift, the backs of them grazing my jaw in a way that makes my breath hitch, not from tenderness, but from the warning.

"Tell me you understand."

I don't. Not in the slightest.

My heart slams against my ribs. I don't want to give him the satisfaction of obeying, but something in his expression, something *dark*, tells me that this is not the time for pride.

I give the smallest nod. "I understand."

His eyes flick over my face, searching, making sure I mean it. Then, satisfied, he straightens and reaches for the door.

The door swings open with a slow, groaning creak, and I step through. Before I can take another step, the Prince catches my arm, winding it through his and holding tight. The grip is not gentle, but possessive, a silent command to stay close. I don't fight him. Something about the way his fingers pressed firmly against my skin makes my pulse stutter in uneasy anticipation.

My breath comes in shallow flutters, my nerves stretched thin. I scan the corridor, expecting horrors to leap from the shadows. But at first, I see only walls. Endless, rough grey stone, stretching into the dimness.

Until I don't.

The narrow passage spills into a large hall, its ceiling looming higher than I expected. And lining its walls, where doors should be, are open archways, dark and gaping, each leading into shadowed rooms.

The Prince moves us forward. My steps falter as we pass the first open space. A woman kneels in the center of the dim room, her head bowed, chin resting against her chest. She doesn't move. Not even a shudder of breath disturbs the stillness of her form.

The next room is the same. Another kneeling figure, silent, unmoving.

But in the third, there is motion.

A young woman stands, scrubbing at a wooden table with slow, rhythmic strokes. Over and over. Wiping the same spot with methodical precision, her gaze fixed on the surface as if it holds the key to her existence.

I tear my gaze away, my unease mounting, but another scene grips me further down the hall.

A sharp crack of leather against stone. A muffled cry.

I flinch, my steps stalling completely.

Inside the room, a man dressed in black uniform stands over a kneeling woman. His voice is clipped but I hear the steel edge beneath it. A reprimand. The woman bows lower, pressing her forehead to the ground as if trying to disappear. Her shoulders tremble. My stomach lurches.

The Prince does not slow. His grip on my arm remains steady as he guides me past the scene as though it is nothing more than a passing conversation.

"These are the training halls for the household staff," he explains, his voice calm, nearly indifferent. "This is where they learn to obey without question. To perform their tasks efficiently." He gestures slightly toward the dim archways. "Most require little guidance. They understand their purpose here."

I almost trip over my own feet.

Purpose.

A word that should carry dignity, direction. But here, it is twisted into something else. Something stripped of choice.

"Servants here are willing," the Prince continues as if he can read my thoughts. "Most enter this service knowing what is required of them."

I keep my silence.

As we walk past another doorway, I see a girl no older than me, scrubbing the floor with shaking hands. No matter what the Prince says, I see no choice in this.

He guides us off down a narrower corridor, leading us away from the servant training hall. His stride remains steady, purposeful, as he continues his cold education.

"Servants leave this hall when their trainer is confident that they know their place and will be an obedient asset to the castle staff. You will know a servant by their grey uniform. They do not speak unless spoken to and do not discuss subjects above their place. Occasionally, those who prove themselves useful are promoted to Mistress status, like Mistress Myra." His gaze flickers toward me at the mention of Myra.

"Mistresses wear black and take on greater duties. They manage the lower servants beneath them and interact with people of higher standing. Then there are the Madames. They were red and oversee entire wings of the castle or even noble households."

We reach a large, iron-bound door. The Prince pauses, one hand resting on the latch.

"You may ask one question before we enter the next section."

The first thing that comes to mind is not about the women in grey or the silent halls we've left behind. Instead, I recall the boy from the feast, young and well-mannered.

"What about the boy servants?" I ask, before I can think better of it. "What happens to them if only Mistresses and Madames hold higher positions?"

His expression remains unreadable as he answers, "Boys leave servitude when they come of age. They are sent to the military or the guard program."

He waits a beat, but I stay silent. Then, just for a moment... a flicker. A shift in his features. A hesitation. The same brief glimpse of concern I saw before, as if some part of him does not want me to see what lies beyond this door. But it's gone as quick as it came. His usual, impassive, royal mask slides back into place, smoothing over any weakness. He tightens his grip on the latch.

He reminds me, voice quiet but firm, "Do not forget what I told you before we entered." His fingers tighten on my arm, just enough to ensure I understand. "Do not incite them."

He pulls the door open. The smell hits me first.

Rot. Filth. Blood.

The heavy stench of unwashed bodies, sweat, despair thick in the air. It clings to my throat, sour and suffocating.

A cold shudder snakes through me. I feel it in my bones.

This is not like the servants' hall. This is something much worse.

The Prince steps forward and I follow. I have no choice. The corridor beyond is darker, the walls damp, the air heavier. A sickly, oppressive weight settles on my chest as I take it all in.

Then we pass the first archway.

The sight nearly stops my heart.

Chains hang from the walls, rusted, stained. The floor is covered in filth, straw, dried blood, things I don't want to identify. The air is thick with the reek of human suffering.

Worse than all of that is the woman inside.

She kneels on the floor, her clothes torn, dirt smeared across her skin. She does not move, does not even seem to register our presence. Her head is tilted slightly downward, her eyes locked on the stone wall in front of her. Vacant. Empty.

Broken.

The crack of a whip splits the silence. A scream follows. I flinch violently, my whole body locking up. A fresh wave of sobs echoes from further down the corridor.

I freeze. I don't want to go any further.

I don't want to *see.*

I dig my heels in without realizing it, and the Prince feels it. He stops. For a long moment, he says nothing, only watching me. My breath quickens as I stare at the woman in the room, as the reality of this place cuts through like a blade.

I don't need the Prince to explain.

I *know.*

She is a slave. Torn from her family, either sold or taken. Brought here, stripped of everything, reduced to nothing but a shell waiting for orders. Broken so completely that there is no trace of the person she used to be.

The thought makes me sick.

I want to help her. *Lands, I want to help her.*

But I can't.

Even if I could, it's already too late. She's broken.

This is what the Prince wanted me to see. *This* is the consequence of standing out to the crown. A warning wrapped in flesh and bone, in the silence of a soul long since shattered.

And they want *me* to be part of it.

They want me to come to heel, to bind myself to the throne, to let the crown dig its claws into me and strip me of everything I am.

Tears prick my eyes. My chest tightens. I can feel the edges of panic creeping closer, knotting in my chest, suffocating.

Not here. Not *now.*

I force myself to breathe, to swallow it down, to keep myself from falling apart in a place designed to shatter people.

Then I move. Just one step. Lifting my chin, I meet the Prince's gaze, my eyes burning. *I understand.* That's what I want him to see. *I understand and I want to leave. I've received the message. Get me out of here.*

His fingers tighten on my arm, his expression hard. He pulls me forward, deeper into the suffering.

With watery eyes, I desperately try not to look into the rooms as we pass, knowing each one will break my heart more than the last. The sounds of suffering leaking into the hall are enough. The sobs, the pleading, the sharp crack of a whip against flesh… it seeps into me, settling like a sickness.

I focus on breathing. In. Out. Slow. Controlled. I *will not* let the panic take me here.

The Prince's pace is steady, deliberate. He says nothing.

"Your Grace!" A man steps out from one of the rooms ahead, bowing deeply before striding toward us.

The Prince inclines his head. "Darius."

The man's eyes slide to me, assessing. I remember the Prince's warning and keep my gaze firmly averted.

"She's a pretty one," he remarks, his voice tinged with interest.

"Indeed," the Prince replies coldly.

Darius grins. "She new? I'll happily take her."

The Prince's grip tightens, pulling me closer. Possessive. A silent declaration that *I am his.*

"No." The word is final.

"Pity." Darius' gaze slides over me again, appraising.

The Prince clears his throat to regain Darius' attention. "Tell me about your current project."

"She's a stubborn chit." Darius chuckles. "Been working on her for over a week now."

"Darius." The Prince's voice holds a reprimanding edge, but it's lighter than I've heard from him.

"I know, I know. Like I said, stubborn."

It hits me suddenly that the *project* they're referring to is breaking someone.

"Show me," the Prince says, like it's the most ordinary request.

Darius' grin widens and he turns, leading the way with a slight skip in his step. I try to resist, but the Prince doesn't allow it, tugging me along beside him.

"She's a discard from the auction," Darius calls over his shoulder, glancing back with a look of amusement. "Guess she was too much trouble. No one wanted her. The Ashen crew defaulted her to us."

"The Ashen crew can not get anything right," the Prince mutters.

"Right? Should've never picked up half their defaults," Darius agrees, shaking his head. "In here." He turns into an archway on the left.

I hesitate, panic clawing at my chest, but the Prince doesn't give me the option to stop. We follow Darius into the room. And even though I want to look away, even though every fiber of my being is screaming not to, I can't help but see.

In the center of the room is a girl, younger than me by at least a year or two, kneeling on the hard floor, her hands shackled and fixed to the ground. She can't move. Her dress is worn and shredded in several places. Her blonde hair matted and dirty. Her bronze skin is marred with bruises and cuts. My breath catches in my throat.

"She's pretty, but feisty," Darius says, a grin spreading across his face. At his words, the girl's head snaps up. Her eyes lock onto the Prince's. Hatred burns in her stare.

Darius sprays something in her face. She winces, blinking the tears away.

"That's your royal sweetheart. You do not look at him," he chastises. I wince on her behalf.

"Over a week and she has not mastered deference. I am disappointed in you Darius," the Prince chides.

"I know, I know," Darius says with a shrug. "I'm sure it would take no time with your expertise."

The Prince ignores him, his attention fixed on the girl. The room falls into silence, broken only by the sound of her labored breathing.

"What's her name?" I whisper, before I can think better of it.

The Prince's fingers dig into my arm, tightening painfully, and I realize too late that I've broken one of the rules.

A wide, fiendish smile spreads across Darius' face as he swings around to stand in front of me. "Well, well. Looks like you have a project of your own there, Your Grace."

The Prince sighs heavily. "Quite possible."

His eyes flicker to me, then back to the girl.

"Explain training and breaking to her." His gaze sharpens, and I know that I won't be asking any more questions. "Perhaps it will resonate more deeply coming from you."

"I'd love to!" Darius practically purrs, stepping closer to me.

I take a quick, instinctive step back, but the Prince's grip holds me firmly in place.

"What do you know of training?" Darius asks, his tone eager, predatory.

"She is from the Outlands. Start at the beginning," the Prince answers for me.

"Ohhhhh." Darius' grin stretches impossibly wide. "Right. Servants are easy. They just need some lessons on court expectations or some practice with their obedience. Usually a mix of lessons and training. Training is repetitive practice of the skills they need, kneeling, chores, speaking properly, eye contact. Sometimes it's to the point of pain, mental strain, punishment for failure, what have you. They learn to obey, but they still hold a little piece of themselves. They don't lose their spirit unless they're pushed too far."

His words make me sick, but I can't look away.

"But slaves..." He hums, taking another step into my space. "Slaves are different. They're not people anymore. They're tools, objects. You take everything that makes them who they are, and you break it." Darius gestures toward the girl chained to the floor. "Take her. Her fire, her resilience, her fight, her loves, her hates. You strip those down until her thoughts no longer belong to her. They belong to you."

I feel bile rising in my throat, and I can't stop myself from trembling.

"You break her, but not too much," Darius continues, his voice lowering to a whisper as he leans in closer. "You need her broken but useful. If you break her too fast, too hard, she'll crack and be useless. But if you find her weakness... her deepest fear, her deepest regret, and you push it... you can make her *obedient*. You can make her *yours*. You find her weakness, and you *push* it until she breaks."

The words are poison. Sinking in, chilling me to my core. I try to breathe through the suffocating horror building in my chest.

"Darius," the Prince warns. Darius smirks and steps back, clearly relishing the lesson.

"Sorry, mate. Instincts and all." He shrugs, not at all apologetic.

"Some trainers prefer brute force," he continues, as if giving a lecture. "We got rid of most of them here in the castle. You'll still find plenty in noble houses and slaver camps, though. But force will get you a dead girl more often than not."

He says it so casually.

"But essentially, you break her soul. You break her so completely that nothing of her remains except what you tell her to be. Nothing is left except unquestionable, unwavering obedience. Done right, she'll lick your boots clean if you tell her to."

I sway on my feet. I don't know if it's from the blow to my head, the drugged tea, the lack of food, exhaustion, or the sheer horror of this place. The Prince's grip tightens, steadying me.

Darius jerks his chin toward the girl. "I could use your help with this one. Planning to return anytime soon?"

"No." The Prince's reply is firm.

"Your Grace," Darius starts, but the Prince cuts him off.

"Another day, Darius," he says shortly. "Thank you for your time."

He looks behind Darius to the girl staring daggers at him.

"Come see me about your project later."

Then he pulls me out into the hall.

His strides are long and purposeful, forcing me to keep up, but I don't care. I just want to *get out.*

At the end of the corridor, he shoves open a heavy door and drags me through, slamming it shut behind us. The moment it closes, my stomach revolts.

I double over, gasping, hands bracing against my knees as bile rises in my throat. My entire body shakes with the effort of keeping it down.

The Prince says nothing. He just waits.

When I finally straighten, my breath still unsteady, I meet his gaze. Revulsion burns through me. *Hate.*

He is part of this. A willing piece of the system that allows such horror to exist. That enables it, profits from it.

I don't say it out loud. But he sees it. I know he does.

His expression remains impassive, but his voice is softer when he finally speaks.

"Now you know what it means to be broken."

Bile rises again. That is what he's threatening me with. That is what the King is threatening me with. Then, a chilling realization... *that* is what my father threatened me with every time he threatened to sell me.

The Prince's fingers curl around my arm again. "We will discuss your request in my study."

The world feels distant, muffled. My legs move, following him, but my mind is still trapped in that hall, in that *place.* The air still carries the scent of blood and filth, clinging to my skin, filling my lungs.

His words finally register. *We will discuss your request.*

Verti.

My heart stutters. I blink, reality snapping back into focus.

Verti. My home.

I glance over my shoulder at the door behind me and a stone weight settles in my chest. I will never see Verti again. I will never return to that life, to the little bit of freedom I once knew.

But Verti still has a chance.

I turn forward again, forcing my spine straight, despite the tremble in my limbs.

I will save them.

Chapter
Forty-One

The Prince's pace isn't punishing this time as he leads me through the winding halls. He slows to match my exhausted tread, supporting my wobbling frame. The journey is silent, but I feel him watching me. Assessing. As tired and shaken as I am, I don't really care what he finds in his assessment.

My legs are barely holding me up when we finally reach his study. The door is open, allowing me a glimpse of the impressive room before we enter. A large, deep-colored wooden desk dominates the space, flanked by two high-backed chairs carefully placed in front of it. Behind the desk, a smaller version of a throne sits with an air of authority. A curved sofa for two, with arms that sweep out, rests against one wall. Shelves holding books, papers, daggers, and other various pieces line the opposite side. Behind the throne, a peaked window overlooks the courtyard outside.

"Sit, before you faint." The Prince instructs firmly as we enter the room. I oblige, but only because I'm not sure he's entirely wrong. I lower myself into one of the chairs, grateful for the reprieve but still anxious.

"Will you tell me why the King isn't saving Verti now?" I jump right back to our conversation before the nightmare that just transpired.

He sighs heavily, closing the door before turning to me.

"I told you. You defied him."

He moves through the room, but doesn't sit on his throne. Instead, he lounges on the sofa.

"I don't understand."

"Verti is in the Outlands, where the whispers of succession are strongest. Your defiance confirms those rumors in his mind. He will let Verti be an example of what happens to those who question Barbast's might, *his* might, against Sunstien. Verti is where you are from. He will let Verti burn as punishment to *you* for continuing to defy him."

I shake my head, heart pounding. "That doesn't make sense. If he lets Verti fall, won't that prove the whispers right? That he *can't* protect us from Sunstien? That he's losing ground?"

The Prince watches me as the realization sets in.

Verti will die because of me.

Mariselle said it herself.

He continues after a moment.

"You can not keep defying him, Narina. If you are lucky, your obedience will satisfy him. If you learn the rules of court and submission like the nobles, perhaps even the servants at this point, he may not pursue anything further." His voice is quiet, as though the King were standing right outside. "But if you continue to challenge him, he *will* demand that you are broken."

"I won't be broken!" I stand too quickly, swaying slightly.

"You have learned nothing from your trip to the training halls." He rises as well, stepping toward me.

"And you would know, of course," I sneer.

Because I had learned. I learned that I could easily be the girl shackled to the floor, but I'm not and I will not let myself be broken. I will fight to my last breath to keep that from happening.

"The great Prince, ever certain of what people are and are not."

"I *know* because you are *still* speaking like this. Because you are refusing to *yield*."

"And that's what you want, isn't it? For me to yield. To forget my home. To drop to my knees and be the perfect prisoner of a mate."

"I want many things, darling. But I do not want to break you."

I realize with a start that he's moved closer, maneuvering us, trapping me against the wall. My heart rate spikes.

"I was a trainer for this castle, you know," he murmurs, leaning in. He places his palms against the wall on either side of me, caging me in.

"I was... I am the *best* trainer. I can break the most stubborn in a matter of days." His deep blue eyes hold mine. "It would be so easy."

He leans even closer, leaving but a hairsbreadth of space between our noses. I fight to keep my breathing under control.

"I know your weaknesses, Narina," he says in a low whisper. "Do not make me break you."

Then, he pushes off the wall and steps back, releasing me from his stare.

"Tell me why you still care about Verti."

I take a moment to collect myself before answering.

"Verti is my home."

"This is your home, now."

"Verti is my home, with people I love. My parents. My—" I hesitate. "My friends." That's a lie. I don't have friends, but he doesn't need to know that. "And—"

He smirks knowingly. "And your lover."

I blush, but nod.

He returns to his seat. "You are here. The town you left should not matter to you anymore."

"I didn't leave. I was taken!" I cry out.

Why doesn't he care?

"So that's the plan?" I ask. "Taking a mate may have been a tradition once, but under our laws, a mate cannot be bound without the approval of her family's patriarch."

Diamo and I had been terrified that my father wouldn't grant his permission.

"You're just going to let them die?" My voice cracks, desperation forcing the words out. "My father and my betrothed. You're going to let them die so you don't have to get his approval."

The Prince chuckles darkly. "I don't need him to die, darling. Your father has already granted his approval for you to be mine."

I collapse into the chair, the words stealing my breath.

"He would never."

But even as I say it, I know it's not true. He would. He'd relish the idea of denying me happiness with Diamo. A loyalist to the bone, he wouldn't even consider denying the crown anything they asked of him.

"But he did." The Prince muses, tilting his head, "All it took was the right price. I can tell you how much gold you are worth if you would like."

"My father…"

Sold me. The truth settles over me. My father sold me to the crown.

"Barely even blinked. And graciously accepted his compensation, I am told."

The Prince watches me closely as I stare at the ornate rug in disbelief. I know my father hated me, but could he really be so callous? So unfeeling?

The Prince leans back, arms crossed. "If it comforts you," he says after a moment of watching me soak in the news of my father's betrayal. "Your previous betrothed was much less gracious about his compensation than your father."

My head snaps up. "He was compensated as well?"

"Yes. He has been denied an asset he was promised." His tone is matter-of-fact, dismissive. I roll my eyes at the word, asset, like I'm nothing more than livestock.

"He refused to relinquish his promise until he was ordered to do so." The Prince continues. "And was then compensated for his loss."

My Diamo.

My father may not care about me, but my Diamo does.

I swallow hard, forcing down my emotions. "And my mother?"

The Prince exhales, his gaze unwavering. "I do not have news on your mother."

My heart sinks a bit with disappointment. I had hoped for an update on her as well.

I steel myself. "What about Verti?" I ask, determined to return to what truly matters.

The Prince watches me carefully. "Your father asked the envoy if I was sure you were the one I wanted."

I scoff. "Sounds like him."

He smirks faintly, but it doesn't reach his eyes. "I had originally thought a lack of discipline was your problem. But your father advised I would need a strict hand with you. So, I assume you were disciplined for your disobedience with him."

The reminder makes my skin crawl. "Yes." I answer shortly. "What about *Verti?*"

"Tell me how," the Prince demands.

I shake my head. "I don't think that…"

"Tell me how he disciplined you, Narina." His stare is expectant. I know what he wants. An answer for an answer, like before.

"A belt, strap, his hand…" I snap. "Whatever was most convenient."

The Prince's gaze sharpens. I wait, my chest rising and falling with each rapid breath. But he doesn't answer in kind.

"Moots said your hand was badly bruised when you arrived. Older than the ones from the guards. A curious injury."

I shift uncomfortably, saying nothing.

"Explain it."

I hesitate. The topic's drifting. This wasn't part of the deal. We're supposed to be talking about Verti.

Still, I'm at his mercy, so the truth pulls free. "It was from a book."

"A punishment." His expression doesn't shift.

I nod, jaw tight. "For reading it without permission."

Silence.

"*What about Verti?!*" My voice rises, sharp with frustration.

"It is the King's decision," he says evenly.

My hands curl into fists. "The Sunstienians will kill them all."

"That is likely." He nods, unfazed.

"Don't you care about your people?" I demand.

His gaze flickers before he straightens. "It is a small village practically sitting on the border. The King sees it as an acceptable loss."

"People who provide labor and food to you are an acceptable loss?!" My voice cracks with anger.

"It is the King's decision on matters regarding the war with Sunstien and where he deploys his men." His words are carefully measured, distant, but there's tension in his jaw.

I step closer, desperate. "His decision is wrong and you know it! Verti is on the border but they are loyal to *you*."

His expression darkens slightly. "The King you mean."

"The crown. They are loyal to the King but they are loyal to you, their future monarch as well."

"Loyalty. It means a great deal."

"Yes. They give it willingly with the understanding that they will be protected for it.

"Protection for loyalty."

"Yes."

The Prince studies me, his gaze sharp. "You are not loyal."

That stops me for a moment. I reach for a response. In the end, I decide on the truth.

"Why should I respect a monarchy that doesn't even see me as a person?"

His eyes soften. "I see you, Narina."

The gentleness in his words catches me by surprise.

"I see the fight in your soul. I see your unyielding resolve. I see the fire in your eyes." He leans forward, bracing his elbows against his knees, his gaze locking onto mine. "I see that you are still trying to fight when you have already lost."

My throat tightens. "And what of my loss?" I ask, my voice barely above a whisper.

That makes him raise a brow.

"Where is my compensation, then?"

"You are becoming a Princess." He says it as if that should be enough.

My fingers curl into my fists at my sides. "I don't want to be a Princess. Find someone else."

"Impossible. The King has chosen you."

"I am being bound to *you*. You can find someone else."

He leans in closer, smirking as if he enjoys my defiance. "The King has ordered our union. I hope you are not suggesting I commit treason and defy him, darling."

I grit my teeth. "Verti, then. Save Verti."

The smirk fades. He straightens. "You want me to put my men at risk to save your village. You want me to take men that are here, protecting us and send them to the Outlands for the sake of your old life."

"To save your *people*," I correct sharply.

"Say I take this risk, defy the King and save your beloved." He pauses, his voice dipping lower. "Tell me what you would do for me in return."

I stare at him, stunned. He wants to trade? He wants to barter with the lives of people? My mind scrambles for an answer. What could I possibly give him? He's the Prince, he has everything.

"What do you want?" I ask, wary.

He stands swiftly. I rise as well, my pulse quickening with nervous energy.

"As I said, darling, I want many things." His tone is almost casual. Almost. "However, I do not want a constant fight with my mate. I do not want to have to stand between her and my King because she does not know when to stop fighting."

I watch him carefully, my breath uneven. What is he getting at?

He takes a step closer, leaning down so we are at eye level. "I *love* the fire in your eyes, Narina. I do not *want* to break you." He straightens, his expression turning impassive once more.

"Protection for loyalty."

I hesitate. "Yes…" I murmur, still confused.

"That is what I am offering." He looks down at me. "I will offer Verti and its people my protection in exchange for *your* loyalty."

"I don't—"

"No more running." He cuts me off. "No more fighting. No more disobedience. No more pushing the King. No more."

My mouth hangs open, floundering for words. His stare penetrates me, freezing me.

"I will save your village," he continues, "and you will be the perfect prisoner of a mate, as you so eloquently put it."

My throat tightens. "You want me… to be broken?" My voice is quieter than I'd like. Didn't he just say he didn't want to break me?

"Of sorts. I like your fire, I would hate to see it disappear." He studies me. "I do not care how you act here, behind closed doors with me. But in front of the King, the court, the servants even, you will be the perfectly obedient mate."

I stiffen. He isn't just asking me to obey, he's telling me to submit, to surrender. To wear chains wrapped in silk. He wants me to agree to give up my freedom. He wants me to enter this engagement willingly. To stop fighting. Stop trying to get home. To do all the things I have sworn not to do.

"There is a guard outside," he says, already rounding his desk. "He will escort you to your quarters, where you can consider your options. You may return here when you have made your decision."

Dismissed. Just like that. It's over.

I turn sharply and leave, the heavy door thuds shut behind me.

The guard outside stiffens at my approach.

"The Prince said to take me back to my room," I murmur, voice hollow.

He nods once and motions for me to lead the way, keeping a safe distance behind me. Not trusting me at his back.

My steps are slow, my body aching, my mind heavier than my limbs. The Prince's words play in my head over and over.

To act broken. To be a puppet at court. To stand by the Prince's side and pretend that it doesn't crush my soul. To be a Princess.

A quiet, bitter laugh escapes me. Any other girl would jump at the chance. But me?

I swallow hard, my thoughts darkening.

Is Verti worth it? Is my family's life worth it? Is Diamo's fate worth tying myself to the Prince?

Diamo's face flashes in my mind. His dark hair, his hazel eyes alight with amusement, his easy, confident smile. I can almost hear his laughter, the warmth in it, the way it always made me feel like I belonged. He has stood by my side my entire life.

I halt so suddenly that the guard nearly collides with me. I can feel him watching me warily.

My hands tremble at my sides.

This is no choice.

My eyes sting, my chest tightening.

There are no options.

I spin on my heel and storm back to the Prince's study, my mind a whirlwind of conflicting thoughts. For a moment, I pause at the door, my hand hovering over the handle. The urge to knock is there, but it quickly fades, replaced by a final act of defiance. I swing the door open.

The Prince's gaze snaps up from the paper he had been reading, his brow lifting in quiet surprise, but his expression quickly shifts to one of calculated patience. He leans back in his chair, waiting for me to speak.

"Protection for loyalty," I say, my voice steady, though my chest cracks with each word. I hadn't expected my voice to hold, but it does.

He puts the paper down slowly, the rustling sound of it louder than it should be in the tense silence. For a moment, he studies me as though trying to gauge my resolve. Then, without hesitation, he stands and moves around the corner of his desk, his footsteps measured, each one sending a quiet tremor through the air.

"I agree to obey, and you will save my village. You will save..." My throat tightens. I can't say his name without feeling my heart threaten to shatter into a thousand jagged pieces.

The Prince steps closer, his gaze hardening, but his voice remains even, calm.

"Your lover. Your family. Your village. They will all live." He stops in front of me.

I swallow, trying to push past the crushing ache in my chest.

"You swear it," I demand. The words come out more broken than I intend. The desperation is clear in my voice.

"I swear to you, Narina. They will live." His words are an ironclad promise, yet they don't offer me any comfort.

I take a shaky breath, struggling to steady myself. "And I just have to *pretend.*"

He dips his head. "As I said, in private, you may do as you wish, but in public—"

"I am yours." I finish for him.

"I have no desire to see another mark across your back, darling. But make no mistake, if you slip up in front of someone, anyone, I will be forced to correct you. It will be expected."

I force myself not to flinch. Instead, I brush the words aside, dismissing them like dust. They don't matter. This is the price. This is what I have to endure. All that matters is saving them. My family. Verti. Diamo.

To save him... I will give him up. I will sacrifice everything... for him.

"Protection for loyalty, then." The words taste bitter as I seal my fate, locking the key to my own cage.

He nods. "I will arrange for my men to set out for Verti at dawn." He hesitates for just a moment, as if considering something else. "Attempt to escape again, and they will be recalled immediately."

"Will they get there in time?" I hate the vulnerability in my voice.

"I will make sure of it."

His gaze lingers on me, measuring, weighing if there is more I need to say. But there isn't. The deal is done. My heart heavy with the price of this promise.

"May I return to my room now?" The words are quiet, almost distant, as if I am no longer truly here.

Our business is finished. My mission is complete. Verti will be saved. Diamo will be saved.

The Prince pauses, his gaze softening for a brief, fleeting moment, almost pitying if I didn't already know better.

"Yes. You look like you could use the rest."

Without another word, I nod, solemnly turning away from the man I now belong to. His gaze burns into my back as I leave the study behind me. The door clicks shut softly behind me, a seal on my fate.

Chapter
Forty-Two

I don't remember the walk back to my room. The hallways blur around me. My muffled footsteps are the only background noise to the chaos inside me. The guard follows just behind, his voice occasionally slicing through the fog of my thoughts to give directions. His words don't reach me fully. I nod, but the motion is automatic, not registering in my mind.

When I reach the door to my room, I stop for a moment, standing there, frozen.

This is it. This is my cage. My life.

The door clicks closed behind me, but I don't move.

I agreed to this. I agreed to stay here, in this cold, lifeless place, belonging to him. To the crown.

How did I get here? How did it come to this? My entire life I've done everything I could to be my own person. I close my eyes for a moment, trying to push away the knot in my throat, but it only grows tighter.

I can't do this.

I can't be the person they expect me to be. The obedient little mate who answers to a man I never asked for. I've never been obedient in my life... not once. Diamo is the *only* person to ever understand that.

And I let him go.

And now, his life depends on that obedience.

How can I pretend? How can I wear the mask of submission when all I've known is resistance?

I take a step farther into the room. I stand there, rooted to the spot, wondering how I'm supposed to do this. How I'm supposed to live like this, when everything inside of me screams to fight. What if I fail? What if I can't act the way they need me to, the way *he* needs me to? It won't just be my own ruin, it will be theirs.

This is the cost of their lives. My obedience. My silence. My soul, perhaps.

It's the only way.

I remind myself, but the thought doesn't make it any easier to breathe. Doesn't make the loss of freedom any easier. Doesn't make the loss of my future with Diamo any easier. My chest feels hollow.

I drag my feet to the mirror, the only thing in this room that seems to hold any life, any truth. It's cold and distant, like everything else here, but at least it's real. I force myself to look into it.

The girl staring back at me is a stranger. Her eyes are swollen, her face pale and drawn. She looks defeated.

I look defeated.

I run my fingers through my hair, tugging at the strands as though it could ground me. It doesn't. It just makes the emptiness inside grow louder.

I am Narina Brevou. I will not be broken.

The tears I've been holding back fall, one after another, blurring the reflection. I try to stop them. I try to force them back. But they fall freely, unstoppable.

I hate them.

I press my hands to the cold glass, feeling the chill seep into my palms. But she's still there. The reflection of a girl who just sold herself. A girl who gave up everything for a promise, for a village, for a man she loves.

Endlessly.

My tears fall for her. Grieving. Trapped by my own choices. Caged by my own stubbornness. Imprisoned by the very freedom I thought I was seeking. If I had just been more obedient...

I stare at the reflection, watching the life I thought I would have slip away with the tears that streak down my cheeks. The pain in my chest, the grief of losing the love of my life, swells to a point it feels like I might shatter.

I'll never see him again. Never hold him again. Never hear his voice again. I am no longer his.

I slam my fist into the mirror. The glass cracks, sharp under my knuckles. It's strangely satisfying, the first release of a pressure that's been building too long. Cracks spider across the glass, splintering the reflection.

I hit it again, and more cracks appear. The tears keep falling, but now, they're broken, just like me. A scream rips from my throat as I strike the mirror once more. It shatters and the jagged shards rain down to the floor.

It's not as satisfying as I hoped it would be. The tears still fall. The pain in my chest still throbs. I still feel the wrench of my heart.

I knock over the mirror's frame in a fit of rage, the wood crashing to the ground, fracturing. I scream again, a raw, desperate sound, as I turn toward the bed. I tear the furs and blankets from it, ripping them apart in my hands. The chest beside me follows. I kick it over, spilling its contents across the floor.

The white dresses inside taunt me, fueling the fire inside me. Another ravaged cry rips from me as I clutch the fine fabric in my hands, shredding it, watching the delicate threads unravel beneath my fingers.

I collapse in a heap in the middle of the room, surrounded by the chaos I've created. The tears keep coming, unstoppable, and I hate myself for it. So, instead of fighting it, I let the pain out.

Every bit of it.

Chapter
Forty-Three

On the day of the annual Fire Festival, the main square was transformed, adorned with vibrant decorations that only made an appearance on this one occasion each year. The Fire Festival was a stark contrast to the Moon Festival. Where the Moon Festival had been quiet and mysterious, the Fire Festival was bold and alive. The square was filled with laughter, music, and color, buzzing with excitement. Banners and streamers fluttered from rooftops and the stalls that lined the square. Flowers of every color were scattered in conspicuous spots, their sharp, sweet scents filling the air as we passed by.

Diamo had chosen to bring me to this festival. He asked my father for permission to escort me alone, instead of joining our families as we usually would. There was something different about that day. He looked handsome, his deep blue pants and crisp white shirt standing out against the lively chaos around us. I wore a flowing orange dress that brushed just past my knees, with ribbons braided into my hair that fell down my back, an extra touch just for that occasion.

As we walked, we were met with smiles and greetings from the people around us, the joy of the festival touching everyone. We visited the tents spread across the square, winding paths leading between them, full of trinkets, clothing, games, and fortune tellers. The music filled the air, lively drums and flutes calling us to join in, and the tempting smells of food drifted by, making our stomachs growl.

Diamo and I joined in the dancing, spinning and twirling to the rhythm of the music, laughing until we felt light-headed. For a while, we forgot about everything; our only concern was enjoying each moment. The sterner folk gave us disapproving looks, but we didn't mind. That night was not about them. It was about the celebration, about feeling alive.

The Fire Festival was more than just fun. It marked the burning of the fields and pastures after the crops had been harvested. The ash, scattered across the land, nourished the soil through the winter, ensuring fresh growth for the next year. It was a ritual of renewal. A way of cleansing the land of any negativity and welcoming the promise of prosperity. The festival was our way of honoring the harvest and hoping for a bright year ahead.

As the evening deepened and the sky darkened, the torches were lit, casting flickering shadows across the square. The professional dancers from court arrived, moving gracefully and hypnotically, their movements mesmerizing and full of life. The entire village gathered, sitting in rapt attention, as the dancers called forth the spirits with their elegant gestures. The crowd was entranced. Scarves swirled and bells tinkled, adding to the illusion. The dancers were offered food and drink by onlookers as they tired, their smiles radiant under the glow of the torches.

When dawn began to hint at its arrival, the torches were dimmed and the music slowed. Diamo took my hand, and together we walked slowly back to my father's house, savoring the quiet of the early morning and the closeness between us. We recounted the highlights of the evening, sharing laughter and soft words, the world outside feeling distant and far away.

At the door to my father's house, Diamo paused and pulled from his pocket a simple band, its silver gleaming faintly in the soft light. He held it out to me, his eyes full of sincerity.

A promise to me. A promise to become my protector, my provider, and my guide. A promise to be my mate.

I don't know how long I've been sitting here. Time feels warped, stretching and folding in on itself. It was a long while before the tears finally stopped, but the emptiness remains. A hollow ache that gnaws at me. Somewhere in the middle of my wailing, a guard peeked in, perhaps to ensure I wasn't being harmed. I hardly noticed him, too consumed by my grief.

Now, I sit surrounded by broken glass. The shards are scattered across the floor like the remnants of my own shattered heart. The emptiness inside me is a gaping wound that refuses to heal. I stare at the mess, but it doesn't matter. Nothing does.

A soft knock on the door interrupts the silence. I don't bother to move.

The servant enters, eyes widening at the sight of the chaos in the room. She hesitates, frozen by the wreckage. Her gaze flicks to me, nervous and unsure. Without a word, she sets the tray of food and teapot down, then quickly retreats, leaving me alone once more.

The room is still. Silent. A reflection of the hollow space within me.

Then, the door opens again.

The Prince steps inside. He surveys the room, taking in the broken mirror, the scattered shards, the mess of blankets and dresses strewn across the floor. A long sigh escapes him, though there's no anger. He steps forward slowly, his eyes lingering on the destruction before they finally meet mine. I turn away from his gaze, tucking my face into my elbow.

Without a word, I hear him cross the room, carefully picking his way through the mess. He kneels before me. He reaches out, cupping my chin gently, lifting my face to meet his. There's a tenderness in his movements, in the way his gaze softens when it falls on me. His eyes study me, searching for something, perhaps an emotion that isn't so distant, so empty.

He lifts me into his arms, out of the chaos, cradling me against him with a gentleness that surprises me. Each step is deliberate as he carries me to the bed. Lowering me onto the edge, his hands linger a moment longer before he finally pulls away. He crouches, studying me with an intensity that sends a fresh ache through my chest.

I can't meet his gaze, not fully. But he stays there, waiting, until at last, my eyes lift to his, void of anything but exhaustion. I bite my cheek lightly. I won't apologize and he doesn't ask for one.

"Narina," the Prince whispers at last, my name barely more than a breath.

I brace myself, waiting for the reprimand, the lecture, but it doesn't come. Instead, he takes my hands, his thumb brushing over the small cuts across my knuckles. The tenderness in the act threatens to unravel me all over again. I blink rapidly, forcing back the fresh wave of tears.

He pushes a strand of hair away from my face, his fingertips grazing my skin.

"You need rest, darling," he murmurs softly.

I shake my head numbly. Sleep won't come, not when my mind is a battlefield, not when my heart feels like it has been carved out of my chest. Reaching into his pocket, he pulls out a small purple vial.

Immediately, I push it away.

"You don't have to drug me. I'm not going anywhere." My voice is raw.

"Try some tea then."

"It's drugged too."

His lips twitch, amused. "Clever girl."

There's no mockery in his tone.

"I am not trying to drug you."

I glance pointedly at the vial in his hand, arching a brow.

He exhales, tilting his head. "I am trying to help you."

"I'm fine."

His gaze sharpens, no longer amused. "Tell me the last time you ate something."

I open my mouth, ready to answer and then realize I can't. I don't know.

"Precisely." His voice is quiet, "But I know you are not going to eat right now."

Just the thought of food turns my stomach, and I shake my head.

"You need rest, Narina. This will *help* you rest."

I shake my head again, refusing. I don't care if it gets me in trouble. We're behind closed doors, I'm not breaking the bargain.

His hand lifts, I flinch but his palm is warm and gentle against my cheek.

"You are hurt, betrayed, angry." I suck in a breath, as every word cuts deeper. "Sleep will let it pass easier. You do not have to take it again. But I want you to take it now."

He unstops the vial. "Sleep, Narina," he whispers.

I look at the bottle in his hand, my resolve wavering.

The Prince doesn't move, doesn't push. He only watches me, holding out the vial like it's an offering instead of an order. His earlier words creep back into my mind, unbidden.

You are still trying to fight when you have already lost.

I blow out a slow breath. Maybe I don't know when to stop.

But I know now.

It's over. I *have* lost.

I take the vial from his fingers, my grip steady despite the tremor beneath my skin. He doesn't gloat. He doesn't smirk. He only watches as I tip the contents back and swallow. The liquid is smooth, slightly sweet on my tongue, gone in a single moment.

The Prince takes the empty bottle from me, his touch careful. He rises to his feet, and for a moment, I think he's going to leave.

Instead, he guides me to lie back against the mattress. His voice is soft, steady, as he searches for a blanket that hasn't been torn to shreds.

"The King has arranged for a tutor," he says, draping the fabric over me. "Two actually. Brielle and Benton."

A sliver of unease cuts through the fog creeping into my mind. My muscles tense, my body fighting the pull of the draft. "Training?" I push myself up, my fingers curling into the blanket. A cold fear grips me.

The Prince catches my shoulder, firm but not forceful, easing me back down.

"*Lessons*," he corrects, his tone calm. "Like school. You will learn court history, etiquette, the noble hierarchy, and your duties."

The words swirl in my head. Lessons. Those went so well with my father...

But my body is growing heavier, sinking into the bed. I barely feel him tucking the blanket around me.

"You will meet with them tomorrow," he continues, his voice even quieter now. "After you have rested." A pause. "And eaten." The last part leaves no room for argument.

My limbs sink into the softness beneath me. I blink slowly. "I have to tell you something."

A hum of acknowledgment. An invitation to continue.

"I hit Mariselle," I mumble, sluggish. Sleep pulls at me, taking my mind somewhere I can't follow.

Somewhere in the haze, I hear a quiet chuckle. Followed by his voice, low and distant.

"Rest, Narina."

Chapter
Forty-Four

I wake, eyes bleary. My limbs feel leaden, my mind sluggish as I stretch, rolling onto my side with a groggy sigh. The blankets slide softly against my skin, tucked neatly around me.

Blinking the sleep from my eyes, I scan the room. It's a stark contrast to the chaos I remember. The shattered mirror is gone. In its place, a new one stands in the corner, its surface unblemished. The floor has been cleared. Every sign of my outburst erased. Even the torn fabrics have been replaced, folded neatly in the chest that has been righted.

My gaze lands on the chair beside the door, one that wasn't there before. Myra sits in it, her posture straight, hands resting lightly in her lap. She's watching me, waiting.

I sigh, pressing the heels of my hands against my eyes before dropping them back to the mattress.

"Why are you here?" My voice is rough with sleep.

"To ensure you don't have another tantrum when you wake," she replies evenly, as if this is the most natural arrangement in the world. "And to make sure you eat before your lessons."

I drag a hand down my face. "Lessons," I echo dully.

The Prince had mentioned them last night, but exhaustion had stolen any room I had to care.

Myra doesn't react. She simply reaches for a tray on the small table beside her, lifts it, and sets it down on the bed within my reach. The scent of warm bread drifts up.

"Eat," she instructs.

I don't move right away, my gaze shifting between the tray and her. She returns to her seat, her posture as rigid and composed as ever.

"Are you going to sit there and watch until I do?"

"Yes."

Of course she is.

I exhale slowly, glancing down at the tray again. I know this isn't a request. It's an order.

"Is this the Prince's doing?"

"He tasked me with ensuring you ate when you woke, yes."

Naturally.

I still don't reach for the food. Instead, I prop myself up on my elbows, studying her. She doesn't fidget. She doesn't shift under my scrutiny. She simply waits, as if she has all the time in the world, as if she knows, in the end, I'll do as I'm told.

"So, you're my nursemaid now?" I ask, letting the bitterness show.

"I am whatever I need to be," she replies. "Right now, I need to be the one ensures you eat before your lessons."

Whatever she needs to be. Whatever she's told to be. Images from the training halls flash through my mind. I try to look at her differently now, to understand what that must feel like. What it must cost.

I sit up and tear off a piece of bread, popping it into my mouth. It tastes bland, but I chew slowly, forcing it down.

Myra watches but doesn't comment. The only sign of approval is the slight release of tension in her shoulders, the first shift in her stance since I woke.

"What time is it?" I ask after a moment.

"Nearly midday."

I pause, surprised. I hadn't realized I'd slept that long. The draft must have been stronger than I thought.

"When are my lessons?"

Myra stands, smoothing out the skirts of her simple dress. "When you have finished eating and are dressed."

She turns to the chest, pulling out a new white dress. My stomach churns, but I don't say anything.

This is my life now. The fight is over.

I finish the last bite and push the tray away.

"Good," Myra says, setting the dress on the bed beside me. "Let's get you dressed."

She helps me dress in silence, her hands swift and efficient as she fastens the buttons on the back of my gown. The fabric is smooth, light. I try not to cringe at the white. I'm so tired of white. I glance at myself in the new mirror before looking away just as quickly.

She doesn't comment on the way I hesitate, on the way I stand there awkwardly. Instead, she gathers my wild hair back, securing it with a simple ribbon before turning away. I think we're finished, but she kneels, placing a pair of shoes in front of me. I stare at them.

That's when I realize. They know I won't run. There's no need to keep shoes from me any more, because they *know* I won't run.

I slowly slip my feet inside.

Myra straightens. "Come," she says, already turning for the door.

I follow, the soft rustle of my skirts the only sound between us. The halls feel emptier than before, the air cool against my skin.

After a moment, I clear my throat. "How long have you been here?"

Myra doesn't answer.

I press my lips together, then try again. "Have you been a Mistress long?"

Still nothing.

I sigh, rolling my shoulders. "You know, you could at least pretend to be friendly."

Not even a flicker of acknowledgment.

She leads me down a corridor I don't recognize. The ceilings arch higher here, the light spilling in brighter. At the end of the hall, a pair of double doors stand slightly ajar. Myra pushes them open without hesitation, revealing a lavish sitting room.

Two people stand near a grand table, their dark hair gleaming under the light filtering through the tall windows. They're both dressed in fine silks, their clothing flowing with an effortless elegance. The moment we enter, they turn in unison.

The woman's lips curve in a polite, almost playful smile.

"Ah, there you are. It's about time, Mistress," Brielle, I assume, says, her tone light but with an edge of impatience.

Myra ignores them both and turns to me. "These are your tutors, Brielle and Benton. I will return for you in a few hours." Then she's gone, leaving me alone with them.

Benton merely inclines his head, his gaze assessing but not unkind. "You're late."

Brielle clasps her hands together, "Well, then! Let's get started, shall we?"

She steps uncomfortably close as she studies me. Her gaze flicks over my dress, my hair, my face, her lips pressing together.

"You're smaller than I expected. Prettier too, for an Outlander."

I blink, forcing my spine straight, biting back the unease.

"Brielle," Benton says sharply.

"What? It's a compliment." She huffs over her shoulder at him, then sighs dramatically. She steps closer and brushes a nonexistent speck of dust from my sleeve. "Really, it's a shame they won't let me dress you properly. White washes you out terribly."

Benton hums in agreement, having yet to move from his position by the table. Brielle turns, gliding back toward Benton. He catches her hand as she passes, pressing a slow kiss to her knuckles.

"Sit," Benton instructs me.

I do as he says, conscious of their gaze, the air heavy with their scrutiny.

Benton takes the seat opposite me. Brielle perches on the arm of his chair instead of taking her own seat. She trails her fingers through the ends of his dark hair, letting them linger against his shoulder before turning back to me with a bright, assessing gaze.

"Your ceremony is in just a couple days," she says brightly. "You'll need to learn everything. How to sit, how to bow, how to speak. You won't want to embarrass yourself in front of the royals."

I try not to flinch at the reminder.

Benton leans forward slightly. "It's not just about how you look or what you say. The court has a certain rhythm, and you need to learn how to move within it, understand the unwritten rules. There's much more than just appearances." He pauses, his dark eyes on me. "You'll have to master it quickly. There's no time to waste."

I nod slowly, the situation already suffocating.

Brielle waves a dismissive hand. "We'll begin with the basics. I'm sure an Outlander doesn't know much about court etiquette. We'll see how quickly you can learn."

I'm not sure how to respond, but my mouth is dry. I fidget with my fingers, reminding myself that this is my life now. This is what I've agreed to.

The hours pass in a blur. Benton drills me on the proper phrases, the right gestures, when to make eye contact, and when to look away. Brielle, though more concerned with how I present myself, watches with a critical eye, occasionally making notes or offering unsolicited suggestions on my posture.

The room is thick with their expectations. I repeat the phrases, trying to get them just right, my throat dry and my head spinning from the constant stream of information.

At first, the hours feel like a relentless wave of instruction and correction. But now, as the sun starts to dip, fatigue settles deep in my bones, each minute stretching longer than the last. My mind grows sluggish, my body aching from sitting too still, holding poses that feel foreign.

Brielle's voice breaks the silence, a sharp reprimand as I fumble a proper court greeting. I can't seem to get it right.

"Again," she says, tapping her foot impatiently. Her eyes narrow, and there's a barely concealed sigh of annoyance. "You *must* learn this. OR are you completely incompetent?"

I try to calm my frustration. Before I can even answer, she rises from her seat, her movements graceful but purposeful.

"You're wasting time." Her voice is tight with displeasure. "Right now, you're nothing but a disappointment."

I shrink back in my chair, feeling the heat of her words. I open my mouth to defend myself, but remember that the Prince sent me here to learn. I should be doing better.

"I'm trying," I mutter. "It's just been a long few days." My eyes drop to the floor, unable to meet their harsh gazes any longer.

"No one cares how tired you are," Brielle snaps, stepping closer. "When you're embarrassing the crown, no one is going to care what excuse you have."

Benton, who's been quiet up until now, suddenly slams his hand on the table with such force that I jump.

"You *will* learn this," he says, a familiar edge of finality in his tone.

I flinch, my heart pounding in my chest. They're both watching me expectantly. Waiting for me to speak, to move, to do something, anything that will prove I'm capable of grasping what they're teaching.

But I feel like I'm drowning.

Just then, the door opens with a soft creak, and Myra's familiar face peeks around the corner.

"We are not finished here," Benton says firmly, his eyes still locked on mine, not diverting his attention.

"My apologies, but she has other obligations," Myra says confidently as she steps into the room. "I'm afraid she must come with me now."

I try to conceal relief, but it's impossible. I stand quickly, almost knocking over the chair I'd been sitting in. I never thought I'd be grateful for Myra's presence, let alone as much as I am right now. But in this moment, she's a lifeline I can't ignore.

"Tomorrow, then," Brielle chirps, moving to stand behind Benton, lightly resting her hands on his shoulders.

He makes a sound of mild frustration, but nods. "We'll pick up where we left off."

Myra nods, her eyes flicking to me. Without another word, I follow her out of the room.

This is my life now.

Chapter Forty-Five

The next few days blur into a haze of repetition and instruction. Twice a day I visit the twins for lessons on court etiquette, while the rest of my time is spent in my room alone, including meals. I haven't seen the Prince since the night we made our bargain. There have been no updates about Verti. Myra is consumed with preparations and has avoided my anxious questioning. A guard now escorts me to and from lessons, his presence a constant reminder of my new reality.

Today, the lesson is even more grueling than usual. Sweat clings to my skin as I hold the curtsy, my body trembling with the effort. Benton's sharp gaze never leaves me and the cold snap of his cane against the back of my knee forces me to bend deeper. Air stalls in my throat as the pressure mounts, but I don't dare move.

I can feel the burn in my legs, the strain in my back, but I force myself to hold the position. Benton's eyes are unwavering, his focus sharp. There's no mercy in his silence. The cane hovers, a constant threat as he waits for the slightest misstep.

"You've learned nothing if you can't even hold a simple curtsy," he mutters under his breath.

I try to steady and center myself, but the frustration simmers just beneath the surface. The room feels stifling. I think of the days that have passed, each one blending into the next. Lessons. Silence. More lessons.

"Again," Benton orders, his voice cool and commanding.

I straighten, trying to shake off the discomfort, but it lingers, settling deeper. The cane taps against the floor, a reminder of the standards that are now my burden to carry.

"Make it fluid this time," Brielle says from her seat, her voice lilting with an air of superiority as she watches me struggle. "Elegance, grace... not just a motion."

The words drip with judgment. My face flushes with irritation but I swallow it down. This is my life. I can't have the Prince getting word that I'm failing here. I shift back into position, forcing my legs to bend again, forcing my body into the posture they expect.

The cane snaps against the side of my thigh, sharp and stinging.

"Not like that," Benton corrects, his tone as firm as the strike.

A startled breath escapes me. I tighten my jaw to stop anything else from slipping free. My leg stings, but I stay silent.

"Again," he orders.

I force my body to obey, even as the ache lingers. I dip lower, smoother, letting the movement flow instead of merely performing it. Each inhale is slow, controlled. My back stays straight despite the ache.

"Better," Brielle murmurs, but there's no warmth to it. Only a distant acknowledgment that the bare minimum has been met.

I release the curtsy, trying to hide the slight tremor in my hands. I know the break won't last long. They'll find another flaw, another imperfection. It's the price I pay for the life I've been thrust into.

Brielle exhales and uncrosses her legs with deliberate grace, every inch a performance. Rising to her feet, she steps toward Benton, her silk skirts whispering against the floor.

She doesn't speak right away, simply lets her fingers trail across the back of his shoulders as she comes to stand beside him. The touch is light, absentminded, yet possessive in a way that makes my skin crawl.

"Our time is up," she announces.

Relief crashes into me so fast I nearly collapse under it. I don't want to be in this room a second longer. I don't want to endure their scrutinizing gazes or their amusement over my failures. I just want to leave.

Benton, however, isn't finished. "Practice," he instructs, his tone allowing no argument. "I expect it to be flawless tomorrow."

I nod stiffly, my limbs still taut with exhaustion.

They don't dismiss me outright, but I take the moment for what it is, barely resisting the urge to bolt as I turn on my heel and head for the door. My fingers fumble the handle.

The guard outside greets me with a short nod. "Come."

I'm eager to be anywhere but here and follow without argument. But instead of leading me back to my room, he turns in the opposite direction.

"Where are we going?" I ask, slowing my footsteps.

"I'm to take you for a walk in the gardens," he answers without slowing. "Prince's orders, says he wants you to get some fresh air."

I blink, hesitating. Every part of me resists the idea of going anywhere, of doing anything outside the routine I've settled into. Lessons. Solitude. Self-pity. Repeat.

"I'd rather go back to my room," I murmur, half to myself.

The guard doesn't acknowledge my reluctance. His expression remains neutral, but there's something in the way he stands that tells me he isn't going to argue with me. Or rather, he isn't going to let me argue with him.

I glance down the hallway in the direction of my chambers before letting my shoulders drop in surrender. It's not like I have a choice.

Without another word, I trail behind him as he leads me through the halls.

It's not long before we reach the door that opens to a stretch of green and sunlight spills over me. I blink against the brightness, momentarily blinded after days spent in dimly lit rooms. The warmth touches my skin, sinking into me, chasing away a lingering chill I hadn't even realized was there. I tilt my face toward it, letting it soak in.

A narrow path of stepping stones cuts through the green lawn, leading toward a tall, arching iron gate. The guard steps aside, no longer guiding me. Just watching, now. Glancing at him, I hesitate but step forward, following the path through the gate.

The hedges rise around me, towering and dense, their leaves starting to dull with the change of seasons. The flowerbeds are fading, petals curling and crisping at the edges. Small stone statues peek from unexpected corners, caught in playful poses as if frozen mid-movement. Benches sit along the path and tucked away in little alcoves, half-hidden behind climbing ivy and the last of the late-blooming roses.

I inhale deeply, something inside me loosening just slightly. Maybe this isn't so bad. Maybe a little fresh air is exactly what I need. A moment where I can breathe. A moment away from the darkness I'd found myself in since surrendering myself to my fate.

Following the path, I trail my fingers across the edges of leaves on the brink of falling, skimming the tips of petals barely holding on. The garden is quiet, save for the rustling of the breeze through the hedges, the distant chirp of birds.

I wonder if the Prince's men have reached Verti. Did they make it in time? How would I know? Even if word reached me, I have no way of knowing if I'm being told the truth.

Are they still alive? Is *he* still alive?

The thought settles like a stone in my chest. As much as it hurts to know I'll never see him again, as much as the ache gnaws at me whenever I think about what my life will be without him, I would rather live with that than consider a world where he no longer exists. If there's even a slim chance that being here keeps him safe, then it's worth it. I would endure a thousand lessons with the twins if it meant sparing his life.

A sharp metallic scrape snaps me out of my thoughts. I turn, frowning. My heart stutters. The guard's sword is unsheathed, the tip gleaming in the sunlight as he levels it at me. His shoulders rise and fall in a ragged rhythm, his eyes wild. I freeze.

"You don't belong here," he growls. My hands lift instinctively, palms out.

"I—I don't have a choice," I manage, taking a slow step back.

He follows. His strides are longer than mine, closing the distance faster than I can widen it.

"Then you will be removed."

Cold panic sets in. My hands shake, air rasping in shallow bursts.

"I *tried* to leave!" I say desperately. If I can keep him talking, make him see…

"You failed." His voice is eerily calm. "I will not."

The sword swings. Sunlight lances off the blade as it cuts through the air. I drop, the blade slicing just above my head. A sharp gasp rips from my throat as I stumble, shoving myself into motion. My feet barely catch me as I break into a run.

"Please!" I beg, as I move too slow.

"You don't deserve the title of Princess!" he bellows as he chases me.

I throw myself around the nearest corner, my foot slipping on the loose dirt. My balance wavers, nearly sending me to the ground before I manage to catch myself and keep running. The pounding of boots behind me is too close. He's gaining.

I pump my arms, willing my legs to move faster, but they're heavy, sluggish from holding endless positions under the twins' relentless instruction. My breath comes in sharp gasps, my skirts tangling around my ankles as I push forward.

Then, voices. Distant, but close enough to hear.

Hope sparks. I suck in a breath and scream. "Help! Someone, please—"

Take Her

A rough shove slams into my back.

The force propels me forward, my feet flying out from under me. For a fleeting second, I have no control. The impact jars through me. My head collides with the worn corner of a stone bench. A sickening crack splits the air, pain splintering through my vision.

This is it. This is when I die.

Familiar darkness wraps itself around me. I greet it like an old friend.

Chapter Forty-Six

I wake to a stabbing pain behind my eyes, my temples pounding in time with my heartbeat. Blinking against the dim light, I take in my surroundings and find none other than the Prince standing at the foot of my bed, arms folded, a hard glare locked on me.

I sit up too fast. The room spins, and I squeeze my eyes shut until it steadies. When I dare to look again, he hasn't moved a muscle.

"What happened?" I mumble, my voice rough.

"I thought we had a bargain, Narina."

Confused, I sit up straighter. The only bargain I've made with him was to save Verti. And I haven't broken that. Have I? My thoughts are slow, muddled.

"I don't understand." Maybe it's the pain in my skull, making everything hazy.

"Do not play with me, darling." His tone is razor-sharp.

I give him a look that I hope conveys just how lost I am.

"You were in the garden," he continues.

"Yes," I say slowly, the memory still piecing itself together. "Following your orders to get fresh air. The guard took me, as you said."

"And that guard told me everything."

A cold rush of memory slams into me. The gleam of a sword. The rough shove. The crash of my head against stone.

"Told you what?" I demand, the last of my drowsiness vanishing. "I was walking through the garden, and he attacked me."

"You tried to run," the Prince states flatly, anger sharpening the edges of his words. "Again."

That yanks my full attention to him. He thinks I broke our agreement. That I ran. And if he truly believes that...

"I did not!" A bolt of panic shoots through me as I swing my legs off the bed, willing the dizziness to stop. I meet his stare head-on. He waits.

"I did not run," I say again. "I went for a walk. With a guard."

"You have one chance to tell me what happened. The truth only, Narina." His voice is cold, edged with warning.

So I do. I recount everything, every aching detail I can remember. The warmth of the sun. The crunch of gravel beneath my feet. The flash of the sword. The chase. The way my head struck stone.

When I finish, his arms unfold, his hands disappearing smoothly into his pockets. He is silent for too many beats. His unreadable expression sends a sharp spike of fear through me. Without thinking, I slip off the bed and onto my knees before him.

For this, I would beg. For Verti, I would beg.

"Please," I whisper, voice raw. "I swear I didn't run. Well... I did, but it was from him. *Only* from him."

"Narina." His voice is hard, cutting.

I keep my gaze fixed on the scuffed toes of his boots, swallowing down the panic clawing its way up my throat.

"You said once, in the woods, that you would believe me over them. Please, believe me now."

"Narina."

"Your Grace—" My voice cracks, but I press on. "I promise it was just a walk." The last word fractures with emotion, and I feel like everything's slipping out of control.

"Narina," he says sharply, gripping my chin, forcing my gaze up to meet his. Pain flares at the sharp angle, my bruised head protesting, but I don't pull away.

His eyes narrow. "You are about to become the Princess of the crown. You kneel for no one."

With firm hands, he pulls me to my feet, guiding me back onto the bed. I swallow, glancing up at him cautiously. He still wears the mask of anger. Dread twists its way through me. I open my mouth to plead again, but he cuts me off.

"I believe you."

Everything inside me goes still.

"Calm down," he says, voice softer now. "I did not doubt you. The guard's story was scattered and pitiful. There were nobles in the garden who heard you yell for help. But I had to be certain before taking action against him." His expression hardens. "Be assured, darling, he will be dealt with."

A shudder runs through me at the cold certainty of his words. Beneath the lingering fear, relief takes root. He doesn't believe I broke our bargain.

I cradle my head, pressing my fingers lightly against my temple, willing the sharp throb to dull.

"Why is this happening?" I ask quietly, though I don't expect an answer.

He sighs, dragging the chair over to sit in front of me. "I believe the assassination attempt and this attack are connected. There are people who are unhappy that the King chose you to be my mate over a noble."

I barely have time to process that before he reaches out, taking my head gently in his hands. He examines my wound. His fingers are surprisingly careful. I still flinch when they graze the tender skin.

"I didn't choose this," I mutter, watching his grey-blue eyes as they move over my face. "Why are they coming after me?"

"I suppose they think if they can eliminate you, the King will select a noble in your place."

"Oh."

The word is soft, nearly lost in the space between us. I can't fault them for their frustration. I never wanted this, either. But to know that there are people that want me dead...

"Verti?" I ask, anxious for an update and to distract from the thought that death may loom around any corner.

"My men arrived and the Sunstienians retreated, as expected." He lifts my face to meet my eyes. "Verti is safe," he reassures me.

I let out a shaky breath. *Thank the stars.*

He releases me, but I barely notice, too caught up in the flood of relief washing over me.

Verti is safe.

My shoulders sag, the tight knot inside me loosening slightly. I close my eyes briefly, forcing back the sting of tears.

"Thank you," I whisper.

When I open my eyes again, he's still watching me. The silence stretches between us. I clear my throat, shifting my focus to the flickering candlelight on the table.

"So... what happens now?"

His expression hardens, the softness from a moment ago vanishing.

"I will find out who is behind this."

I glance at him warily. "And if you do?"

His fingers drum once against his knee before stilling. "When I do. I will deal with them."

Another chill prickles down my arms, at the deadly promise his words hold. I should be horrified. Maybe a part of me is. But mostly, I'm just tired.

Tired of fighting.

Tired of being hunted.

Tired of a fate I never chose.

The Prince shifts slightly. "I am no longer comfortable with you having a rotating guard." I blink up at him. "I am assigning you a personal guard," he continues. "Someone loyal. Someone who will not leave you vulnerable."

The words settle as I try to picture a guard that would match that. Then, I remember him. A gentle face in a dark room.

I hesitate before speaking, doubting my opinion will carry any influence in his decision.

"What about the guard who found me in the safe room after the assassination attempt?"

His brows furrow slightly. "He turned you into the King."

"He followed orders. But he *did* try to defend me before the King dismissed him."

He watches me for a beat, then gives a single nod. "I will consider it."

I nod in return, surprised he didn't shut my suggestion down immediately. Suddenly, the full drag of exhaustion pulls at me.

I run a hand over my face, wincing when my fingers brush the sore spot on my head.

"I need to rest," I murmur, unable to hold myself upright any longer.

His finger grazes my cheek. "You need to see Moots."

"I'll be fine. I just need some rest."

"I do not like the number of times your head has taken blows," he argues.

"Please don't bother him," I mumble, already half asleep as I lean back into the mattress.

He stands without a word, the chair scraping softly against the floor as he returns it. I expect him to leave, but he hesitates at the door.

"Narina."

I glance up.

His eyes meet mine, something flickering behind them. Then, just as quickly, it's gone, replaced by the mask of the monarch.

"Sleep," he orders, his voice quiet but firm. "I will handle the rest."

Then he's gone, leaving me alone with nothing but the steady thrum in my ears.

Chapter Forty-Seven

Once again, when I wake, Myra is sitting in my room, watching me. A groan slips out before I can stop it.

"It wasn't my fault this time," I mumble, my voice still thick with sleep.

She hums in agreement, crossing one leg over the other. "I know."

She's perched on the chair beside the fireplace, her posture pristine as always.

Pushing myself up onto my elbows, I wince at the dull throbbing at my temple. My head still aches, a dull, persistent reminder of the garden.

I blink at her. "Then why are you here... again?" I rub at the sore spot lightly.

Myra tilts her head, her expression as haughty as ever. The firelight flickers across her features, giving her an almost eerie glow.

"I was told to watch you. To ensure your head injury didn't cause complications."

I slump back against the pillows. "I'm alive. Much to your disappointment, I'm sure, Myra."

She clicks her tongue. "Mistress," she corrects coolly. "And don't be ridiculous."

I roll my eyes but mutter, "Mistress," under my breath.

The room is cast in the dim, flickering glow of candlelight, just as it always is. It could be morning or midnight, there's no way to tell without windows. My body feels stiff, my limbs sluggish with exhaustion. I force myself to move, stretching slowly beneath the blankets.

"I suppose I have lessons soon?" I ask, dreading the answer.

"No," Myra replies simply.

That's... unexpected. I frown at her, pushing myself up fully this time.

"No?"

She folds her hands primly in her lap. "The Prince wants you to rest instead. But it's getting late, so you do need to get ready soon. You are to have dinner with him this evening."

I freeze mid-stretch, my body tensing. "Am I?"

"Yes." Myra shifts in her seat, her usual mask of indifference faltering just enough to make me wonder what exactly the Prince must have said to make her, of all people, nervous.

I hum in thought, tilting my head. "Doesn't sound much like a request."

She stills, her moment of unease vanishing as she fixes me with a hard stare. "It isn't. And I will ask you not to make my job more difficult."

"I wouldn't dream of it," I purr, flashing her an overly sweet smile.

She snorts, unimpressed. "Right." Her skeptical look lingering. "So, you really should be getting up soon."

My stomach twists with uncertainty. Dinner with the Prince. A reprieve from lessons perhaps, but my encounters with the Prince have been… unpredictable at best.

"Well," I throw back the blankets and rise, swallowing a wince as I try to ignore the ache tapping at my temples. "It's not like I have anything better to change into. Shall we go?"

Dinner with the Prince is not on the list of things I'd like to do, but I have no desire to see Myra in trouble because of me. So, I dutifully follow her through the maze of the castle, bracing myself for whatever awaits me.

She leads me to an area I'm not familiar with, stopping in front of a set of ornately carved double doors. The rich wood gleams under the flickering candlelight of the wall sconces, the intricate patterns a silent testament to wealth and power.

She turns to me. "The Prince requested we wait outside. He would like to escort you in himself."

I scoff, shifting my weight and crossing my arms. "You and I both know the Prince doesn't *request* anything."

Myra doesn't argue. She merely steps aside, positioning herself in front of me, her posture straight and unreadable.

I lean against the cool stone wall and let my mind wander, my gaze falling to the soft crease in the back of her black uniform.

Why does the Prince suddenly want to share a meal with me? The last time we dined together had ended with sharp words. Maybe he truly meant it when he said he didn't want our union to be a fight.

Our union.

The words still feel so wrong, foreign and sour on my tongue. I am to be united with the Prince. The one and only heir to the throne. The very throne I have hated since I was young enough to understand this world. And now… I am to be bound to it. A part of it. Forever.

I wonder how the people of Verti reacted when the Prince's men arrived. My father probably assumed I had landed myself in trouble. Perhaps he thought the guards had come as a threat against me. In a way, they had. Or at least, their absence was.

Does Diamo think the same?

A sharp pinch squeezes my heart at the thought of him. Did he confront my father after learning of the King's decree? Did he demand answers, demand to know how my father could allow such a thing?

How ironic that if my father had refused, if I had refused, Verti would have been razed to the ground.

If the King hadn't chosen me.

If I had never stumbled across him in that field.

If I had just kept my head down.

Would they all be dead? Or, if I hadn't been so defiant, would the King have saved Verti anyway?

A familiar anger simmers at the thought, burning away any lingering uncertainty. The King was willing to abandon his people without hesitation, without even granting them the mercy of a warning. If he had his way, the village wouldn't have even had the chance to flee.

And the Prince, the man I'm to bind myself to for life, was willing to let it happen. I am binding myself to a man who would have let innocent people die.

"You are very deep in thought, darling."

My eyes snap up at the sound of his voice. The very man who had been plaguing my thoughts now stands before me. Myra has already retreated down the hall, leaving us alone. I hadn't even noticed.

The Prince smirks. "I do not suppose you will share what thoughts had you so deeply enthralled."

"No." The word comes out sharper than I intend, the anger still simmering just beneath my skin.

His smirk deepens. "Very well." He gestures to the doors. "We are dining here this evening. I do not believe you have been here yet."

I shake my head silently.

He holds his hand out expectantly and I take it. His fingers close around mine with surprising warmth. He loops my hand around his elbow, guiding me forward through the door. As soon as we step into the room, I freeze, stunned by the sight before me. I don't even notice the door quietly shutting behind us.

A low chuckle sounds from beside me. I can feel the Prince's eyes on me, but I'm too mesmerized by the grandeur of the space to care. The stories I'd heard about the castle's magnificence had done it no justice. People had spoken of its splendor, but I have only seen cold stone walls and ordinary meeting rooms. Yes, they are large, but nothing that felt breathtaking. The throne room had been grand, yes, but this... this is something entirely different.

The room before me is vast, bigger than anything I've ever seen. The floor is made of polished white stone, so smooth that the light from the flickering candles reflects and bounces in every direction. The stone seems to glow softly, a pale shimmer that dances in the warmth of the room.

The far wall is half stone, rising up to waist height, where it transitions seamlessly into a wall of glass so clear, it's as if the room itself is part of the night sky. Through the glass, I can see the jagged peaks of the mountains in the distance, their silhouettes outlined by the stars. The other two walls shimmer with the same ethereal light, and my gaze is drawn upward, where the ceiling arches into a magnificent dome. The dome is crafted from flawless glass, offering an uninterrupted view of the night sky. The stars twinkle as though they're within reach, and the nearly full moon casts a soft, silver glow across the room.

Goosebumps rise on my skin as I take it all in. The room seems to hum with quiet beauty. Small, raised platforms of the same ivory stone are scattered across the space, each filled with lush, overflowing greenery. Vines spill over the edges of the boxes, their leaves a deep, vibrant green, contrasting with the soft gleam of the stone. The air feels light, fresh, as though the room itself breathes in rhythm with the stars above.

I feel like I've stepped into another world; one that exists in the space between the stars and the land. Everything about this room is designed to feel open, airy, and impossibly beautiful. The gentle shimmer of the stone, the light play of the candles, and the soft glow of the moon all come together in perfect harmony. It's as if the room were crafted to reflect the very wonder of the night sky.

I feel unmoored, overwhelmed by the beauty, as I take it all in.

"Lands divine," my voice feels too loud in the midst of the beauty surrounding us. "How?"

The Prince's voice is soft, as he responds. "There are no written records on its origin. No one knows which King built it."

I marvel at the view, my eyes still wide with awe. How does something so magnificent exist in a place so shadowed by the dark? It feels like a dream, a fragment of light that doesn't belong in this world.

"My theory," the Prince continues, drawing my attention back to him, "is that it was a gift."

"A gift?" I turn to look at him, incredulous.

"It is an old tradition for a King to give his Queen a gift when she gives him an heir. My father built a section of the gardens for my mother when I was born." His expression is still unreadable, but his eyes glimmer slightly.

"So, you think this," I wave my hand, encompassing the splendor around us, "was a gift like that?"

I can hardly fathom such a gesture. What kind of King was capable of seeing this kind of beauty, let alone have the imagination to create it.

The Prince shrugs, a simple motion that seems oddly out of place coming from him. "There are not too many more plausible explanations beyond someone just wanting it."

I mull it over, still stunned. "I suppose."

The words feel empty compared to the room around us, but they are all I can muster. My mind is still trying to piece together how such a place could exist.

"Come," he says, gently pulling me deeper into the room, his arm still cradled around mine. His touch is firm but unhurried, guiding me through the space as though we belong in this place together. I don't resist, too caught up in the enchanting room to care about anything else.

He leads me toward the back of the room. The plants grow lush and wild, spilling over the edges of their boxes in rich shades of green.

Each one seems to thrive in this perfect, ethereal space, their leaves catching the light from the candles scattered around us.

I'm still lost in the beauty of it, my gaze dancing over the starry dome above us, when the Prince comes to a stop in front of the large window that dominates the back wall. My eyes widen as I take in the view.

The window is like a living frame, its glass so clear it seems to disappear entirely, leaving only the view of the world beyond. The mountains in the distance are dark shadows against the night sky. The stars twinkle in such abundance, they look as if they're part of the room itself. It's as though the world outside is reaching in, becoming part of this breathtaking space.

But what really stops me in my tracks is what lies centered just in front of the window. A quaint table set for two. The candlelight flickers softly, casting warm shadows on the pristine white tablecloth. There are plates full of food and two glasses of water sparkle faintly in the candle's glow. It's not a grand banquet, no. It feels... intimate. Unexpected. It makes my stomach flutter in a way I'm not prepared for.

His gaze flickers over to me, studying my reaction carefully.

The entire atmosphere of the room, the plants, the stars, the table, has me feeling exposed in a way I can't quite explain. It's beautiful, yes, but it's also...personal. There's no grand display, no other guests. Just us. It feels too close. Too intimate. I can't shake the feeling that this moment is something different from the cold formality I've come to expect from him.

I glance at the table again, at the plates, the quiet candlelight, and the gentle glow of the stars. The Prince watches me silently, waiting for my response. I swallow, feeling the gravity of the moment.

"Why?" I ask, my voice quieter than I expect. I'm not even sure what I'm asking of him.

The Prince steps closer. His expression is still masked, but his eyes flicker with something I can't quite decipher.

"I told you, Narina," he says, his voice also quiet. "I do not want a constant fight with my mate. That is easier to do when you are not strangers."

"And this?" I ask, still struggling to understand what exactly he's offering.

He gestures to the table, the food, the stars beyond the window. "This is simply a moment for us to talk," he says. "Without the walls of the court between us. Without the weight of titles or duties pressing down on us. Just two people, getting to know each other."

I blink, unsure whether to be relieved or confused.

"You want to... what? Break bread with me like this is some casual gathering?"

He chuckles softly, the sound surprising me. It's not mocking, just a quiet amusement.

"No, not casual. I want us to have the chance to speak without the tension. There is much I need to explain, much you may want to ask. But first, we need to remove some of the distance between us, Narina."

I glance at the table once more, at the food, the warmth of the room, the moonlight casting its glow over everything. It feels strange, this kind of softness coming from him, but there's something undeniably real about it. I don't know whether it's his way of reaching out or a calculated move to soften me, but it's disarming, in a way.

I bite my lip, unsure what to say. There's so much I want to know, so many questions swirling in my mind, but can't seem to form them into words.

Instead, I simply nod, a quiet acceptance. "Alright."

The Prince watches me intently for a moment, then steps closer. He pulls out a chair, guiding me to sit. I lower myself into it, my hands lingering in my lap as the Prince takes his seat across from me. The soft light of the candles flickers between us. I glance down at the plates before us, the aroma of the food reminding me that I haven't eaten since this morning. The silence stretches out.

"Well," I say, trying to force a lightness into my voice, "at least the food looks good."

His lips twitch, just a hint of a smile, and for a moment, it almost feels like we're two normal people sharing a meal. Almost.

"Eat, darling. I can hear your stomach from here."

I grin and nod. The food is unfamiliar, but enticing. A delicate soup with rich flavors, fresh bread that breaks apart with a soft crumb, and a platter of roasted vegetables that smell divine. I dip my spoon into the soup, the warmth filling me with a sense of comfort I hadn't expected.

He watches me eat for a moment before speaking again.

"I imagine the meals in Verti were not quite as elaborate."

I swallow my bite of bread, raising a brow. "You mean the plain loaves and thin stew?" I tilt my head. "No, I suppose not."

His lips quirk slightly. "A shame. I hear the markets there sell excellent honey."

"They do," I admit, surprised. "The beekeepers in Verti take great pride in their work. It takes a skilled hand to achieve what they do. There's nothing quite like warm bread with fresh honey."

He nods, as if tucking the information away. "Perhaps I will have some sent to the castle."

Something about that thought unsettles me, but I push it aside. "Do you have a favorite food?" I ask, more to keep the conversation going than anything.

He leans back slightly. "I suppose you would be disappointed if I say something predictable, like roasted pheasant in a spiced glaze."

"Immensely."

His smirk returns. "Then I suppose I will have to lie and say it is a humble bowl of vegetable stew."

I snort. "Right, I'm sure it is." I catch his gaze and decide to push a little. "Come on, *stranger*, share the secret. It can't be that embarrassing."

He takes a measured breath as if deciding whether he will answer or not.

"There is a particular kind of citrus that only grows in the west. It is preserved in syrup, and the peel is softened until it becomes sweet enough to eat."

I blink, taken aback. "Candied fruit?"

His lips curve slightly, just enough to tell me he notices my surprise. "It was my mother's favorite. She shared them with me when I was young."

I glance at the spread before us and try to picture him as a child, sitting beside the Queen, peeling apart slices of sweetened fruit. It's too human, too normal. The image doesn't fit with the cold, unshaken Prince before me, and yet... it's there, lingering in my mind.

"You don't seem the type for sweets," I say carefully.

"I am not." He picks up his glass, studying it. "But I suppose it reminds me of simpler things."

I scoff. "Says the man who lives in a castle of gold?"

"It is not *all* gold."

I tilt my head, watching him as he takes a slow sip of his drink. "Then what is it all for?"

His gaze flickers to me. He cocks his head, in silent question.

"This." I gesture vaguely to the room, to the gleaming stone, the flickering candlelight, the lavish spread of food before us. "The grandeur. The wealth. If you prefer simple things, why surround yourself with all this?"

He sets his glass down with quiet precision. "It was never my choice."

The words are spoken so simply, so matter-of-fact, but they settle between us like lead. I don't know what I expected him to say. Probably some carefully curated line about legacy, duty, and the burdens of the crown, but not that.

I don't push any further. I take the moment for what it is. A raw glimpse into the person behind the mask of the monarchy.

I glance at the meal before us, at the lavish glimmering room, at the man across from me who was born into a life he might not have chosen, and one I certainly never wanted.

"And yet, here we are."

His deep blue eyes linger on mine for a moment before he finally says, "Yes. Here we are."

A thought slips out before I can stop it. "What will my gift be?"

The moment the words leave my lips, I regret them.

The Prince's brow lifts, his lips curling into a full, amused smile. "I did not imagine you would be fantasizing about having my children quite so soon, darling."

I roll my eyes with exaggerated flair, spearing a carrot and popping it into my mouth instead of dignifying him with a response. But his teasing fades as he watches me, his smile slowly disappearing.

"I have not yet decided," he admits, his voice softer now. "But I would hope it is as worthy of the life you give. Of the gift of a child."

The air between us shifts. There's no jest in his words, no glib remark waiting on his tongue. I hadn't meant anything by the impulsive question. It was nothing more than a fleeting curiosity. But now, faced with the sincerity in his gaze, a bitter thought follows.

"And if it's a girl, and not a precious heir?" I ask coldly, my grip tightening on my fork as I spear another carrot.

Before I can bring it to my lips, his hand moves, gently circling my wrist. His touch is firm but careful, his fingers warm against my skin. I go still under his gaze, that's now sharp and unwavering.

"She will be just as great a gift," he says, his voice steady, certain. No hesitation. No doubt.

For a moment, I can't breathe.

Because the strangest part isn't that he said it. It's that I believe him.

Everything about this place, about the life I've been forced into, has told me otherwise. Every law, every tradition, every whispered conversation has proven that a daughter is never enough. That she is *only* as valuable as the alliance her marriage can forge.

And yet, here he is. The Crown Prince. The man raised by this very system, bred to uphold it, contradicting that.

I pull my wrist from his grasp, not forcefully, but deliberately. I need space. I need to think. He lets me go without resistance, his hand retreating, but his gaze remains on me.

I busy myself with my plate, though I'm no longer hungry. The food that had smelled so enticing now sits untouched.

"You speak as if it's so simple," I murmur at last.

The Prince picks up his glass, taking a sip before answering. "Because it is."

I scoff. "For you, maybe."

His lips press together in something almost like frustration, but when he speaks, his voice is even.

"You believe everything here is cruel, and I cannot blame you for that." He sets his glass down, fingertips resting against the rim. "But not every tradition is law. And not every belief is mine."

I don't know how to respond to that.

The Prince doesn't wait for one. "You have been given no reason to trust me, Narina. I know that." His voice lowers with something heavier than the teasing or the calculated charm. "But I will not let you believe that our daughter, should we ever have one, would be seen as anything *less*."

I see it, the smallest crack in the mask he wears so well.

"You were a trainer." My voice is quieter than I intend, but the words land sharply all the same. "You bragged about it. How can I believe you?"

Something flickers in his expression, so brief I almost miss it. Not guilt. Not shame. Something else.

"I did not brag," he says, "I stated a fact."

I huff out a bitter laugh. "Oh, well, that makes it so much better."

His eyes darken. "Despite what you would seem to prefer, I do not lie, Narina. I spent years breaking women into obedience. I was the enforcer of the very system that brought you here."

I clench my jaw. "I'd *prefer* you to at least acknowledge the contradiction."

The Prince exhales, slow and steady. "There is no contradiction, Narina. I was raised to believe one thing. I followed the path laid before me without question."

He pauses just long enough that I feel a hint of what he isn't saying.

"Until I didn't."

I frown, the words pressing into me. He doesn't elaborate, doesn't justify. Just lays the truth between us, bare and unapologetic.

I should push further. Demand more. But something in me hesitates. Because I'm not sure I want to know his answers.

I shift uncomfortably in my chair, the strain of the conversation still lingering. I don't know how to ease it. I can't help but feel like I've pushed something too far, said something I shouldn't have.

"May I be excused?" I murmur, my voice quieter than usual.

The Prince tilts his head, almost imperceptibly narrowing his eyes.

"I'm still tired, and my headache from earlier hasn't quite gone away…"

I trail off, not wanting to make this moment harder than it needs to be. I don't know why I say it, I'm sure he can see through the excuse. Maybe because it's easier than admitting how overwhelmed I feel.

There's a brief flash of disappointment in his eyes, quickly hidden again, but he says nothing. Instead, he stands his chair scraping softly against the floor as he moves around the table.

"Of course," he says, his voice neutral, almost distant.

He steps toward me and offers his arm with the same cool grace he always does, but now it feels more ceremonial than before.

I take it, though, the warmth of his arm only serves to make the tension in my chest worse. He walks me to the door, unhurried. The castle feels quieter now.

As we reach the door, I see his usual cold mask slide into place, smoothing over any cracks our brief evening may have revealed. Outside, standing at attention just beyond the door, is a young guard. His posture is perfect, his uniform pristine. I recognize him immediately as the guard from the safe room.

"Your new personal guard," the Prince says, his voice firm. "This is James. He will be your shadow."

"It is an honor to serve, milady." James' voice is steady with resolve.

I nod at James, offering a small smile, more out of politeness than anything else.

"The only time he will not be at your side, is when he is sleeping and my own guard, Andre, will take his place."

A burly man I've often seen near the Prince gives a curt nod as he's introduced.

The Prince watches the exchange quietly, before turning to me.

"Tomorrow is our ceremony."

The words hit me brutally. I blink, shocked, struggling to grasp what he's saying.

"Tomorrow?" I repeat, my voice faint, as if hearing it again will make it sink in.

I lost track of the days. All I could focus on was the present, this moment, this dinner, this strange encounter between us, and now the surety of what's coming crashes down on me.

"Yes," the Prince replies, his eyes steady. "There are some customs you may not be familiar with, but I will not leave you alone." His voice softens, just enough to hint at something more than the detached ruler. "If you can't trust me, trust the process."

I nod, unsure of what else to say, my mind still reeling from the shock of tomorrow's reality. He's already stepping back, his eyes never leaving mine.

"Rest well, Narina," he says, and without another word, he turns and leaves.

I stand there for a moment, processing as James watches me, waiting.

Tomorrow.

The ceremony, and everything that comes after.

Chapter
Forty-Eight

The halls are quiet and empty as James walks me back to my room, the silence a clear sign of how late it is. I step into my room, the door closing softly behind me. The stillness of the space only amplifies the nervous energy pulsing through me. My fingers brush the edges of the table as I pace back and forth.

Tomorrow.

The ceremony.

The thought scrapes through me, leaving my insides buzzing.

The ceremony will seal it. Bind me to him. To this life, this fate. It cannot be undone once it happens. There will be no escaping this future, no matter how much I want to fight it.

I should rest. I know that. My head throbs with a dull ache and my body feels heavy, as if it's trying to pull me into sleep.

But I can't.

Not with tomorrow hanging over me.

My eyes flick to the small purple vial resting on the table. I know what it is, what it does, why they left it. A quick fix. A way to numb the mind, to silence the thoughts, to sleep. But I don't want it. Not now. Not for this. I can't escape the truth of what's happening, no matter how much I wish I could. Taking the drug would just be another way of running from it all.

With a low exhale of frustration, I turn away from the vial, pushing the temptation aside. The only thing I can do now is face the inevitable.

Tomorrow will come. The ceremony will happen.

And somehow, I have to find a way to survive it. Somehow, I have to find a way to say goodbye to my life with Diamo, once and for all.

Diamo.

Suddenly, the room is too small. Too confined. Too much like a cage. I wrench open the door, the chill of the hallway rushing in. The guard standing there looks surprised.

"Where's James?" I demand, eyeing Andre.

"I have the night shift. James will be with you tomorrow," he replies, his tone stiff, but his stance polite.

Tomorrow.

I don't bother to acknowledge him any further.

"I'm going for a walk."

I brush past him, not waiting to see if he follows. My footsteps echo through the silent hallways as I retrace the path of my first venture through these halls. The one where the Prince found me and carried me back to my room. With each step, the cold air from the corridor seems to grow more intense, and I wonder if this path will lead me outside, where I can breathe freely. Fresh air. It's exactly what I need to ease the quiet pressure building.

The further I walk, the more the hallway stretches before me. But soon, I come to a fork in the path. Two statues stand at each corner of the intersection, both of them lifelike, poised as though caught in the midst of some eternal moment. I pause, drawn to them. These statues are different. Not the cold, emotionless men I've seen scattered throughout the halls. These are women, two of them, carved with such detail it almost seems impossible. The artist who made these must have been remarkable.

The first woman is depicted with flowing hair, cascading past her shoulders. The drape of her dress moves around her body, light and wispy. Her face holds a quiet sadness, and no matter how closely I stand, her eyes seem to look past me, into something I can't see.

A strong gust of wind pulls me out of my trance. The cool breeze makes me shiver, urging me to leave the statues behind and follow the path the wind had come from. My body moves quickly, my pace picking up as the sharp, cool air beckons me.

I stop short, my eyes wide at the sight ahead. Two tall glass doors are open wide, leading to a balcony. Etched into the glass of each door are the delicate outlines of a tree. Its branches twist and climb over the glass in intricate patterns. As I move toward the entrance, the frigid air hits my face, sharp and biting, making my eyes water and my hair swirl around me.

I reach the railing, which is made of the same shimmering white stone as the room I had seen earlier. As I run my fingers along the cold, smooth surface, I notice the details carved into it. Tiny, almost imperceptible patterns so delicate, they could have been painted on air. It's as though every inch of this place has been touched with care, crafted with a reverence.

The view beyond the balcony takes my breath away. Before me stretches the mountain range that borders Barbast. The peaks rise high, piercing the starry sky like jagged teeth. The moon hangs low, glowing orange as it hovers just above the tips of the mountains, casting a dim glow across the land. In the soft light, the mountains appear almost purple, their slopes steep and rough.

Halfway down, the rocky terrain gives way to thick forests, their deep green a contrast against the pale, moonlit rock. The tree line stretches endlessly, reaching toward the base of the mountains before spilling out into more wilderness. The dense thicket continues far beyond what I can see.

Beyond the trees, the landscape opens up into a broad pasture, with a ribbon of silver from the river that cuts through it. The moon reflects off the water's surface, shimmering even from this distance. At the edge of the pasture, neat fields stretch outward, rows of wheat and corn growing in perfect, precise lines. The fields seem to run almost all the way to the castle wall. A strip of bare ground encircles it; no plants, just space for the guards to patrol, to keep watch.

Inside the castle walls, the space is sparse, save for a well-kept lawn that is dotted with a few scattered trees. Their branches are mostly bare now, the last of the leaves clinging to the limbs in a stubborn attempt at survival. Soon, they will be completely naked, but I can almost imagine the vibrancy of them in the spring, when they're full of life again.

In the middle of the lawn, a fountain trickles quietly. Two half-circle benches are placed around it, inviting anyone who wishes to sit and watch the water dance in the pale light.

I breathe in deeply, the fresh, cool air filling my lungs. It calms me, clears my thoughts. For a moment, I close my eyes, letting the peace of the night sink into my bones. The stillness is absolute. Too quiet, perhaps, but for once, I don't mind. I let the silence soothe the restless churn inside me, if only for a brief moment.

"Beautiful."

The quiet word disturbs the stillness, sending a jolt through me. My eyes snap open at the sound of his voice. How does he always do that? He moves like a shadow, silent and unshaken. I keep still, uncertain, but he speaks again, his voice hushed.

"My mother didn't want to disturb the beauty of nature too much, so she only added the fountain. This balcony was her favorite place in the entire castle."

I don't look at him, unsure if the fragile calm will hold.

"It's amazing," I say finally, just as quiet.

He doesn't respond right away, simply steps forward to stand beside me at the railing. I stop trying to decide what's appropriate.

"Where is she?" I ask softly. Since arriving, I've heard no mention of the Queen. The only thing they taught about her in school was that she had been bound to the King and provided an heir.

His gaze sweeps over the distant mountain range, his breath barely more than a sigh.

"She is with the stars," he murmurs after a moment.

The silence returns, but it is not the uneasy kind that filled the space between us before. It is the silence of the night itself. The kind that you can only find in the deep of night, wrapping around us in a quiet that feels almost like peace. We linger in it, each of us deep in our own thoughts.

"Is it wrong," I begin quietly after a long while, my voice faltering slightly, "that I can't help but feel like I'm betraying him?" A pang of guilt cuts straight through me. "I never wanted this. I didn't choose this." The words taste bitter on my tongue and my mind flashes with memories of Diamo, his kindness, the way he'd always made me feel.

The Prince shifts next to me and regret settles in. He doesn't want to hear about my love for another man. I brace for his indifference, his coldness. But instead, his voice comes softly.

"You are not betraying anyone, Narina. You are not the one who decided to tear apart everything you knew."

I draw in a shuddering breath. "I'm sorry," I whisper. To the Prince, for bringing it up. To Diamo, for leaving him. To myself, for every failure. To the night, for disturbing it with my grief.

"I understand your loyalty," he says quietly. "It is not something you can turn off overnight."

The night envelops us again, a gentle breeze stirring the air, carrying with it the scent of the mountains and the distant whisper of rustling leaves. The wind shifts, cool against my skin. A shiver runs through me.

"I did not choose this either," he says at last, his words low and vulnerable. "You are not alone in this."

313

Words tangle at the back of my throat, and I hesitate. The Prince steps away from the railing, pausing, just for a moment.

Then, softer than before, he says, "It is never wrong to love, Narina."

Without another word, he turns and slips into the shadows, leaving me alone with the night.

Chapter
Forty-Nine

I stand before the mirror, watching the slow transformation overtake my image. The transformation of a ritual bride. I haven't been here long, but I hardly recognize the woman staring back at me. She looks like me, but she doesn't.

There's something in her eyes that doesn't belong to me, or perhaps it's something they're lacking. Something that I'm so used to seeing but is absent now. Or perhaps something new has taken its place. It's difficult to tell which.

Four women move around me, working in practiced silence. Their movements are quick and efficient. They are confident in their tasks, never getting in each other's way. Dressed in simple grey shifts, their long brown hair twisted into identical buns, they are immaculate and uniform in every way. Even their feet are covered in soft grey slippers, muffling their steps against the stone floor. They do not speak. And not once do their eyes meet mine.

Two of them scurry around the room, stripping the bedding, scrubbing the furniture, clearing away any trace of my presence. When they finish, there will be no sign that I ever spent time here. It's an odd feeling to know one's presence can be erased that easily. I wonder if my parents have done the same. If, in my absence, they've cleared away the remnants of me. Did they just erase me? The disappointment of a daughter, finally gone.

I return my attention to the servants at work, back to the hands working through my hair. Braiding. Twisting. Looping. Intricate knots take shape as my curls are pinned into place. I swallow against the sudden lump in my throat, the practiced fingers triggering a memory so sharp it steals my breath. My mother. Her hands in my hair each morning, struggling with the unruly curls, taming them with quiet determination. That was before. Before this place. Before this life.

When I was young, my mother hummed a spritely tune as she wrestled with my hair. I knew that tune; she sang it when she was happy. She finished my braid, wrapping it around my head and pinning it into place. Then she grabbed my hands and pulled me to my feet. Still humming, she twirled me around the room, lifting me into the air, spinning me in circles until we were both overtaken with laughter.

I giggled as we danced together, our movements wild and unrestrained. Then my father stepped into the doorway, watching in silence. Usually, that was enough to put an end to our joy. But sometimes, on the rare occasions when his mood allowed, he stepped forward and joined us.

He took turns spinning me in his arms and dancing with my mother, his boots striking the floor in time with her melody, adding a steady rhythm to the song. I laughed and clapped along, caught in the moment. Because even then, even before his love for me soured into something cold and bitter, moments like these were scarce. He had always been a strict man, duty-bound and severe. But every once in a while, when something inside him softened just enough, he let us have this.

Eventually, my little legs tired, and I sat on the floor, watching as my parents danced to the music they made together. I watched them laugh, my mother leaning into my father's embrace, smiling up at him as he held her close, guiding her around the room. They looked so happy. Someday, I wanted a love like that.

The women finish with my hair, and I ache for my mother. For the soft hums she would weave into each braid, for the warmth of her behind me, steady and strong. I long to see her reflection in the mirror. Her face, gentle with concentration. Her hands, sure and careful. I crave her presence so fiercely it hurts. But she is gone. Lost to me forever.

Two more women enter, each carrying a wooden bowl and a cloth. They kneel beside me without a word, dipping the cloths into warm, perfumed water. One starts at my feet, the other at my hands, washing me in slow, deliberate circles.

The scent rises, lavender, rose, and something else I don't recognize. It fills my nose, clings to my skin. The warmth of the water soothes, but I hate this. Hate that I am not allowed to bathe myself. It has been this way since I arrived.

A few days. I have been here barely a fortnight, yet it feels like a lifetime.

When they finish, all but one leave. The last stands behind me, silent as ever, holding a white robe. I step into it, the fabric lush and heavy as it settles over my skin. I clutch it tightly around me, nodding once. She gives me nothing in return, not a glance, not a word, before slipping out the door.

Alone again, I walk to the mirror and sink down in front of it, crossing my legs on the cool stone floor. My reflection stares back at me, eyes hollow, mouth tight. Accusing. Hating. Sad.

This is my fault.

I was the one who stood out when I should have blended in. I was the one who defied when I should have obeyed. In a society of quiet, obedient women, I dared to be something else. That is why they chose me.

Foolish, foolish girl.

I bury my face against my drawn-up knees, wrapping my arms around myself as if I could hold everything in, keep it from shattering.

Why couldn't I have just listened? Obeyed my mother. Heeded my father. Been like the other girls… the good ones, the ones who don't fight their fate. The ones who dream of this, who would sit here now with their heads high and hearts full of pride.

They know their place.

They do their duty.

They serve. They belong.

So why am I sitting here, wiping away tears that have no place in this moment?

"Narina! Psst, Narina!"

The urgent whisper yanked me from sleep. I groaned, rolling onto my side before forcing myself up and stumbling toward the window.

"Diamo?" I blinked, still half-asleep, as his face came into focus in the moonlight. "It's the middle of the night. What are you doing? Do you know what my father will do if he catches you?" I rubbed my eyes, stifling a yawn.

Diamo grinned. "You mean what he'll do if he catches us."

I frowned. "What are you talking about?"

"I have to work the farm the next several weeks," he said, his expression turning serious. "I won't be able to see you." Then, his usual smile returned, warm and inviting. "I couldn't bear the thought."

He held out his hand. How could I resist that?

Without hesitation, I took it, and he helped me through the window. As soon as my feet touched the ground, he took off, pulling me along behind him. The dirt road felt cool beneath my bare feet, and I matched his pace easily, our laughter swallowed by the night air.

We raced through the village and beyond, past the last of the houses, until he slowed, leading me into a field that had been left to rest this season.

Diamo stopped in the middle of the field, releasing my hand. He spread his arms wide, spinning in a slow circle.

I watched him, amused. "What's going on?"

He grinned. "Let's play!"

I glanced around, expecting to see a ball or a pile of sticks, but all I saw were scattered stones. "Play what?"

He rolled his eyes, stepping beside me and pointing at the ground. I looked closer, realizing the stones weren't scattered at all. They were arranged in careful circles and lines.

I gasped. "Diamo, this is the biggest setup of Stones I've ever seen. This will take forever!"

"Good thing we have all night." He winked, then suddenly pulled me close, pressing a quick kiss to my cheek. "Take a toss, love."

Laughing, I picked up a stone and made the first throw.

We spent the entire night playing, our quiet giggles breaking the silence of the fields. By the time he walked me back to my window, the first light of dawn crested over the horizon.

Stop it! Stop it. I can't do this to myself. All that is gone. He's gone. I'm here and he's gone. I have to pull myself together. I'll never see him again. I have to forget it. I have to forget him. Forget all of it.

I stare at my reflection, my eyes raw and red from crying, and I resolve that this will be the last time I wipe tears away.

A woman enters behind me, her red attire striking against the dullness of the room. In the mirror, I watch her move with purpose, setting down bowls of various sizes on the two tables before exiting again. Soon, she returns, accompanied by a woman dressed in black and two of the women from earlier. One of them carries a low stool, which she places between the tables, silently gesturing for me to sit.

I rise unsteadily, struggling to maintain some semblance of modesty in this flimsy robe. It's a challenge, but I manage to sit without embarrassing myself, though my hands shake slightly. I glance at the bowls, their contents various shades of liquid with brushes laid out next to them. What is this?

The woman in red speaks, her voice smooth and practiced. "I am Madame Kristi. I will be overseeing this portion of your preparations. Please, tilt your head back."

I do as instructed, pushing my questions deep down where they won't surface. They won't answer them.

As my eyes close, I feel a cool brush glide over my cheek, the liquid cold against my skin. Another brush touches my eyelid. Are they painting my face?

I try to relax, but it's hard. This is my life now. Silent rooms, strict instructions, things I don't understand. It's strange, knowing I'll soon walk through a binding ceremony with a man I barely know. A man I've barely spoken to. And none of our interactions have been promising. Except... last night, on the balcony, things had been different. I remind myself that this is what I agreed to.

Back home, our ceremonies didn't involve these strange customs. No perfumed water, no lavish robes, no silent servants. In my village, it was always the girl's family helping her prepare. For me, that would have been my mother. She would've been quiet, but kind. She would've answered my questions, offered advice, maybe laughed with me about the oddities of it all. She would've been the one standing beside me, her hand gently guiding me. Her soft smile would have comforted me, and we would've shared a moment of understanding.

A touch on my shoulder pulls me from my thoughts, and I open my eyes slowly, squinting at the bright light. I stretch my neck, trying to ease the stiffness that has settled in my shoulders. I notice that the women are removing the bowls, their work finished.

One of the girls stumbles, and before anyone can react, a bowl crashes to the floor. The sharp sound of cracking wood fills the room, followed by the splash of red paint splattering across the stone. Madame Kristi's eyes narrow in irritation, but she remains silent, offering only a scathing look. The girl hurries out of the room without a word.

Not a moment later, another girl steps in, her movements fluid as she skirts around the mess on the floor. She carries a cloth, its fabric shimmering with the slightest movement. She drapes it over the small bed, the material swaying delicately in the air.

I eye the cloth warily, unconvinced that the bed is the best place for it. Madame Kristi gestures impatiently for me to stand. When I hesitate, she exhales sharply, annoyance clear in her expression.

"Come along, girl. We haven't the time to waste. We must get you into the dress for your ceremony."

Confused, I point toward the golden cloth. The woman looks up toward the ceiling, as if seeking help, then sighs, "Yes, now here we go."

I can't help but chuckle softly. That dress is for me? I've never owned anything so stunning. In fact, I don't think I've ever seen anything so beautiful. Standing, I take a step closer, inspecting the fabric more closely. It looks so fine, so delicate, I'm afraid to touch it. Another quiet chuckle escapes me. I will look far better in this than I did when I first stood in front of the Prince.

Kristi's impatience is palpable as she watches me, her hands hovering over the dress. I roll my eyes, irritated once again that I am denied the right to dress myself. She gathers the fine fabric in her arms, and I huff softly, stepping back to remove my robe.

With a swift motion, she places the gown over my head, guiding my arms through the appropriate holes. The rest of the dress falls into place effortlessly, sweeping the floor with grace.

Oh my.

I take in the full effect of the gown. It is truly lovely, more than I ever could've imagined. The fabric is so smooth and soft against my skin that I can hardly feel it. It's like wearing air. The gown molds to my body, flattering every curve. I stand still as the Madame pulls the laces of the intricate bodice tighter, securing the back with a practiced tug, before securing them in a final knot. I'm mesmerized by how different I feel in it.

The bodice is a delicate contradiction—elegant yet daring, structured yet revealing. Ivory fabric, soft as silk, wraps around my shoulders in an intricate cross-over design, leaving my collarbones and the tops of my arms bare. The fabric gathers at the center of my chest before parting again, covering my breasts and revealing a sheer panel that plunges in a deep V down my torso. Gold embroidery glistens across the translucent fabric, swirling in delicate, leaf-like patterns, strategically placed to provide a hint of modesty while still exposing far more skin than I'm used to. Every movement makes the beading catch the light, tiny stars scattered across my skin.

My waist is cinched tightly, the structured boning of the bodice pressing against my ribs, making me feel both secure and exposed at once. The sides of the bodice are just as sheer, the golden embroidery fading into nothing where the fabric clings to me. Cool air whispers against my skin, making me all too aware of how much more I'm showing than I ever have before.

I resist the urge to fold my arms, to shield myself from the eyes that would surely linger. My fingers twitch, aching to tug the fabric higher.

The skirt is just as breathtaking and just as unnerving. Layers of ivory tulle spill from my hips, ethereal and weightless, but any illusion of modesty is shattered by the twin slits on either side. The fabric parts with each step, revealing golden lace that clings to my thighs, shimmering against my skin before disappearing back into the folds of the skirt. No matter how I shift, there is no escape from the exposure, no way to stand or move that doesn't make me feel bare. The back of the skirt pools into a gentle train, trailing behind me like a veil of stardust.

I shift uncomfortably, trying to pull the fabric closer around me, but there's no hiding in this gown. It was made to be seen.

"Is there more to the dress?" I ask, my voice a little too hesitant.

Madame Kristi laughs in response, the sound catching me off guard. A flush of embarrassment spreads across my cheeks. The ceremony is to take place in front of the entire court, and the thought of presenting myself to such a large group, dressed in so little, sends a flush creeping up my neck.

Madame Kristi doesn't say anything, but she guides me toward the mirror, her hands steady. As soon as I see my reflection, I freeze.

The image staring back at me is almost unrecognizable. I can't help it. The laughter spills from my lips before I can even think. It feels wild, almost hysterical. Madame Kristi watches me with a look of disbelief. If the roles were reversed, I wouldn't blame her. My reflection has caught me so off guard that I can't contain it. The paint on my face, which I feared would make me look ridiculous, somehow doesn't. Instead, it enhances me in ways I never expected.

My skin looks smooth, almost luminous. The dark lines around my eyes contrast against the gold on my eyelids, making them look brighter, more alive. My lips are painted a deep, bold red… unnaturally perfect. And the dress… it clings to my body in a way that I never thought possible. The fabric hugs every curve, shimmering softly with my every movement, creating the illusion that my skin is glowing.

I stop laughing, pushing the bewilderment aside, and try to focus on the transformation. I no longer look like the ragged girl who arrived here just days ago. No, now I look like…

A Princess.

Elegant, radiant, untouchable.

I twist, turning this way and that in front of the mirror, trying to take it all in. The hair, the makeup, the dress, it's all so… beautiful.

And then, it hits me.

I feel beautiful.

The realization leaves me stunned. I feel almost giddy but I'm not supposed to feel this way. Or should I?

As I stand there, caught between wonder and guilt, Madame Kristi clears her throat, and I snap back to reality. I look up, realizing that I've completely forgotten about her watching me. Her eyes are still fixed on me, waiting for me to process what I'm seeing. I glance at her, a bit sheepish, but still unable to shake the awe that lingers.

"We're moving on to the next room now. Follow me."

A chill creeps through me as I pull my arms tightly around myself, trying to shield from the cool air in the hallway. My bare feet pad softly against the cold floor, offering little protection against the chill. The dress, though beautiful, is far from practical in this stone castle.

Kristi stops and opens another door, stepping inside. I follow, but pause just before entering.

The room is full of people. They bustle about, too busy to notice me at first, but I can't count how many there are. Most wear uniforms of various colors, and the noise of their activity fills the space.

Kristi seems to notice my hesitation. Her return is silent but grounding, a still point in the noise. As soon as she steps back, the room begins to take notice of me. Eyes, too many eyes, lock onto me, and I feel them like a thousand needles against my skin. Slowly, they start to find their seats, but their gazes remain fixed.

"You must kneel before the table," Kristi whispers beside me, her voice barely a sound over the murmurs. I hardly hear her at all. My mind races.

A sharp nudge in my back jolts me forward, and I exhale deeply, steadying my nerves. One breath. Two. I force myself to take a step toward the front of the room, where the table stands, set and waiting. The room has quieted, everyone now seated. But the murmurs linger, low and distant, like a buzz of insects.

I refuse to meet anyone's stare. I fix my eyes on the table, focusing only on putting one foot in front of the other until I reach the small pad at the base. When I kneel, the fabric is soft against my knees. I hold myself steady, determined to keep my gaze fixed on the spot in front of me.

Out of the corner of my eye, I notice a man step across from me at the table. His hair is peppered with grey, and his robes are a crisp white that stands out sharply in the room. He raises his hands, and the words that come from his mouth sound foreign to me. I don't understand them, but I recognize the cadence of the old language.

His movements are erratic and seemingly random. He pushes the bowl to one side of the table, then back to the other. He raises the candle, then sets it down again. Every few minutes, the crowd murmurs something in unison, and I can't help but wonder if I'm supposed to be doing something, too.

The pain in my knees grows sharper with each passing moment, but it's only when the man's words become louder and more pronounced that I realize he's nearing the end of whatever ritual this is. With a final, deliberate motion, he blows out the candle. The room shifts immediately. Everyone stands, repeats the phrase, and then exits in silence.

How strange.

I quickly glance around, but Madame Kristi has already disappeared. Perfect. Struggling not to step on the hem of my dress, I push myself up to my feet, but my balance falters. Just as I'm about to stumble, a voice catches me off guard.

"Milady."

A servant stands in the doorway, curtsying before retreating back into the hallway. I hurry after her, desperate not to lose sight of her. The hallway is dark, and she moves swiftly, her pale skin and light hair almost blending into the shadows of the stone walls. Her grey robes make her almost invisible in the gloom.

Ahead, I see her turn a corner. I quicken my pace to follow, but as I round the corner, I nearly crash into her. I lurch to the side to avoid the collision, and my heart skips a beat. There's no reaction from her, no surprise, no alarm. Her expression is unnervingly blank. It's unsettling.

I apologize quickly, but she doesn't respond. I step into the room we've stopped in front of, relieved that it's empty. The door shuts behind me with a soft click, and I'm left alone in silence.

With nothing else to occupy me, I begin pacing the room. There are no chairs, no beds, no mirrors to reflect back my frustration. I stop in my tracks, staring at the door. My hand itches to reach for the handle, to test it, to see if it will open, and to run.

Run.

Run as fast and as far as I can. Run until my legs give out, until my lungs burn and my heart races. Run from this place. Run from what is waiting for me. Run from the fate that seems inevitable.

Just run.

Chapter Fifty

Tightening my hand into a fist, I force myself to turn away from the door.

There will be no running for me.

The Prince made it clear. Run, and Verti will no longer be protected.

I've forced his hand, and he's forced mine.

A frustrated shout escapes my lips, echoing in the empty room. This is maddening. No matter how many beautiful dresses and obedient servants surround me, a cage is still a cage. And right now, I feel like a caged animal, pacing in restless circles.

It's taking every ounce of self-respect and strength I have not to collapse onto the floor, screaming, crying, tearing my hair out. This beautiful dress, the meticulously styled hair, the paint, the perfume… all of it to make me look like I'm worthy of being the Prince's mate, like I'm fit to go through with this ceremony.

But I don't want it.

I don't want any of it.

I look around the room I've been pacing. A single lit fireplace and a small window on the far wall are the only things to occupy my attention. I cross the room, drawn to the window, hoping to glimpse more of the world outside. Peering out, I'm surprised to find myself on the third floor of the castle. Below, a courtyard stretches out with winding pathways. Beyond that, the green expanse of land stretches out, bordered by the tall stone walls of the castle.

What I wouldn't give to feel the breeze my face, or to feel the cool grass between my toes.

Minutes, or maybe hours, slip by as I lose myself in thoughts of escaping into the mountains, far from this place. When the door opens, I don't bother to look up.

What's the point? It's always just another servant of the King, coming and going.

Doors opening, doors closing.

People coming in, people going out.

They'll make themselves known eventually.

"I am Madame Kenya. This is the final stage of your preparation."

I push away from the wall and turn to face her. Her voice is softer than the others, kinder, and for a moment I almost feel an ember of relief. She holds a small wooden bowl in her hands, and I wonder if there's more painting to come.

She leads me to the fireplace, positioning me so the light dances on my skin, and starts her work. Yes, more painting. She takes the brush and begins at my shoulder, her hands moving expertly down my arm. Curiosity gets the better of me, and I glance down to see what she's painting. Symbols. Three columns of intricate gold markings. They look strikingly similar to the moon glyphs.

I start to ask what they're for, but I stop myself. What's the use? There's no point in wasting my breath when I know I won't get an answer. Instead, I turn my gaze back to the fire, watching as the flames flicker and dance.

How do these women know exactly what to do? There hasn't been a ceremony in the castle since the King bound himself to his mate, and this woman is far too young to have been part of that. Was she trained for this, or was she only told what to do recently? No, her hands are steady and confident. Her focus is precise. She's not struggling to recall instructions, but working with purpose, as though this is second nature to her.

A soft pop from the fire breaks my thoughts, and a spark flies out onto the stone floor, flickering briefly before fading into the darkness.

The entire village had just finished clearing trees from a block of land for more farming space. The trees were piled high in one massive heap, and someone had set fire to it. The air was thick with the crackling heat, the smell of burning wood, and the wild energy of the young people. It was a rare night for us. The adults turned a blind eye, hoping some mating matches would come from the gathering. We were free to let loose, away from the expectations of work and duty. Dancing, yelling, and drinking, everyone was lost in the moment, enjoying the carefree celebration.

I was laughing, caught up in the fun, when suddenly hands gripped my hips, lifting me into the air and spinning me around. I gasped, breathless, as I landed back on the ground. Diamo stood before me, a mischievous grin plastered on his face.

"Come on, love," he said, his voice full of playful challenge. "Let's paint our bodies and dance naked like the Tryto peoples do." He spun around awkwardly in a small circle, his movements fueled by the drink someone had given him.

"Diamo Reddrit!" I exclaimed, but I couldn't help the laughter bubbling up. "That is very inappropriate!"

He pouted dramatically. "Ah, yes. It would be so wicked, inviting, and… entertaining." His grin only widened as he crept closer to me. "Besides, Narina Reddrit, you're going to be my mate in a few months. What harm would it do?"

I shook my head, trying to suppress my smile. If only he knew what he looked like. His hair sticking out at odd angles and that ridiculous grin on his face. The words that followed stuck in my throat, making it difficult to deny him.

"But I'm not yet Reddrit," I said, my voice quieter now. "And not yet your mate, so I must turn down your... offer. I wish you a safe journey home tonight."

I walked away, heading back toward my father's house. The night was already filled with so much chaos, but just as I turned to leave, a crackling noise came from the fire behind me. A burning branch, still glowing with embers, snapped free from the pile and fell, careening toward the ground.

"Narina!" I heard Diamo shout before I was roughly shoved to the side.

I hit the dirt, mouth full of the grit. When I looked up to see who had pushed me, my heart skipped. There stood Diamo, cradling his arm tightly to his chest. His friends were rushing toward him, but I was there first. His arm was badly burned, the skin raw and blistered from the flames.

I wrapped my arm around him and led him back to my father's house, determined to take care of him. We didn't speak as we walked; our footsteps slow and quiet in the silence. The energy from the gathering still buzzed around us, but it felt distant now.

Inside, I worked quickly to clean and bandage his wound, my hands shaking as I tended to the burn. He saved my life. But we didn't talk about it. Not while I carefully wrapped the cloth, not as we sat in silence after.

Finally, after several hours, Diamo broke the silence with a soft, hoarse voice. "I would do anything for you, Narina."

I looked at him, my heart tight. I tried to joke, to lighten the air. "Yes, apparently including sparring with a flaming tree."

He shook his head slowly, his expression serious. He leaned back, closing his eyes as the exhaustion from the night took over.

"There, all finished now." Madame Kenya sets the bowl down at her feet and takes a step back, inspecting her work. Just as I let out a shaky breath, there's a knock at the door. She grabs my hand, her touch steady and warm.

"It's time. Let's go."

Her words hit me like a ton of bricks.

It's time.

Time for me to seal my fate.

She helps me into a pair of flat, golden shoes right outside the door. Shoes. Finally. A small comfort in all this madness.

We start walking down the hallway, her hand firmly in mine.

I can't stop the wave of panic that crashes over me. I pull her to a stop.

"Please, I don't know what to do. There's an entire ceremony, and I have no idea what's expected of me. How am I supposed to act?" I plead, my voice tight with fear.

She smiles softly, patting my hand. "It's alright, dear. Nothing to fear. It's simple really. When you walk out onto the dais, just move through the smoke to the Prince's side. Then follow his lead. He will guide you. The only thing you need to do is say yes when they ask it of you." She gives me another reassuring smile before tugging me forward again.

Right. Sounds simple enough. But something tells me it won't be. Nothing ever is.

The sound of the crowd reaches my ears before I even see it. Shouts, cheers, voices, all so close. We round the corner, and the end of the hallway opens up into blinding light. My eyes struggle to adjust, and then I see it. The castle square. The hallway leading right out to the dais. This is it. My heart races.

"Hold out your hands," James says, standing in front of me.

I hesitate, unsure what he means.

"My dear." Madame Kenya's voice is softer now. "The Prince's mate is taken." She gestures to the rope he's holding. Of course. This couldn't be more surreal.

But then I remember the Prince's words, his insistence that I trust the process. So, with an unsteady inhale, I hold out my hands. The guard places the loops over my wrists, tightening them before holding onto the loose end. The twisting vines of panic threaten to squeeze the air from my lungs. I shove them back. I can't fall apart now.

James gives the rope a light tug, silently urging me forward. I step into the light, squinting against the brightness.

A roar of cheering from the crowd freezes me where I stand. I can't comprehend the sheer number of people here. It seems like everyone within a day's journey has gathered. I'm exposed for the world to see. A dull pounding roar fills my ears.

Another tug reminds me that I'm supposed to be moving.

Inhale. Left foot. Exhale. Right foot. Inhale. Left foot. Exhale. Right foot.

The screen of smoke swirls around me as I move forward, each step more reluctant than the last. Then, I pass through it, and there he is.

The Prince. Standing tall, proud, and handsome. His presence is commanding, regal in every way. He's wearing a deep blue tunic that hugs his broad shoulders, gold trim tracing the edges of the fabric in sharp lines that seem to catch the light. His high collar is adorned with gold buttons, each one a small glint that pulls my eyes to them and down the length of his chest. His dark hair is swept to the side, the slight waves soft against the sharp angles of his face.

But it's his eyes that strike me most.

They lock onto me as soon as I step forward, darkening, sending a shiver down my spine. It's not anger this time, not the usual irritation I've come to expect. It's something far more unsettling. Hunger flashes as his gaze drags over me like fingers across bare skin. The kind of hunger I've seen before, but only in Diamo's gaze, only in the eyes of the one person who's ever made my heart race in that way. Diamo, my best friend, my love, the one who always knew me. That look, that fierce intensity… it should be his. Not the Prince's.

I feel the flush creep up my neck, heat spreading across my chest. The exposed dress, so delicate and revealing, suddenly feels like a skin I can't escape, like the air is too thick, too tight. I can feel every inch of my body under his gaze, every curve, every breath I take. The fabric clings to me, leaving nothing to the imagination. I want to hide from him, hide from that look. But I can't. His eyes are on me. Something tightens under my skin, every nerve on edge. My body betrays me, reacting to his stare.

I can't bring myself to meet his gaze. I lower my head instinctively, my eyes falling to the floor. But no matter how I try to hide, I can't escape the feeling of being exposed, of being laid bare in front of him, in front of this crowd.

The tether pulls gently, an unspoken reminder that I'm supposed to move forward. I step, my feet drag, but they carry me toward him anyway, the rope tight against my wrists. I stop when James does, he passes the rope to the Prince. He bows and backs away, leaving me with him. Alone.

The crowd's murmurs fade into the background, their eyes all on us, but it's his eyes that make my skin burn. Then, in a voice low enough for only me to hear, his words whisper against my ear.

"Head up. Now is the time for that strength of yours." His breath is warm against my skin.

Who are you?

I am Narina Brevou.

I force myself to straighten, to meet his gaze, but it's like staring into a storm. Dark, heavy, intense. A flutter of something dark and dangerous stirs deep within me. He still has that look of hunger, but it's edged with something softer, something *more*.

He gives me the slightest of nods before turning to face the crowd. His movements are practiced, fluid, and sure, as though he's done this a thousand times before. With a graceful motion, he raises his hand into the air, and the entire room immediately falls silent in response. The command is effortless, and the crowd obeys without hesitation.

I try to mimic his confidence, lifting my chin slightly, staring out into the sea of faces. But beneath the surface, my knees are shaking. The pressure of so many eyes on me is suffocating.

The Prince moves forward, leading me to the left side of the dais. My feet move automatically, following his lead as we approach a small, ornately decorated table. The man in white with the grey hair is already standing there, waiting. He doesn't acknowledge us directly, his eyes focused on the small candle in his hands.

The Prince pauses in front of the table and kneels, pulling me down with him. I lower myself onto the soft cushion, the fabric of my dress brushing against the ground. It feels like this ritual is almost identical to the one I went through earlier, but the energy is different.

The man in white lifts the candle, his movements deliberate, and the flickering flame casts dancing shadows on the walls. His voice starts low as he chants in the old language, the words flowing smoothly, rhythmically, but still foreign to my ears. The heat from the flame mingles with the cool air, creating a strange tension. As he speaks, the wax drips slowly from the candle, landing in the bowl below. The scent of melting wax fills the air, and I try to calm my breathing, ignoring the uncomfortable feeling crawling up my spine.

The man finishes his chanting and lowers the candle back to its resting place. Without hesitation, he dips his thumb into the wax, then leans forward, placing it on the Prince's forehead. The Prince remains still as the man traces a symbol onto his skin. The crowd repeats the chant in unison, their voices rising and falling like a wave.

The man then turns to me. He dips his thumb back into the bowl and leans forward. I stiffen, bracing myself for the sensation, unsure of what to expect. The moment his thumb touches my skin, I feel a slight burn, more of a tingle, really. It's not painful, just enough to make me inhale sharply. The sting lingers for a moment before fading.

If my hands weren't bound, I would try to rub it off. My wrists ache slightly from the bindings, but I focus on not reacting. I don't want to show weakness.

We're on our feet again, and the Prince leads me across the stage to the center. The space feels even larger now, the crowd's presence pressing in from all sides, their attention sharp and unrelenting. At the center of the stage stands an elderly woman with a table in front of her. Five small bowls are arranged in a circle.

She takes a handful of blue powder from the first bowl and a handful of red powder from the last, combining them together in the empty bowl in the center. The powders mix, creating a swirl of color. She doesn't speak a word as she carefully scatters the mixture in a circle around us, her hands steady, her movements deliberate.

Once the circle is complete, she takes two small white flowers from one bowl and a large orange flower from the other. With great care, she places them atop the center bowl. Then, she grinds them together, her focus intense as she works. My eyes can't help but follow the rhythmic motion, fascinated by her steady hands and the quiet concentration in her face.

Finally, she turns toward us, holding out her hand. The Prince places my left hand, palm up, into hers. Without warning, she takes a knife from her belt and drags it swiftly across my palm. The pain is sharp, and I gasp, instinctively trying to jerk my hand back. But she holds it fast, moving it over the center bowl, the blood pooling in the powder. She keeps my hand steady until several droplets fall, before releasing me. I quickly retract my hand, the sting sharp and raw.

Again, she holds out her hand, and this time the Prince offers his. Without hesitation, she repeats the same action on him, dragging the blade across his palm with a swift motion. I watch, fascinated and slightly stunned as he doesn't flinch. The blood falls into the bowl with mine, mingling together in a way that feels intimate.

Once our blood has been added to the mixture, we're moving again, the Prince guiding me to the far side of the stage. This time, there's no table. Just the man in white, holding a length of rope entwined with blue satin. I know exactly what this is. This is the binding, the final step. This is where I become forever tied to this man.

A cold shiver runs through me as reality hits. In that instant, it strikes me that I don't even know his name. I'm about to pledge myself to someone I've barely spoken to, someone whose name has never been shared with me.

I close my eyes, trying to quell the flood of anxiety that threatens to swallow me whole. But there's no escaping it now. It's too late to back out, too late to run.

I open my eyes when I feel my hands being unbound, and find myself locked in the gaze of two eyes, the deepest blue I've ever seen. I'm faintly aware that the old language is being spoken again, and that the woman is spreading the mixture around us in a circle, but I can't seem to pull my focus away from him. His stare is unwavering, as though he can see right through me. Only when my hands are freed does he briefly flick his gaze to the man presiding over the ceremony.

The man places my injured hand in the Prince's, palms facing each other, our wounds mirrored. The Prince's touch is cool, his grip gentle, as the man takes the binding cord and winds it around our joined hands, up our arms. This is it. Once this ceremony is completed, there is no turning back. The actions taking place here cannot be undone, unless by death. The knot in my stomach tightens.

Once the man finishes tying the cord, he steps back, taking a deep breath. His voice rings loud and clear, resonating across the stage and through the space.

"Your grace, we stand here today in a ceremony of binding. As per centuries of tradition, your mate has been chosen by your predecessor. She has been found worthy and desirable by this court. As our future leader, we will look to and follow you. Here, on this day, before your court and your subjects, do you accept this woman? Do you swear to protect her, shelter her, guide her, and be her voice? Will you take her as yours and share her with no man? Do you promise to take this woman and bind her to you from this day forth? Will you take this woman as your mate?"

There's no hesitation in the Prince's voice when he responds. The word is strong, confident, undeniable.

"Yes."

The man then turns to me. My heart pounds so loudly, I fear the entire room can hear it. His gaze is unwavering, stern.

"Narina. You have been chosen by his majesty to be bound to his one and only heir. You have been chosen for showing admirable qualities that are desired of and expected in future heirs. His grace has accepted you as his own and has committed to providing you shelter, protection, and a strong figure to follow. Here, on this day, before his court and his grace's subjects, do you accept this man? Do you swear to follow and obey him? Will you be his and accept no other man? Do you promise to fulfill your duties and bind yourself to him from this day forth? Will you take this man as your mate?"

Happiness. Pure, unshakable happiness.

Diamo knelt before me, a plain silver band resting between his fingers. His eyes, warm and unwavering, held mine as he spoke.

"We've been friends forever. I love your spirit, your humor. I love your eyes and that sweet smile of yours. I love how you dance, how you laugh. I love your strength, the way you defy the rules set before you." He took a steady breath, his voice softer now, but no less sure. "Narina, I love you. Will you be my mate? Will you be mine?"

Pure happiness.

I swallow hard, once… twice, forcing back the memory. A single tear slips down my cheek.

"Yes."

The officiant takes our joined hands, lifting them high as he turns us toward the crowd.

"Before you today, your heir has accepted his mate and completed the binding ceremony. I present to you… His Grace, the Prince, and Her Grace, the Princess."

Chapter
Fifty-One

Princess.

The word slams into me, ringing louder than the deafening cheers that erupt around us. The crowd roars its approval. Whistles, drums, and wild shouts blend into a relentless, rolling wave of sound. But all I can hear is that one word. *Princess.*

It doesn't feel real. It doesn't feel right.

The Prince tugs me forward. Our hands remain bound as he guides me toward a set of stairs at the center of the dais; stairs I hadn't noticed before. Unease twists as I realize where they lead.

Straight into the crowd.

The number of people, their eyes, their attention, sends a fresh wave of panic crashing over me. I can't do this. I can't walk into that. I pull back, resisting.

The Prince stops, irritation flashing across his face. But then, something shifts, his expression softening as he takes in whatever he sees in mine. He doesn't speak, doesn't push. Instead, he steps toward me, close enough that the noise and chaos feel just a little farther away.

Then, he nods. A small gesture. A reminder. Reassurance. Strength.

With a steady pull, he draws me nearer, guiding me forward. Together, we descend into the sea of waiting people.

As we reach the front line of the crowd, we pause. A ripple moves through the people, and in unison, they bow. The magnitude of it stuns me into stillness, a silent wave of deference that makes my skin prickle.

When we start moving again, the crowd parts before us, but they are still unbearably close. Their voices surround me, a constant stream of well-wishes, greetings, and congratulations. Some swear their loyalty, others profess their admiration, some with reverence, others with bold enthusiasm. It's overwhelming.

We cross the vast space, passing through a wide opening in the rear wall. The moment we step through, I am greeted by a dazzling sight.

The square is bathed in the golden glow of the setting sun, its light stretching long shadows across the ground. Torches flicker along the walls and pathways, adding their warm, steady glow. Towering castle walls enclose the space, but it doesn't feel confining. It feels alive.

Blue and gold ribbons adorn everything. They hang from the walls, drape over wooden stands, stretch across doorways, and flutter in the hands of laughing children who weave through the crowd.

The scent of flowers is thick in the air, overwhelming in its richness. More flowers than I've ever seen. Bursts of every color and variety imaginable, decorating tables, wrapped into wreaths, woven into garlands that hang from posts and archways.

In the center of the square, a large space has been cleared and lined with seating. A group of musicians with flutes and drums plays a lively tune in one corner, their melody weaving through the hum of voices and the rustle of movement. It's a space for dancing.

Along the perimeter, market stalls spill into every available space, bursting with goods. Fragrant meats sizzling on open grills, baskets overflowing with ripe fruits and fresh bread, bolts of vibrant cloth catching the breeze, jewelry and metalwork glinting in the firelight, musicians selling their handcrafted instruments.

People fill every corner, laughing, talking, moving in an endless tide of celebration.

I stand there, caught in the moment, staring.

It's like the fire festival, but grander, brighter, more alive.

A low chuckle from my side pulls me from my thoughts.

"I have been told court celebrations are a thing of legend," he murmurs in my ear, his voice cutting through the noise.

"Yes, but I never imagined this." I can't tear my eyes away. It's beautiful and overwhelming all at once.

"Well, it is not every day that the heir is bound. A grand occasion calls for a grand celebration."

I nod, still absorbing the spectacle, and he chuckles again.

"Come," he says, leading me forward. "Tell me where you would like to go first."

The first stall we approach belongs to a cloth maker, her area overflowing with bolts of fabric in rich colors and fine textures. She looks up and gasps, her eyes lighting up as she sees us. Immediately, she dips into a deep bow, hands trembling as she presses them together. "What an honor," she says breathlessly.

The Prince smiles, shaking her hand before placing a brief, charming kiss on the back of it. The woman's wrinkled cheeks flood with color, and she clutches a hand to her chest as if steadying her heart.

"What can I do for you, milord?" she stammers.

He gestures to the piles of fabric. "Show me what you have for my beautiful new mate."

Her eyes widen with delight, and she scurries around, gathering samples from various stacks, pulling down bolts of cloth with impressive speed. In moments, she has six exquisite fabrics laid out before us.

"I have many that will look wonderful on milady," she says eagerly.

The Prince turns to me. "Show me what you like."

I blink up at him, confused. I haven't been allowed to choose anything during my stay here. I wasn't even permitted to bathe myself.

The Prince inclines his head toward the clothier. "Esmeralda is the finest at her craft. Pick what you like, and we will have dresses made for you." Then, he leans in, his breath warm against my ear. "Unless, of course, you intend to go without."

My face burns. My glare only makes his smirk deepen.

I quickly turn my attention to the fabrics, my fingers grazing over the samples laid out before me. I point to three: a deep red with a subtle shimmer, an emerald green, and a soft, pale pink.

"These are very nice."

"Perfect," the Prince says. "Deliver these to Thalia at the castle tomorrow. She will handle the rest."

Esmeralda beams, bowing once more. The Prince returns it with a graceful nod, then takes my hand again, leading me onward.

We move through the rest of the vendors, the Prince engaging each of them in conversation. He asks about their business, whether they have an apprentice, their thoughts on the market, and if they have any concerns. It's effortless, natural. Nothing like the cold, commanding demeanor he wears in court.

I can't help but feel lighter, watching the way he speaks to them, how they respond with genuine warmth and enthusiasm. He listens intently, nodding at their words, sometimes laughing, sometimes offering a few quiet ones of his own. They are not afraid of him. They adore him.

Nearly every vendor insists on gifting us a piece of their wares, delicate pastries, small trinkets, and tokens of good fortune. They all refuse payment, shaking their heads adamantly when the Prince attempts to offer them coin. But each time we leave a stall, there is a small blue purse that wasn't there when we arrived.

Three guards trail us, close enough to watch but not intrude. The Prince doesn't seem to consider his people a threat. He charges the guards, James included, with carrying the growing collection of parcels.

Through it all, our hands remain bound together with the blue satin cord, a physical reminder of the vow we've taken. The silk tightens when I try to put too much distance between us, a constant, inescapable tether.

Only after we've visited the final stall does the Prince stop. He tugs me gently toward him, then begins to unravel the binding cord. His fingers work deftly, the fabric sliding free, leaving behind a warmth on my wrist where it had pressed against my skin.

He coils the cord neatly and turns to James, placing it in his hands. James nods, tucking it away.

I flex my fingers, rubbing my wrist where the silk had pressed against my skin. The absence of it feels strange. My gaze drops to my palm. I turn it over, inspecting the small cut left from the ceremony. The blood has dried, dark against my skin, and the wound is little more than a faint sting now. It's not deep, but it's a reminder of what happened tonight.

I run my thumb lightly over the edge, lost in thought, until I feel the Prince's eyes on me. When I glance up, he's watching. Without a word, he takes my hand, his thumb brushing over the cut in a barely-there touch before he flips my palm back over and laces his fingers through mine.

"Come," he says, smooth and coaxing.

The Prince leads me out to the dance area.

"What are we doing?" I ask him, feeling a bit out of place. He halts and turns, facing me with a look that's both amused and expectant.

"It is a celebration," he says, a playful glint in his eyes. "I am going to dance with my new mate." He laughs softly, his smile confident. There's something almost daring in the way he looks at me. I nod in response, unsure why his words make a nervous flutter tickle to life inside me.

He wraps his arm around my waist, pulling me tight, and takes my hand. We step onto the dance floor. I can't help but notice how close we are; how his body presses gently against mine as we move in sync. The music shifts, and we move with the rhythm, my body still adjusting to the unfamiliar feel of it all.

The musicians play a mix of songs, some I know, others are new to me. At times, I stumble or falter, but the Prince is always there, steady and patient, guiding me through. He's strong, his movements sure and controlled, leading me without issue. For a moment, I almost forget where I am, lost in the dancing.

But I can't help but wonder about the man spinning me around. He's so different now. The Prince who was threatening and volatile in that meeting hall, who I feared, seems to have vanished. This version of him is laughing, enjoying himself, his smile wide and genuine.

I try not to focus on the feel of his hand on my lower back, the gentle but insistent pull of his body guiding mine. His warm fingers slide against my skin, every step feeling more intimate than the last. The space between us shrinks until it's barely there at all.

I know he feels it too. The way his grip tightens ever so slightly. How his movements are just a bit more deliberate now. His breath is warm against my ear when he leans down, his mouth brushing against my cheek as we twirl. The intimacy of it sends a shiver through me.

Pausing, the Prince turns to face me fully, his eyes locking onto mine with a piercing intensity that pins me in place. I can't read him. I can't begin to guess what thoughts are shifting behind that gaze, but something about it makes my pulse stumble. He steps closer, drawing me in by degrees, until the heat of his body brushes mine and the faint drift of his hands sends tingles spiraling beneath my skin. For a heartbeat, he lingers there, as if reluctant to let the moment end.

Slowly, he exhales and pulls away. The warmth vanishes. His expression hardens, shoulders straightening as he turns toward the guards. With a single raised hand, he signals James forward, and the moment is gone.

"Take milady up to my quarters," he instructs, his voice losing its earlier warmth. "Direct the Madame to her and linger in the hallway."

He looks at me again. "I will be up shortly."

The soft edge of earlier gone, replaced by the stranger Prince I've grown accustomed to. He bows his head to me and I respond with a small, respectful curtsey.

As I follow James, I glance back. The Prince walks the other way, his shoulders squared, his expression distant. Whatever warmth I glimpsed in him moments ago has vanished, like the man I danced with never existed at all.

Chapter
Fifty-Two

I am led through more winding corridors of the castle, my footsteps echoing off the stone walls. We turn a corner and are met by a tall woman dressed in red.

"His Grace will be up shortly," James announces before turning, placing his back to the wall, and assuming a formal position. The woman nods, then begins walking down a long hallway. I assume I am meant to follow.

"This is His Grace's private quarters. There are several rooms within this wing, all belonging to him. If he wishes you to see any of them, he will show you. I am Madame Elle, and I will help you prepare for the claiming."

The words *the claiming* hit me, freezing me in my tracks.

Of course.

I am now bound, and tonight will seal the union between the Prince and me, ensuring he is the first and the last to share my bed.

Hesitantly, I continue following Madame Elle through a pair of solid double doors. The room we enter is drastically different from the chambers I stayed in before. Three large windows break up the stone of the walls, offering stunning views of the mountain range, fields, and the King's Road. A balcony stretches out from one of them, open to the cool evening air. A plush, thick rug lies in the center of the room. The deep color contrasts with the lighter tones of the stone.

There is another, unmarked door in one wall. A massive bed occupies one wall, piled high with soft blankets, pillows, and furs, promising warmth and comfort. A mirror, large and ornate, covers half of another wall, with a set of drawers beside it. On the opposite side of the room, an armoire and a heavy chest stand as silent sentinels. The intricate etchings in the dark wood are breathtaking, each detail, a work of art. I make a mental note to study them later, after the night's events are behind me.

Madame Elle steps to the middle of the room and turns to face me, her gaze measuring, thoughtful. After a moment, she tilts her head, as if contemplating something. Then she speaks, her tone calm and matter-of-fact.

"Normally, my duty is to help you undress and prepare, but His Grace has requested that I simply answer any questions you may have before his arrival." She looks at me expectantly.

I stand there, frozen for a moment. My mind is swirling, but nothing coherent forms. For once, I have no questions. The expectation of the night presses on me, and I manage to shake my head. Madame Elle gives a small nod, then exits the room, leaving me alone.

I move toward the far windows. The mountain range stretches across the horizon, dark peaks towering against the dimming sky. A small flock of black birds flutters among the trees at the base of the mountains, their shadows blending into the growing dusk. The vast, open sky offers little comfort, and I feel small in the quiet stillness of the room, caught between what has been and what is yet to come.

I watch the last of the daylight slip behind the mountains, the world sinking into shades of twilight. The dark peaks loom, casting long shadows. I can feel the pull of the past creeping in, and I can't stop my mind from wandering to what tonight might have been if things had turned out differently.

If Diamo were here, with me.

I can almost hear his soft laughter, feel his steady presence beside me. His touch, warm and familiar, would have been comforting, pulling me close as if nothing else mattered. I close my eyes, imagining his arms around me, his breath on my neck, and for a fleeting moment, it's as if the world outside doesn't exist. I can hear my mother's words echoing in my mind. *He's a good man. He will take care of you.* It was simple, so full of hope. A future that will never be.

That warmth is gone now, replaced with an unfamiliar chill. I glance down at my hand, my fingers tracing the cut on my palm, the pain still faint. It's the mark of the binding, a tangible sign of my tied fate. As much as I want to cling to the comfort of the past, I can't deny it any longer. There's no undoing this. The Prince is my future now. This night will change everything. I am bound to him.

The pull of Diamo still tugs at me, an ache in my chest I can't quite shake. But I know... lingering on him, on what we lost, will only bring me more pain. Tonight is a turning point. The claiming will seal everything, mark me as the Prince's, body and soul. There will be no undoing it. It will be forever.

Maybe it's time I accept that. Embrace it. If I stop fighting the inevitable, maybe the burden of it won't be so suffocating. Maybe, in accepting the Prince, this union, I'll be able to let go. I will be his, irrevocably, and that will mark the end of what was and the beginning of what is to come.

I don't know if that will make it easier, but I have no choice.

As I stand there, my heart torn between the past and the present, the door creaks open behind me, the sound slicing through my thoughts.

"Do not turn around," his voice is low, the usual certainty replaced with an unfamiliar trace of hesitation. I still, my gaze lingering on the darkening sky and the birds that continue to circle.

I wait, the quiet pressing in.

"I have convinced my father to forgo the traditional witnesses," he continues softly, almost as if he's testing the words as he says them. "The claiming will be... just the two of us."

I feel a rush of relief, something I hadn't known I needed until this moment. Witnesses. The thought makes my stomach churn. The idea of having to endure the judgment, the eyes on me... I can't even imagine how humiliating it would have been. The claiming alone is daunting enough without an audience of expectant onlookers.

He continues, his voice steadying. "I will not force the issue. I will not make you share my bed tonight, Narina. You have but to say the word and I will leave right now. No consequences. No guilt. No obligation."

I glance down at my hand, still resting lightly on the windowpane, feeling the coolness of the glass beneath my palm.

"But," he says, stepping closer, his voice quiet, "if you will allow me, I believe we should go through with the claiming." There's a pause and I can hear the slight shift of his weight, like he's trying to gauge my reaction. "For us. For the sake of being properly mated. My father will not have reason to suspect anything. After tonight... you never have to share my bed again, if that is not something you ever want."

A silence stretches between us. His words, his offer, settle over me. A part of me wants to resist, to send him away immediately and another part feels... almost grateful. Grateful for his honesty, his offer of freedom. The idea of never having to be in his bed is oddly comforting.

"What about heirs?" I ask before I can stop myself, the question slipping out with an urgency that surprises even me. My mind spins. I think of Diamo, of what could have been. The tug of the past pulls at my heart, making me question everything.

When he answers, the calm assurance has returned to his voice. "I will never force you to my bed, Narina. Obligation or no. I will never *expect* you in my bed. I do not *want* you in my bed, unless you wholly *want* to be there. But tonight..."

"Yes," I say, my voice steady despite the nerves running through me as I cut him off.

There's a pause in his breathing, just enough to show I've caught him off guard. I know it's not what he expected. He doesn't rush to touch me, to pull me close. Instead, he stands there for a beat too long, as if waiting for me to change my mind.

"Narina..."

"Yes," I say firmly. "Yes. I need..."

Closure. I need this. I need to stop lingering in the shadows of what was.

"Close your eyes."

His quiet, unrushed voice tells me he accepts my answer. He understands.

I'm not sure I like the thought of not being able to see, especially when his moods tend to shift drastically within seconds. But there's something about the calm in his voice that settles my nerves, even as my breath hitches with nervous anticipation.

His heavy footsteps approach me slowly. I tense, my heart thumping louder with each step.

"Always fighting me," he murmurs from right behind me.

His hands move to my hair, the touch surprisingly gentle as he starts to remove the pins, one by one. I can feel the tension in my scalp as each pin is released, the weight of the braid loosening slowly. My breathing is still unsteady, unsure of what to expect next, but I wait for him to speak. His hands work with ease, undoing the careful arrangement that had taken so much time earlier.

When he finally has all the pins removed and the braids undone, I feel his fingers weave through the curls, his touch lingering, gentle.

"Beautiful," he murmurs, the words catching me off guard. "I love your hair down."

Take Her

The compliment is intimate, disarming in its simplicity. It's not the kind of thing I would expect from him, and I find myself unsure of how to respond.

"Relax." His voice is a whisper, warm and close against my ear. "I'm not going to hurt you, Narina. I promise."

I nod, swallowing the lump that has formed in my throat. I can't find my voice, but his assurance soothes something deep inside me, the sincerity in it undeniable.

"Now, close your eyes," he says softly.

I hesitate for a moment longer, uncertainty swirling within me, but I obey. My eyelids flutter shut, and the world around me blurs into darkness.

"Tell me why you still fight me." His voice shifts, now in my other ear, the words quiet and firm.

The words barely make it past my lips.

"I don't know you."

He laughs softly, the sound warm.

"Tell me what you would like to know, darling."

His proximity is overwhelming. I feel the heat of him, the slight brush of his clothing against my back as he stands so close. My breath comes too fast, the rush beneath my skin impossible to ignore.

"Your name," I finally murmur.

A low chuckle escapes him again, but this time, there's something softer beneath it.

"Ryden," he says quietly, almost as if it's a secret. "My name is Ryden."

He moves, his fingers brushing against my hair, pushing it off to one side. His touch trails down my shoulder, then along the curve of my side.

"Look at you. You are ravishing."

I stiffen instinctively at the contact, my body reacting before my mind has time to process. The Prince feels it. He exhales lightly, resting his forehead against my shoulder for a moment. But then, he pulls back,

350

stepping away just enough to give me some space. The air between us feels charged.

His voice, when it comes again, is quiet.

"Tell me his name."

I shake my head, confused, my thoughts have muddled beneath the heat of his touch. Everything else blurs, my focus narrowing to the feel of him, too close, too much.

"Tell me the name of your lover. The one you are trying to leave behind tonight." His words are steady, but there's an edge to them now.

I falter, thrown by the reminder, by the fact that he's brought him up. But he knows. He understands why I need this. Knows I need this to close a door I can't leave open.

"We weren't lovers. Only betrothed." The words tumble out, sharper than I intend. Nothing had been shared beyond a few kisses.

"His name, Narina."

He doesn't ask. He commands, and the authority in his voice sends a ripple through me and raises the hair on my arms. His hand glides over my shoulder blades, slow and deliberate, drawing tension from every nerve.

"Diamo," I whisper, my throat tight with the name. Saying it feels like another tie that binds me to the past, but I can't stay there anymore.

The Prince grunts softly, satisfied. His fingers press against the button at the nape of my neck, and it pops undone with barely a sound, the crisscrossing fabric of my dress loosening.

"You were not lovers."

His voice is thoughtful now, almost as if he's piecing something together. His finger traces down my spine, sending a shiver through me.

It's hard to focus on anything as he tugs at the tie holding the laces of my dress tight.

I shake my head.

"Good," he murmurs, the word almost a growl. "I do not share."

Another chuckle slips from his lips, low and private, as if he's found some kind of dark amusement in the idea.

He moves to stand in front of me. My eyes stay shut, but I feel him there, the shift in the air, the warmth of him brushing close. My breath stutters, and my body tenses, caught somewhere between pulling away and leaning in.

"My mate is blushing." His voice is playful, teasing, and it sends a flush of heat straight to my face.

He places a light kiss on my cheek, his lips soft against my skin. I can't help it. I feel the heat spread, my face on fire. I force myself to inhale deeply, but it does nothing to settle the frantic flutter as I drag in the unfamiliar scent of him. He smells of cedar and leather, laced with something that reminds me of steel and secrets, familiar and foreign all at once.

"Let me help you forget him." His words come in a soft whisper, his breath tickling my ear. His hand finds its place on my back again.

He steps closer, urging me back with a careful press of his hand. I stumble, but he's there to steady me, close enough that I can feel the heat of him brushing against my skin. We move like that, a slow retreat, the plush rug beneath my feet sinking with each step.

I try to slow my breath, but anticipation is wound tight inside me, impossible to ignore. When the backs of my knees brush the bed, a jolt of nervous energy rushes through me, like I'm teetering on the edge of something I can't quite name, and it's already too late to turn back.

His strong hand gently cups my cheek, the touch soft, grounding. My heart is thundering in my chest.

"Look at me," he commands quietly, his voice gentle.

I obey, meeting his dark searching eyes, but there's an undeniable gentleness there.

"You can change your mind, Narina."

His offer is unexpected in its softness, in how easily he's willing to let me go. For a moment, I can only look at him. Then I shake my head, small but certain.

He nods once, like he's understood me completely without needing to ask again.

His hands slide to my lower back, firm and possessive, drawing me in. He presses a kiss just beneath my ear, and I find myself tilting toward him, offering more. My movements aren't conscious anymore. My body responds on instinct, caught in the slow unraveling of restraint. His lips trail warmth against my neck, sending a slow shiver through me. My breath catches, pulse quickening, not just from nerves this time, but something deeper. Something I no longer want to deny.

The fabric of my dress slips from my shoulder, his fingers guiding it down with quiet care. His mouth traces the line of my jaw, each kiss unhurried and deliberate. My body answers before I can think, arching into him. Every nerve hums, every breath caught between hesitation and hunger. And still, I lean in, drawn to him.

Chapter Fifty-Three

He pulls back just enough to see me, his gaze locking onto mine. One hand lifts to caress my cheek, his fingers brushing softly against my skin. I don't look away. The intensity in his eyes holds me there. He leans in, his thumb brushing across my bottom lip, an unspoken question.

I tilt my head, the answer in the motion. A quiet yes.

His lips meet mine, slow at first, tentative, as if he's waiting for me to pull away. I don't. I lean in, drawn by the warmth of him, the quiet steadiness he offers. With every second I stay, the heat between us builds, deepening into something that hums beneath my skin.

The kiss grows fuller, more consuming, pulling me under in a way that should terrify me, but doesn't. I let go. The constant churn of thoughts, the doubts, the grief, the ache… they all fall away, replaced by the nearness of him. The now. Just this moment, and the way he makes everything else go quiet.

Hesitantly, I wrap my arms around him, unsure where they belong, but wanting it. My fingers thread into his hair, tugging him closer. His hands roam with purpose, mapping the curve of my body, each touch sending sparks dancing across my skin. I feel alive, every nerve awake as he deepens the kiss.

He presses into me, and I lean into it, caught in the rhythm of him. His lips leave mine, trailing down to my neck. A shiver rolls through me at the brush of his breath, at the way he finds that spot just below my ear and lingers there. Then lower, placing soft, heated kisses along my collarbone, until he pauses.

He draws back only far enough to meet my gaze, searching, as if he needs to see my thoughts to trust what we're building. There's a question in his eyes, even now. Not for the kiss, but for everything else that might come after.

"I am not going to hurt you," he murmurs, the promise in his voice unmistakable.

"I know," I whisper, nodding, my throat tight with everything I can't yet say.

His lips find mine again, and this time, it's different. There's no hesitance, no question. He kisses me with certainty, claiming me with a confidence that matches my own as I melt beneath him. His hands roam lower, over the curve of my waist, slipping between the folds of fabric to my thighs. In one fluid motion, he lifts me against him like I weigh nothing at all.

He moves with slow, deliberate ease, pushing the top of my dress down. The fabric slips over my hips and pools at my feet, baring me to the air. I tense, just slightly, as the coolness grazes my skin, as the last of my defenses fall.

"Let go," he breathes against my ear. "You do not have to fight anymore."

And I believe him. I feel it in the way he touches me, one hand firm at my hip, the other cradling the back of my neck. I feel it in the

355

way he kisses me, soft but sure, tenderness in each one. I saw it in his eyes before I closed mine, that promise not to hurt me. He doesn't want to conquer me. He wants me to choose him. To accept what this has become. To stop resisting him.

I'm so tired of fighting.

So I don't.

I close my eyes, letting the words settle inside me like a balm. The tension drains from my body, as I surrender to the heat building between us, to the rawness of what's unfolding. He feels the shift. His gaze sweeps over me, intense but not demanding, just watching, like he's trying to memorize every part of me. A flicker of self-consciousness rises at being seen like this, so bare before him, but I push it aside.

When his lips find mine again, I meet him with equal fervor, my fingers tangling in his hair to pull him closer. The kiss is deeper now, more certain, full of meaning I don't have words for. The last of the tightness in my chest unspools. His hands roam lower, worshipping every inch of skin, and a shuddering breath escapes me. Each kiss, each touch, draws me further under, dissolving what little doubt still lingered.

He eases me back until the bed catches me, soft beneath my spine. Then he pulls away, slowly, his eyes lingering on mine for a moment before sweeping over me. There's hunger in them, yes, but it's tempered with reverence, with something far gentler than I expected.

He draws a deep breath, steadying himself, as though holding back is the hardest thing he's ever done.

His fingers graze the buttons of his tunic, undoing them with ease. The fabric slips from his shoulders and down his arms. I watch, breath caught, as smooth skin and sculpted muscle come into view, each shift flexing across his chest. He lets the tunic fall, never looking away.

There's a quiet command in the way he stands, in the stillness of his gaze. I can only follow him with my eyes, tracing the shape of him, the way his arms move as he bends to remove his boots, unhurried and sure. When he rises again, his hands move to the last layer between us.

He slides his trousers down slowly, each motion filled with control. My pulse spikes, the air thick with anticipation as he steps free of them. The sight of him, bare and unguarded, pulls a quiet gasp from me. I don't look away. I let myself take him in, all of him, before meeting his eyes again.

He stands there, proud and still, his body lit by the soft glow of the room. There's a quiet, compelling power in the way he looks at me, a mix of dominance and something unexpectedly gentle. Protective, even.

He steps closer, his hands lifting to cradle my face, thumb tracing the line of my jaw. His touch is warm and gentle, despite the intensity simmering between us. There's hardly any space left now; the heat of him wraps around me.

He leans in, his lips brushing mine in a kiss softer than any before, slow, lingering, savoring. When he pulls back, he doesn't release me. Instead, he coaxes me gently onto the bed, following as I sink into it. His body moves over mine, settling between my legs, skin to skin. The contact sends a shiver rippling through me.

His fingers trail down my arm, brushing my wrist before sliding to my waist, drawing me closer. The nearness is overwhelming, almost too much, and yet, I lean into it. Into him. My chest rises and falls in uneven breaths, but I don't pull away.

His lips brush against my forehead, soft and sure.

I become acutely aware of how my body responds to him, how easily it yields. My hands grip his arms, instinctive, grounding me as my body presses flush against his. He props himself on one elbow, his hand sliding into my hair, fingers tangling gently.

His free hand roams the length of me, brushing over my shoulder, grazing my collarbone, then lower. Across my chest, over the swell of my breast. A shiver rolls through me as his touch circles my nipple, then glides to the other side, repeating the motion.

His mouth follows, lips dragging soft, lingering kisses along my jaw, down the curve of my neck, leaving warmth, and goosebumps, in their wake.

He pauses, meeting my eyes, as he nudges against me, offering one last moment to change my mind. My lips part on a soft exhale. I nod, just barely.

"I trust you," I whisper, the words fragile, but they feel true.

A slow smile touches his lips. His hand moves to my waist, anchoring me to him as he pushes forward, filling me completely. A gasp escapes me, but he catches it with his mouth, kissing me deeply as he stills, giving me time to adjust. He scatters kisses over my closed eyelids, across my cheeks, down the line of my jaw, his patience wrapping around me as surely as his arms.

"Breathe," he murmurs, his voice warm against my skin. I let out a slow exhale, sinking into him.

He waits, tense with restraint, his fingers stroking slow, soothing patterns along my waist. His lips brush the corner of my mouth, coaxing, reassuring. I shift beneath him, the discomfort fading, replaced by a warmth that spreads low and deep, like slow-burning embers.

Another breath leaves me, steadier now. My body softens in silent permission. He feels the change, kisses me again, lingering, then begins to move.

A slow, careful roll of his hips. My breath stutters. He finds my hand, guiding it to his shoulder, encouraging me. His other hand stays firm at my waist, keeping me close as he sets a rhythm built on care, on intention, on making sure I feel every inch of this.

The tension I've held for so long begins to unravel, thread by thread, with each movement, each whispered breath against my skin. His mouth never strays far from mine, brushing kisses to my jaw, my throat, my shoulder. Never demanding. Only offering. His touch is reverent, like he's trying to memorize me.

I tilt my hips instinctively, and he groans softly against my neck, his fingers tightening as his rhythm deepens. A spark ignites my core, the growing pleasure unexpected, overwhelming. I cling to him, nails digging into his shoulders. He shudders, answering with a kiss that's no longer patient but desperate, consuming.

The room fades. There's only this, the warmth of his body, the way he looks at me like I am something to be cherished.

Each movement pulls me deeper into something I can't quite name. His hands roam, down my sides, over my hips, into my hair, as if needing to touch every part of me. His mouth finds the hollow of my throat, leaving open-mouthed kisses in his wake, each one scattering sparks that catch and spread until I'm burning beneath him.

The tension coiling in my belly tightens with every slow, purposeful thrust. My fingers dig into the muscles of his back, as sensation crests higher, threatening to pull me under. He groans, breath hot against my neck, his pace quickening, more urgent now, more desperate.

He lifts his head, searching for me. The way he looks at me, like I am the only thing that exists in this moment, sends another rush of heat through me.

I can't stop the breathless sounds that escape me, my body responding as the pressure builds, tightens, spirals. He must feel it too, the way I tremble beneath him, the way my nails bite into his skin as it winds tighter, holding me on the edge. His hand slips between us, fingers finding the center of me with perfect precision. My back arches, a cry breaking from my throat as the pleasure shatters through me.

And then I'm lost. Falling into the sensation, coming undone beneath him. He groans against my mouth, his movements faltering, his grip on me tightening as he buries himself deep.

For a long moment, neither of us moves. We stay there, bodies tangled, breath uneven, the air around us still pulsing with heat.

His forehead rests against mine, his chest rising hard against mine with every breath. Then he kisses me, slow and sure, like he's marking the moment into both of us.

"You are mine, now," he whispers against my lips.

And for the first time... I don't think to fight it.

He holds himself above me for a moment, his breaths still uneven, his body taut. His fingers skim over my side, soothing, grounding, before he slowly pulls away. A sharp gasp escapes me at the loss, my body too sensitive, and I flinch without meaning to. He instantly peppers me with soft kisses. His hands roam gently, smoothing over my heated skin, easing the shudder that follows.

He lingers for a beat, then rises and slips from the bed. I watch him through heavy-lidded eyes as he moves across the room, naked, unbothered, his presence filling the space with quiet confidence. At the basin on the table, he dips a cloth into the water, wrings it out, and returns to me.

The bed dips under his weight. The cloth is cool against my skin, jarring against the heat still lingering along my thighs. He's careful and tender in his attention. When I startle, his gaze flicks up, watchful. My eyes catch on the pale pink staining the cloth. My stomach twists.

He sees.

"It's normal," he murmurs, tossing the cloth aside. He leans in, pressing a kiss to my forehead. "You're alright."

I nod, though I don't quite trust my voice yet. He doesn't push. Instead, he shifts, settling beside me. Strong arms wrap around me, pulling me into the curve of his body. His lips brush slow, featherlight kisses that trail lazily up the curve of my neck and along my spine.

Little by little, the tension melts away as his touch lulls me into a hazy calm. The stroke of his fingers over my hip, the steady rise and fall of his chest against my back, the way he holds me like he doesn't intend to let go… it all weaves together.

Sleep comes slowly, inevitably. His lips brush my skin one last time before I drift off, a touch that feels less like possession, and more like something neither of us meant to find.

Chapter
Fifty-Four

I groan and roll over, trying to escape the light filtering through the windows. I pause when I hit something solid... warm, unyielding flesh. An arm drapes across my stomach, anchoring me in place, and a rush of memories from last night crash over me.

I shift slightly, just enough to test the distance, but his arm tightens, pulling me back until my spine rests against the firm line of his abdomen. Heat radiates from him, seeping into my skin, wrapping around me like a tether.

I force my breathing to stay steady, willing myself still. Maybe if I pretend to sleep, he won't realize I'm awake. Maybe I can slip away before things turn unbearably awkward.

A single abrupt knock splits the quiet.

My whole body goes rigid. Before I can move, he grunts and pulls the blanket higher, draping it over both of us just as the door groans open.

"Stay asleep," he murmurs against my neck, his breath warm against my skin. His arm holds tighter, just briefly, then he says louder, voice edged with annoyance. "Sean."

"Forgive me, Your Grace," Sean stammers from the doorway. "His Majesty requests an audience with you and your new mate." A pause. "Immediately."

Right on cue, the sound of heavy footsteps echo behind him.

"Ah, good morn, son." The King's familiar baritone vibrates off the walls. "I see you are enjoying yourself."

Mortification floods me. We're tangled beneath the covers, barely hidden, leaving nothing to the imagination. My face burns. Thank the skies he had the sense to pull the blanket over us before his father entered.

"Your Majesty," the Prince replies with a sigh that barely masks his irritation.

"Did you claim her?"

"I think that is obvious," he mutters.

"Watch your tongue, boy. I am still King here." His voice sharpens with authority before shifting his focus. "Wake her. I wish to hear it from her."

I barely breathe. The Prince exhales hard through his nose, jaw tense. "Yes, milord." Then he leans closer to me, whispering against my ear. "Keep your eyes down."

His voice rises again. "Narina, wake up."

I let my lashes flutter, feigning sleep-tinged grogginess. I keep my gaze low, refusing to look toward the center of this wretched power play.

"Look at me, girl."

I hesitate, then the Prince spares me the choice. "Do as he says," he instructs, voice firm, meant for the King as much as for me.

My gaze lifts slowly. A shiver slips through me as it meets the King's frigid stare.

"Did my son claim you?"

"Yes, Your Majesty," I barely whisper.

His eyes rake over me, dissecting more than just my words. Then he nods once, satisfied. "Good."

He turns without ceremony, robes swishing across the stone. Sean hesitates, then quickly follows, shutting the door behind them.

The Prince releases a long breath. His body softens against mine as he buries his face into the crook of my neck.

I stay stiff, unsure of what to do, what to say. After a moment, he shifts again, easing me onto my back, hovering above me with concern in his eyes.

"Tell me how you are, darling."

Infinitely uncomfortable lying here naked with you. The words sit on the tip of my tongue, but I bite them back, saying nothing.

He clears his throat. "I imagine you might be a bit sore." He gestures vaguely toward the bedside table. "There are some pain drafts. If you need them."

I glance over. Three small vials, emerald-green and faintly glowing in the morning light.

"That's... considerate of you," I say at last.

To my surprise, he throws his head back and laughs. A real, open laugh that breaks the lingering strain.

"I am not a monster, Narina." His eyes catch mine, and this time, I look away.

He reaches for my chin, gently guiding my face back toward his. "I am not a monster," he says again, softer now, as if he truly needs me to believe it. "You would be here regardless of our deal."

"I know." The words slip out small and honest.

His eyes study mine, searching for something. "You finally let yourself relax last night," he murmurs. "And now you are back to fighting me. Tell me why."

I don't answer.

"There have been very few stolen mates who have tried to run more than once. Believe me, I checked. And despite the glimmer of hope I was given last night, I have no doubt that if it were not for the consequences your village would suffer… you would still be trying to escape."

He leans in slightly, his voice softer but no less intense. "Tell me why you fight this so strongly."

"It's just…"

I hesitate. He waits.

"I'm trapped," I admit, voice trembling. "I didn't have a choice. Even when I agreed to stay, it wasn't a real choice. Everything I knew, everything I loved, was taken from me. And now I'm bound to a stranger." My breath catches. "To you."

Silence.

"It is not my choice either," he says after a moment. "This tradition exists to preserve the bloodline." He watches me closely. "But, if I am honest… I am not sorry that it was you."

I wait, searching for some hidden meaning in his words.

"My father could have chosen some dim-witted, simpering girl. Compliant. Easy. Like Coraline." He traces a finger along my arm. "But he chose you."

I don't know what to say. I'm not sure what I *can* say.

His hand stills. "I may not regret that you are here," he continues, "but I am sorry for what you had to lose."

The sincerity in his words is unexpected. I find myself unable to speak, not trusting myself to respond without my voice betraying me. I fight against the tears that threaten to fall.

"Narina," he prompts.

"I don't know what to say. Or feel. Or do." My throat tightens. "There's just so much I don't understand."

His thumb brushes against my temple, wiping away a tear I didn't notice had escaped.

"So ask, sweet Narina." His voice is gentle now. "We are alone. Ask your questions. I know you have many."

My brows lift, cautious. Was he serious? After being denied answers at every turn since I arrived, he was offering them freely now? He nods, patiently waiting.

I sit up, wrapping the blanket around myself more securely. He leans back against the headboard, folding his hands as if to prove he means it.

I test his offer with a simple question, one I hadn't even thought of until just moments ago.

"Where was the King yesterday? I didn't see him."

He answers easily. "On the dais, toward the back. You were... preoccupied. He did not attend the celebration."

True to his word, he answers every question I have, filling in the gaps of everything I haven't understood since I arrived.

The crowded room, the foreign tongue, it was part of an ancient blessing, one that had to be witnessed. He'd gone through the same ceremony.

The symbols painted on my skin are more blessings. Marks of luck, faith, health, fertility, happiness, obedience, and peace. As he names them, his fingers trace each one with a reverent touch, his voice softer now, almost distant.

"Why don't you have any?"

His hand stills. "Because a woman's body is a precious vessel," he says after a beat. "The blessings are hers to bear."

He walks me through the rest, each part of the binding I hadn't understood.

The smoke was to cleanse the body.

The mark on the forehead, the soul.

The blood we both gave, *that* bound our spirits.

And the final act... bound our bodies.

I ask more. And he keeps answering, never once turning away or retreating behind cold silence.

And then, quietly, I ask the question that's haunted me all morning.

"This?" My voice comes out smaller than intended, unsure. "What is it you want from me?"

After everything else, this is the one that matters.

The Prince—Ryden—was right about one thing. We *are* strangers, bound by a decision neither of us made. And yet... there's something about this moment that feels like more than just a shared duty.

The Prince's gaze softens just slightly. There's a quiet understanding there, something more than the guarded facade he's shown me so far. "I am not asking for anything, Narina," he says. "I am simply trying to make this easier for both of us. We can not change what has been done. But we *can* choose how to move forward."

I lower my eyes, watching my fingers fiddle with the edge of the soft fur beneath us. His words echo through me. *How to move forward.*

The ache in my chest sharpens. Diamo's name is never spoken, but still there. Still *mine*.

"I don't know how to do that." I admit, almost too quiet to hear.

He brushes a strand of hair behind my ear, leaning in just enough to meet my eyes. "You are not betraying him, Narina."

I meet his eyes, searching for some hint of mockery, but there's none. He speaks with a strange sincerity, and it confuses me further. If this union is so unwanted for both of us, why does he seem so determined to make it easier?

"Are you telling me to forget him?" The question scrapes its way out. I brace myself for the answer.

"No," he says, his voice steady. "I do not need that. But I would like something else."

The back of his hand trails softly along my cheek, down my neck, a touch that asks, not takes.

"I would like the chance to make this something other than just a fight. We can not pretend that this is not our reality, Narina. But it does not have to be a battle."

Something shifts in my chest, a quiet pang, like a fracture I hadn't known was there. The idea of peace, of *choosing* to make this union work... it *feels* like a betrayal to Diamo. But the Prince's words settle over me in a way that I can't quite shake. I don't *have* to fight him. But if I keep resisting, keep bracing for battle… am I only making it harder for both of us?

"I don't know if I can just *accept* this," I say softly. "But I don't want to keep fighting it either."

Ryden is silent for a moment, his gaze steady on me if weighing my words carefully.

"That is all I want, Narina," he says at last. "Not acceptance. Not perfection. Just the willingness to try, without the constant battle."

The words settle between us, quiet and unresolved. Part of me still wants to resist, to rail against the inevitability of all this. But another part, the one that's tired of carrying so much grief and fury, just wants to let go. To stop fighting. To breathe without the strain of resistance.

I wonder if that might be enough.

"I'll try," I murmur. The promise is more for me than for him.

His gaze softens, something flickering behind it, relief, maybe. "That is all I ask."

A tentative knock breaks the stillness.

The Prince's jaw tightens, irritation flickering at the interruption.

"Enter," the Prince calls, voice edged with impatience. I almost pity whoever's on the other side of the door.

It creaks open, and Sean peeks through the crack, "Apologies, Your Grace."

"Speak quickly." The Prince's warning is sharp.

"There is a subject in the throne room with a formal complaint, Your Grace. His Majesty requests the presence of you and your mate."

Sean lowers his head, clearly bracing for the response.

The Prince exhales, dragging a hand along his jaw. "You may tell him we will be there shortly. Send milady's attendants to prepare her."

He waves Sean off, already done with the conversation. The boy bows and disappears, leaving the door ajar behind him.

I shift, uneasy. "Why would the King want me there?"

The Prince casts a glance my way but doesn't answer. Instead, he rises, the mattress dipping beneath his weight. "Formal complaints are rare. Members of court are bound to be there. So, try to remember yourself, remember your lessons."

His brow lifts in a silent warning.

I lift my hands in mock surrender. "I'll try. But aside from a flawless curtsy…" My voice trails off as a flash of memory hits. Benton's cane snapping against my legs. I flinch. "I'm not sure how useful those lessons will be."

His look turns skeptical. "Stay close. If you must speak, look to me first."

He steps toward me, and that's when I realize, with a jolt, that he's still completely unclothed. My gaze drops fast, heat rushing to my face.

He leans in, voice low and amused. Warmth radiates from him. "It is a little late for that shy blush, darling."

A sharp knock spares me from a response. He chuckles at my flustered silence before calling out, "Enter."

Two servants in dove-grey step into the room, heads bowed. If the Prince minds his current state, he gives no sign.

"Dress her quickly. We are expected in the throne room. The blue gown will do."

I blink, startled, glancing over at him. Now he's choosing my clothing?

Before I can object, he's already turning away. "Make it quick," he calls over his shoulder, disappearing into the adjoining chamber and closing the door behind him.

The servants move with quiet efficiency, skirts whispering against the stone floor as they glide through the room. I watch, half dazed, as they work in a rhythm so precise they never collide, never pause.

Before long, I am laced into a deep blue gown with flowing sleeves and a fitted bodice. My hair is swept into an elegant pile of curls atop my head. The fabric slides like water through my fingers. So fine, so unlike anything I have ever owned. I don't know if I'll ever get used to such fine things.

The adjoining door opens again.

The Prince strides in, now dressed in a stark black dress uniform. The only ornamentation is the double row of silver buttons down the center of his jacket. Atop his dark hair rests a silver crown. Bare of any jewels, the intricate silver pattern twists and weaves back around itself, creating the illusion of twisted branches.

The servants curtsy low as he surveys me, eyes dragging from head to toe. A slow, smug grin curves across his face.

"You look quite lovely when you are not covered in mud."

I frown. Does that count as a compliment?

"Sean!" His sudden bark makes me jump.

Sean appears, carefully balancing a red velvet pillow in his hands. I choke on a cough. Atop it sits a delicate silver circlet, a smaller version of the Prince's. Its dainty twisting vines cradle a large sapphire at the center. Small ivory pearls accent the intricate metalwork.

"A gift," the Prince says. "For the new Princess."

I stare. "I can't wear that!"

It's too extravagant, too delicate, too... beautiful.

The Prince doesn't waver. He lifts the circlet from its cushion as Sean bows and quietly retreats.

"Of course you can," he says, stepping toward me. "And you will."

He settles the crown gently amidst my curls, his hand sure and steady. Then he steps back, gaze sweeping over me in silent appraisal. After a pause, he gives a small nod.

"You are ready, milady."

"Am I?" The words slip out barely above a whisper.

I turn to the mirror, and a stranger looks back at me. The girl in the glass is poised, regal, every inch a princess. I lift a hand, fingertips grazing the fine metal. The truth lands hard.

Once, I stood beneath ancient trees, laughing as I told a blacksmith's apprentice that I had no need for fancy things.

Now, the most exquisite thing I've ever touched sits upon my head.

A symbol to the world of the oath I've made.

Continue for...

A *Take Her* bonus chapter!

&

A Sneak Peek of Book Two!!

Acknowledgments

The biggest acknowledgment and thank you goes to my parents. They have supported me and my writing my entire life. They set up my first author website for my 13th birthday (eons ago) and have asked when this book will be done for the last ten years. No, actually… they've asked when Book Two will be done. I wouldn't be here without them and their encouragement. I love you.

Thank you to my kids. My babies. They will never know how much joy they have brought to my life. And I hope they never know how much strength they have leant me when I didn't know if I had any left. More than the whole big moon.

Thank you to my fiancé. He has supported all my dreams, no matter how crazy they are. He recognizes how important writing is to me and helps ensure I have time to do just that. I can't wait to marry you this August. <3

Thank you to my sister. You know what for.

Thank you to Mimi. She's always been in my corner and that's something I will never be able to thank her enough for. Just between you and me.

Thank you to Aamna and her team at Etheric Designs for such beautiful artwork. You've been a joy to work with. I can't believe you were able to take my rambling thoughts and illegible scribbles and create some incredible designs that have just made me fall in love with this book even more.

Thanks to Ellie for being a beta reader. Your advice and notes pushed parts of the story to be the best it can be as well as giving some much needed encouragement.

I also have to thank the writers, authors, editors, and readers that have inspired, supported, and encouraged this journey.

Here's to you.

Author Bio

Kinsley Kane writes stories of ruin, romance, and resilience.

When not lost in fictional worlds of her own, she explores the worlds of others with a good book. Otherwise, she can be found with a cup of tea and a notebook full of random notes.

Kinsley Kane has been writing for over 20 years with her first novel being published under a pen name in 2015.

Let's Connect:

Website: authorkinsleykane.com
Facebook: /authorkinsleykane
Instagram: @authorkinsleykane
TikTok: @authorkinsleykane

Also By Kinsley Kane

Take Her Bonus Chapter

Get a bonus chapter from *Take Her* in Diamo's POV!

You know how her story began... now witness the moment that shattered him.

He loved her wild. Loved the way she defied the world with every breath.

But he always feared what it might cost.

And when the worst happens... when she's ripped from his arms and punished for daring to be free... he's left helpless, watching everything he swore to protect slip away.

This is the moment he broke.

https://authorkinsleykane.com/take-her-bonus-chapter/

Book Two Sneak Peek

Break Her

Chapter One

"We must go," the Prince—Ryden, urges gently.

I know he's right. We shouldn't keep the King waiting. But… I can't reconcile with the reflection in the mirror. She's me, but she's not.

The dress flows through my fingers like water, smooth and impossibly fine. A huge contrast to the plain white gowns I've worn since I arrived. Nothing in Verti could compare. I don't think even the elegant attire I've seen the nobles wear could. This surpasses them all.

My hand lifts again, skimming over the delicate crown resting against my hair. *Princess.* The word doesn't fit, doesn't settle.

"Narina."

I lower my hand and glance at Ryden. He watches me, his expression as unreadable as ever, though something lingers in his gaze. Whatever it is, it doesn't ease the uncertainty twisting inside me. And I have no time to dwell on it.

He holds out his arm to me. A silent command. There's no way I'm ready for whatever is about to happen next. Being summoned by the King is never a pleasant encounter in my limited experience. But with no other choice in sight, I take it.

The Prince's grip is steady, as he guides me through the castle's winding corridors.

Torches flicker as we pass, throwing long shadows against the stone walls. The further we go, the more the air seems to shift. Servants pause in their duties to bow as we pass. Nobles, the same.

Whispers trail behind us, hushed voices threading through the halls like strands of silk. I keep my chin level, refusing to let the sound stab at what little confidence I have, though my fingers tighten slightly against Ryden's sleeve.

One day, I will commit these hallways to memory. Today, however, my mind is too busy trying to keep from spiraling to pay much attention. Except for the familiar double doors of the throne room that come into view, standing as tall and imposing as I remember. I'm beginning to hate these doors, despite the gorgeous art carved into their planes. The guards at either side see us approaching and move in perfect synchronization, pulling the doors open.

A deep breath fails to steady me as my gaze sweeps the room. Inside, the chamber is filled with nobles, their fine fabrics and jeweled adornments gleaming under the glow of the chandeliers. Some stand with their mates, others in small clusters, heads inclined toward one another. Conversation dwindles as we pause at the doorway, the shift in attention unsettling.

At the far end, at the center upon the dais, the King sits upon his throne. His presence is unmistakable, a figure of unwavering authority. His crown glints in the light, and I can't help but feel that *his* belongs. Mine feels like a plaything, like something that doesn't belong to me.

Then my eyes land on them.

Two guards stand at the center of the room, positioned over the royal seal embedded in the floor. Between them, a lone figure stands.

My heart stops.

Even before I can fully register the face, I *know*. I'd know that silhouette anywhere.

"Diamo!"

His name is past my lips before I know it.

I move to run to him, to cross the room and close the impossible distance between us, but the Prince's arm is around my waist in an instant. His grip is unyielding as he pulls me back and down the side hallway. The throne room vanishes from view, replaced by stone walls and flickering torchlight. Behind us, I hear the double doors shut with a soft thump, sealing Diamo away from me once again.

I twist against the Prince's hold, pushing at his arm.

"Let me go!" My voice is sharp with desperation, but his hold remains firm. He doesn't hurt me, but he doesn't let me go either.

"Narina," the Prince murmurs near my ear. "Narina, *stop this*." His tone is impatient, but not unkind.

I whirl on him, incredulous. "I have to go to him!"

I shove at his chest, anger and desperation crashing through me in waves. Does he seriously believe that I will stay here while the love of my life stands only steps away? I may be bound to this man but my heart was bound to Diamo a long time ago.

"You cannot," he says, low.

My heart pounds against my chest, "You don't understand! I have to—"

"I do understand." There's no mockery, no condescension. Just quiet certainty. "Which is why I stopped you."

I wrench back enough to face him fully, my breath coming fast. His expression is calm, but there's something beneath it, something measured. Watching me closely, calculating my next move.

Diamo is here. *Here.* Not a memory, not a dream, not some distant part of my past I can never touch. He's *real*, standing in that throne room, and I am *so close*.

I swallow against the knot forming in my throat. "Why is he here? Is he in trouble?" The words barely come out as panic claws at me.

The Prince studies me for a moment before answering, his expression unchanging. "I assume your lover is here to lodge a complaint. To request your return from the King."

A wild, foolish hope sparks. Maybe, just maybe, the King will see reason, show mercy, let me go home.

"Narina."

The gentleness in his voice is enough to shatter that fragile hope before it even has the chance to take root. Reality settles in. Our ceremony was yesterday. I am bound. Even if I wasn't, I made a deal. I traded my freedom for Verti's safety.

I clench my jaw, blinking hard against the moisture gathering in my eyes.

"Why—" My voice breaks. I inhale slowly, forcing composure back into place. He waits. "Why would the King allow this?"

The Prince lowers his gaze, something almost like embarrassment flickering across his face. "For this reason."

He lifts his head, his fingers cupping my chin, tilting it up until I meet his eyes. "To get a reaction from you. From him."

My breath stutters.

"This is cruel," I whisper.

"It is."

I bite the inside of my cheek, trying to steady myself, but it's useless. Diamo is so close, and I can't have him. I pull away from the Prince's touch. He let's me.

"What am I supposed to do?" My back meets the wall, my body giving way to defeat. My world crashing down around me as a roar in my ears.

"You must summon that strength of yours and keep yourself together until we are dismissed. You can fall apart as much as you like after."

I shoot him a glare, but he steps closer, gripping my arms with urgency. "This is serious, Narina. If the King believes that you can not let your lover go…" He pauses, searching my face. "He will execute him."

My stomach drops. "What?!" I shove him away.

What kind of person would punish someone for a love that was fostered and grown over years? What kind of monster expects me to erase years of devotion just because he took me?

I shake my head, my voice trembling. "The King can't possibly expect me to forget about Diamo simply because he *stole* me away."

The Prince catches my wrist before I can pull away again. "He can and he does. He is the *King*, Narina. He can do anything he pleases.

That includes killing your lover if he decides *you* are betraying the crown by wanting him."

My pulse thrums in my ears. He holds my gaze, and for the first time, I see something in him I haven't before. I don't know what it is. It scares me.

His voice softens. "I understand this will be one of the hardest things you will ever have to do, but I urge you to keep yourself collected. You love him. I know that. You agreed to be my mate to save his life. Do not let that sacrifice be in vain."

I close my eyes, forcing back the flood of emotions twisting through me. He's right. I sold my soul to the crown to save Diamo's life. If I let my love for him show now, I'll be the reason he dies.

I tip my head back, blinking at the ceiling. The tears don't fall. Not yet.

"What do I have to do?" I whisper, unable to speak any louder.

The Prince slides his hands to mine, holding them gently. "Be strong."

I nod, still blinking furiously.

"You do not have to speak unless you are told to," he continues. "Just stand there and let the King deny his complaint. You are bound. Our souls are bound for life. There is no undoing it. That is the truth and the end of it."

I exhale shakily. "And if I have to speak?

"Speak the truth." A pause. "Just... try to sound loyal to the crown when you do it."

I roll my eyes despite everything. Of course. Just another impossible expectation to add to the list. Try not to offend the King more than I already have in the short amount of time I've been here.

But Diamo... this is going to crush him. How am I supposed to stand there and witness his heart break?

My voice trembles. "What if I can't do this?" I whisper, my eyes pleading with the man in front of me.

Don't make me do this.

His jaw flexes, but his voice remains steady. "You do not have a choice. You have been summoned."

He straightens, extending his arm toward me. "We must go. We are already late."

I stare at him. My entire body feels locked in place, my feet refusing to move. He steps closer, his arm still outstretched.

"I will be right there. I will not let you do something that will get you into trouble with the King."

Except it isn't me I'm worried about.

The next few minutes will literally determine the fate of the man that my whole world revolves around.

As if reading my thoughts, the Prince adds, "I will not let you do anything that will reflect poorly on your lover either. My deal was to protect his life. I will uphold it."

He glances toward the throne room, his voice now firm. "We really must go now."

Instead of waiting for me to take his arm, he takes mine, looping it through his before leading me back to the double doors.

I stop just before the doors, staring at the intricate carvings, willing myself to breathe.

I am Narina Brevou—

My hands shake violently, betraying me.

The doors swing open, and my heart stops.

The scene is unchanged. Except now… Diamo is on his knees between the guards.

My breath hitches.

The Prince moves forward, pulling me with him. My legs feel like lead, like my body is resisting every step.

A voice rings out through the vast chamber.

"Announcing, His Royal Grace, Prince Caltrava, Heir of Barbast and his mate, Princess Caltrava."

Princess. There's no chance I'll ever get used to that.

Diamo's head snaps toward me at the announcement, his sharp gaze locking onto mine. He tries to stand, but the guards shove him down, hands pressing against his shoulders.

A million tiny knives sink into my chest. Seeing him like this, helpless, restrained, shatters something inside me. Tears sting my eyes.

My soul yearns for him, aching to embrace his familiar warmth.

"Narina."

The Prince's voice is low, a warning meant for me alone. Reluctantly, I force my gaze forward.

The walk to the front of the room is the longest trek of my life. *So many eyes.* Watching, waiting. Their stares burn holes in my fragile composure.

We reach the dais. Behind us, I can still feel Diamo's presence.

The Prince bows low. "Your Majesty."

I follow his lead, lowing into a deep curtsy, keeping my eyes trained downward.

"Your Grace. Milady." The King returns the greeting, the words carrying easily through the chamber.

I rise alongside the Prince and we move again. He leads me to a set of stairs built into the side of the platform. His hand finds mine, steadying me as I ascend. I'm grateful for the assistance; my knees are weak and I doubt I'd make it up on my own.

At the top, we take our places. The Prince stands beside the King. I stand beside him.

Instinctively, my gaze searches for Diamo's. I easily find the adoration that's always been there. He's about to suffer because of me.

I'm sorry.

"I understand you have a complaint." The King's baritone voice echoes through the room.

"Yes, Your Majesty." Diamo shifts his attention to the throne. My heart tugs, his voice is confident as always. My Diamo.

"Speak it," the King commands.

"I request the crown to return my betrothed to me. She -"

The King lifts a hand, cutting him off.

I release the breath I'd been holding. At least the King wasn't going to let him go through the entire plea just to reject it.

"You are but a day too late for that, boy." The last word is spat with disdain. Diamo's brow furrows in confusion.

"Do you not see the crown she so elegantly wears?"

Diamo's gaze shifts to me. Dread fills his eyes. He knows perfectly well what the King means. He just doesn't want it to be true.

"Perhaps you can clear this up for him, Milady Narina."

The world tilts. All the air has been knocked out of me. I squeeze the Prince's arm, afraid I might faint.

This is it. The moment from my nightmares.

What I say next will determine whether Diamo lives or dies.

I try to speak but all that comes out is a strangled breath.

Those pleading hazel eyes hold me captive.

The Prince squeezes my hand, whether in reassurance or warning, I can't tell.

"Speak, Narina," he says quietly.

I clear my throat.

"Diamo."

Preorder *Break Her* today!

Just visit my shop at:

authorkinsleykane.com/shop